D0093731

TO SAVE THE SUN

Tor books by Ben Bova

As on a Darkling Plain
The Astral Mirror
Battle Station
The Best of the Nebulas (ed.)
Colony
Cyberbooks
Escape Plus
Future Crime
Gremlins Go Home
   (with Gordon R. Dickson)
The Kinsman Saga
The Multiple Man
Orion
Orion in the Dying Time
Out of the Sun

Peacekeepers
Privateers
Prometheans
Star Peace: Assured Survival
The Starcrossed
Test of Fire
To Save the Sun
   (with A.J. Austin)
The Trikon Deception
   (with Bill Pogue)
Vengeance of Orion
Voyagers
Voyagers II: The Alien Within
Voyagers III: Star Brothers
The Winds of Altair

TO SAVE THE SUN

Ben Bova and A. J. Austin

A TOM DOHERTY ASSOCIATES BOOK   NEW YORK

TETON COUNTY LIBRARY
JACKSON, WYOMING

This is a work of fiction. All the characters and events
portrayed in this book are fictitious, and any resemblance
to real people or events is purely coincidental.

Parts of this novel were originally published in slightly different form
in *Stellar Science Fiction Stories #4,* copyright © 1978 by Random
House, Inc., and in *Analog Science Fiction/Science Fact,* copyright
© 1991 by Davis Publications, Inc.

TO SAVE THE SUN

Copyright © 1992 by Ben Bova and A. J. Austin

All rights reserved, including the right to reproduce this book, or portions
thereof, in any form.

This book is printed on acid-free paper.

A Tor Book
Published by Tom Doherty Associates, Inc.
175 Fifth Avenue
New York, N.Y. 10010

Tor® is a registered trademark of Tom Doherty Associates, Inc.

Library of Congress Cataloging-in-Publication Data

Bova, Ben
    To save the sun / Ben Bova and A. J. Austin.
        p.   cm.
    "TOR book."
    ISBN 0-312-85177-4
    I. Austin, A. J.   II. Title.
PS3552.O84T6   1992
813'.54—dc20   92-25453
                                                                    CIP

First edition: September 1992

Printed in the United States of America

0 9 8 7 6 5 4 3 2 1

For Barbara, of course.—B.B.

For Sally, who makes everything possible, and for Courtney, who makes everything fun.—A.J.A.

And for Gordy, with our deepest thanks for his unfailing kindness and generosity.

PART ONE

DECISION

ONE

The Emperor of the Hundred Worlds stood at the head of the conference chamber, tall, gray, grim-faced. Although there were forty other men and women seated in the chamber, the Emperor knew he was alone.

"Then it is certain?" he asked, his voice grave but strong despite the news they had given him. "Earth's Sun will explode?"

The scientists had come from all ends of the Empire to reveal their findings to the Emperor. They shifted uneasily in their sculptured couches under his steady gaze. A few of them, the oldest and best-trusted, were actually on Corinth, the Imperial planet itself, only an ocean away from the palace. Most of the others had been brought to the Imperial solar system from their homeworlds, and were housed on the three other planets of the system.

Although the holographic projections made them look as solid and real as Emperor Nicholas himself, there was always a slight lag in their responses to him. The delay was an indication of their rank within the scientific order, and they had even arranged their seating in the conference chamber the same way: the farther away from the Emperor, the lower in the hierarchy.

Some things cannot be conquered, the Emperor thought to himself as one of the men in the third rank of couches, a roundish, balding, slightly pompous little man, got to his feet. *Time still reigns supreme. Distance we can conquer, but not time. Not death.*

"Properly speaking, Sire, the Sun will not explode. It will not become a nova. Its mass is too low for that. But the eruptions that it will suffer will be of sufficient severity to heat Earth's atmosphere to incandescence. It will destroy all life on the surface. And, of course, the oceans will be drastically damaged; the food chain of the oceans will be totally disrupted."

Good-bye to Earth, then, thought the Emperor.

But aloud he asked, "The power satellites, and the shielding we have provided the planet—they will not protect it?"

The scientist stood dumb, patiently waiting for his Emperor's response to span the light-minutes between them. *How drab he looks,* the Emperor noted. *And how soft.* He pulled his own white robe closer around his iron-hard body. He was older than most of them in the conference chamber, but they were accustomed to sitting at desks and lecturing to students. He was accustomed to standing before multitudes and commanding.

"The shielding," the bald man said at last, "will not be sufficient. There is nothing we can do. For several centuries neutrino counts have consistently shown that the core of Earth's Sun has become stagnant. Sometime over the next three to five hundred years, the Sun will erupt and destroy all life on Earth and the inner planets of its system. The data are conclusive."

The Emperor inclined his head to the man, curtly, a gesture that meant both "Thank you" and "Be seated." The scientist waited mutely for the gesture to reach him.

The data are conclusive. The integrator woven into the molecules of his cerebral cortex linked the Emperor's mind with the continent-spanning computer complex that was the Imperial memory.

Within milliseconds he reviewed the equations and found no flaw in them. Even as he did so, the other hemisphere of his brain was picturing Earth's daystar seething, writhing in a fury of pent-up nuclear agony, then erupting into giant flares. The Sun calmed afterward and smiled benignly once again on a blackened, barren, smoking rock called Earth.

A younger man was on his feet, back in the last row of couches. The Emperor realized that he had already asked for permission to speak. Now they both waited for the photons to complete the journey between them. From his position in the chamber and the distance between them, he was either an upstart or a very junior researcher.

"Sire," he said at last, his face suddenly flushed in embarrassed self-consciousness or, perhaps, the heat of conviction, "the data may be conclusive, true enough. But it is *not* true that we must accept this catastrophe with folded hands."

The Emperor began to say, "Explain yourself," but the intense young man never hesitated to wait for an Imperial response. He was taking no chance of being commanded into silence before he had finished.

"Earth's Sun will erupt only if we do nothing to prevent it. A colleague of mine believes that we have the means to prevent the eruptions. I would like to present her ideas on the subject. She could not attend this meeting herself." The young man's face grew taut, angry. "Her application to attend was rejected by the Coordinating Committee."

The Emperor smiled inwardly as the young man's words reached the other scientists around him. He could see a shock wave of disbelief and indignation spread through the assembly. The hoary old men in the front row, who chose the members of the Coordinating Committee, went stiff with anger.

Even Prince Javas, the Emperor's last remaining son, roused from his idle daydreaming where he sat at the Emperor's side and seemed to take an interest in the meeting for the first time.

"You may present your colleague's proposal," the Emperor said. *That is what an Emperor is for,* he added silently, looking at his youngest son, seeking some understanding on his handsome untroubled face. *To be magnanimous in the face of disaster.*

The young man took a pen-sized data stick from his sleeve pocket and inserted it into the computer input slot in the arm of his couch. The scientists in the front ranks of the chamber glowered and muttered to each other.

The Emperor stood lean and straight, stroking his graying beard absently as he waited for the information to reach him. When it did, he saw in his mind a young dark-haired woman whose face might have been charming were she not so intensely serious about her subject. She was speaking, trying to keep her voice dispassionate, but was almost literally quivering with ex-

citement. Equations appeared, charts, graphs, lists of materials
and costs; yet her intent, dark-eyed face dominated it all.

Beyond her, the Emperor saw a vague, star-shimmering image
of vast ships ferrying megatons of equipment and thousands
upon thousands of technical specialists from all parts of the
Hundred Worlds toward Earth and its troubled Sun.

Then, as the equations faded and the starry picture went dim
and even the woman's face began to pale, the Emperor saw the
Earth, green and safe, smelled the grass and heard birds singing,
saw the Sun shining gently over a range of softly rolling, ancient
wooded hills.

He closed his eyes. *You go too far, woman.* But how was she to
know that his eldest son had died in hills exactly like these, killed
on Earth, killed *by* Earth, so many years ago?

TWO

H e sat now. The Emperor of the Hundred Worlds spent
little time on his feet anymore. *One by one the vanities
are surrendered.* He sat in a powered chair that held
him in a soft yet firm embrace. It was mobile and almost alive:
part personal vehicle, part medical monitor, part communications system that could link him with any place in the
Empire.

His son stood. Prince Javas stood by the marble balustrade
that girdled the high terrace where his father had received him.
He wore the gray-blue uniform of a fleet commander, although
he had never bothered to accept command of even one ship. His
wife, the Princess Rihana, was at her husband's side.

They were a well-matched pair physically. Gold and fire. The
Prince had his father's lean sinewy grace, golden hair and star-
flecked eyes. Rihana was fiery, with the beauty and ruthlessness

of a tigress in her face. Her hair was a cascade of molten copper tumbling past her shoulders, her gown a metallic glitter.

"It was a wasted trip," Javas said to his father, with his usual sardonic smile. "Earth is . . . well," he shrugged, "nothing but Earth. It hasn't changed in the slightest."

"Thirty wasted years," Rihana said.

The Emperor looked past them, beyond the terrace to the lovingly landscaped forest that his engineers could never make quite the right shade of terrestrial green.

"Not entirely wasted, daughter-in-law," he said at last. "In cryosleep, you've aged hardly at all . . ."

"We are thirty years out of date with the affairs of the Empire," she snapped. The smoldering expression on her face made it clear that she believed her father-in-law deliberately plotted to keep her as far from the throne as possible.

"You can easily catch up," the Emperor said, ignoring her anger. "In the meantime, you have kept your youthful appearance."

"I shall always keep it! *You* are the one who denies himself rejuvenation treatments, not me."

"And so will Javas, when he becomes Emperor."

"Will he?" Her eyes were suddenly mocking.

"He will," said the Emperor, with the weight of a hundred worlds behind his voice.

Rihana looked away from him. "Well, even so, I shan't. I see no reason why I should age and wither when even the foulest shopkeeper can live for centuries."

"Your husband will age."

She said nothing. *And as he ages,* the Emperor knew, *you will find younger lovers. But of course, you have already done that, haven't you?* He turned toward his son, who was still standing by the balustrade.

"Kyle Arman is dead," Javas blurted.

For a moment, the Emperor failed to comprehend. "Dead?" he asked, his voice sounding old and weak even to himself.

Javas nodded. "In his sleep. A heart seizure."

"But he is too young . . ."

"He was your age, Father."

"And he refused rejuvenation treatments," Rihana said, sounding positively happy. "As if he were royalty! The pretentious fool. A servant . . . a menial . . ."

"He was a friend of this House," the Emperor said.

"He killed my brother," said Javas.

"Your brother failed the test. He was a coward. Unfit to rule." *But Kyle passed you,* the Emperor thought. *You were found fit to rule . . . or was Kyle still ashamed of what he had done to my firstborn?*

"And you accepted his story." For once, Javas' bemused smile was gone. There was iron in his voice. "The word of a backwoods Earthman."

"A pretentious fool," Rihana gloated.

"A proud and faithful man," the Emperor corrected. "A man who put honor and duty above personal safety or comfort."

His eyes locked with Javas'. After a long moment in silence, the Prince shrugged and turned away.

"Regardless," Rihana said, "we surveyed the situation on Earth, as you requested us to."

Commanded, the Emperor thought. *Not requested.*

"The people there are all primitives. Hardly a city on the entire planet! It's all trees and huge oceans."

"I know," he said drily, "I was born there."

Javas said, "There are only a few millions living on Earth. They can be evacuated easily and resettled on a few of the frontier planets. After all, they *are* primitives."

"Those 'primitives' are the baseline for our race. They are the pool of original genetic material, against which our scientists constantly measure the rest of humanity throughout the Hundred Worlds."

Rihana said, "Well, they're going to have to find another primitive world to live on."

"Unless we prevent their Sun from exploding."

Javas looked amused. "You're not seriously considering that?"

"I am . . . considering it. Perhaps not very seriously."

"It makes no difference," Rihana said. "The plan to save the Sun—to save your precious Earth—will take hundreds of years to implement. You will be dead long before even the earliest steps can be brought to a conclusion. The next Emperor can cancel the entire plan the day he takes the throne."

The Emperor turned his chair slightly to face his son, but Javas looked away, out toward the darkening forest.

"I know," the Emperor whispered, more to himself than to her. "I know that full well."

He could not sleep. The Emperor lay on the wide expanse of warmth, floating a single molecular layer above the gently soothing waters. Always before, when sleep would not come readily, a woman had solved the problem for him. But lately not even lovemaking helped.

The body grows weary but the mind refuses sleep. Is this what old age brings?

Now he lay alone, the ceiling of his tower bedroom depolarized so that he could see the blazing glory of the night sky of Corinth, capital planet of the Hundred Worlds.

Not the pale tranquil sky of Earth, with its bloated Moon smiling inanely at you, he thought. This was truly an Imperial sky, brazen with shimmering lights that glittered and sparkled like a thick sprinkling of gleaming gemstones. But they were not true stars, the Emperor knew. The inner reaches of the Procyon system were strewn with rubble, asteroids, the makings of planets that never coalesced because of the star's massive gravity field. *Debris,* thought the Emperor. *Still, they shine beautifully.* No moon rode in the sky; none was needed. There was never true darkness on Corinth.

A few true stars shone feebly through the glittering haze. One particularly bright one: diamond-hard, brilliant. Procyon's dwarf-star companion. A star that was halfway toward death.

That is what the Sun will look like one day, the Emperor realized. Once that companion had been a normal star, fully as large and bright as Procyon itself. When it collapsed it spewed out lethal waves of heat and radiation that scrubbed all life from the surface of Corinth. When the first explorers from Earth had found the planet, it was blackened and barren, its atmosphere just beginning to stabilize after its terrible ordeal.

That is why Corinth was made the capital of the Empire. It was useless for any other purpose. No one wanted it, so the Imperial Court was free to build on it without hindrance.

And yet Earth's sky seemed so much friendlier. You could pick out old companions there: the two Bears, the Lion, the Twins, the Hunter, the Winged Horse.

Already I think of Earth in the past tense. Like Kyle. Like my son.

He thought of the Earth's warming Sun. How could it turn traitor? How could it . . . begin to die? In his mind's eye he hovered above the Sun, bathed in its fiery glow, watching its bubbling, seething surface. He plunged deeper into the roiling plasma, saw filaments and streamers arching a thousand Earth-spans into space, heard the pulsing throb of the star's energy, the roar of its power, blinding bright, overpowering, ceaseless merciless heat, throbbing, roaring, pounding . . .

He was gasping for breath and the pounding he heard was his own heartbeat throbbing in his ears. Soaked with sweat, he tried to sit up. The bed enfolded him protectively, supporting his body.

"Hear me," he commanded the computer. His voice cracked.

"Sire?" answered a softly female voice in his mind.

He forced himself to relax. Forced the pain from his body. The dryness in his throat eased. His breathing slowed. The pounding of his heart diminished.

"Get me the woman scientist who reported at the conference on the Sun's explosion, thirty years ago. She was not present at the conference; her report was presented by a colleague."

The computer needed more than a second to reply, but finally: "Sire, there were four such reports by female scientists at that conference."

"This was the only one to deal with a plan to save the Earth's Sun."

THREE

Medical monitors were implanted in his body now. Although the Imperial physicians insisted that it was impossible, the Emperor could feel the microscopic implants on the wall of his heart, in his aorta, alongside his carotid artery. The Imperial psychotechs called it a psychosomatic reaction. But since his mind was linked to the computers that handled all the information on the planet, the Emperor knew what his monitors were reporting before the doctors did.

They had reduced the gravity in his working and living sections of the palace to one-third normal, and forbade him from leaving these areas, except for the rare occasions of state when he was needed in the Great Assembly Hall or another public area. He acquiesced in this: The lighter gravity felt better and allowed him to be on his feet once again, free of the powerchair's clutches.

This day he was walking slowly, calmly, through a green forest of Earth. He strolled along a parklike path, admiring the lofty maples and birches, listening to the birds and small forest animals' songs of life. He inhaled scents of pine and grass and sweet clean air. He felt the warm sun on his face and the faintest cool breeze. For a moment he considered how the trees would look in their autumnal reds and golds. But he shook his head.

No. There is enough autumn in my life. I'd rather be in spring-time.

In the rooms next to the corridor he walked through, tense knots of technicians worked at the holographic systems that produced the illusion of the forest, while other groups of white-suited meditechs studied the readouts from the Emperor's implants. Even though the machinery was so highly automated as to be virtually sentient, Imperial tradition—and bureaucratic insistence—kept triply redundant teams of humans on duty constantly.

Two men joined the Emperor on the forest path: Academician Bomeer, head of the Imperial Academy of Sciences, and Su-

preme Commander Fain, chief of staff of the Imperial Military
Forces. Both were old friends and advisors, close enough to the
Emperor to be housed within the palace itself when allowed to
visit their master.

Bomeer looked young, almost sprightly, in a stylish robe of
green and tan. He was slightly built, had a lean, almost ascetic
face spoiled by a large mop of unruly brown hair.

Commander Fain was iron gray, square-faced, a perfect picture of a military leader. His black and silver uniform fit his
muscular frame like a second skin. His gray eyes seemed eternally
troubled.

Emperor Nicholas greeted them and allowed Bomeer to spend
a few minutes admiring the forest simulation. The scientist called
out the correct names for each type of tree they walked past and
identified several species of birds and squirrel. Finally the Emperor asked him about the young woman who had arrived on the
Imperial planet the previous month.

"I have discussed her plan thoroughly with her," Bomeer said,
his face going serious. "I must say that she is dedicated, ener-
getic, close to brilliant. But rather naive and overly sanguine
about her own ideas."

"Could her plan work?" asked the Emperor.

"Could it work?" the scientist echoed. He had tenaciously held
on to his post at the top of the scientific hierarchy for nearly a
century. His body had been rejuvenated more than once, the
Emperor knew. But not his mind.

"Sire, there is no way to tell if it could work! Such an operation
has never been done before. There are no valid data. Mathemat-
ics, yes, but even so, there is no more than theory. And the costs!
The time it would take! The technical manpower!" He shook his
head. "Staggering."

The Emperor stopped walking. Fifty meters away, behind the
hologram screens, a dozen meditechs suddenly hunched over
their readout screens intently.

But the Emperor had stopped merely to repeat to Bomeer,
"Could her plan work?"

Bomeer ran a hand through his boyish mop, glanced at Commander Fain for support and found none, then faced his Emperor again. "I . . . there is no firm answer, Sire. Statistically I
would say that the chances are vanishingly small."

"Statistics!" The Emperor made a disgusted gesture. "A refuge for scoundrels and sociotechs. Is there anything scientifically impossible in what she proposes?"

"Nnn . . . not *theoretically* impossible, Sire," Bomeer said slowly. "A star's life span *can* be increased; it has been known for centuries that some stars rejuvenate naturally. Massive stellar collisions at the centers of the globular clusters have been known to transform dying red giants into young blue stragglers, although the process is obviously highly destructive in itself. But her theories involve something entirely different, and in the practical world of reality . . . it . . . it's the *magnitude* of the project. The costs. Why, it would take half of Supreme Commander Fain's fleet to transport even the most basic equipment and material needed for such a venture."

Fain seized his opportunity to speak. "And the Imperial fleet, Sire, is spread much too thin for safety as it is."

"We are at peace, Commander," said the Emperor.

"For how long, Sire? The frontier worlds grow more restless every day. And the aliens beyond our borders—"

"Are weaker than we are. I have reviewed the intelligence assessments, Commander."

"Sire, the relevant factor in those reports is that the aliens are growing stronger and we are not."

With a nod, the Emperor resumed walking. The scientist and the Commander followed him, arguing their points unceasingly.

Finally they reached the end of the long corridor, where the holographic simulation showed them Earth's Sun setting beyond the edge of an ocean, turning the restless sea into an impossible glitter of opalescence.

"Your recommendations, then, gentlemen?" he asked wearily. Even in the one-third gravity his legs felt tired, his back ached.

Bomeer spoke first, his voice hard and sure. "This naive dream of saving the Earth's Sun is doomed to fail. The plan must be rejected."

Fain added, "The fleet can detach enough squadrons from its noncombat units to initiate the evacuation of Earth whenever you order it, Sire."

"Evacuate them to an unsettled planet?" the Emperor asked.

"Or resettle them on the existing frontier worlds. The Earth residents are rather frontier-like themselves; they have purposely been kept primitive. They would get along well with some of the frontier populations. They might even serve to calm down some of the unrest on the frontier worlds."

The Emperor looked at Fain and almost smiled. "Or they might fan that unrest into outright rebellion. They are a cantankerous lot, you know."

"We can deal with rebellion," said Fain.

"Can you?" the Emperor asked. "You can kill people, of course. You can level cities and even render whole planets uninhabitable. But does that end it? Or do the neighboring worlds become fearful and turn against us?"

Fain stood as unmoved as a statue. His lips barely parted as he asked, "Sire, if I may speak frankly?"

"Certainly, Commander."

Like a soldier standing at attention as he delivers an unpleasant report to his superior officer, Fain drew himself up and monotoned, "Sire, the main reason for unrest among the frontier words is the lack of Imperial firmness in dealing with them. In my opinion, a strong hand is desperately needed. The neighboring worlds will respect their Emperor if—and only if—he acts decisively. The people value strength, Sire, not meekness."

The Emperor reached out and put a hand on the Commander's shoulder. Fain was still rock-hard under his uniform.

"You have sworn an oath to protect and defend this realm," the Emperor said. "If necessary, to die for it."

"And to protect and defend you, Sire." The man stood straighter and firmer than the trees around them.

"But this Empire, my dear Commander, is more than blood and steel. It is more than any one man. It is an *idea.*"

Fain looked back at him steadily, but with no real understanding in his eyes. Bomeer stood uncertainly off to one side.

Impatiently the Emperor turned his face toward the ceiling hologram and called, "Map!"

Instantly the forest scene disappeared and they were in limitless space. Stars glowed around them, overhead, on all sides, underfoot. The pale gleam of the galaxy's spiral arms wafted off and away into unutterable distance.

Bomeer's knees buckled. Even the Commander's rigid self-discipline was shaken.

The Emperor smiled. He was accustomed to walking godlike on the face of the Deep.

"This is the Empire, gentlemen," he lectured in the darkness. "A handful of stars, a pitiful scattering of worlds set apart by distances that take years to traverse. All populated by human beings, the descendants of Earth."

He could hear Bomeer breathing heavily. Fain was a ramrod outline against the glow of the Milky Way, but his hands were outstretched, as if seeking balance.

"What links these scattered dust motes? What preserves their ancient heritage, guards their civilization, protects their hard-won knowledge and arts and sciences? The Empire, gentlemen. We are the mind of the Hundred Worlds, their memory, the yardstick against which they can measure their own humanity. We are their friend, their father, their teacher and helper."

The Emperor searched the black starry void for the tiny yellow speck of Earth's Sun, while saying:

"But if the Hundred Worlds decide that the Empire is no longer their friend, if they want to leave their father, if they feel that their teacher and helper has become an oppressor . . . what then happens to the human race? It will shatter into a hundred fragments, and all the civilization that we have built and nurtured and protected over all these centuries will be destroyed."

Bomeer's whispered voice floated through the darkness. "They would never—"

"Yes. They would never turn against the Empire because they know that they have more to gain by remaining with us than by leaving us."

"But the frontier worlds," Fain said.

"The frontier worlds are restless, as frontier communities always are. If we use military might to force them to bow to our will, then other worlds will begin to wonder where their own best interests lie."

"But they could never hope to fight against the Empire!"

The Emperor snapped his fingers and instantly the three of them were standing again in the forest at sunset.

"They could never hope to *win* against the Empire," the Emperor corrected. "But they could destroy the Empire and themselves. I have played out the scenarios with the computers.

Widespread rebellion is possible, once the majority of the Hundred Worlds becomes convinced that the Empire is interfering with their freedoms."

"But the rebels could never win," the Commander said. "I have run the same war games myself, many times."

"Civil war," said the Emperor. "Who wins a civil war? And once we begin to slaughter ourselves, what will your aliens do, my dear Fain? Eh?"

His two advisors fell silent. The forest simulation was now deep in twilight shadow. The three men began to walk back along the path, which was softly illuminated by bioluminescent flowers and fireflies flickering through the dark.

Bomeer clasped his hands behind his back as he walked. "Now that I have seen some of your other problems, Sire, I must take a stronger stand and insist—yes, Sire, *insist*—that this young woman's plan to save the Earth is even more foolhardy than I had at first thought it to be. The cost is too high, and the chance of success is much too slim. The frontier worlds would react violently against such an extravagance. And," with a nod to Fain, "it would hamstring the fleet."

For several moments the Emperor walked down the simulated forest path without saying a word. Then, slowly, "I suppose you are right. It is an old man's sentimental dream."

"I'm afraid that's the truth of it, Sire," said Fain.

Bomeer nodded sagaciously.

"I will tell her. She will be disappointed. Bitterly."

Bomeer gasped. "She's here?"

The Emperor said, "Yes. I had her brought here to the palace. She has crossed the Empire, given up more than two decades of her life to make the trip, lost half a century of her career over this wild scheme of hers . . . just to hear that I will refuse her."

"In the palace?" Fain echoed. "Sire, you're not going to see her in person? The security—"

"Yes, in person. I owe her that much." The Emperor could see the shock on their faces. Bomeer, who had never stood in the same building with the Emperor until he had become Chairman of the Academy, was trying to suppress his fury with poor success. Fain, sworn to guard the Emperor as well as the Empire, looked worried.

"But Sire," the Commander said, "no one has personally seen the Emperor, privately, outside of his family and closest advisors"—Bomeer bristled visibly—"in years . . . decades!"

The Emperor nodded but insisted, "She is going to see me. I owe her that much. An ancient ruler on Earth once said, 'When you are going to kill a man, it costs nothing to be polite about it.' She is not a man, of course, but I fear that our decision will kill her soul."

They looked unconvinced.

Very well, then, the Emperor said to them silently. *Put it down as the whim of an old man . . . a man who is feeling all his years . . . a man who will never recapture his youth.*

She is only a child.

The Emperor studied Adela de Montgarde as the young astrophysicist made her way through the guards and secretaries and halls and antechambers toward his own private chambers. He had prepared to meet her in his reception room, changed his mind and moved the meeting to his office, then changed it again and now waited for her in his study. She knew nothing of his indecision; she merely followed the directions given her by the computer-informed staff of the palace.

The study was a warm old room, lined with shelves of private tapes and ancient paper tomes that the Emperor had collected over the years. A stone fireplace big enough to walk into spanned one wall; its flames soaked the Emperor in life-giving warmth. The opposite wall was a single broad window that looked out on the real forest beyond the palace walls. The window could also serve as a hologram frame; the Emperor could have any scene he wanted projected from it.

Best to have reality this evening, he told himself. *There is too little reality in my life these days.* So he eased back in his power-chair and watched his approaching visitor on the viewscreen above the fireplace of the richly carpeted, comfortably paneled old room.

He had carefully absorbed all the computer's information about Adela de Montgarde: born of a noble family on Gris, a frontier world whose settlers were slowly, painfully transforming a ball of mineral-rich rock into a viable habitat for human life. He knew her face, her life history, her scientific accomplishments

TETON COUNTY LIBRARY

JACKSON, WYOMING

and rank. But now, as he watched her approaching on the view-screen built into the stone fireplace, he realized how little knowledge had accompanied the computer's detailed information.

The door to the study swung open automatically, and she stood uncertainly, framed in the doorway.

The Emperor swiveled his powerchair around to face her. The viewscreen immediately faded and became indistinguishable from the other stones.

"Come in, come in, Dr. Montgarde."

She was tiny, the smallest woman the Emperor remembered seeing. Her face was almost elfin, with large curious eyes that looked as if they had known laughter. She wore a metallic tunic buttoned to the throat, and a brief skirt. Her figure was childlike.

The Emperor smiled to himself. *She certainly won't tempt me with her body.*

As she stepped hesitantly into the study, her eyes darting all around the room, he said:

"I am sure that my aides have filled your head with all sorts of nonsense about protocol—when to stand, when to bow, what forms of address to use. Forget all of it. This is an informal meeting, common politeness will suffice. If you need a form of address for me, call me Sire. I shall call you Adela, if you don't mind."

With a slow nod of her head she answered, "Thank you, Sire. That will be fine." Her voice was so soft that he could barely hear it. He thought he detected a slight waver in it.

She's not going to make this easy for me, he said to himself. Then he noticed the little stone that she wore on a slim silver chain about her neck.

"Agate," he said.

She fingered the stone reflexively. "Yes . . . it's from my home-world . . . Gris. Our planet is rich in minerals."

"And poor in cultivable land."

"We are converting more land every year, Sire."

"Please sit down," the Emperor said. "I'm afraid it's been so long since my old legs have tried to stand in full gravity that I'm forced to remain in this powerchair . . . or lower the gravitational field in this room. But the computer files said that you are not accustomed to low *g* fields."

She glanced around the warm, richly furnished room.

"Any seat you like. My chair rides like a magic carpet."

Adela picked the biggest couch in the room and tucked herself into a corner of it. The Emperor glided his chair over to her.

"It's very kind of you to keep the gravity up for me," she said.

He shrugged. "It costs nothing to be polite . . . But tell me, of all the minerals for which Gris is famous, why did you choose to wear agate?"

She blushed.

The Emperor laughed. "Come, come, my dear. There's nothing to be ashamed of. It's well known that agate is a magical stone that protects the wearer from scorpions and snakes. An ancient superstition, of course, but it could possibly be significant, eh?"

"No . . . it's not that!"

"Then what is it?"

"It . . . agate also makes the wearer . . . eloquent in speech."

"And a favorite of Princes," added the Emperor.

Her blush had gone. She sat straighter and almost smiled. "And it gives one victory over her enemies."

"You perceive me as your enemy?"

"Oh no!" She reached out toward him, her small, childlike hand almost touching his.

"Who, then?"

"The hierarchy . . . the old men who pretend to be young and refuse to admit any new ideas into the scientific community."

"I am an old man," the Emperor said.

"Yes . . ." She stared frankly at his aged face. "I was surprised when I saw you a few moments ago. I have seen holographic pictures, of course . . . but you . . . you've *aged.*"

"Indeed."

"Why can't you be rejuvenated? It seems like a useless old superstition to keep the Emperor from using modern biomedical techniques."

"No, no, my child. It is a very wise tradition. You complain of the inflexible old men at the top of the scientific hierarchy. Suppose you had an inflexible old man in the Emperor's throne? A man who would live not merely seven or eight score of years, but many centuries? What would happen to the Empire then?"

"Ohh. I see." And there was real understanding and sympathy in her eyes.

"So the King must die, to make room for new blood, new ideas, new vigor."

"It's sad," she said. "You are known everywhere as a good Emperor. The people love you."

He felt his eyebrows rise. "Even on the frontier worlds?"

"Yes. Most of them know that Fain and his troops would be standing on our necks if it weren't for the Emperor. We are not without our sources of information."

He smiled. "Interesting."

"But that is not why you called me here to see you," Adela said.

She grows bolder. "True. You want to save Earth's Sun. Bomeer and all my advisors tell me that it is either impossible or foolish. I fear that they have powerful arguments on their side."

"Perhaps," she said. "But I have the facts."

"I have seen your presentation. I understand the scientific basis of your plan."

"We can do it!" Adela said, her hands suddenly animated. "We can! The critical mass is really minuscule compared to—"

"Megatons are minuscule?"

"Compared to the effect it will produce. Yes."

And then she was on her feet, pacing the room, ticking off points on her fingers, lecturing, pleading, cajoling. The Emperor's powerchair swung back and forth, following her intense, wiry form as she paced.

"Of course it will take vast resources! And time—more than a century before we know to a first-order approximation that the initial steps are working. I'll have to give myself up to cryosleep for decades at a time. But we *have* the resources! And we have the time . . . just barely. We can do it, if we want to."

The Emperor said, "How can you expect me to divert half the resources of the Empire to save Earth's Sun?"

"Because Earth is *important,*" she argued back, a tiny fighter standing alone in the middle of the Emperor's study. "It's the baseline for all the other worlds of the Empire. On Gris we send biogenetic teams to Earth every twenty years to check our own mutation rate. The cost is enormous for us, but we do it. We have to."

"We can move Earth's population to another G-type star. There are plenty of them."

"It won't be the same."

"Adela, my dear, believe me, I would like to help. I know how important Earth is. But we simply cannot afford to try your scheme now. Perhaps in another hundred years or so—"

"That will be too late."

"But new scientific advances—"

"Under Bomeer and his ilk? Hah!"

The Emperor wanted to frown at her, but somehow his face would not compose itself properly. "You are a fierce, uncompromising woman," he said.

She came to him and dropped to her knees at his feet. "No, Sire. I'm not. I'm foolish and vain and utterly self-centered. I want to save Earth because I know I can do it. I can't stand the thought of living the rest of my life knowing that I could have done it, but never having had the chance to try."

Now we're getting at the truth, the Emperor thought.

"And someday, maybe a million years from now, maybe a billion . . . Gris' sun will become unstable. I want to be able to save Gris, too. And any other world whose star threatens it. I want all the Empire to know that Adela de Montgarde discovered the way to do it!"

The Emperor felt his breath rush out of him.

"Sire," she went on, "I'm sorry if I'm speaking impolitely or stupidly. It's just that I know we can do this thing, do it successfully, and you're the only one who can make it happen."

But he was barely listening. "Come with me," he said, reaching out to grasp her slim wrists and raising her to her feet. "It's time for the evening meal. I want you to meet my son."

Javas put on his usual amused smile when the Emperor introduced Adela. *Will nothing ever reach under his everlasting facade of polite boredom?* Rihana, at least, was properly furious. He could see the anger in her face: A virtual barbarian from some frontier planet. Daughter of a petty noble. Practically a commoner. Dining with them!

"Such a young child to have such grandiose schemes," the Princess said when she realized who Adela was.

"Surely," said the Emperor, "you had grandiose schemes of your own when you were young, Rihana. Of course, they involved lineages and marriages rather than astrophysics, didn't they?"

None of them smiled.

Emperor Nicholas had ordered dinner out on the terrace, under Corinth's glowing night sky. Rihana, who was responsible for household affairs, always had sumptuous meals spread for them: the best meats and fowl and fruits of a dozen prime worlds. Adela looked bewildered by the array placed in front of her by the servants. Such riches were obviously new to her. The Emperor ate sparingly and watched them all.

Inevitably the conversation returned to Adela's plan to save Earth's Sun. And Adela, subdued and timid at first, slowly turned lioness once again. She met Rihana's scorn with coldly furious logic. She countered Javas' skepticism with:

"Of course, since it will take more than a century before the theories behind the project can be proven, you will probably be the Emperor who is remembered by all the human race as the one who saved the Earth."

Javas' eyes widened slightly. *It hit home,* the Emperor noticed. *For once something affected the boy. This young woman should be kept at the palace.*

But Rihana snapped, "Why should the Crown Prince care about saving Earth? His brother was murdered by an Earthman."

The Emperor felt his blood turn to ice.

Adela looked panic-stricken. She turned to the Emperor, wide-eyed, open-mouthed.

"My eldest son died on Earth. My second son was killed putting down a rebellion on a frontier world, many years ago. My third son died of a viral infection that *some* have attempted to convince me"—he stared at Rihana—"was assassination. Death is a constant companion in every royal house."

"Three sons . . ." Adela seemed ready to burst into tears.

"I have not punished Earth, nor that frontier world, nor sought to find a possible assassin," the Emperor went on icily. "My only hope is that my last remaining son will make a good Emperor, despite his . . . handicaps."

Javas turned very deliberately in his chair to stare out at the dark forest. He seemed irked by the antagonism between his wife and his father. Rihana glowered like molten steel.

The dinner ended in dismal, bitter silence. The Emperor sent them all away to their rooms while he remained on the terrace and stared hard at the gleaming lights in the heavens that crowded out the darkness.

He closed his eyes and summoned a computer-assisted image of Earth's Sun. He saw it coalesce from a hazy cloud of cold gas and dust, saw it turn into a star and spawn planets. Saw it beaming out energy that allowed life to grow and flourish on one of those planets. And then saw it age, blemish, erupt, swell and finally collapse into a dark cinder.

Just as I will, thought the Emperor. *The Sun and I have both reached the age where a bit of rejuvenation is needed. Otherwise . . . death.*

He opened his eyes and looked down at his veined, fleshless, knobby hands. *How different from hers! How young and vital she is.*

With a touch on one of the control studs set into the arm of his powerchair, he headed for his bedroom.

I cannot be rejuvenated. It is wrong even to desire it. But the Sun? Would it be wrong to try? Is it proper for puny men to tamper with the destinies of the stars themselves?

Once in his tower-top bedroom he called for her. Adela came to him quickly, without delay or question. She wore a simple knee-length gown tied loosely at the waist. It hung limply over her childlike figure.

"You sent for me, Sire." It was not a question but a statement. The Emperor knew her meaning: *I will do what you ask, but in return I expect you to give me what I desire.*

He was already reclining in the soft embrace of his bed. The texture of the monolayer surface felt soft and protective. The warmth of the water beneath it eased his tired body.

"Come here, child. Come and talk to me. I hardly ever sleep

anymore; it gives my doctors something to worry about. Come and sit beside me and tell me all about yourself . . . the parts of your life story that are not on file in the computers."

She sat on the edge of the huge bed, and its nearly living surface barely dimpled under her spare body.

"What would you like to know?" she asked.

"I have never had a daughter," the Emperor said. "What was your childhood like? How did you become the woman you are?"

She began to tell him. Living underground in the mining settlements on Gris. Seeing sunlight only when the planet was far enough from its too-bright star to let humans walk the surface safely. Playing in the tunnels. Sent by her parents to other worlds for schooling. The realization that her beauty was not physical. The few lovers she had known. The astronomer who had championed her cause to the Emperor at that meeting nearly fifty years ago. Their brief marriage. Its breakup when he realized that being married to her kept him from advancing in the hierarchy.

"You have known pain, too," the Emperor said.

"It's not an Imperial prerogative," she answered softly. "Everyone who lives knows pain."

By now the sky was milky white with the approach of dawn. The Emperor smiled at her.

"Before breakfast everyone in the palace will know that you spent the night with me. I'm afraid I have ruined your reputation."

She smiled back. "Or perhaps *made* it."

He reached out and took her by the shoulders. Holding her at arm's length, he searched her face with a long, sad, almost fatherly look.

"It would not be a kindness to grant your request. If I allow you to pursue this dream of yours, have you any idea of the enemies it would make for you? Your life would be so cruel, so filled with envy and hatred."

"I know that," Adela said evenly. "I've known that from the beginning."

"And you are not afraid?"

"Of course I'm afraid! But I won't turn away from what I must do. Not because of fear. Not because of envy or hatred or any other reason."

"Not even for love?"

He felt her body stiffen. "No," she said. "Not even for love."

The Emperor let his hands drop away from her and called out to the computer, "Connect me with Prince Javas, Academician Bomeer and Commander Fain."

"At once, Sire."

Their holographic images quickly appeared on separate segments of the farthest wall of the bedroom. Bomeer, halfway around the planet in late afternoon, was at his ornate desk. Fain appeared to be on the bridge of a warship in orbit around the planet. Javas, of course, was still in bed. It was not Rihana who lay next to him.

The Emperor's first impulse was disapproval, but then he wondered where Rihana was sleeping.

"I am sorry to intrude on you so abruptly," he said to all three of the men, while they were still staring at the slight young woman sitting on the bed with their Emperor. "I have made my decision on the question of trying to save the Earth's Sun."

Bomeer folded his hands on the desktop. Fain, on his feet, shifted uneasily. Javas arched an eyebrow and looked more curious than anything else.

"I have listened to all your arguments and find that there is much merit in them. I have also listened carefully to Dr. Montgarde's arguments, and find much merit in them, as well."

Adela sat rigidly beside him. The expression on her face was frozen: She feared nothing and expected nothing. She neither hoped nor despaired. She waited.

"We will move the Imperial throne and all the Court to Earth's only moon," said the Emperor.

They gasped. All of them.

"Since this project to save the Sun will take many human generations, we will want the seat of the Empire close enough to the project so that the Emperor may take a direct view of the progress."

"But you can't move the entire capital!" Fain protested. "And to Earth! It's a backwater—"

"Supreme Commander Fain," the Emperor said sternly. "Yesterday you were prepared to move Earth's millions. I ask now that the fleet move the Court's thousands. And Earth will no longer be a backwater when the Empire is centered once again at the original home of the human race."

Bomeer sputtered, "But . . . but what if her plan fails? The sun will explode . . . and . . . and . . ."

"That is a decision to be made in the future."

He glanced at Adela. Her expression had not changed, but she was breathing rapidly now. The excitement had hit her body, it hadn't yet penetrated her emotional defenses.

"Father," Javas said, "may I point out that it takes *fifteen years* in realtime to reach the Earth from here? The Empire cannot be governed without an Emperor for that long."

"Quite true, my son. You will go to Earth before me. Once there, you will become acting Emperor while I make the trip."

Javas' mouth dropped open. "The acting Emperor? For fifteen years?"

"With luck," the Emperor said, grinning slightly, "old age will catch up with me before I reach Earth, and you will be the full-fledged Emperor for the rest of your life."

"But I don't want . . ."

"I know, Javas. But you will be Emperor someday. It is a responsibility you cannot avoid. Fifteen years of training will stand you in good stead."

The Prince sat up straighter in his bed, his face serious, his eyes meeting his father's steadily.

"And son," the Emperor went on, "to be an Emperor—even for fifteen years—you must be master of your own house."

Javas nodded. "I know, Father. I understand. And I will be."

"Good."

Then the Prince's impish smile flitted across his face once again. "But tell me . . . suppose, while you are in transit toward Earth, I decide to move the Imperial capital elsewhere? What then?"

His father smiled back at him. "I believe I will just have to trust you not to do that."

"You would trust me?" Javas asked.

"I always have."

Javas' smile took on a new pleasure. "Thank you, Father. I will be waiting for you on Earth's Moon. And for the lovely Dr. Montgarde as well."

Bomeer was still livid. "All this uprooting of everything . . . the costs . . . the manpower . . . over an unproven theory!"

"Why is the theory unproven, my friend?" the Emperor asked.

Bomeer's mouth opened and closed like a fish's, but no words came out.

"It is unproven," said the Emperor, "because our scientists have never gone so far before. In fact, the sciences of the Hundred Worlds have not made much progress at all in several generations. Isn't that true, Bomeer?"

"We . . . Sire, we have reached a natural plateau in our understanding of the physical universe. It has happened before. Our era is one of consolidation and practical application of already-acquired knowledge, not new basic breakthroughs."

"Well, this project will force some new thinking and new breakthroughs, I warrant. Certainly we will be forced to recruit new scientists and engineers by the shipload. Perhaps that will be impetus enough to start the climb upward again, eh, Bomeer? I never did like plateaus."

The academician lapsed into silence.

"And I see you, Fain," the Emperor said, "trying to calculate in your head how much of your fleet's strength is going to be wasted on this old man's dream."

"Sire, I had no—"

The Emperor waved him into silence. "No matter. Moving the capital won't put much of a strain on the fleet, will it?"

"No, Sire. But this project to save Earth—"

"We will have to construct new ships for that, Fain. And we will have to turn to the frontier worlds for them." He glanced at Adela. "I believe that the frontier worlds will gladly join the effort to save Earth's Sun. And their treasuries will be enriched by our purchase of thousands of new ships."

"While the Imperial treasury is depleted."

"It's a rich Empire, Fain. It's time we shared some of our wealth with the frontier worlds. A large shipbuilding program will do more to reconcile them with the Empire than anything else we can imagine."

"Sire," said Fain bluntly, "I still think it's madness."

"Yes, I know. Perhaps it is. I only hope that I live long enough to find out, one way or the other."

"Sire," Adela said breathlessly, "you will be reuniting all the worlds of the Empire into a closely knit human community such as we haven't seen in centuries!"

"Perhaps. It would be pleasant to believe so. But for the moment, all I have done is to implement a decision to *try* to save Earth's Sun. It may succeed; it may fail. But we are sons and daughters of planet Earth, and we will not allow our original homeworld to be destroyed without struggling to our uttermost to save it."

He looked at their faces again. They were all waiting for him to continue. *You grow pompous, old man.*

"Very well. You each have several lifetimes of work to accomplish. Get busy, all of you."

Bomeer's and Fain's images winked off immediately. Javas' remained.

"Yes, my son? What is it?"

Javas' ever-present smile was gone. He looked serious, even troubled. "Father . . . I am not going to bring Rihana with me to Earth. She wouldn't want to come, I know—at least, not until all the comforts of the Court were established there for her."

The Emperor nodded.

"If I'm to be master of my own house," Javas went on, "it's time we ended this farce of a marriage."

"Very well, son. That is your decision to make. But, for what it's worth, I agree with you."

"Thank you, Father." Javas' image disappeared.

For a long moment the Emperor sat gazing thoughtfully at the wall where the holographic images had appeared.

"I believe that I will send you to Earth on Javas' ship. I think he likes you, and it is important that the two of you get along well together."

Adela looked almost shocked. "What do you mean by 'get along well together'?"

The Emperor grinned at her. "That's for the two of you to decide."

"You're scandalous!" she said, but she was smiling, too.

He shrugged. "Call it part of the price of victory. You'll like

Javas; he's a good man. And I doubt that he's ever met a woman quite like you."

"I don't know what to say . . ."

"You'll need Javas' protection and support, you know. You have defeated my closest advisors, and that means that they may become your enemies. Powerful enemies. That is also part of the price of your triumph."

"Triumph? I don't feel very triumphant."

"I know," the Emperor said. "Perhaps that's what triumph really is: not so much glorying in the defeat of your enemies as weariness that they couldn't see what seemed so obvious to you."

Abruptly, Adela moved to him and put her lips to his cheek. "Thank you, Sire."

"Why, thank you, child."

For a moment she stood there, holding his old hands in her tiny young ones.

Then, "I . . . I have lots of work to do."

"Of course. We may never see each other again. Go and do your work. Do it well."

"I will," she said. "And you?"

He leaned back into the bed and smiled wryly. "I have to hold this old Empire together long enough to see that you will succeed."

PART TWO

HE WHO MUST DIE

FOUR

Anastasio Bomeer hated the dress tunic he was desperately trying to button properly. He hated the way it pinched at his neck, and the way it made him stand straighter and with more formality—against his will—when at public gatherings. He hated the fact that Court protocol required the ancient-looking academician's garb and wished, not for the first time, that tradition would allow him to wear a more modern, more comfortable, Imperial uniform jacket instead. But above all else, he hated the occasion for the formal attire.

Damn! he thought. *What have they done to this*— With a last grunted effort he managed to get the stiff collar of the tunic fastened and stood, nearly out of breath at the exasperating effort of merely getting dressed, staring at himself in the full-length mirror in his plush suite.

His face had reddened, and the skin of his neck lapped ever so slightly over the constricting collar. Had the tunic shrunk? Surely he had not put on that much weight in his relatively short stay on the Moon. Glancing at the straining buttons midway down the front of the dress tunic, he frowned deeply, remembering that this was only the second time he'd donned the outfit in the whole year since his arrival. The first had been on the dreadful day he'd landed here, beginning what he considered a near exile on Earth's only natural satellite.

His frown deepened when he recalled that he'd put the tunic

away himself shortly after the welcoming ceremonies and that it had not been tailored or otherwise altered in any way since.

Angrily inserting a finger into each side of the collar, he tugged hard, nearly cutting off his windpipe momentarily, and managed to loosen the fit slightly. Or at least enough that the redness began to slowly drain from his face. A small sound, like a single chime, stopped him before he could struggle with the collar again.

"Wait," he said aloud, moving back into the living area. He glanced quickly at the identification banner on the comm screen, verifying the caller as his personal aide before accepting the call. "Audio only. Answer."

The screen brightened, showing the youthful face and slight build of a man who, were it not for the impeccable tailoring of his uniform, might have looked too young to be in the Imperial service. "Academician Bomeer," he said urgently. "You asked to be kept informed of the Emperor's progress . . ." The aide's voice trailed off somewhat, apparently concerned that his end of the call had remained dark.

"I've not finished dressing for the reception," Bomeer lied. "You said you had information of his whereabouts?" Hands clasped behind his back, he walked slowly to the wide expanse of ray-shielded plastiglass that made up the entire far wall of the suite. He gazed out at a barren landscape that had been described by one of the earliest explorers as "magnificent desolation." Where others may have found beauty, he found only revulsion.

"Yes, sir. We've been informed that the Emperor's landing shuttle will pad down in ten minutes."

Ahead of schedule, Bomeer thought. *Just like the old fool.* He leaned close to the surface of the window and squinted into the distance where a bright pinpoint approached rapidly from the east. From his vantage point he might be able to see nearly the entire approach of the lander as it skirted the edge of the city, before finally disappearing as it proceeded to the landing area.

"Academician?"

Without turning: "Thank you, Kandel. That will be all." There was a tiny chirp sound as the aide disconnected.

Bomeer stared solemnly over the lunar landscape. His suite on the north side of Armelin City in the Tycho district had one of the best views of any of the lunar cities. With most of the industrial and support buildings located to the south and west, the tenants at this level paid dearly for the pristine scenery, unobstructed by the towers, receiving dishes and traffic patterns which were common sights from most of the residential areas. Those who even *had* windows, that is.

He watched the approaching dot of light for several moments, and as it grew larger confirmed it to be the Emperor's shuttle. Even at this distance it looked huge. "I never believed that I would think of you in as shameful a manner as I do now," he said softly. The bright dot moved steadily closer, oblivious to his mutterings. *Save Earth's Sun?* he thought bitterly, and plainly saw his frown reflected back at him from the surface of the plastiglass. *Save these Earthers?* He turned disgustedly away from the window.

He crossed quickly to the couch and sat stiff-backed on the edge of one of the cushions, again cursing the tunic, and touched the keypad set into the bottom of the comm unit. A series of coded numbers flashed and changed briefly, finally stopping on an eight-digit number. Pressing the manual call bar, Bomeer carefully tapped the number into the keypad.

After several long seconds, a gray-haired man wearing a formal tunic that closely matched Bomeer's appeared in the screen. The man looked frustrated, and Bomeer noted with satisfaction that the collar of his tunic was still undone.

"Anastasio! I was just about to head—"

"There's been a change," Bomeer interrupted. "His shuttle is already on its way."

The look of frustration on the man's face disappeared, replaced by an expression of surprised shock. "But he wasn't due for nearly an hour! There's no way we can assemble in time."

Bomeer knew what was going through his mind. "My thought exactly. This is Javas' work, I'm sure. He's purposely having his father arrive early, hoping to catch us off guard, hoping to get whatever edge he may to gain the support of the Hundred Worlds for this foolish plan of his father's."

The other nodded thoughtfully, just a hint of anger in his eyes.

"Listen," Bomeer continued, glancing at the golden timepiece on his wrist, "I'm leaving immediately. His shuttle is landing right about now, but it should be at least another fifteen or twenty minutes before his party appears on the platform. I think I can get there before then."

"What about the rest of us?" The other man deftly buttoned the collar on the tunic and smoothed the satiny fabric with the palms of his hands, further annoying Bomeer.

"Round up as many of the others as you can, and get down there. Use this same code once I've broken the connection." Bomeer touched the keypad once to send the code to the other terminal, waited a moment for a nod of confirmation that it had been received, then touched the disconnect bar, being certain to leave the code in place on his own unit.

His eyes darted around the room. "Lights at half. Security on." The room lights dimmed immediately and a tiny red light suddenly flickered in the center of the door.

Nice try, Javas, he thought as he quickly exited the room. *But you haven't won this round yet.*

On the other side of Armelin City, in his private receiving chamber near the shuttle landing pad, Prince Javas frowned.

"I'm sorry, Sire," the synthesized voice of the comm unit repeated, "but the circuit is still engaged. A code lock is in place. Shall I implement an override?"

Javas could have Bomeer's code lock broken, of course. One quick order from the acting Emperor could not only have the circuit opened in less than a millisecond but could also have reprimand orders cut, processed, filed and sent to whichever technician had installed the system in the academician's suite. But there was no need; knowing that Bomeer was still at home was all the information he needed just now.

"No. However, please monitor the circuit and inform me when it is clear." The unit responded with a confirming chirp, and the blue screen dimmed immediately.

The Prince allowed himself a moment of wry pleasure as he wondered what the man was up to. He was certain he'd caught Bomeer and his cadre of academicians unprepared by insisting that the Emperor's shuttle arrive earlier than expected. Commander Fain had protested, of course, as had most of his father's attending Court when he'd made the suggestion via holoconference earlier that morning. But an insistent nod from him and a knowing look from the Emperor was all it took for his father to put the order to action.

How odd, he thought idly. *And how close we seem to have become; how like each other we seem to think.* Had the years of separation really made that much difference in the way he thought? Or was it the experience gained from fifteen years as acting Emperor? In the last several weeks, as his father's ship drew ever closer to Earth, the conferences and talks between the two had grown more and more numerous. Javas smiled inwardly at the realization that his father had come to know him better in these last weeks, while still separated by millions of kilometers, than in years of living together on the Imperial planet.

It suddenly occurred to him what it was: trust. The single suggestion of pushing up the landing by an hour, mentioned in just the right way, told his father *I am in charge here.* It was all that was necessary for Emperor Nicholas to immediately give Supreme Commander Fain the order for the schedule alteration.

A chime from the room system interrupted his thoughts momentarily. "Incoming message, Sire. Port Director Mila Kaselin."

"Yes, I'll accept." He swiveled his chair to face the small screen in the desktop comm unit once more. A woman appeared, talking off screen to someone as she waited for her call to go through. She turned quickly to him, a hint of embarrassment briefly crossing her youthful features. She wore the light green coveralls and matching hard hat and headset of the port authority; only the markings on her sleeve indicated she was anything other than one of hundreds of other port techs. Javas knew better: Kaselin ran the tightest, most efficient landing facility on Luna.

"Director Kaselin?" he said simply.

"Sire, the Imperial shuttle will pad down in five minutes. We're about to start landing procedure—" She turned her attention away from him abruptly, and without apology. Cupping the microphone of her headset with one hand, she spoke rapidly while studying the electronic clipboard held in her other. Like most civilians on Luna—or anywhere, for that matter—Kaselin spoke with deference, even timidity, to members of the royal family. But with Kaselin, all pretense of formality disappeared instantly when her duties interrupted. She followed protocol to the letter when necessary, but made no secret that her job, and the safety of the hundreds of people who depended on her, came first. If formality and protocol suffered as a result, so be it. Javas liked that, and silently wished that certain members of his own staff felt as strongly about their duties. He waited patiently.

The interruption dealt with, she turned back without apology and continued. "Landing procedure has begun, Sire. Your father will arrive in . . ."—again, a glance to the side—"four minutes twenty-two seconds." She nodded curtly and, not waiting for a reply, broke the connection.

"Give them hell, Mila," Javas said softly. The Prince stood. He removed his jacket from the back of the chair and slipped it on, deftly fastening the gold buttons as he approached a grouping of several plush chairs facing the opposite wall. "System," he commanded, sitting in the leftmost chair.

"Sire?"

"Open my receiving room, please. I wish to view the landing. Interior lights off for the duration."

The room dimmed and a glow formed several centimeters over the entire surface of the wall as the air shield came on. A thin shaft of light beamed into the room in a straight line along the edge where wall met ceiling, then widened as the entire wall slid noiselessly into the floor, exposing the huge landing bay.

Leaning forward, Javas looked directly below his chamber at the private viewing section reserved for members of the Court and invited guests. Nearly all the seats were filled. All, that is, except one row near the front of the section that had been reserved for Bomeer and his associates from the Academy of Science. He chuckled to himself, pleased that the academician had been so easily sidestepped. His eyes swept farther down to the floor of the chamber, fully a hundred meters below his position, where hundreds of technicians scurried about, attending to God-only-knew-what important duties that were essential to the safe landing of the ship. He squinted at the workers on the floor and in the dozens of catwalks and workstations that lined the curving walls of the circular expanse, and wondered which of the moving figures might be Kaselin.

Prince Javas shook his head slowly in awe at the tremendous sight, and allowed the corners of his mouth to turn up in a boyish grin.

"I never get tired of this," he whispered to himself, settling back in the comfort of the chair. Then, aloud, "System, please place an audio-only call to Commander Fain aboard the incoming shuttle, and inform me when through."

The public access conduit was crowded. Hundreds of people hurried down the wide, curving hallway that surrounded the landing bay. Many of them stopped momentarily to sneak a glance at the seating passes in their hands while looking for the large, painted numbers identifying each side passage in an attempt to find the spectator gallery to which they'd been assigned for the landing ceremonies.

Two men stood near a side passage identified as "Gallery 29." The shorter of the two looked nervously around at anyone who passed nearby, lowering his voice whenever he thought someone might be within earshot.

"But there are so many in each section," he was saying. He wrung his hands as he spoke and shifted his weight first to one foot, then the other. "How will I know if I'm in the right one?"

"Don't worry," replied his companion. "We've checked her seating assignment. She'll be sitting in the front row of the gallery. After the ceremonies have concluded, just wait in your seat for her to exit, then give her the letter." He seemed much calmer than the other; at ease, in fact. His exact expression, however, was hidden behind a thick beard.

"I'm not certain about this. What if—"

"Listen!" snapped the bearded man. His powerful voice cut instantly through the small man's agitation and forced him to gaze up into the bearded man's wolflike eyes; forcing him—as effectively as if he'd violently grabbed him by the lapels of his coat—to give his total attention. "Our cause is right. We must do whatever it takes to make His will succeed. Here . . ." He reached into a side pocket of his leather jacket and retrieved a gold bracelet. "Wear this, and show it to her when you identify yourself."

He obediently slipped the bracelet over his wrist, examining the engraved picture on its surface as he did. "A phoenix?"

"A trinket; it means nothing. It serves only to identify you." The bearded man took a few steps into the stream of pedestrian traffic and located an info screen he'd remembered seeing

mounted a few meters down the far wall. "They'll be sealing the
galleries in a few minutes. Better get in."

The man nodded, absently fingering the bracelet on his wrist,
and headed down the passageway.

The bearded man stood unobtrusively in front of the passageway, pretending to be waiting for someone, until he heard a large
doorway close. A quick look toward the gallery confirmed that
it had been sealed; an armed guard stood before it.

Satisfied that no one would be leaving the gallery until after
the ceremonies, he casually strolled away from gallery 29, careful
not to attract attention.

The huge landing shuttle continued its deceleration as it approached Armelin City. Still five kilometers out, the spherical
craft reoriented slightly and slowed even further—an observer on
the ground might even have assumed it had stopped all forward
motion entirely.

"Imperial shuttle *Bright Cay* now in approach position, awaiting final clearance."

"You are in pattern, *Bright Cay,* and we have you in approach
mode. You may proceed at your convenience."

"Roger, approach mode. Stand by, please." The pilot turned
in her chair to face the uniformed man seated in the log officer's
station behind her.

Supreme Commander Fain stirred uneasily in the chair, feeling
useless and unnecessary on the deceptively small control bridge
of the shuttle. Indeed, the log officer had to be reassigned to an
auxiliary position on the bridge afterdeck just to make room for
him behind the pilot.

Protocol.

There was no real need for him to even be here. He knew the
five-person crew could handle this or any other landing in their
sleep—Fain had, in fact, personally selected them from among
his own officers on the flagship now orbiting the Moon—but
protocol demanded his presence all the same.

"Commander?" The pilot was still looking at him expectantly.
The copilot had also turned to face him, and Fain wondered how
long he'd hesitated.

"You may proceed with final approach," he said firmly, then
sat straighter in his chair to see over the pilot's shoulder and

watch the landscape below as it began to slide past the shuttle once more.

The new landing facility was clearly visible on the southern tip of the settlement, where all major traffic in and out of Armelin City was handled. There were numerous landing domes of various sizes located here, but the largest of them, built especially to handle Imperial traffic, was separated from the rest and appeared to be a miniature city in its own right. Smaller domes and external, unenclosed pads surrounded it. An irregularly shaped structure Fain recognized as an independent power facility stood out bright orange against the dull gray of the regolith.

"Now at one and one," the pilot said, indicating the ship was at a distance and height of one kilometer.

"One and one confirmed. Come to five hundred meters for final lock-in."

"Coming to five hundred."

Fain felt a twinge of envy. How long had it been since he'd actually piloted a ship like this with his own hands? The personnel of the port authority were controlling a good portion of the landing now, but the final hand-off was yet to come. Fain sighed and leaned back in the chair; as they neared the dome and the vertical angle increased, there was not much to be seen through the front viewport anyway. He could watch the rest of the approach on the small viewscreen set into the log officer's station.

"Commander Fain?" said the communications officer to his left. "I'm receiving an automated ground-based message for you."

Now? "Put it through, then."

"It's coded private, sir; audio-only."

Fain exhaled heavily and thumbed a switch on the armrest of his chair, putting his headset into private mode. "This is Fain," he said, then waited for confirmation that his voiceprint ID had been verified.

"Stand by for a transmission from Prince Javas," said a synthesized voice. Fain's brow knitted in concern: The call was automated through the Prince's personal system, and not being handled by Luna. "Ready to receive?"

"Yes." There was a one-second delay before the transmission started, but it seemed much longer.

"Commander, I hope you are in good health?"

"I am, Sire. But I must admit to being somewhat puzzled by your call."

The Prince's chuckle buzzed in the headset.

"I'm sorry if I alarmed you. You'll be landing in a few moments and I'll see you personally then on the receiving platform, but there's something I wanted to say to you now.

"When you bring the ship down, you'll also be bringing to an end the long and hard transfer of the Imperial Court to Earth. I'm sure I don't need to remind you of the scope of this undertaking, nor of its ultimate importance to my father's project. But—" He paused, and for a moment Fain thought the young man might be at a loss for words, perhaps for the first time since he'd known him.

"I've relied on you these last fifteen years more than you know," he continued. "My father's health is not good. You know that, have known it, for many years now. But you may not realize just how close you are to my father's favor."

"Sire, I—"

"Let me finish, Commander. You've served my father well, as both Commander of the Imperial fleet . . . and as a friend. He's depended on you for personal advice as much as for professional competence, and I'm convinced he would not have survived the trip without you. Thank you, Fain."

Fain sat, stunned, and could think of no response. His jaw moved soundlessly, but the Prince, apparently aware of his discomfort, spared him further embarrassment by quickly adding in an upbeat voice, "I'll see you soon, Commander." There was an almost imperceptible click in the headset, indicating that the signal had disconnected.

"We're at five hundred meters, Commander, and holding," the pilot said over her shoulder. Fain quickly recovered and thumbed the headset off private.

"Give me an underside view, please." His viewscreen switched immediately to show the landing dome below them. Concentric targeting rings glowed brightly around the perimeter of the dome in a bull's-eye pattern. A dark circular portion in the center of the rings, the massive landing bay doors, was easily discernible even in the tiny screen.

"I have the Port Director now, sir; would you care to give the hand-off?"

Fain looked at her, and caught the slight smile before she turned back to her control panel. "Thank you." He thumbed the armrest. "Director Kaselin, what is your status?"

"We're now in full lock-in, and are ready for pad-down."

"The *Bright Cay* is ready. Bring us in."

"Yes, sir." She disconnected immediately. A quick shuddering grasped the ship as the gravity harness engaged. The sensation ended almost at once, and the ship started moving smoothly toward the dome, completely under ground control now. Fain watched in satisfaction as the well-trained crew began the shutdown procedures. All thrust was reduced to standby levels and the background noise and vibration of the engines—so ever-present during their entire flight—decreased, leaving the control bridge in relative silence.

As the crew finished the procedures, there was little left for them to do except monitor the systems on standby and enjoy the remainder of the ride. All video monitors in the small room showed the landing dome, now only a hundred meters directly below them.

Fain relaxed for the first time since the shuttle left the flagship and joined the others in watching the landing. He returned his attention to the screen just as an opening appeared at the crown of the dome.

The landing bay of the Imperial dome was the largest single enclosed space Adela de Montgarde had ever seen. The port facilities on Gris were tiny by comparison. Even the starport on the Imperial planet, certainly the largest on any of the Hundred Worlds, had nothing like this.

She sat in the fifth row of a special section reserved for those personally invited by the Imperial Court, accompanied on either side by members of her scientific staff. She recognized many of the other invitees despite their formal attire, but realized that there were even more that she had never seen before. She quickly surveyed the section and noted that, with the exception of the row directly in front of hers, nearly every seat was filled. Adela wondered inwardly, looking along the empty row, why that obnoxious Bomeer and his group of sycophants had not yet arrived. Surely he had been informed of the change in arrival time. *Probably wants to make an entrance,* she thought.

Her eyes scanned the vast chamber, trying to take it all in. The ceiling was fully four hundred meters above her, and it was necessary to look closely to make out the separation lines between the movable doors at the top of the dome and the gently curving walls that rose to meet them. There were several catwalks regularly spaced on the walls, and the lighted windows of numerous workstations, viewing rooms and technical facilities glowed brightly on the various levels.

Below the lowest of the catwalks were the spectator galleries which, like the dome itself, had been constructed especially for this momentous occasion and nearly sparkled in their newness. Arranged irregularly around the perimeter of the landing bay, the galleries gave the facility the appearance of a sporting arena, although the odd layout of sections throughout the dome reminded Adela of no athletic event she could imagine.

Each section was packed, with few empty seats visible. The dome had begun filling many hours ago: The spectators had been waiting patiently for the Emperor's arrival through most of the afternoon. The gallery level was well separated from the upper, technical reaches of the dome, and each section was widely spaced from the next. Adela noted the hundreds of lightly armed security personnel, each in formal dress uniform, who strolled the lower catwalk as well as the wide areas between the sections themselves.

The entire area was dominated—or perhaps dwarfed would be a better word—by the enormous landing platform below, crisscrossed with a glowing grid pattern. It was the grid markings themselves that gave astute observers a clue to the true size of the place: Adela knew the grid lines were spaced twenty meters apart, but from this distance they looked as close together as lines on graph paper.

A heightened buzz swept through the crowd and she turned in her seat to see the source of the excitement. Immediately above them a viewing room had opened, and the Prince himself sat ready to witness his father's arrival. He stood, raising a hand in salute to the crowd, and the room swelled with the sounds of cheering, applause, whistles and shouts.

The joyful noise continued unabated until the Prince rose and moved to the rear of the room, out of Adela's line of sight. He returned minutes later and she assumed by his unhurried manner

that he'd merely taken care of some routine business or had been
called away momentarily by an aide. Javas remained standing at
the edge of the room, hands clasped behind his back, and
scanned the Imperial section, picking her out. When their eyes
met, a smile came to his face and he nodded in greeting. His eyes
lingered a few moments longer before sweeping out across the
crowded chamber. He waved again to the crowd and took his
seat.

A faint humming sound, more felt than heard, and a sudden
brightness in the air took her by surprise. She looked up and
watched as an air shield snapped into place around her entire
section. Elsewhere around the massive landing bay, shielding was
coming on section by section, and the surprised gasps of scattered spectators not familiar with the security precaution reached
her ears. Gasps invariably gave way to nervous laughter, however, when those more used to the technology explained to their
neighbors what was happening.

The air filled with three sharp blasts of a warning horn that
immediately silenced the crowd. Dozens of rotating lights ringing
the topmost catwalk drew all eyes upward. Another shield was
forming at the top of the dome. It brightened as it formed,
gradually expanding until the entrance doors in the ceiling were
completely covered.

The crowd stared in silent awe as a soft hissing sound filled the
chamber. The spectators did not seem as startled by the sound as
Adela might have expected, and she had assumed that the unini-
tiated had been forewarned that the evacuation of air from the
space between the air shield and the doors themselves was normal procedure.

The hissing faded away, punctuated by a single, steady blast of
the horn, and the doors parted in the center with a rumbling that
sent vibrations through the entire dome. Although the landing
bay was brightly illuminated, even Adela was not prepared for
the brilliance of the shaft of light that burst through the opening.
Many in the crowd looked quickly away, eyes stinging from the
sudden brightness, and watched the path of light as it rapidly
widened on the landing platform below until they grew accustomed to the intensity and returned their gaze to the opening
above just in time to see the doors clank into place at their widest
point.

Nothing happened for what seemed a long time, then a sudden chattering and a collective gasp spread through the crowd. It started at the lowest rows, where spectators nearer the center saw it first, then spread quickly up through the galleries.

My God, it's huge, Adela thought as the landing gear and the underside of the shuttle appeared over the opening. The sunlight reflecting off the spacecraft's gleaming, white surface brought tears to her eyes and she squinted, rubbing them occasionally on the backs of her knuckles. Above the air shield dust and smoke swirled violently in incongruous silence in the narrow open space just inside the doors, but the swirling abated immediately when the standby thrusters were shut down. Caught securely in the landing bay's gravity harness, the ship lowered smoothly and steadily through the opening.

The landing feet touched the air shield first, causing the entire glowing surface to shimmer momentarily. The air sparkled around the gear as the craft lowered through the shield, and glowing ripples spread across the width of it as on the surface of a pond. As the shuttle came through the shield, Adela became aware of the increasing sound level. Mechanical hums and the descending whine of the thrusters as they continued through their shutdown cycle came from within the craft itself, while sections of the gleaming metal skin popped and creaked as it began to equalize to the internal dome air temperature.

The shuttle had just barely cleared the shield when the doors started slowly closing again. As it happened, the doors thunked shut at nearly the exact instant the shuttle came to rest dead center on the landing platform. The full weight of the craft settled suddenly on its gear as the gravity harness was released. Adela looked at the massive lander, her eyes sweeping along the front where the smoothness of its surface was marred only by the bulge of the control bridge halfway to the top. She could see the crew moving inside the cramped space, going through their postlanding checks.

She'd never seen anything like it, and neither had the thousands of people who had turned out for the event. A mighty roar went up from the galleries, virtually drowning out the sound of the bay's recirculating fans as they eliminated the last of the thruster exhaust from the chamber.

Adela turned once more to the Prince's viewing room behind

their section. He was nodding, the relief evident on his features. After a moment, he stood and joined in the general applause.

She looked back to the ship and, unable to contain herself, rose with the crowd and began to clap her hands.

Only moments before, the occupants of *Bright Cay* not involved in the actual landing process itself were unaware of the magnificence of the huge doors about to open as the shuttle approached. The Emperor of the Hundred Worlds sat comfortably in his powerchair, in spite of the stiffly formal uniform he wore, and enjoyed the natural pull of the world below him, the first natural gravity he'd felt in years. The closest of his personal physicians back on Corinth, the former Imperial capital, used to chide him about being able to tell the difference between the artificial light gravity they'd prescribed for his personal quarters there and natural gravity. But, like the bio-implants he'd more than grown accustomed to, he knew, *sensed* somehow, the subtle differences that lesser men missed.

"How long till we land?" he asked Brendan, the full-time aide assigned to him for the duration of the long voyage. He refused to think of Brendan as anything but his aide, even though common sense and practicality constantly reminded him that he was an aide in name only; that he was, in reality, a twenty-four-hour nurse. His lips drew together in a tight line of disgust every time the word "nurse" flashed in his mind, but despite the unwelcome feeling, the Emperor liked the young man and enjoyed his company.

It was a sign of either good training or insight that Brendan refrained from jumping to the Emperor's side at the question in an overbearing attempt to reassure him of the safe progress of the vessel—certainly the Emperor had had enough of *those* kinds of aides—and he appreciated, not for the first time, Brendan's candor and approach to his position. As it was, the younger man only turned slightly in his seat and, glancing at the timepiece on his wrist, replied simply, "About five minutes, Sire." He was watching the progress of the landing on the large viewscreen set into the opposite wall.

As if an afterthought had occurred to him, he added casually, "There's still time to ride out the landing in your stateroom, Sire, should you prefer."

The Emperor studied the young man. Even though his medical condition was constantly being relayed to the Imperial computer and then to the medical staff, his aide had his own implants and constantly monitored his medical readouts. Even now, he knew, Brendan was comparing respiration, heart rate, blood pressure and other biolevels with those found to be acceptable for the Emperor in a variety of conditions. *My pulse must be up slightly,* thought the Emperor, *or he would not have suggested a move designed to get me back into bed.* He made a conscious effort to relax, breathing slowly and easily to calm his excitement at the imminent conclusion of the lengthy trip.

Brendan turned to him once more, right eyebrow arched slightly at an angle nearly matching the half-smile appearing on his face. "I guess not, then."

The Emperor knew his efforts at subterfuge had been read and interpreted correctly, and returned a knowing smile. *I can't keep much from you, can I?* he added silently.

There was a brief shuddering, followed by a decrease in the slight, almost imperceptible background noise of the cabin. The progress of the shuttle smoothed then, as they resumed their forward-and-down movement toward the landing dome.

The Emperor had been kept advised of Javas' progress as his son set up the seat of Empire on the Moon. He'd even approved personally the plans for the facility they now approached. All the same, he was impressed with what he saw on the viewscreen.

He watched in silence as the viewscreen feed reoriented to an underside view, allowing a perfect angle for observing the doors—now directly below them—and their final descent.

The landing itself proceeded more rapidly than he might have expected, and it seemed as if only moments had passed when the contact warning horn sounded softly over the room system. There was a slight jar as the landing gear touched the pad, then another as the gravity harness released. The Emperor accessed the shuttle computer through his integrator and quickly verified that the landing had been perfect in every way, although he expected no less from Fain's handpicked crew. He issued a silent command, giving commendations to each member of the shuttle crew.

Brendan stood solemnly, a rare look of seriousness on his face. "Sire, I . . . I'd like to request permission to remain aboard until after you've been transported to the Imperial residence."

"Oh?" The Emperor scrutinized the young man's features, looking for some clue to his discomfort. "Why is that?" The aide tensed under his gaze. Accessing his own implanted integrator, he observed that Brendan's pulse and respiration were both elevated. *We are linked inextricably,* he mused. *Patient and caretaker, linked more closely than Siamese twins.* He softened his tone. "Brendan, if we cannot speak freely to each other after these many years together, then I know you less than I had believed. Please, do you have a concern of which I should be made aware?"

The change in the Emperor's voice seemed to relax the man, and he continued, more sure of himself this time. "Sire, your medical readouts are already being switched over from the ship to the Imperial computers here, plus I'll continue to monitor you personally, of course. But when you leave the ship in a few minutes, it will mark the first time you've been seen publicly in many years. I understand that the ceremonies are being carried on all the Sol system and Imperial nets, not to mention the thousands who have traveled here for the honor of being on hand for this historic moment . . ." He stopped, took a deep breath. "Do you really want to be seen with your, uh, nurse standing by your side?"

The words now in the open, Brendan exhaled heavily and gazed steadily into the Emperor's face. The Emperor absently rubbed his white-bearded chin with his thin, frail fingers and nodded silently. The thought had simply not occurred to him. *I must truly be getting old, to overlook such an obvious point,* he admitted inwardly. He looked at the young man and extended a bony hand.

"You're right, Brendan," he said, feeling the strength in the other's grasp. "Thank you for pointing it out." Disengaging the powerchair from the magnetic landing restraints, he glided quietly to the viewscreen. "Inform Commander Fain that I am ready to leave, at his soonest convenience."

"Yes, Sire." Brendan bowed slightly and turned immediately for the door.

It took nearly fifteen minutes before the room system informed him that Commander Fain was on his way, and another ten before they arrived at the shuttle's elevator. Most of the accompanying members of the Imperial Court were already waiting in formation outside the ship, and the two men, alone on the lift, rode in near silence until the elevator tapped softly down on the platform of the landing bay itself. The Emperor cocked his head to one side, listening intently to a steady vibration that seeped through the walls of the cubicle. Fain caught the motion and offered, "It's the crowd, Sire."

"Well, then," he replied, "we had best not keep them waiting any longer." He nodded once, and Fain touched a small keypad set into the front wall of the lift.

The door slid aside instantly, and both men were hit by what seemed like a solid wall of sound. The Emperor of the Hundred Worlds smoothly powered the chair forward onto the crowded platform, Commander Fain walking steadily at his right. Imperial officers, flagship crew and shuttle crew members, support personnel and numerous other dignitaries parted as he passed, and fell into position behind him. Fain escorted the Emperor to a large circular receiving area that had obviously been set up for the reception, then took two steps back as the Emperor himself glided into its center.

Lights dimmed slightly in the chamber and a spotlight illuminated the circle. He raised a hand in greeting, and the crowd exploded once more into tumultuous applause that continued for several long minutes. He raised both hands now in an effort to quiet them, and waited patiently for the noise to die slowly away. He glanced to Fain, who touched his earpiece once and nodded, indicating that the audio pickups in the landing bay were operative and ready, then turned to face the crowd.

"I thank you deeply for your warm welcome," he said simply, his strong voice reverberating from the curved walls of the immense room. "It is good to be home."

The crowd burst into approving applause, and the Emperor thought better of attempting an address at this time. Instead, he extended a hand to a point just above the nearest gallery, the one reserved for Imperial guests, and motioned directly at the Prince's viewing room. Another spotlight arched across the room, catching the Prince in its center, and all eyes turned to face Javas as he rose, bowed briefly, then turned swiftly and disappeared from view. He reappeared seconds later at a door at the top of the gallery flanked by two color guards and, with a single wave to the crowd, started down the steps set to one side of the private section. He walked slowly, purposefully, down the narrow aisle until reaching the fifth row. He stopped, and held out a hand to a formally dressed woman sitting a few seats down the row. The woman hesitated, but at the insistent urging of those around her she rose and edged carefully down the row to stand nervously at the Prince's side.

He extended his arm and escorted her forward to the bottom of the gallery. The Prince's color guard separated and quickly took position on either side of a short set of steps leading to the landing grid itself. A section of the air shield at the top of the steps quivered visibly and changed color momentarily, allowing Javas and Adela to pass through, then solidified when they continued on to the reviewing area where the Emperor now waited.

They were nearly on the platform itself before the Emperor recognized the woman being escorted by his son as the tiny girl who, in his bed chamber one night that seemed a thousand years ago, convinced him of her plan to save Earth's Sun. *The years have aged her,* he thought as she curtsied formally before him. He studied her face and realized that behind her eyes was a subtle look of surprised shock, a look that reflected her own concern at how much *he* had deteriorated.

Prince Javas bowed deeply and moved to stand at the front of the receiving circle, where he looked out over the crowd and raised an arm to silence them. When he was satisfied that the noise level had subsided to his liking, he carefully removed the Imperial sash and held it above him in both hands, turning slowly so as many people as possible could see what he was about to do. Ceremoniously he knelt at the side of his father's power-chair and placed the sash over the older man's head, smoothing the glistening, satiny material across his shoulder. He leaned close and whispered in his father's ear, "Things are going well." He nodded to the empty row in the reserved gallery and enjoyed the look of understanding in the old man's eyes as he realized that Bomeer had been sidestepped. He stood upright again and faced the crowd.

"Ladies and gentlemen," the Prince said forcefully, proudly, in a voice more powerful and commanding than the Emperor had remembered. "I give you Nicholas, Emperor of the Hundred Worlds!"

There was no restraining the people now as they erupted into applause and shouts of approval that seemed to shake the very walls of the landing bay. Javas stepped briskly to a smiling Commander Fain, offering a hand that the other grasped and shook vigorously. As the Prince turned formally and stood on his father's right, Fain immediately crossed behind the Emperor and took position on his left, completing the ceremonial transfer of power. As the threesome remained in formation for the audience review, the Emperor noticed that Adela, unfamiliar with Imperial protocol, stood awkwardly at the edge of the receiving circle. He looked up and caught his son's eye, nodding in her direction. Javas raised an eyebrow in silent request and, when the Emperor nodded approval, slowly extended his arm, indicating that she should join him at his side.

The noise was so loud that it took several moments before anyone noticed the commotion off to the right side of the reviewing platform. Dozens of security personnel had surrounded one of the public galleries, and the people in the gallery itself seemed to be scrambling in an effort to escape.

There was a sudden flash in one of the backmost rows of the gallery and the entire wedge-shaped area suddenly turned crimson as the explosion was contained by the shielding. The flash subsided immediately, leaving only a smoke-filled cube behind.

A sudden crackling filled the air as the shield surrounding the landing area—until now at a normal setting—snapped to maximum, adding a translucent haze around the perimeter of the platform that made it difficult to observe what was happening in the gallery. Javas lunged for his father's powerchair in an instinctive attempt to cover the Emperor with his own body, but a dozen members of the Imperial security staff had immediately surrounded him, separating him from the Emperor for safety's sake, just as Fain and Adela were being hustled under equally heavy guard to different secure areas. The Emperor tried desperately to make out what was happening in the landing chamber, but he was already being placed into the protective custody of the shuttle crew.

If what he suspected was true, the entire gallery—effectively contained by the air shield—had been turned into an oven, guaranteeing the death of everyone in the section. The Emperor shook his head, realizing that his greatest fear had come true.

So, he thought. *It begins.*

FIVE

"**D**ead. All dead."

The Emperor of the Hundred Worlds hadn't realized he'd spoken the words aloud, although softly, and was startled momentarily by the confused beeping of the info system built into the walls of his study. The system had mistaken the words as an incomplete command.

"Cancel—" he started to say, then thought better of it. He hesitated, knowing how great the pain would be if he acted on the sudden thought. He sighed heavily, feeling the tiredness of the last twenty-four hours wash over him, and glided the powerchair to a position facing the center of the large viewscreen on the far wall of his study.

"Interior lights off." The room's artificial lighting dimmed immediately, but the screen cast a soft, comfortable glow over the room. "Give me a single-screen biographical file on each of the victims of yesterday's explosion in gallery 29, alphabetically."

"Manual or continuous rotation?"

"Manual." The Emperor's reply was a whisper. Although easily picked up by the system, another person in the room would have heard only the slightest mumbling. *The mutterings of an aging man,* he thought bitterly.

"The specified files will require some time to cycle manually, Sire. Would you prefer an integrator download?"

Emperor Nicholas didn't answer, and instead stared intently at the screen. The first bio was already displayed, and showed a young man with disheveled sandy hair and a beaming smile. *James Altann,* read the file. *Age: 32. Home: Alphonsus, Luna. Occupation: Cargo Driver, Exterior. Marital status: Married, one child.*

"Would you prefer an integrator download?" the room system repeated.

"No, audiovisual only. Next file." The screen display changed instantly, showing a freckle-faced woman with long blond hair and sparkling blue eyes. *Miriam Altann. Age: 31. Home: Alphonsus, Luna . . .*

As useful as the integrator was, the Emperor had come to loathe it and used it only when necessary; when alone, he nearly always shunned it. The information his personal link with the Imperial computer provided was extremely valuable—and frequently indispensable—but he had come to believe that it made the information it imparted too unfeeling, too "clean." The integrator could have provided all the files in a matter of seconds, but the Emperor wanted to observe them with his own senses, individually, one at a time.

"Sire," the system intoned, accompanied by an insistent chiming. "I have an incoming communication, coded as important."

"Store all messages for later retrieval. Next." The Emperor moved the powerchair closer and felt a sudden chill wash over him as he scanned the file. "Five years old," he whispered.

There was a single beep from the system, indicating confusion once more at what it interpreted as another incomplete command. He ignored it and concentrated instead on the bio file of little Tracy Altann, noting how the child's freckles and deep blue eyes closely matched her mother's.

"Next file." The Emperor went through the files slowly, one after another. There were numerous single entries, with no apparent connection to those who had died in the seats next to them. Some were Armelin City employees, some were tourists. There were members of the Imperial research staff and local shopkeepers. There were other whole families who, like the Altanns, had traveled for the rare privilege of witnessing the Emperor's arrival.

All dead.

He started cycling through the files again. "This is a code one override." The room system's persistent tone broke Emperor Nicholas from his unpleasant task and he turned sharply away from the viewscreen. "This is a code one override," it repeated. He had no way of knowing how many times the system had paged him since he'd disabled it several minutes earlier, but he did know that the override page would repeat until it was acknowledged. His physicians, rightly concerned for the aging leader's continually deteriorating health, had ordered the override code installed in his personal page program. The Emperor also knew that if he ignored the code one page *too* long, Brendan and the medical staff, escorted by a full security team, would cut through the door with torches if necessary to determine why he had not responded. He reluctantly issued a mental command to reopen the communications program in the room.

"I do not wish to be disturbed!"

"Father, are you all right?" It was Javas. "I've been trying to reach you for some time and grew concerned. May I come in?" The Emperor did not answer immediately, and Javas' tone grew more insistent. "Father, I must speak with you about the accident in the landing bay."

The Emperor sighed, resigning himself to the fact that he had postponed this meeting long enough. Through the integrator, he ordered the system to abandon voice mode and return the room lighting to normal levels before admitting the Prince. "I'm sorry, Javas," he said as his son entered, "but I was reading the files of those killed in the blast and, well, I'm afraid I got a bit more involved than I had intended." He studied the Prince for a moment and, knowing that the young man would someday perform similar tasks, smiled briefly before adding, "It never gets any easier."

Javas nodded politely, staring over his father's shoulder. *Display off,* he commanded silently, but realized Javas must surely have seen Tracy Altann's file on the screen. Javas quickly returned his attention to him as the display winked out and was replaced with an external view of the lunar surface surrounding Armelin City, simply nodding at his father's remark rather than pointing out the obvious. *Thank you, son, for allowing me a moment of private pain,* he thought.

"Please, be seated."

Javas chose a firm, straight-backed swivel chair in front of the huge desk that dominated the room, and turned it to face the older man. The massive piece of furniture, handmade of the finest woods and inlaid with precious metals from a dozen planets, had been a welcoming gift from Javas. The Prince had arranged for its construction shortly after arriving on the Moon, giving orders that it be installed in the Emperor's study before his father arrived.

The two men regarded each other silently for several moments, each feeling the awkwardness of this first face-to-face meeting alone in so many years. The Emperor noted that Javas' manner had changed significantly since entering his study. The anger and frustration of dealing with the tragedy had shown plainly on his face when he'd first arrived, but now he seemed more nervous than the awkwardness of the situation warranted. The young man sat stiffly upright in the chair, not touching the backrest, and fidgeted uneasily. The Prince seemed to have difficulty keeping eye contact with him, but those moments when their eyes did meet, the Emperor saw a glint of something—a mixture of pain and regret?—in his son's face. He called up a diagnostic readout on the Prince's personal biomonitors. The information came to him quickly and confirmed what he'd suspected: His son's heart rate, respiration and brain activity were all at high readings, despite his son's best efforts to hide his discomfort.

Their eyes met briefly, and the Emperor knew that Javas had guessed what he was doing. *My turn to save you a bit of embarrassment,* he thought.

"You are shocked at my appearance," he said simply, bluntly. "But what did you expect? I was an old man before we embarked on this grand adventure thirty years ago. I age. The Emperor always ages." He leveled his gaze at Javas and looked deeply into his son's eyes, then added, "As will you, when you become Emperor and are forced to stop rejuvenation."

"Father, I—"

"No, Javas. It's all right." His words carried a tone of understanding as he spoke. All trappings of Emperor and Prince abandoned for the moment, he spoke instead as father to son. "I do not need the integrator to tell me what you're thinking. The many holoconferences we've held in recent months are one thing, but seeing me alone now, here in this room, you've been forced to come to terms with your own future. A future that, I fear, may be coming to pass much sooner than either of us would like."

Javas nodded silently, then looked into his father's eyes.

"These fifteen years here have not been easy," he began. "When I first set about my task of relocating the Imperial throne here, I had many questions about the wisdom of this undertaking. In the last year I'm afraid I asked too many of those questions of Bomeer and listened too closely and too often to his answers. But for every reason he expressed that this was but a"—the Prince paused, regarded his father a moment before going on—"a fool's mission . . ."

The Emperor gave an amused snort. "Well, there is at least one thing, then, that the years cannot change."

"Each time he attempted to win me to his side on a particular issue or procedure surrounding our purpose here, Adela—Dr. Montgarde—convinced me of each issue's validity."

The Emperor raised an eyebrow. "I see."

"Academician Bomeer has done his best at every turn to convert others to his side of the argument, as well, even as he follows your orders—"

"Son," the Emperor interrupted, feeling his demeanor change. Where before he had been disturbed, even shaken, by the tragedy of the day before, he now summoned up his inner strength and once more spoke as Emperor. "I have seen the reports; those that you have been so thoughtful as to provide as well as my own private intelligence. I am aware of the problems you've faced here and of your many successes. I am quite familiar with the situation, as it stands now." He glided the powerchair to its workstation behind the desk, a silent order opening a cabinet set into the wall behind him as he pivoted around and took a bottle and two glasses from the well-stocked shelves inside. He smiled to himself as he turned back to the desk, amused at what his physicians would think if they knew of this secret cache, installed at Javas' order to match the one in his study on Corinth. He gave another silent order, this time to suppress those particular bio-monitors that would relay certain information—specifically, information concerning his intake of alcohol and its effect on his system—to Brendan, who was certainly monitoring his readouts around the clock.

"In fact," he went on, pouring two drinks, "even though I've been in the system but a short time, I'm sure I can provide you with more useful information than you might imagine." He handed one of the drinks to the Prince, then held his own up in a brief salute before taking a long sip of the liquor. "Are you aware, for example, that there is to be an assassination attempt next week at the Hundred Worlds Planetary Council?"

Javas stared at his father, the glass frozen mere centimeters from his lips.

"Lost your taste for drink, son?" The Emperor sipped at his glass, set it down near the terminal screen built into the desktop.

"Father! You can't be serious." Javas downed his own glass in a single bolt.

The Emperor shook his head. "Fine liquor should be savored, not gulped. Yes, I'm quite serious. As we address the collected representatives of the Hundred Worlds, there will be another attempt on our lives; yours and mine. And probably Dr. Montgarde's as well."

Javas, quickly regaining his composure, set the empty glass slowly on the desk in front of him. The Emperor studied his son carefully and raised a pleased eyebrow when he noted that the momentary blip in the young man's bio-readout had returned quickly to normal.

"I can understand why you have become a target, Father," he said bluntly, "and, to a lesser extent, myself. If I've learned anything these last fifteen years here, it's that your project has not been well received by all. There would be many who would like to see the plan defeated with the end of your reign. But why should Dr. Montgarde's life be in danger? Surely any opposition would realize that without the full power and support of the Emperor to back her work, the plan would end here and now, whether she was part of the project or not."

"Would it, then?" He looked steadily at his son, allowing the meaning of his words to sink in. "If I were dead, you would immediately assume the throne. And, whether you realize it or not, it is already widely known through many of the Hundred Worlds that you would continue the work where I left off." He reached once more for the bottle and refilled each glass. He sipped once of the dark brown liquor before continuing. "And son, unless I'm misinterpreting both my information and my own senses, it is also obvious to many that you will certainly be working much more closely with Dr. Montgarde than I ever would have."

The Prince sat quietly, then rose and approached the viewscreen. Staring at the sparkling lunar landscape, he sipped at his drink. "I've been a fool," he said quietly, turning back to face the imposing figure seated behind the huge desk. "I've been entirely too open about my feelings for this project." He paused, then added, "And, yes; I have grown close to Adela de Montgarde."

The Emperor waved a hand to dismiss the small confession and indicated the chair before the desk, waiting until the Prince sat before going on. "You've not been a fool. In fact, your unbridled enthusiasm for the Doctor's theories will probably, in the long run, work to your advantage. Consider this: Many think my backing of this plan to be merely the dream of a weak old man, clinging to the last strings of power before the inevitable occurs." The Emperor paused, allowing a tiny smile to spread across his lips as he absently studied the empty glass in his wrinkled hand.

"Well, perhaps there is some truth in that. In any event, you are well liked and respected. Your work here has impressed many of the representatives of the Hundred Worlds. For them to see your conviction and enthusiasm has, no doubt, won many more followers than Bomeer's frenzied rantings."

While Javas considered what he'd just heard, the Emperor issued another silent command, then leaned wearily back into the comfort of the powerchair. A green light flashed several times on the right armrest of the chair. The Emperor pressed the light briefly, extinguishing it, then said aloud, "Enter."

Prince Javas turned his head toward the opposite side of the study and stood as a door, previously invisible in the intricate woodworking of the room's far wall, slid noiselessly into the matching paneling surrounding it.

The newcomer was of medium height and build, quite unimposing really, and wore—not a fleet uniform or an Imperial jacket, as might be expected of someone entering the Emperor's private study in so sure a manner—but plain, civilian clothing in a style currently popular in the larger, more cosmopolitan lunar cities. A closer examination of his clothing, however, showed that his outfit was not as inexpensively tailored as a casual glance would lead one to believe; that it had, in fact, been purposely designed to look quite ordinary, as though the wearer wished to be able to blend into a crowd without calling attention to himself. The door closed behind him and the newcomer suddenly adopted a much more formal attitude as he approached the massive desk, stopping barely a meter away. There was no mistaking that when he stood, he stood at attention. The Emperor nodded once and the man relaxed, clasping his hands casually in front of him.

"No, you have not been foolish to show your excitement,"

the old man went on, returning his attention to the Prince. "However, you have been careless in some matters. Oh, please meet Marcus Glenney." Again, the Emperor leaned back, watching the reaction on his son's face. *So, the old man can still surprise, eh?*

Javas extended a hand in cordial greeting, but he tilted his head to one side, narrowing his eyes as a look of haven't-I-seen-you-somewhere-before spread openly across his features. "Do I know you?"

Glenney took his hand with a strong, firm grasp. "No, not officially. But it is good to finally meet you, Young Prince."

"We've met . . . unofficially, then?"

The Emperor chuckled softly, enjoying the small joke, and indicated that both men be seated. He fetched a glass and poured a drink for the newcomer, who thanked him but nonetheless set the glass down without drinking.

"Marc has been with you for nearly, what, twenty-five years now, subjective time?" Glenney nodded. "And with my arrival becomes head of Imperial security here on Luna. He has been your constant companion—without your knowledge, I'm afraid—since your wedding day. I assigned him as your personal protector the same day"—he paused, the sound of contempt plain in his voice even to him—"that *she* entered our House."

"So, it seems I have a guardian angel," Javas replied, ignoring his father's aside at his former wife. An amused smile appeared momentarily on his lips before his voice lowered, assuming a no-nonsense tone. As he spoke, Glenney sat a bit more upright in his chair. "My father would not be revealing your identity, indeed, your very existence to me, if there were not a point to all of this. What have you to report?"

The Emperor watched and listened closely to his son, pleased at how quickly he had adjusted to this new situation, how readily he had taken charge. *You have matured greatly,* he thought. *I should have set you to an important task much sooner.*

"Young Prince, I regret that there have been no fewer than three assassination attempts since your arrival here on the Moon."

"Three!" A look of surprised shock. "I know of one, eleven months ago. My own security team"—Javas shot a quick look at his father—"informed me of their suspicions long before the threat was realized. Those involved were apprehended and dealt with."

Glenney looked steadily at the Prince and said, not a hint of apology in his delivery, "I know. Your security team was given a great deal of help. By me. The information was channeled secretly, of course. They had no way of knowing that they'd not defused the situation as a result of their own efforts."

Glenney glanced to the Emperor, who nodded curtly, then continued. "The second was taken care of without the knowledge of your personal security. In this case, however, those responsible were rounded up early on at Landsdowne, on the far side, with the threat never even making it to Armelin City."

"I see." Javas sat, unmoving, and stared intently at the security man. "And the third?"

For the first time since entering the study, Glenney squirmed uneasily in his chair. He turned to the Emperor, awaiting a sign to continue, when Javas pounded a fist on the table.

"Don't look to my father for permission to speak! I asked you a question!" Glenney sat bolt upright, as if snapped to attention on a parade ground, but before he could answer, the Emperor held up a withered hand.

He looked to Javas, feeling a mixture of pride at the sudden strength exhibited by his son and regret at having kept secret what he was about to say.

"The explosion yesterday was not an accident." He waited a moment for the words to sink in, and watched as a look of realization crossed the Prince's features. The Emperor had ordered that the tragedy be explained as accidental, that the rupturing of a compressor line below the galleries had caused a flash fire responsible for the deaths of nearly 160 people.

"Not an accident?" The anger drained from Javas' face and he eased back into the swivel chair. "But any attempt on your life from the galleries would have been contained by the shielding. Any assailant would realize that. I'm not sure I understand."

Glenney reached into his jacket, extracting a thin sheet of stiff plastic, and handed it to the Prince. "Do you know what this is?" he asked.

Javas examined it, read the markings: *Gallery 29, Row 1, Seat 11.* It was dated for the previous day. "Obviously it's a seating pass for the landing ceremony. Did you recover this from one of the victims?" He looked first at Glenney, then, when the security man remained mute, to his father.

"No," he answered for Glenney. "There was not much to be recovered. This was Dr. Montgarde's pass. She had originally been assigned to gallery 29." He observed Javas carefully, noting how his brow furrowed in pained concern, his lips drew into a tight line. "Without knowing it, you saved her life, as well as the lives of several members of her research team."

"When you invited her to sit in the Imperial gallery," Glenney added, "we no longer felt the need to concentrate our efforts in 29. Fortunately no other members of the Imperial staff or the Doctor's team were seated there."

Javas' mouth opened in obvious disbelief at the callous statement, and he was immediately on his feet. For a moment, the Emperor thought the Prince might strike the man but he watched as his son turned suddenly, disgustedly, away and crossed to the other side of the study.

"A hundred and sixty people," he said softly. The Prince sighed and shook his head reverently, but the inner reflection lasted only a few seconds before a look of fiery determination glowed in his eyes and he turned his full attention to the security man. "I want those responsible, Glenney, do you understand?" The Emperor started to speak, but Javas cut him off before he could say anything. "No! Father, this is mine."

Glenney cleared his throat. "I'm afraid that won't be possible, Sire. The cause of the explosion was chemical in nature, and those responsible died along with the others. Which is partially the reason, incidentally, for our not being able to detect this attempt in advance."

"Oh? And why is that, *security* agent?" Javas made no attempt to hide his sarcasm and stared at him, unblinking, until he continued.

"From spectrographic analysis of what little we've been able to recover, it seems this was an individual attempt on Dr. Montgarde's life. One person, certainly no more than two, apparently brought volatile chemicals into the gallery; most likely by saturating articles of clothing. Alone, the chemicals were harmless, but combining them—perhaps with an effort as simple as crossing his arms so the sleeves made contact with one another— created a nearly instantaneous reaction. With the shielding in place, the assailant knew he didn't even have to sit near his target. The explosion, in fact, originated in the last row. Ironically, from that location the assailant probably wasn't even aware that the Doctor wasn't seated in the gallery."

The Emperor kept silent and observed the fortitude his son displayed in handling what was surely one of the most difficult experiences he'd had since arriving on the Moon. He smiled inwardly, pleased at the Prince's self-control.

Javas crossed the room and sat down. He rubbed his eyes wearily with the backs of his hands and the Emperor noticed for the first time how tired his son appeared. He had not been the only one, he realized, who had slept very little the night before.

The Prince leaned an elbow on the armrest of the chair and stroked his chin absently for several moments before swiveling the chair to address Glenney.

"You've missed something," he said. His words came slowly, evenly, and he waited until he had the other's full attention.

Glenney sat straighter, cocking his head slightly in puzzlement and curiosity at what the Prince might be suggesting, but remained silent.

"The explosion occurred," he went on, "several minutes after Dr. Montgarde was in plain sight on the landing platform. Tell me, security agent: Why would an assailant, acting alone and in control of his own actions, attempt to kill a target that was plainly no longer available?"

SIX

"I don't like this," said the gray-haired man. "I don't like any of it. At all." He leaned back, sinking deeply into the comfort of the thickly padded sofa, but despite his efforts looked positively anything but comfortable.

"You think I do?" Bomeer shot back. He paced briskly before the enormous window, nervously looking from time to time at the box resting on the low table between the sofa and the two matching chairs that faced it. Seeing that the top surface of the small cube glowed green and, satisfied that the audio blocker was functioning properly, he continued. "I don't like the native Earthers any more than I trust them, but face facts: Now that Javas fully intends to support the Old Man's fool project—and carry it on when he himself becomes Emperor—we can't afford to be too particular about whose help we accept." He paced steadily, glancing occasionally at the comm terminal to check the time.

"Academician! Would you kindly sit down?"

Bomeer halted in mid-stride and regarded his companion. With a bemused snort, he crossed to one of the chairs opposite the sofa and fell heavily into it.

"You're right, Wynne," he said, checking the time yet again. "My apologies." Bomeer reached for a glass on the same serving tray where he'd placed the blocker, but a soft chiming from the door stopped him. He spoke tersely at the comm. "Identify." The screen glowed immediately, an external camera showing a tall, slim man standing outside the suite.

"Is that him?" Wynne asked, leaning forward to study the screen more closely.

"Yes." Both men rose, and Bomeer crossed quickly to the entranceway. "I'll say this for Earthers, they're punctual," he said to the other academician under his breath, then, louder: "Admit."

The newcomer was tall, Bomeer realized as soon as the door slid aside; surprisingly so. The external security camera had not given a true feeling for the man's sheer size any more than it had given a clear look at the intricacies of his face. Although hidden by a thick beard, his features appeared mostly North American or European; but Bomeer could detect a hint of Asian stock somewhere in the man's background. He wore a neat but casual outfit dominated by shades of browns that closely matched the color of his hair and beard. His jacket, Bomeer noted, was a finely brushed leather. Not waiting to be invited in, he strode purposefully into the room as soon as the door had completely cleared the frame.

"On behalf of myself and my fellow academician," Bomeer said to the man's back, "I'm honored you have agreed to—"

The man spun about, the angry glare of his dark eyes immediately silencing the academician, and drew a quick finger across his throat in a cutting motion. He just as abruptly turned away again and walked to the seating area in the center of the room. Ignoring Wynne completely, he hurriedly scanned his surroundings and reached into the pocket of his jacket, producing a thin cylinder—it looked to Bomeer like a pen or stylus—and twisted the top once, clockwise, and clipped it to the jacket's narrow lapel. The tip of the object blinked softly, steadily. He turned to face Bomeer, the leather of his jacket creaking subtly as he clasped his hands casually behind him, and allowed a polite smile.

"All right, then. You were saying?" His deeply resonant voice was deceptively calm and out of place with the rugged image he presented.

Bomeer pursed his lips a moment and forced down the annoyance he felt at his visitor—dismissing his manners as peculiar, but normal perhaps, to Earthers. Clasping his own hands behind his back, Bomeer stepped down to the seating area and stood facing the newcomer. The two men stared at each other for several seconds, neither making an effort to extend a hand in greeting to the other. Bomeer's neck began to stiffen as he stared up at the giant of a man, and he immediately regretted trying to imitate his actions.

"Your blocker was not necessary," Bomeer said finally, indicating the blinking object clipped to the Earther's jacket. "We've already seen fit to take all practical caution."

"Is that so?" The man's hand flashed into his coat and, before the two academicians realized what was happening, held a pin laser leveled at Bomeer's face. "It wouldn't be easy to kill you with this, Mr. Bomeer, but I could blind you in two seconds." He punctuated his remark by flicking the weapon back and forth several times mere centimeters from Bomeer's eyes. An unpleasantly sadistic smile crept across his features as he added, "Of course, with my foot planted firmly on your chest and fifteen or twenty seconds to work, I *could* slice open your throat." He lowered the laser and waved it at Bomeer's neck, whispering softly on each pass, "Zip. Zip. Zip."

Bomeer stood frozen and felt sweat trickle down his neck, back; his armpits burned, and at the same time an incongruous wave of cold swept over him. He moved his lips several times to speak, but no sound came out. He glanced pleadingly to Wynne, still standing at the sofa, but realized that the older academician was even more terrified by what was happening than he was. The standoff continued a few agonizing moments longer before the bearded man laughed aloud and turned away, smoothly replacing the laser into his coat, and sat nonchalantly in one of the chairs opposite the sofa.

"Perhaps a review of what you feel to be 'practical caution' is in order, Mr. Bomeer?"

Bomeer tugged at his tunic, nervously trying to regain his composure, and sat on one side of the sofa. He regarded Wynne, still standing speechless, and managed to relieve his own anxiety somewhat by concentrating on just how much more afraid Wynne was than he. He cleared his throat once, then again.

"Wynne, please be seated," he said, using every bit of will he possessed to make each word sound calm, steady. He watched the visitor carefully as Wynne sat, trying to take the measure of this stranger from Earth, and at the same time trying to utilize every additional second of silence to further calm himself.

"As I started to say," he went on, feeling more of his confidence returning, "I'm pleased that you've asked to meet with us this afternoon. This is Plantir Wynne, Director Emeritus of the Imperial Academy of Science." He nodded at Wynne, who sat looking even less comfortable than he had before the Earther had arrived. Wynne extended a quivering hand.

The bearded man regarded Wynne with disdain, and even Bomeer had to admit, if only to himself, just how pitiful his colleague appeared. "Please refer to me as 'Johnson' in this and any other transactions we may have," he said, reaching to shake hands finally.

"I must be frank," Bomeer went on, anxious to get this meeting started—and ended. "I was a bit surprised to receive your message several days ago. However, I'm not sure exactly what it is we have to discuss."

"Johnson" stared at him, half smiling through his beard. "It's very simple. You wish to stop this plan to save the Sun. The entire 'Academy of Science,' as you call it, has been on record as opposing the project from the beginning, but the two of you have been the most vocal in your disagreement, am I correct?"

And just how much else do you know? Bomeer wondered to himself. "I have been loyal to the Emperor all my life," he said, "but I've not kept secret my feelings that this project will severely undermine the Empire, potentially bankrupting it. I have gained few friends among the Imperial Court for my beliefs, but to keep silent about my feelings would be a disservice."

"I see." Johnson nodded thoughtfully, then turned sharply to Wynne. "And you? Do you mimic every thought of your colleague, or do you actually have a voice of your own?"

Wynne seemed to have regained some of his composure and raised an eyebrow to the Earthman. "The Emperor has been a good leader for many years," he said without hesitation, surprising Bomeer with the unexpected confidence in his voice. "But this plan will destroy the very fabric of the Empire."

"I see," Johnson repeated. Rising from his chair, he approached the window and stared solemnly out over the lunar landscape for a moment before turning to face the two once more. "I, and those I represent, could not possibly care less about the so-called 'fabric of the Empire.' " For the first time since entering the suite, the Earthman allowed genuine emotion to show in his voice—whether intentionally or not, Bomeer couldn't be certain.

"We do not care for *your* Empire," he went on, the disgust plain in his voice. "Your goals are not ours. Your values, your government, your very way of life is abhorrent to those of us here who strive to cleanse ourselves of your influence."

"You've damn well accepted the benefits of membership in the Hundred Worlds, though, haven't you?" Bomeer countered, feeling his own anger beginning to rise. "The powersat network. Medical and agricultural research. Somewhat hypocritical of you pure, clean Earthers, eh?"

"It is a compromise that benefits us, yes!" Johnson hesitated as he returned to his chair, where he sat and crossed his legs, resuming the nonchalant manner he'd exhibited earlier. When he spoke again, all traces of emotion had disappeared from his voice. "We're not stupid backwater natives, as is so popularly believed among the Worlds. We like our life the way it is, and accept those benefits from the Empire that we see fit to accept. Our dealings with the Empire these many centuries have been regarded as a necessary evil to maintain our life-style.

"Sol system is a harmonious system. Those Earthers not wishing to be a part of the life-style on the home world are free to settle elsewhere, and many relocate here on the Moon or in the Orbitals. Some have joined the project to reclaim Venus or have settled on the moons of the gas giants; still others accept the Imperial way of life or elect the harsh life on one of the frontier worlds. They do so with our blessings, leaving our values, and theirs, intact. Is that so difficult for you to understand?"

Bomeer looked once at Wynne, then regarded Johnson steadily. "What I seem to understand," he said, rising from his spot on the sofa, "is that there is apparently little purpose to our continuing this discussion." He reached for the blocker on the tray, but Johnson's hand on his wrist stopped him. The man's grip was incredibly strong. Bomeer stared at the Earther's hand, envious of the great strength hidden in his deceptively thin fingers, and noticed a gold bracelet encircling his wrist. But for an etching of a majestic flame-enshrouded bird on the metal's curved, gleaming surface, the bracelet was plain and otherwise unadorned.

Bomeer looked up and found himself gazing squarely into Johnson's face. This close to the man, he noticed a musky scent about him that mingled pleasantly with the smell of his leather jacket. Further, there was something about the look in Johnson's eyes as he leaned close that made Bomeer want to listen, something that made him want to trust the man.

"Let us understand this, then: We are a different people, you and I, and have differences in philosophy." He released Bomeer's arm and, sitting upright once more, addressed both academicians. "But in this instance we share the same goal. You, to maintain the physical integrity of your Empire, wish this project stopped. So do we. Only our motives differ."

Bomeer idly rubbed his wrist. "And just what *are* your motives?"

Johnson was silent a moment, then, "We believe that the death of the Sun is part of the natural order of things, part of His plan for us. We wish to maintain our spiritual integrity."

"Religious fanatic," Wynne spat once the door had slid shut. "I've detested them wherever I've encountered them."

"I heartily agree," Bomeer said, retrieving his glass from the tray. The ice had melted, diluting his drink, and he crossed to a waist-high cart placed to one side of the room to fix himself another. "But they have their uses. Did you see his eyes? There was something there, something that made me want to— When he grabbed my wrist I wanted to reach out and throttle him. But something in his eyes, in the tone of his voice, made me stop, made me listen. That's a powerful strength. If he can control and convince his followers, his own people, as easily as he did us . . ." Bomeer shuddered with the memory of the man's stare.

"Yes, but can we control him?"

Bomeer exhaled heavily and, turning to stare out at the landscape, added, "Perhaps a better question would be: Do we dare try?"

Rihana sat before the dressing table in her private chamber, studying her reflection in the mirror as she slowly brushed her long coppery hair. She was not displeased with what she saw. Before leaving Corinth, she had accepted the fact that she would most likely need a rejuvenation upon arriving at Sol system, but a smile came to her lips as she observed just how little the trip had affected her.

There was a soft, polite tapping at the door. "Mistress Valtane?"

She paused, mid-stroke, at the interruption but finished with the brush and set it on the table before responding.

"Yes, what is it, Linn?" She made no effort to turn to face her attendant when she entered, and instead concentrated on her own image in the mirror as she considered which jeweled comb would best accentuate the outfit she'd selected for this meeting.

"The Ambassador's liaison is here, Mistress. He is waiting in the receiving room."

On that, Rihana did turn. "His liaison? Not the Ambassador himself?" Since it was the Ambassador who had requested this meeting, she was surprised at the news. "Very well," she said, "I'll be there directly."

The attendant nodded and quickly left the chamber. Rihana went to a full-length mirror near one of the room's several closets and examined herself. She'd selected her outfit specifically with the Ambassador in mind, being careful to choose a color pattern visible to the alien. She quickly undressed, tossing the expensive gown casually across a chair, and selected a two-piece pantsuit of shiny satin. Only slightly less expensive than the outfit now lying in a heap on the chair, it was considerably more comfortable. Glancing in the mirror, she confirmed that it would also be more appealing to the all-too-human eye of the Ambassador's liaison.

He was already standing when she entered, idly watching the comings and goings in the small landing facility adjacent to the receiving room. Over his shoulder she could see the Sarpan shuttle parked and being tended to by members of her staff. He wore a loose open-collar white shirt, short-sleeved, with pants of a matching light material and looked more like a man on holiday than an official emissary for an alien race. Another of her attendants had remained with him since his arrival, and she nodded to dismiss him. The Ambassador's liaison had his back to her, and he started slightly at the sudden movement behind him and turned. Rihana recognized him as the same man who had contacted her to arrange the meeting the day before.

"Mistress Valtane," he said with a polite nod that was almost, but not quite, a formal bow. "On behalf of Ambassador Press, thank you for receiving me."

"Please, be comfortable." She led him to a circular sofa grouping at one side of the room and waited until they were both seated before continuing. "I must admit Mr.—Carrigan, is it?— that I'm a bit surprised. When we spoke yesterday, I was of the impression that the Ambassador himself wished to speak with me."

Carrigan cleared his throat, but if he was at all nervous or unsure of himself, he didn't show it. "I apologize for any misunderstanding, Mistress Valtane, but the Ambassador never meets in person with anyone, including members of his own race, during what they refer to as a 'first touching.' It is customary for important members of the Sarpan race to meet first through an intermediary, even when all are present in the same room, and they have extended that custom to members of the Hundred Worlds as well. I'm sorry, but I'd assumed you knew."

"First touching," she replied, almost to herself, and extended a tentative hand. "Very well, then."

He took the offered hand. "Ambassador Press extends his greetings and good wishes to the House of Valtane."

She nodded agreement and Carrigan started to release her

hand, but Rihana held it a bit longer, studying his reaction, before slowly letting go. Again, he seemed in complete control of his actions.

"Now," she asked, leaning back into the chair, "may I inquire as to the purpose of this meeting?"

"Since it is widely known that House Valtane is no longer linked with that of the Emperor, the Ambassador is curious, Mistress Valtane, as to the reason for your presence here on Luna," he said without hesitation. "May he inquire as to your purpose?"

Rihana smiled inwardly. *You do get to the point, don't you?* she thought. *Why not?* "Yes. He may."

"Very good. Let me go over a few points of protocol before you meet him."

Rihana was taken aback. "He's here?"

"Yes; on the shuttle in which I arrived. I thought I made that clear."

Rihana was grateful for the quick lesson in interspecies protocol that Carrigan had given her as she waited for the Ambassador to enter his side of his shuttle's small receiving room. The chamber was divided by an air shield similar to that used in the shuttle bays. Each side of the room, as far as she could tell through the haziness of the Sarpan-normal atmosphere on the other side, mirrored the other, with three chairs facing the shielding on either side. Closer scrutiny, however, showed several differences. While the chairs on the alien's side were roughly of the same size and design, they were padded with thick cushions of waterproof plastic. The chair in which she sat was fabric-covered. Moisture dripped freely down the walls on the other side, and even the window-shield fogged slightly from time to time as moisture adhered to it. The Sarpan shield was nonpermeable and kept the wetness inside, but was not designed for insulation; considerable heat radiated from the window's surface, and her side of the room was uncomfortably warm. The reason behind Carrigan's choice of light clothing became suddenly clear.

"Ambassador Press," she said when he entered his side of the chamber, remembering to look him directly in the face, "it is with great honor that I welcome you to my House." She swept an arm to indicate, not the shuttle itself, but rather the landing bay in which it was parked. Carrigan, seated next to her, nodded and she rose and approached the window-shield, tentatively placing the palm of her hand flat on the sultry surface. The shield was firm, but gave slightly beneath the pressure of her fingertips. The Sarpan was somewhat shorter than she, and needed to reach up to place a webbed, four-fingered hand opposite hers. As their hands met, separated by the molecular thickness of the shield, Rihana could feel the warmth and softness of the alien's fleshy palm against hers. He nodded several times, puffing gill slits at the sides of his neck with each movement. The "touching" completed, he reclined in the centermost chair.

The Ambassador wore a short kilt of bright orange with a matching sash over one shoulder, soft-looking leather boots and little else. The edges of his gill slits were pierced, Rihana noted, and sported several tiny silver bobs that glinted brightly against the gray-brown moistness of his skin when he spoke.

"Mistress Valtane," he said in a strangely melodious voice through the comm speaker. "It is my honor." He turned to his liaison. "Mr. Carrigan?"

"Ambassador, I have informed Mistress Valtane of your interest in her House, and she has agreed to discuss the situation frankly."

"Good." He returned his gaze to Rihana, blinking away excess moisture with transparent nictitating membranes. The drops rolling down his face gave the appearance that he was crying. "Why have you come to Sol system? We know that you are out of favor with the House of the Emperor of the Hundred Worlds. So. Why are you here?"

"Ambassador, my ouster from my husband's House is unprecedented. I have come to make claim on several rights due the wife of the Emperor's son."

"But you are no longer his wife. You no longer have claim."

Had she been speaking to another human, Rihana would have been outraged by such effrontery. She suppressed her feelings of anger and stared evenly at Press, rationalizing that he was speaking candidly and decided to return his frankness. "You are correct in that I am no longer the Prince's wife, but that does not change the fact that I am to be the mother of his son."

Press blinked eye membranes and laced and unlaced his fingers several times as he considered this new bit of information. "So.

I see. Another question, then: Is your"—Press hesitated, groping for the word she had used—" 'ouster' from your husband's House related in any way to that scientific endeavor ongoing now to halt Sol star's rebirth?"

"Yes. I opposed his support of the Emperor's project. But I am confused, Ambassador. My reason for being here has only to do with my rights, and nothing directly related to the project—"

"A moment, a moment," Press interjected, "a moment. Understand. I thought, perhaps because of your estranged relationship to the Emperor's House, that you might be less reluctant to inform me of this project. So?"

"So" indeed. That's it, then. She waited for him to continue.

"Consider, please: We see a massive building of starships by your people. We see your Court moved farther from the Sarpan sphere of influence. We see a traveling of your people from all the Hundred Worlds to here. So. Consider: What are we to think?"

Rihana did consider. The Sarpan were, simply enough, nervous about the Empire's massive buildup of equipment and ships. And why not? The relationship between the Empire and the Sarpan had been tenuous at best, and deadly—on occasion—at worst. How were they to know that the Hundred Worlds hadn't decided it was time to change the relationship to their favor once and for all at the Sarpan's expense?

"To the best of my knowledge, Ambassador, the stated purposes of the Emperor are true and without darker motives."

"But, to stop a star's rebirthing! Surely this is a folly?"

Rihana nodded in understanding. "I know," she admitted, "it does seem foolish, just as I told my former husband." A thought suddenly came to her. "Ambassador, despite the treatment of my House by my former husband, I am not without influence. It would be no difficult matter to confirm or deny the truth of this."

"So? And in return for this truth?"

He's sharp, Rihana thought, a smile spreading across her lips.

"Suppose," she began, "that House Valtane were able to confirm that the nature of the Emperor's endeavor is, indeed, scientific only—that this plan to 'stop the rebirthing,' as you describe it, is exactly that?"

A disturbingly human grin appeared on Ambassador Press' face. "Mr. Carrigan, leave us." The Ambassador's liaison stood, nodding politely to Rihana, and quickly exited the small cham-

ber. "What we say now should be between us only. If House
Valtane could confirm this, then this one of the Sarpan would be
much in debt to House Valtane."

"Perhaps. But it need not be a onetime arrangement," she
hinted. "Think of the future, Ambassador: trade, information,
materials; both my House and yours could profit greatly from
such a cooperation."

Rihana paused as he blinked in consideration, then tilted her
head and smiled wryly, adding, "Think, too, of a human Empire
ruled by a son of my House."

SEVEN

I *was wrong,* the Emperor reflected as he watched Adela de
Montgarde approach. *She hasn't aged; she's matured.* True,
the corners of her eyes showed new lines that hadn't existed
when she'd left Corinth for Earth's Moon. Her figure was fuller
now as well, less boyish than he'd remembered. But if the tasks
ahead of her on this difficult endeavor had aged her slightly, they
had also invigorated her, filled her with a purpose that was easy
to see after so long a separation. Still, despite her newfound
maturity, he took comfort in the childlike way she delighted in
each of the pleasures the royal family's private garden presented.

The scientist walked briskly toward him through the garden.
Smaller than the common green area of the Imperial dome—
which, in turn, was only slightly less magnificent than the main
green of Armelin City itself—the garden was aglow in plants,
birds and flowers in hundreds of colors, from dozens of worlds.

There was a bounce to her step, he noticed, that the lunar-
normal gravity could not quite account for. *She's anxious, excited,* he reasoned. *Do I have the right to make her dream more
difficult?* She slowed her pace as she approached, but before she
could formally greet him, he smiled and motioned her to come
forward.

"There is no need for protocol here," he said, "nor time for the luxury. Please walk with me." The Emperor smoothly rotated his powerchair, gliding it silently down one of the several flagstone paths crisscrossing the garden. As they walked, she discussed the project and the many successes she'd already had in her research. Only half listening, the Emperor studied her as they followed the path. Her bio-readouts were strong, he verified; no less strong than her determination.

"I wanted to speak to you before tomorrow's Planetary Council," he said. "So much has occurred since my arrival, and there's been little time. Are you ready for your presentation?"

She laughed softly. "Sire, I've been rehearsing this presentation, in one form or another, for many years now. I've never been more prepared for anything in my life."

"Yes, I suppose you have at that. Come; this way." The footpath widened, passing through a series of flower beds before ending in a circular clearing perhaps forty meters wide where a number of the garden paths converged. Scattered throughout the area, surrounded by a ring of high shrubbery, were several stone benches. The Emperor directed the powerchair to the nearest of the benches and indicated that Adela be seated. He looked around him at the beauty of the garden and breathed deeply of the scented air. Adela sat straighter on the bench and waited in silence for him to continue. She seemed to have sensed the change in his demeanor, and the Emperor realized he must have let his guard down momentarily. *It's getting harder to hide my feelings,* he thought bitterly. *It's getting harder to lie.*

"Adela, I need to speak to you of two very important matters."

"Sire?" Her tone carried with it a sense of worry. Her eyes darted nervously around the garden and her hands fidgeted in her lap. The Emperor did not need the integrator to tell him that her heart was racing.

She thinks I am taking her dream from her! "First, understand that the project has my full support." She relaxed, but only slightly. "I know that the long years you have spent setting up the groundwork have been difficult. But remember that it is *only* a beginning."

Her smile now long-vanished, she looked deeply into his face.

"I realize that," she said. There was something in her voice that took several moments for the Emperor to identify.

It suddenly struck him what it was and he regarded her differently as he went on. "I'm talking down to you, aren't I? Like an old man to a child."

Adela lowered her eyes, her silence confirming his question.

He chuckled in apology. "Forgive this old man, then, who seems to have developed an old man's habits." She looked back up at him, and he was relieved to see a sparkle return to her eyes.

"Let me speak bluntly, then, one adult to another: Adela, I am dying." She opened her mouth to protest, but he continued before she could speak. "At one point, I was doubtful that I would survive the journey here. I'm afraid that I even resorted to a few drastic measures to assure my healthy arrival on the Moon."

"Drastic measures? I'm not sure I—"

" 'Drastic' is, perhaps, a poor word choice; I should have said 'illegal.' On the voyage here, my medical staff saw to it that I was kept isolated for weeks, even months, at a time for various health reasons. Under my orders, they explained to the Imperial Court that I was 'being prepared,' medically speaking, for the transition from the open environmental and atmospheric conditions on Corinth to the closed lunar environment here." He swept a fragile hand to indicate the huge domework above their heads. "Only my personal medical aide and a handful of the Imperial staff know that I spent a cumulative total of nine years in cryosleep." He waited a moment for the words to sink in. "Even Javas is unaware of this."

Adela rose wordlessly and walked a few meters to a blossom-laden bush. The Emperor accessed his integrator and called up a botanical file that identified the bright yellow and orange foliage as that of a firebush from her native Gris. She absently plucked one of the fire-red blooms and turned back to the Emperor, her eyes avoiding his as he spoke.

"I did not want to resort to violating a law that even I had steadfastly supported throughout my reign," he went on, "but it was a necessary evil."

Adela returned to her place on the stone bench. "Why are you telling me this?" she asked softly, setting the flower next to her on the bench.

He reached out, taking one of her hands in both of his. "I knew that I would not live to reach Sol system. I also knew that without my presence here for the official transfer of the Imperial Court, Javas would have a much more difficult time in gaining initial acceptance for his support of the project, especially with the likes of Bomeer and his followers working at every opportunity to turn sentiment against it."

He sighed deeply and leaned wearily back in the powerchair. "I tell you this now because I want you to realize something: I want you to know that I felt strongly enough about the purpose and validity of your dream that I was willing to do what was necessary to continue my part in it." He paused, then added, "Look at me." Adela lifted her face and regarded the Emperor once more.

"If your cause is right, then you do whatever is necessary to make it succeed. It is not always pleasant, for it often inflicts pain upon you, as well as upon those around you; but Adela, you must adopt this attitude for yourself—or you will fail."

"I know." Her voice was a whisper.

"Much will happen at the Planetary Council and in the days to follow. I will offer what help I can in the time left me, but understand this: Whatever happens, remain true to what you know is right."

The Emperor reached for the flower and brought it to his nose, inhaling deeply of the sweet fragrance.

"It's a firebush," she offered, "from my homeworld. They were lunar-adapted and planted at Prince Javas' request. He . . . knew how much I missed home."

You've captured him, haven't you? Much the way you captured me, he mused silently, and handed the bloom to her. She sniffed at it, then held it to her face, gently stroking the soft petals against the skin of her cheek.

"There . . . is another thing," he said, surprised at his hesitation. The man who ruled a hundred worlds, who had passed judgment on millions, now felt nervous, uncertain for the first time he could remember.

"Yes?" There was a sober fear reflected in her eyes at what he might say next. She dropped her hands to her lap, where nervous fingers twirled the stem of the flower first one way, then the other.

"The explosion in the landing bay was not an accident," he

said abruptly, making no attempt to soften the words. "It was an assassination attempt—directed at you."

Her lips quivered, and a single tear rolled slowly down the same cheek that moments before had felt the caress of a flower, now lying forgotten on the ground at her feet.

"Somehow . . . deep inside me . . . I think I already knew that it was my fault." Her breath came haltingly in heavy sobs, and she lowered her face into her hands.

With only a few hours remaining before the start of the Hundred Worlds Planetary Council, Adela had assembled several members of her staff in the reception area of her office at the Imperial lab facilities. Spirits were high as they talked among themselves in anticipation of the event. Although they had already been hard at work on Luna for several years, today's Council session would mark the official beginning of the project.

"How do I look?" asked Kel Sites, her first assistant. She stifled a laugh as she saw him standing before her in his formal tunic, hands spread at his sides for her approval, and wondered just how uncomfortable and out of place he must be feeling in the formal outfit. Everyone on the lab staff, for that matter, looked like strangers in what they had jokingly referred to as "Imperial costume."

"Better check a mirror," she suggested, pointing to the front of the tunic. He groaned when he realized, to the delight of those nearest him, that he'd fastened the entire row of buttons one buttonhole off from the proper order. Several of the others in the group, no more accustomed to the buttons and hooks found on formal attire than Kel, hastily checked their own appearances.

"Hey, don't worry, Kel," one of them offered. "We'll make them all wait until you figure it out." The room burst into good-natured kidding at Kel's expense. None of them knew what had transpired at her meeting earlier with the Emperor, of course, but Adela felt good at how the mood of everyone in the room had managed to cheer her up. In spite of herself, she joined in the laughter; and enjoyed it.

"Dr. Montgarde?"

Adela turned to find a stranger, hands clasped casually in front of him. While smartly dressed in a modest business suit, something in his manner made it obvious that he was someone's servant.

"Yes? Can I help you?"

He nodded politely. "My name is Poser, attendant to House Valtane. Mistress Rihana Valtane wishes to call on you."

The light bantering in the room faded instantly at the mention of the name.

"I'm afraid now would not be a convenient—"

"She wishes to call on you alone," he went on, flashing his best plastic smile. "I have taken the liberty of arranging an audience for you in your private office."

"In my . . . I see."

The man waited patiently, the smile not wavering. He seemed determined not to budge; but then, knowing Javas' former wife, the man probably feared for his life if he did.

"All right." Adela turned and addressed her lab staff. "Kel, you and the others are dismissed for now. I'll meet you all later at the auditorium." Her visitor waited in silence as the others bid Adela good-bye and filed out of the room, whispering among themselves.

"Well?" she asked once the last of the group had left.

His smile widened, if that was possible, and he stood aside as she walked past him down the hall, then fell quickly into step behind her.

There was a reception desk and terminal station outside her office, and Adela's secretary was on his feet as soon as he saw her approaching.

"I'm sorry, Doctor," he blurted, "but she insisted on waiting in—"

Adela cut him off with an understanding smile and a shake of her head. "It's all right, Stase," she said. "Why don't you take a break."

He nodded eagerly, anxious to get away from what looked like a confrontation, then snapped off the terminal before making a hasty disappearance down the hall.

Poser rapped sharply on the door and another attendant opened it from inside. "Dr. Montgarde is here," he said once the door had slid completely aside.

He motioned for Adela to follow him and took position next

to the open door, announcing her formally as she entered. "Dr. Adela de Montgarde—Mistress Rihana of House Valtane."

As angry as Adela was over her visitor's insistence that she stop what she was doing to grant her an "audience," she could not help but be awed by what she saw. Rihana was even more striking than Adela had remembered when she'd first met the woman at the Emperor's table—and Prince Javas' side—on Corinth years earlier. She wore a clinging gown of cobalt blue that shimmered and sparkled with even the tiniest movement. A torque of sapphire, seemingly carved from a single gemstone, and the matching blue stones at her wrists and ears formed a perfect contrast to the copper hair that was pulled to the side and fastened in such a manner as to sweep in a fiery mass across one shoulder.

Adela bowed, automatically respectful. "Princess Rihana—"

An icy stare cut Adela off before she could finish. "Dr. Montgarde, as I'm sure you are aware, the title of 'Princess' is, well, no longer accurate. 'Mistress' will do fine."

Adela felt an angry heat rise within her, but forced it down and bowed her head slightly once more. "As you wish, Mistress. What can I do—"

"Thank you Poser, Dennie," she snapped, interrupting Adela again. "That will be all for now."

The two nodded curtly, then left, thumbing the door closed from outside. Adela heard a faint click and realized one of Rihana's attendants had taken the liberty of putting the door into private mode.

"What brings you here, Mistress?" Adela asked, keeping her voice as friendly as possible. "I wasn't even aware that you were on the Moon."

Rihana looked thoughtful a moment, then said, "May I be seated?" She indicated a sofa at the far side of the room adjacent to Adela's desk and, not waiting for an answer, approached it.

Adela followed, inwardly impressed at how the woman's gown shimmered as she walked, and wondered for a moment just how much the outfit must have cost. She sat in a chair opposite her guest, folding her arms in front of her.

"As I asked before, what brings you here?"

Rihana picked up a small figurine from the desk, carved from a piece of Grisian rockwood, and examined it, turning it over in her delicate hands as she spoke. "I think we have something to offer one another," she began without preamble. "My House would be interested in offering—for a price, of course—full cooperation toward achieving your, ah, goal." She raised a knowing eyebrow and allowed the sound of a smile to lace her words. "House Valtane has considerable influence on a number of the frontier worlds; influence that may be needed to bring your project to fruition." She set the figurine on top of a stack of reports on the desk and made no move to right it when it toppled over.

"And what of the frontier worlds?" Adela shot back, making little attempt now to hide the rising wave of contempt she felt for her uninvited guest. "Do you see a problem there, *Mistress?*"

Rihana's eyes flashed, her composure slipping for a brief instant before she resumed. "Let's be honest with one another, shall we? Without the full support of every planet of the Hundred Worlds, you can't hope to achieve a successful end to this project. My House has influence that . . . might be put at your disposal"

"I see." Adela raised an eyebrow of her own. "You admit now that my ideas have merit?"

The erstwhile Princess nodded almost imperceptibly in the realization that she was dealing with a strong adversary here. "Let me say this: My people have researched your theories and have found them to be valid. *Technically* valid, that is." She leaned back in the sofa and crossed long legs. Adela noted that the gown was slit up one side and showed the woman's assets to good advantage. "Personally, however, I still feel the endeavor to be a foolish dream of a foolish man trying to make a last, memorable impression on his subjects. But, no matter; I see a great profit in this for my House. And what is so dreadfully wrong in that?"

And just what is it you really want? Adela wondered. *And what might your price be?* "Here is your answer, then: There is nothing wrong with that, Mistress. In fact, I'll certainly need to make use of whatever help I can get. If your influence could become a factor in gaining support from the frontier worlds, then the help of House Valtane would be most welcome."

Apparently satisfied that this meeting was ended, Rihana rose and crossed to the door.

"Thank you for your time, Doctor," she said, tossing a holo-card on the service table. The flimsy card skittered frictionlessly across the surface of the table and fell to the floor. "You can reach me with this to set up any arrangements we deem mutually beneficial." She smiled politely and half bowed, certainly more out of acknowledgment than respect, and knocked once at the closed door. One of her attendants on the other side opened it immediately.

Before exiting, however, Rihana turned briefly, almost as an afterthought. "This project . . . it will take many generations to complete, am I correct?"

"Yes, it will," she replied, rising. "I'll need years of cryosleep and rejuvenation to see it through to its conclusion."

Rihana nodded, a sadistic smile coming to her lips. "Then you will lose him, you know. Just as I did." She turned abruptly and left without another word.

Adela knew it, of course, but had refused to allow herself to think about it. Not now. Not today.

She thumbed the door closed and retrieved the holocard, not-ing that the copper-colored card was apparently blank, translu-cent. Holding it to the light at the right angle, however, the Valtane crest glowed a brilliant cobalt blue.

Emperor Nicholas felt slightly dazed and blinked several times, trying to minimize the stress caused by the lengthy integrator download he'd just accepted. Accessing the Imperial computer system was becoming more of a strain to him, and he reserved its use lately only for periodic bits of quick information, or for those informational files that were too long to be reported orally. Like the one Glenney had just given him.

"They were all killed, then?" the Emperor asked at last.

Glenney lowered his eyes. "Unfortunately yes. We don't have much to go on at this point; and we're getting precious little help from authorities on Earth."

"You are certain their ties lead to the planet itself?"

"Yes, Sire. Further, as I mentioned in the report, I'm begin-ning to believe this group may have been involved in the landing bay explosion, or connected to the group that was." Glenney reached into his jacket and produced a gold bracelet, handing it to the Emperor. "Two of the dead men were wearing these."

The Emperor turned it over in his hands, examining the workmanship of the etching on its surface, and noticed how light it was. He tapped it on the armrest of the powerchair. "Hollow?"

Glenney nodded, adding, "Volatile chemicals could have been secreted in a chambered version, with a tiny valve to intermix the chambers at the right time. The gold itself would have provided excellent shielding. This one, of course, is empty."

"Who were they, and what threat did they pose to the Planetary Council?"

"Uncertain at this time, Sire. However, there is a chance that this group, in itself, posed little or no threat to the Council whatever."

"Meaning?"

"Sire, I suspect they were part of a considerably larger, well-organized effort that felt my people were getting a little too close to uncovering them. I think they set this group up purposely, as decoys, hoping we'd assume they constituted the bulk of their threat and would curtail our investigation. I doubt these five were even aware they'd been set up."

The Emperor considered this last. "Whoever was behind them, sacrificed them."

"Yes, Sire."

" 'He who is willing to die for his cause thinks nothing of killing you for his cause.' Do you know who said that?"

"Sire?"

"A twentieth-century writer of plays." The Emperor shook his head at the irony. "What it means is that you are dealing with a group of people who will stop at nothing to achieve their goals. Remember that. Give the investigation of this group your highest priority."

Glenney nodded in agreement.

"Is your next report lengthy?" Glenney nodded again and the Emperor sighed tiredly. "Very well." He closed his eyes for the few moments it took for the images and information to flow into his mind.

The Emperor took a deep breath and straightened in his powerchair when the download had finished. "She has been extremely busy, has she not?" he finally asked.

"Yes, Sire," Glenney replied, visibly relieved that the Emperor had regained his strength. "Unfortunately we have been unable to determine the exact nature of her discussion with the Ambassador, or her motives in meeting with him, any more than we know why she chose to call on Dr. Montgarde a few hours ago."

The Emperor smiled and raised an eyebrow to the security agent. "The first should not be too difficult to guess: She is obviously looking for an alliance of some type between her House and the Sarpan, although to what end we can only guess—I trust that you will make finding the answer to that question another of your priorities. However, I agree with you that her motives for calling on the Doctor, at present, are unclear."

"I'm certain we could find out more by having her detained," Glenney suggested. "For a civilian, even one with a House as high-ranking as hers, to directly meet with an official representative of the Sarpan without the advance knowledge of the Court—"

"It is unnecessary to quote Imperial law to me," the Emperor snapped. Reaching up, he rubbed his temples with thin, fragile fingertips but made no attempt to apologize before continuing. "Do not detain her. Instead, keep her under a closer watch until you have a better idea as to her motives." He received an urgent, silent query from Brendan and immediately regretted letting the stress of the last several days get the better of him. He exhaled in a wheezing sigh and, even as the medical systems built into his chair started working at a higher rate, gave a silent command to admit his aide.

The door slid open, and the young medical technician walked briskly into the room, although he carefully avoided allowing his features to show anything that might signify undue alarm on his part for the Emperor's condition. Putting duty to the Emperor first, he addressed the aging ruler directly, completely oblivious to the fact that the security man who had jumped instantly to his feet upon his entrance was only now relaxing his defensive posture.

"Sire, your readings are at levels that cannot safely be sustained." He knelt at the Emperor's side and examined the readouts of the chair itself to confirm the information he'd obviously received moments earlier from his implants. Rising, he added respectfully, but firmly, "I must insist that this meeting be concluded or postponed."

The Emperor studied Brendan for a moment and determined that his concern was sincere, but that he was no longer overly worried—a quick check with the computer showed that the young man had mentally canceled the medical emergency code that had brought him to his private study in the first place.

He took another deep breath, then another, and began to feel his strength slowly returning as the efforts of the powerchair's systems became effective. "Perhaps you're right," the Emperor admitted. *I am so tired.*

"I'll wait in the anteroom." Brendan stepped politely back, reserving any further medical discussion until the Emperor had dismissed his guest, and left the room.

The Emperor returned his attention to the agent. "It is time, Marc, that my son be advised of your findings concerning his former wife. Please see to it that he receives the report I just reviewed, and that he is kept up to date on anything else you may uncover regarding her activities."

The man's eyes grew wide. "Sire?"

"Do not question me on this," he said. He narrowed his eyes and looked squarely at the man. "Thank you for your report." He lifted a hand to emphasize that the meeting had ended and started to pivot the chair around, but stopped when he realized that although the man was now on his feet, Glenney had made no move to leave the chamber.

"Sire . . ."

For a moment, the Emperor thought the man was about to ask him to reconsider his request to inform Javas, but Glenney's face—normally unreadable—told him otherwise. "Yes? There is something else?"

Glenney reached into a coat pocket and produced a data stick, rolling it nervously in his fingers as he spoke. "There is an addendum to my report," he began, the barest hint of apology in his voice, "concerning another of Mistress Valtane's meetings, that is not yet in the main system. Because of what it contains, I . . ." He hesitated and licked lips gone suddenly dry. "I wished to present it for your personal review before entering it into the main files." He placed the stick in the Emperor's outstretched hand, a look of relief plain on his features to be free of the thing.

The Emperor slipped the data stick into a matching slot in the arm of the powerchair and stiffened as the images flowed into his

mind. He felt a wave of cold wash over him as he watched
Rihana Valtane conversing in a private dining booth of one of
Armelin City's finest restaurants. She had altered the color of her
hair, and her clothing was entirely out of character, although the
thin disguise was probably intended more to avoid unwanted
public attention to herself than Imperial scrutiny. Her dinner
companion, on the other hand, had made no attempt to alter his
appearance. The visual quality of the surveillance report was
clear enough to easily detect the amount of wine in their glasses,
but the conversation between the two was inaudible. An audio
blocker had obviously been used in the table's vicinity. He mentally speeded the download, noting the time, date and other
particulars of the meeting.

"Their lips were visible through most of what I just saw," he
said to Glenney. "Have you made an attempt to have a computer
reconstruction made of their discussion?"

"No, Sire. As I said, I thought this was important enough to
give to you before I did anything with it."

"Thank you for bringing this to me first." He turned the chair
away from Glenney. "You are dismissed."

Glenney took a step forward. "Shall I enter this with the other
file?"

"That won't be necessary," he lied. He used as much willpower
as he could summon to control not only his bio-readouts but his
emotions as well. "I've already done so."

The Emperor didn't bother to rotate the chair, but the sound
of the door sliding shut, followed by a stillness returning to the
room, confirmed that Glenney had gone. He dimmed the lights
to a more comfortable level and looked at the bracelet, still in his
hand, and marveled at the way it reflected even in the weak light.
A phoenix, he mused. *Life, rising from death.* He waited, lost in
thought. Less than a minute passed, however, before he heard
the door slide open again. He didn't need to turn to identify the
newcomer; other than Prince Javas, only his immediate medical
aide could enter his study without the Emperor personally admitting him.

"Please have a seat, Brendan," he began, a lightness in his
voice belying what he actually felt. He glided the chair around to
face the aide finally, adding, "I gather you wish to reprimand me
for repeatedly ignoring your medical orders of late."

The man raised an eyebrow and smiled, as he always did when reminding the Emperor of his medical needs. "It appears that my reprimands are taken too lightly, sometimes. However, I trust that ,once this business of the Hundred Worlds Council is concluded this afternoon you'll finally be willing to accept the medical order I gave you when we arrived, and the one you've ignored the longest: Rest after a long voyage."

The Emperor allowed a smile to form on his lips for the first time since Glenney had come to see him. "Perhaps so. Perhaps so." He stared into the young man's eyes and concentrated, giving a complicated command that caused the study's viewscreen to spring to life, replaying the visual portion of Glenney's report on the data stick still inserted into the chair arm.

Brendan's face drained of all color as he watched the replay, saw clearly Rihana Valtane talking to him at the restaurant. His eyes darted from the Emperor to the screen, then back again several times. He watched himself fidgeting in the replayed scene, and he saw that he had glanced around several times in fear that he'd be spotted talking to her. He began shaking as he watched, sweat rolled down his brow and his body quivered in spasms even though he sat rigidly upright in the chair.

The bright images cast a flickering reflection on Brendan's face and white tunic in the dimmed room, adding a grotesque enhancement to his obvious fear and discomfort. The Emperor took no pleasure in it.

The replay stopped as abruptly as it had begun, and the lights slowly increased in intensity. Except for the sound of Brendan's rapid breathing, and the minute rustling of the man's clothes as he shook visibly under the Emperor's gaze, the room was silent. The Emperor remained where he was and regarded his aide steadily, saying nothing, asking nothing of him. He carefully, continuously monitored the aide's readouts, despite the drain the effort caused him, and waited.

"There is a debt between our Houses," Brendan offered at last, his voice trembling. "She . . . A representative of her House called on me, insisted that I meet with her. I couldn't refuse."

"We know." The Emperor lowered his voice to a whisper. "What did she want?"

Brendan tried to reply, but each time he opened his mouth to speak he reconsidered what he was about to say and attempted to start over. His brow furrowed in puzzlement and his words came in sobs when he finally got control of himself enough to form a coherent answer. "I don't know! She . . . I . . ." He sat upright once more, averting the Emperor's gaze, and tried desperately to regain his composure.

You're telling me the truth, he thought as he monitored several vital telltales in Brendan's readouts. The Emperor steepled his hands before him and waited for Brendan to continue.

"I . . . I had made up my mind, long before I was to meet with her, to refuse whatever request she made. The debt between Houses is centuries old, and I intended to deny it." He looked up again, his face flush with a mixture of shame and confusion. "I made an oath of loyalty to you, Sire, and have lived by that oath. I intended to invalidate the debt, but she made no request!"

"Think carefully," the Emperor said. He spoke slowly, keeping his words firm, but at the same time letting the controlled power of his voice encourage the distraught young man to speak freely. "What did she say? What did you discuss?"

"Nothing of consequence, Sire, I swear!" His breathing had slowed, and he spoke more calmly now, but he shook his head in frustration as he searched his memory. "It seemed almost, for lack of a better description, like a . . . a family reunion. She asked only about my welfare: Were my duties demanding? Did I need anything? Had the change in location of the Imperial Court put a greater burden on me? Things of that sort."

The Emperor listened as he described their conversation, then nodded in understanding when Brendan had finished. He leaned on an elbow, absently pulling at his thinning white beard as he considered the implications of what he'd heard.

"You were used," he said flatly. "Your talk, her questions, seemed innocent enough; and on the surface, I suppose, they were. But I'm just as convinced that her people observed you constantly."

"Sire, I don't—"

"Your every word, your every action and mannerism, was analyzed as you spoke; probably by the very people who advised her what carefully rehearsed questions to ask of you. She wanted information, Brendan. On how close you are to me. On the current state of my health. On anything to do with my relationship with you or anyone else with whom I interact. And you unknowingly gave it to them."

Brendan sat wide-eyed, his mouth slightly open in shock at the revelation.

The Emperor sighed and shook his head slowly. "The fault was not yours, it was mine." *It was mine,* he repeated silently, *for underestimating the bitch.*

Brendan sank into the chair, overwhelmed with remorse. "Sire, I deeply regret my role in this . . ." Gone was the light banter the Emperor had enjoyed; gone was the assured way the young man had handled his duties these many years while at the same time allowing the Emperor to retain his dignity. Gone, too, was that which the Emperor would miss most: the closeness he'd been able to share with a person who had become more of a companion than a subject.

"This can be remedied," the Emperor said, shaking Brendan from his depression. "But it will require a sacrifice on your part."

"Anything, Sire!" His face beamed with the thought that he still might serve his ruler.

The Emperor watched the change in the man's demeanor at the thought of somehow making amends. "I shall not ask for your agreement in this, for I have already made my decision as to your part in it. Before this day is out you will become the center of Imperial attention; you will be asked many questions by many people." He watched Brendan's reaction, weighed it against the look of puzzlement and foreboding in his eyes. "Say nothing of this discussion. Nothing. Do you understand?"

The young man nodded slowly, uncertainly.

"Say nothing," he repeated. "Answer none of their questions."

"Yes, Sire." Brendan's head hung nearly to his chest, his voice catching in his throat as he added: "I understand, but . . . I am not sure I understand why."

The Emperor glided the powerchair close enough to Brendan that he could have touched him, and held out the bracelet, its shiny surface catching the light almost hypnotically. "Take this," he said. "Its purpose will be explained later." The medical aide obediently slipped the bracelet into a pocket. "Tell me: Would you give up your life for your Emperor?"

The man's eyes widened, but he didn't hesitate in answering. "Yes, Sire. I swore an oath to serve you when I agreed to the implants before leaving Corinth. I would not take back that oath now."

"That is good," the Emperor replied, his voice at once kindly and foreboding. "That is good. Because when this day ends, your life will truly be over."

He glanced at the data stick in its slot and issued a silent one-word command:

Erase.

EIGHT

P rince Javas stood, alone for the moment, at one side of the stage. Everyone else—Imperial staff, aides, ranking members of the Court, and those taking part in the presentation itself—buzzed incessantly all around him.

At the opposite side of the cavernous area were several groups of people. He easily recognized Bomeer and his retinue, and even in the dim lighting could plainly detect the scowl on the man's face. Nearby, Supreme Commander Fain gave last-minute orders to some of his people. By one of the rear entrances, Adela stood with the members of her lab team. As he watched, each of the scientists spoke to her briefly, shaking her hand or giving her a quick hug, before she turned and passed through the security check. He realized the necessity of the security efforts, of course, but still felt uneasy watching her being subjected to them and looked away. He caught sight of Glenney, walking vigilantly among them all, glancing first here, then there, apparently satisfied that his security measures were in place. A wave of nervousness swept over him.

Only an hour earlier he had felt excited, anxious, and had enjoyed the rush of last-minute anticipation that the years of groundwork for his father's project were at last to be replaced by the actual work of the project itself. But the mood of several key people around him—as well as the constant, impatient murmuring of the representatives of the Hundred Worlds Planetary Council filling the auditorium—had affected him greatly in these last moments before the presentation. The raw edge of anxiety in the air had infected him, for the worse, and now he felt simple, common nervousness.

He didn't like the feeling.

The backstage area of the auditorium was enormous, nearly as large as the seating area itself, and Javas felt dwarfed by the massive velvet curtains, open now while last-minute details were being attended to. He stared above him at the flies, noting that Glenney's handpicked men remained at their positions in the catwalks among the hoisted and secured pieces of scenery and theater lighting equipment. He smiled at the intricacies of what went on backstage, things normally invisible to a theater patron but nonetheless essential to a smooth production. *Just like life,* he mused.

Javas stepped around the curtain and glanced at the front of the stage, as he had nearly a hundred times already, and confirmed once more that the shielding was in place at the edge of the proscenium. It would remain, until the start of the proceedings, on an opaque setting. The crowd that shifted in anticipation on the other side of the shield could not see the dimly lighted stage area behind it, but the bright lighting in the house itself enabled Javas to see occasional movement of the audience on the other side. The silhouette of a dozen armed Imperial guards just on the other side of the shielding, their backs to him as they scanned the crowd, did little to ease his tension just now.

"Sire?"

Startled by the sudden intrusion into his thoughts, the Prince turned sharply to his personal aide. "Yes," he snapped. "What is it?"

The aide bowed curtly. "Sire, I've been informed that the Emperor is on his way to the auditorium."

"Very good. Please tell Commander Fain we'll begin as soon as my father arrives."

The man spun about and crossed quickly to the other side of the stage. Javas was about to join Fain himself, but was stopped by a light touch on the sleeve of his dress uniform.

Adela was a vision in a flowing gown of powder blue that fit her exquisitely, accentuating her beauty. Her dark hair, normally restrained or pulled back behind her head, tumbled freely across her shoulders. A polished stone, an agate, hung from a simple silver chain around her neck and she had adorned her hair with a single fire-red flower. She smiled, then turned wordlessly and walked to where Javas had stood just a few minutes earlier behind the gathered velvet curtain.

Javas followed. A security guard in Imperial dress stood near the wall a few meters away. Although forbidden to leave his assigned position, the man made a show of inspecting the flies and catwalks above him. With a smile, he read the guard's name on the pocket of his uniform and made a mental note of it.

He embraced her then and, intoxicated by the way her perfume mixed pleasantly with the natural scent of the flower in her hair, kissed her.

They separated slightly and, still held in his strong arms, Adela lay her head against his chest. "I can't believe it's finally happening," she said at last.

Javas took her chin gently in his fingertips and gazed down into her eyes. "I never doubted that it would." Still cradling her chin in his hand, he kissed her again, more softly this time.

The nearby guard cleared his throat and Javas pulled away slowly, regretfully. The guard nodded across the stage and Javas turned, hands clasped behind his back, to see Fain approaching.

"Commander?"

Fain bowed his head briefly to Adela, then addressed the Prince. "Sire, your father is arriving."

"Thank you."

Fain bowed once more, then hurried to the rear entrance, which, Javas could see, was now bordered on both sides by members of the Court. He smiled at the guard and gave him a curt nod of thanks, then walked across the stage with Adela on his arm.

Academician Bomeer yawned.

They sat in two formal rows at the apron of the stage, a few meters back of the now-transparent shielding that curved invisibly around the edge. There were five places in the first row: Emperor Nicholas sat in his powerchair at center stage, flanked on his right by the Prince—now standing as he addressed the assembly with introductory remarks—and Dr. Montgarde. To the Emperor's left was Fain's chair, then his own just to the Commander's left.

Bomeer paid as little attention to what the Prince was saying as he did to the dozen people sitting in the row behind them. He glanced idly at those seated in the second row of chairs just in front of the closed velvet curtain. Plantir Wynne was there, as was the Emperor's nursemaid, Brendan. One of the scientist's team was there, as well as several other members of the Court whose faces he couldn't immediately place—or particularly care about.

Bomeer returned his attention to the assembly itself, disturbed by the importance of what he'd seen. The auditorium was filled nearly to its eight-hundred-seat capacity with the representatives of the Hundred Worlds and their guests, which was something Bomeer had never expected. And except for a smaller section at the rear of the house where a number of representatives not present on Luna were attending holographically, nearly every one of the attendees had made the long trip to be here personally as the Emperor outlined his foolish project.

Although the time for open discussion at the Council would not come until all the presentations had been made, Bomeer's discreet investigations had already told him that support for the plan was strong among the worlds. He had found a number of representatives who openly opposed the venture, but was unsure if their opposition could be counted on.

As the Prince spoke of opportunity, advancing technology and benefits to all members of the Empire, Bomeer scanned the audience as the representatives listened in rapt attention to Javas' words.

". . . it will be a time of expansion, a time of science," the Prince was saying. "Each world, giving of its resources and talents, will see itself grow in proportion to its contribution. And you may wonder: What of those worlds of lower technological background? What of the frontier worlds and new colonies just beginning that may have less expertise to spare as they work to shape and build their own homes?" Javas' eyes slowly swept the audience as whispers and nods passed among some of the representatives who apparently had been thinking just that.

"These worlds, too, will share in this endeavor. The frontier worlds, while sometimes poor in technology, are rich in materials essential to the successful completion of the most important effort ever undertaken by the Hundred Worlds. These worlds, in return for the construction of ships and manpower, can expect more help in establishing a home than any world has received since the beginning of the Empire . . ."

No wonder there is such a positive feeling among the worlds, Bomeer thought. *Cooperation is easy to acquire when it's paid for.*

The academician looked back out over the audience once more, attempting to tune out the Prince's words, but was again impressed by the assembly. The representatives had been seated, Bomeer realized, according to the distance from Earth of their home planets. Each delegation was identified by a small banner attached to its row displaying the crest or flag of that planet. Those from the nearer worlds sat in the front rows, those more distant in the upper portion of the auditorium. The representatives from Earth, Luna and the Orbitals sat in the first row itself.

Bomeer looked at the Earth delegation, and his heart nearly stopped when he saw a tall bearded man sitting with the group. *My God, what is he doing here?*

As he stared at Johnson the man turned sharply and his eyes met Bomeer's unexpectedly. The Earther's feral, wolflike eyes narrowed and—was the man smiling at him?

The time has come, the Emperor thought as he listened to his son. Ignoring his own tiredness, he took pride in the way the Prince worked the crowd, in how the representatives of the Hundred Worlds hung on each of his words. *You will make a fine leader.*

Javas had finished speaking and had come to his side to assist him as he prepared to address the auditorium. He glided the powerchair forward about a meter in front of the others and placed his hands firmly on the arms of the chair. With Javas steadying him at his elbow, he pushed himself to his feet. He saw the concerned look on his son's face, and smiled to reassure him that the assisters on his legs, as well as the back brace that enabled him to walk, were working fine.

His heart pounded at the effort of each step, and he felt a bead of sweat running down his scalp as he concentrated hard on keeping Brendan from reading the pain caused by the pressure the brace was putting on his back. He turned to his son and embraced him, then regarded the auditorium once more and waited for the applause to fade.

He raised a hand to silence them, then dropped it quickly to his side when he felt it shaking. A pain rose in his chest and he concentrated even harder on suppressing the information his implants would now be trying to relay to the bio-readouts Brendan was monitoring.

"Members of the Hundred Worlds," he began, and as his voice echoed through the auditorium sound system he envisioned his words flowing out, not just to those seated before him, but leaping across space itself to the very reaches of the Empire. "Members of the Court; citizens and friends, all. We embark today on a journey, the likes of which make the Empire itself seem small by comparison."

The speech he gave was not memorized, but there had been no need to. He knew what he wanted, needed, to say. There was additional applause periodically as he spoke, and the Emperor took advantage of each pause in the address to catch his breath and refocus his concentration. At one point, his knees began to shake almost imperceptibly in the assisters Brendan had fitted to his legs, and he felt a weakness flow over him like a wave. At that moment, he sensed Brendan probing him and clamped down even more tightly on his systems to hide what he was truly feeling.

"In just a few moments . . . A young scientist with a vision will address you in a few moments." His will was drifting and, realizing that his words were becoming rambling and repetitive, he tried to pay closer attention to what he was saying. "Her ingenuity, her drive and her dreams are exemplary," he went on. The words came now with great difficulty and a light-headedness swept over him briefly before he managed to force it away. He was sweating freely now and, no longer able to control his hands, kept them riveted at his side to hide their shaking. "But without . . . the cooperation of all of us, working together as one, her dream is nothing. And that, I think, is . . . the real strength of the Hundred Worlds; that each member world, strong in itself, is made stronger by . . . by the association of others."

There was applause again, and the Emperor felt his son's hand on his shoulder. Javas was standing by his side, concern evident in his eyes. The Emperor looked at the other members of the Court seated on the stage. Tears glistened in Adela's eyes and she was plainly frightened. Fain fidgeted in his seat, looking helpless. Even Bomeer appeared uncomfortable as he chewed absently on a lower lip. Javas looked pleadingly at him, then turned to Brendan seated just behind the powerchair and demanded, "Is he all right?"

"I—I don't know!" Brendan sputtered. "His readings are . . . confusing."

The Emperor saw the sheer terror on Brendan's face, and knew that only then did his medical aide realize that he'd been hiding his true condition from him all along.

He felt a squeezing in his chest, a line of pain burning down the length of his left arm. The auditorium spun around him and he felt himself weaving as the pain flooded in, but found that he couldn't fall because the assisters on his legs automatically compensated for the erratic motions.

"Father!"

Everything was happening at once around him, and yet it all seemed to move in slow motion: Javas reaching for him. Brendan on his feet and moving quickly to his side. Fain barking orders into his wrist comm. Adela gasping, a hand over her mouth. Glenney bursting through the curtains. Everyone talking, crying, shouting at once. And through it all, a deathly, stunned silence fell over the auditorium.

Another wave of pain racked him and he pitched forward into Javas' arms. He stopped repressing his monitoring implants, allowing his bio-readouts to flow freely once more, and heard an immediate, sharp gasp at his shoulder. Brendan stumbled backward as the sudden messages of agony momentarily overloaded his implants before he could regain control.

Javas eased him to the floor and knelt there, cradling his father in his lap. The Emperor felt the pressure of tiny fingers on his hand and became aware that Adela was kneeling at his son's side, her face a mask of consuming grief.

Free now of the burden of controlling the readings his implants were sending out, he was surprised at how clear his thoughts had become. Despite the tremendous pain, the Emperor understood now why the auditorium had grown oppressively silent and realized that someone—Fain, probably, or maybe Glenney—had cut off the audio pickup carrying the presentation to the auditorium sound system, and then out over the Imperial net. Closing his eyes tightly, he used the last bit of strength he possessed to search the computer circuitry and found the necessary channel to reactivate the system.

"Hear me," he said, his eyes still closed, in a voice barely more than a whisper. The words echoed in the auditorium and the Emperor smiled weakly as he imagined the signal spreading out. Instantly to Armelin City, then a split second later to Earth, then a few seconds after that to the Orbitals, then a few minutes more to the colonies in Sol system, and finally out across the Hundred Worlds themselves.

"Hear me! This is not . . . an ending, but . . . a beginning." The Emperor coughed violently and struggled for breath before continuing. "Do not allow what has . . . been done to me to stray you from . . . from our noble goal."

He who is willing to die for his cause . . . Gasping for breath, he opened his eyes and found Brendan leaning over him. It was easy to see in the young man's ashen face the realization of what his role in this would become. Part of him wanted to apologize, but he turned away instead.

"As I ask you to work together . . . for understanding in this," the Emperor wheezed, "can I do less than demand the same . . . of myself?"

"Father, please. Lie still." Javas' face reflected the pain he felt inside.

The Emperor looked into his son's eyes. "Prince Javas. Son. I—I have made many decisions during my reign. As my last decision, in the spirit . . . of the task which now falls upon you . . . I forgive those who did this to me. I pardon them." His head rolled unceremoniously to the side, and the life went out of him.

Javas eased his father's body to the stage and grasped Brendan's shoulder in his strong hands, jerking him unsteadily to his feet.

"Why is my father dead?" he demanded. "Why was his condition not relayed to medical?"

On hearing the Prince's words, Glenney summoned several of his nearest men with a snap of his fingers.

Javas held the hapless man by both shoulders now, shaking him as he continued. "You were in constant link with him; you are the only one who could have suppressed his readouts!"

He released his grip on the man's sleeves, allowing him to collapse into a sobbing heap. Javas turned in disgust as Glenney's men dragged Brendan off the stage.

NINE

The sun glowed a brilliant red and streamers of red and orange played through the clouds and jet contrails lacing across the evening sky. As the sun finally dipped below the horizon, the red glow in the sky remained well into dusk as stars appeared one by one through the glow.

Brendan walked along the narrow, hard-packed dirt road with no particular destination in mind, but hoped he'd find the inn soon. A passing farmer had told him there was an inn on the outskirts of the village up ahead where he could get an excellent meal and a room for the night.

He shook his head in bemused confusion as he remembered his short chat with the farmer. The man had been driving a primitive wooden wagon pulled by two of the most beautiful work horses genetic engineering could produce, but when he'd stopped to give him directions to the village, Brendan had noticed that the back of the rickety wagon was filled with an odd array of farming equipment: There were several wood and metal hoes, rakes and shovels, as might be expected, each covered with hardened mud and manure. But jumbled haphazardly in with the hand tools was an electronic hydro-drill—also mud- and manure-encrusted —and a number of water condenser components that obviously came from a state-of-the-art irrigation system.

What a study in contrasts Earth was, with dirt roads and animal-drawn vehicles coexisting with advanced biotechnology and jet aircraft. The oddest thing about it all was that the Earthers didn't even seem to notice the contradiction. *Best to get used to it,* he reminded himself, *since I'll be spending the rest of my life here.*

He found the inn just over the next rise. It had grown dark and he was close enough to hear the sounds of revelry coming from inside the tavern even before he managed to get a good look at it. It was large and inviting, two-storied, and except for the metal sheeting of the roof was made entirely of wood. There was a hand-carved sign that swung precariously above an entrance lighted by two lanterns. Several horses were tied to a horizontal post nearby and pawed the ground nervously each time the swinging sign banged against the siding of the house. Looking up in the dimness, he could just make out the dish of a receiving antenna mounted on the roof.

The inside of the tavern was as much a collection of contradictions as anything he'd seen in the three weeks he'd been on Earth. A roaring fire warmed the room and candles provided most of the lighting at the scattered tables, but a public information screen was mounted just inside the entranceway and music, obviously recorded, filled the room. There were maybe ten people inside; some were eating, some sharing drinks. Three men, their clothing soiled from whatever constituted their daily occupation, talked loudly at a table near the fireplace and occasionally burst into fits of laughter. No one paid him much attention when he entered.

He made his way to the massive wooden bar and ordered a hot meal and a tall mug of the local brew—a bitter but not unpleasant-tasting malt beverage served at room temperature—and took it to an unoccupied table to await his dinner.

"Will you be staying the night, then, sir?" asked the innkeeper when he brought his plate, heaped with steaming food. Seeing him closely for the first time, Brendan realized that he was a mere boy, no more than nineteen years old. He was startled for a moment to see someone so young working at a job such as this, but remembered that this was normal: Native Earthers didn't use life extension. It was commonplace to begin a life's work early here.

"Uh, yes. Yes, I'll need a room for the night."

"Very good, sir." The boy turned to a woman clearing a table on the far side of the room and whistled over the chatter to catch her attention. He held up two fingers. "Room two for the traveler, Sarah," he called out before turning back to his customer. "My wife'll have your room ready by the time you've finished. Will you be having another ale, then?"

"No. Thank you." The boy—no, *young man,* Brendan reminded himself—nodded and returned to his place behind the bar. Brendan finished his meal undisturbed, paid for it and the room and went up to bed.

He was so tired and sore from walking that after removing his boots he fell onto the bed fully clothed. Despite his fatigue, he did not fall asleep easily, which was becoming commonplace of late, and lay staring out the room's single window. The Moon had risen, and cast a pale glow across the floor.

I did what you asked, he thought. *I said nothing, told them nothing.* His head ached slightly, although he couldn't tell if the dull pain was caused by the deactivated implants or the strong ale he'd consumed.

Why? Was it so important to you to see this project begun that you had to sacrifice your life this way? Brendan sighed heavily and tossed fitfully in the small bed. He rubbed tired, burning eyes and silently added, *And mine?*

Hours passed and he was nearly asleep when there came a soft knocking at the door. Not bothering to attempt to light the oil lamp on the table, he stumbled across the room with only moonlight to guide him and opened the door a crack. "Yes?"

It was Sarah, the innkeeper's wife. She carried an electric flashlight and he blinked at the brightness of the beam streaming in through the door. "Sorry to be disturbing you, sir, but the traveler you were expecting has arrived. He and his wife are waiting downstairs at table."

Brendan shook his head to clear it. "What traveler? I was expecting no one."

"I'm sorry, sir," she replied, "but he did not give his name. Shall I tell him you shan't be disturbed until morning, then?"

Curiosity got the better of him and he quickly pulled on his boots. "No. I'll see him." Sarah stepped back and allowed the glow of the flashlight to guide them both down the narrow staircase.

The man stood immediately when Sarah led him into the dining room, surprising Brendan with his size.

"Will you have some more coffee, sir?" She indicated a large pot and several cups sitting on the table.

"No, thank you, ma'am," the bearded stranger said politely in a deep, resonant voice. "We'll be fine for now." He turned his attention to Brendan. "Come, sir, and join me at my table."

Brendan sat down and gratefully took the offered cup of steaming coffee. He sipped carefully of the hot liquid and studied the stranger. The fire had burned down, but the mound of glowing embers in the fireplace cast an eerie light that reflected in the man's feral eyes. And even seated, he still looked taller than any Earther Brendan had yet seen.

"I'm afraid you have the advantage," Brendan began. "Do I know you?"

"My name is Johnson."

Brendan offered his hand and winced at the strength in Johnson's handshake.

"It's good to meet you . . ." Brendan hesitated, looking for the proper salutation. "Uh, Mr. Johnson."

A dying log shifted suddenly in the embers, momentarily bathing the room in orange brightness. In the few moments since Brendan had come downstairs, most of his attention had been focused on Johnson, and he'd paid little heed to the woman sitting at his side. But as the glow in the room increased, he saw her clearly for the first time.

She had darkened her hair and her face was nearly hidden by the high collar of the Earther coat she wore, but as the glow of the fireplace bathed her features in a dance of flickering light, there was no mistaking that the woman playing the role of Johnson's wife was Rihana Valtane.

As he had numerous times since his father's death nearly three weeks earlier, Javas met now with the Emperor's two closest friends and advisors in what was to have been his father's study. There was much to do now that the Planetary Council had, by an overwhelming margin, given official approval to Dr. Montgarde's project, and Javas had consulted with Fain and Bomeer repeatedly. The Commander, having realized the benefits of the project to the Imperial military fleet, had proven himself to be one of its staunchest supporters. Bomeer, too—although still quick to point out every flaw or negative aspect of his planning—seemed, at least, to have mellowed in his opposition.

Commander Fain paced slowly in front of the viewscreen. "Pallatin has been a thorn in the Empire's side since it was colonized three centuries ago," Fain said in a voice now husky from overuse. "They have had little discourse with other worlds, still less trade, and except for minimal representation on the Planetary Council, have preferred to allow themselves to develop without Imperial assistance. They even seem unconcerned about how their gene pools have drifted and have no interest in preserving a genetic baseline. It was no surprise that the representatives from Pallatin's governing body, the 'Joint Dominion,' were among the few of the Hundred Worlds to refuse, outright, their cooperation."

Fain crossed the width of the room quickly, retaking his seat next to Bomeer's. "Unfortunately," he went on, "they also possess more raw materials necessary for shipbuilding than any of the worlds. Their construction facilities, likewise, are among the finest in the Empire—"

"But they *are* a member of the Empire, even if in name only," Javas finished for him. "As such, they cannot, *will* not, outright refuse the needs of the Empire."

Fain shrugged, nodded in understanding. Many of the outermost worlds of the Empire had seen unrest and had shown a certain level of defiance. The chief of staff of the Imperial Military Forces had maintained throughout his career that a firmer hand was needed with the frontier worlds and, while he did not exactly welcome the opportunity to use force, agreed that it was necessary and that he was prepared to use it.

"We need Pallatin's cooperation in this," Javas said firmly. "Do what is required, Commander."

Fain nodded in sharp agreement, the slight hint of satisfaction in his manner telling Javas that he was not displeased with the decision.

This meeting, like so many of the others, had lasted hours. Javas rubbed his face with both hands in an attempt to perk himself up and a sudden feeling of frustration swept over him, interrupting the subject at hand. He blinked the tiredness from his eyes and let them wander over the study. He took in the viewscreen and the handcrafted woodwork of the cabinetry, felt the massive wooden desk beneath his fingertips; he'd personally designed this room and all its contents for the Emperor, had it equipped with every convenience, every comfort his father might want. Javas was surprised, when he reluctantly took the study as his own, at how comfortable the room was, how it seemed to "fit" him. The feeling disturbed him.

"Why did he do it? Why did he pardon his own murderer?" Javas pounded a fist on the desk in frustration, startling both men seated across from him. He leaned forward and rested his chin on steepled fingers, staring intently at the two. "You knew him, Fain, better than anyone. Why?"

"I can't answer that, Sire." Fain sat rigidly in his chair, not quite at attention, and returned the new Emperor's gaze. There was strength in those eyes, Javas realized, but pain and frustration lay behind them as well.

"Nor can I," Bomeer added softly. He ran a hand absently through thick brown hair that was more unruly than usual. "Sire, no one could have detected the extent of the threat your father's—'caretaker' presented to his health. No one." He let his gaze fall to the floor as he chose his words, then regarded Javas seriously, but carefully. "Sire, I served your father all my life, and spoke candidly to him of my feelings in all things—even when my feelings went against his, as they did concerning this project. It is true that the bluntness of my remarks angered him on occasion, but my advice was always accepted at face value. May I be so bold as to speak bluntly now?"

Fain turned slightly in his chair, an eyebrow arched almost imperceptibly.

"If I've learned nothing else from my father, it was to seek—and carefully consider—the counsel of others. Speak freely."

Bomeer cleared his throat softly, and without further hesitation said, "Sire, you are blaming yourself for your father's death."

"Is that so, Academician?" Javas heard the anger rising in his voice. "And how about you, Commander? Do you concur?"

Fain's answer was instantaneous. "I do." He paused then, as if taking further measure of his new Emperor before continuing. "And if I, too, may speak candidly, Sire?"

Javas nodded.

"It is my considered opinion that this preoccupation with your own possible guilt in this matter can serve only to weaken your resolve in achieving your father's goals."

Javas opened his mouth to refute the statement, but realized that the man was right and instead shook his head slowly in resignation, allowing his anger to drain slowly away. Looking first to one, then the other, he saw that each seemed as tired as he himself felt, and he was certain that a glance into a mirror would show the same dark circles under his eyes that he saw under those of his companions.

He pushed away from the desk and crossed silently to the viewscreen on the opposite wall. Arms folded across his chest, he stared idly at the graphic representation of the Pallatin system Fain had been discussing.

They're both right, he thought, still standing before the screen. *I am blaming myself.* He sighed heavily and returned to the desk.

"Thank you for your honesty," said the Emperor of the Hundred Worlds, nodding to each of them in turn. "Commander, when can you have a ship crewed and ready to depart for Pallatin?"

They lay next to each other, legs still entangled in the satin sheets of the huge bed, and stared tranquilly at the branches of the trees swaying gently above them. From time to time the rustling boughs parted enough to see the sky, revealing a field of stars as unfamiliar to Javas as those seen from Luna. He propped himself up on an elbow and smiled at the way the holographic forest around them was augmented by the scent of leaves and flowers, and how the singing of a night bird in the distance seemed to call forth the twin moons now rising brightly through a clearing of thin saplings. He watched her as she lay, taking in the way her hair cascaded over her pale shoulders, the rise and fall of her breasts as her breathing slowed. Her face was turned to watch the rising of the moons, and he couldn't read the expression there. Their lovemaking had been passionate, but preoccupied in the knowledge that she was leaving.

Despite the impression of openness suggested by the holographic forest, the room had grown warm, and as Javas stroked the smooth flatness of Adela's stomach with his left hand, his fingertips glided softly over a thin sheen of perspiration. He furrowed his brow in concentration and silently ordered the temperature lowered a few degrees. An extra moment of will as he concentrated gave rise to a whisper of air that enveloped the bed chamber like a breeze, seeming more a natural part of the "forest" than that of the room's cooling system. Although Javas was still unaccustomed to the integrator, and was still learning to use it with the effortless ease his father had shown, he was already beginning to appreciate some of the finer opportunities it presented.

Adela's breathing had slowed to normal and was now almost inaudible. She took his hand in both of hers and brought it to her lips as she turned to him amid the jumble of sheets. She pulled Javas to her and embraced him in a long, warm kiss. He was about to return the kiss, but she pulled away and swung her legs over the edge of the bed. Without a word, she left his side, crossing to a small settee marking the edge of the room and stood, her back to him, silhouetted against the moons as she admired the vista around them.

"Thank you," she said tenderly, "for the vision of home. I've missed it so."

"I had it programmed some time ago," he replied, still leaning on his elbow. "It was to be a gift." *She's so tiny,* he thought, watching the moonlight shining through the moving trees play across the gentle curves of her body. "Although I'd not intended it as a going-away gift."

It made sense, of course, for her to leave. If anyone could convince the Pallatins to the necessity of their cooperation, it was she. Hadn't she, after all, convinced him? If the ship Fain was sending ultimately had to use force to bring the Joint Dominion into line, it wouldn't be for lack of her persuasive talents. Then there was the time factor. They both had come to terms with the fact that she would need to follow this project through to its conclusion, requiring either long periods of cryosleep or travel at near-relativistic speeds or, more likely, both. The round trip would take forty years, in realtime, while she would age only a few.

A bird flew past so close she started for a moment, then giggled in the realization of how silly it must have appeared to be so completely fooled by something that wasn't even there. Javas smiled. *I love all the childlike, joyously simple things about you,* he thought silently as her gentle laughter reached his ears. *I'm going to miss them.* The thought reminded him of another, more important reason why he hadn't fought her decision to go: her personal safety. Until he'd managed to learn the truth surrounding his father's death, he preferred that she be somewhere else for now.

There was a soft chiming, so faint that it might have gone unnoticed but for its intrusion in the peaceful setting all around them.

"Acknowledged." The chiming stopped. Javas pulled a robe around him, then went to Adela, who had not moved from her spot near the settee. Standing behind her, he encircled her in his strong arms and kissed her once on the neck.

"It's time, isn't it?" she whispered.

"Yes."

He followed Adela as she wordlessly retrieved a light knee-length wraparound from the tangled covers at the foot of Javas' bed and slipped it on, smoothing it down with the palms of her hands before cinching it around her narrow waist.

"I have to go."

Javas nodded and, after taking one last look around at the serene Grisian forest, addressed the room system. "Cancel and store display." The scene instantly dissolved and was replaced by his bed chamber.

He wanted to hold her, ask—no, command—her to stay, but knew better than to try. Instead, he took her upturned face in his hands and kissed her once.

"Good-bye," he said simply.

Adela smiled and, reaching up to his face, played smooth fingertips over the stubble on his cheek. She stood on tiptoe and kissed him, then turned and quietly let herself out of his bed chamber.

And out of his life for the next forty years.

PART THREE

COMING OF AGE

TEN

Eric's breath came in sharp, painful gasps. There was a stabbing ache in his side and a hot, metallic taste in his mouth that burned down the very length of his throat each time he swallowed. The day had been chilly when he'd started his hike, but sweat covered him now as he ran, making the tiny scratches and lacerations on his face and forearms from low branches and briars sting. Fatigue steadily overtook him, causing him to misplace his hurried steps more and more frequently now; he was stumbling more often, and he knew that any lead he once had over his pursuers was beginning to dwindle, if, in fact, much distance remained between them.

He had never taken the main trail this near the town before, and was now beginning to regret having left the grounds at all.

There was a clearing up ahead where the hulk of a fallen tree—an enormous oak, its battered old trunk more than a meter thick—lay across the path. It had been there for some time, apparently, because someone, perhaps a local farmer or one of the townsmen who regularly hunted these woods, had taken the trouble to hack crude steps into the rounded sides with an ax. The steps were little more than boot holds scooped out of the wood and he should have slowed, he knew, and sacrificed a bit of time to scramble carefully over, but instead he made an attempt to leap it. His right leg actually cleared the top as he leaped, but his left shin banged full force into the downed tree, snagging him and sending him tumbling onto the damp, hard-packed dirt of the path on the other side.

Eric rolled onto his back and, staring at the patches of blue sky visible through the treetops, lay still and waited for the ground to stop spinning around him. He closed his eyes, shutting out the dizziness, and enjoyed for a moment the delicious chill seeping through his sweat-soaked shirt from the damp ground beneath him. Listening carefully, he tried to detect the sounds of the boys chasing him, but his breathing was still too labored and, to him anyway, too loud to hear much of anything other than his own blood rushing in his ears at the same accelerated pace as his heart pounding in his chest.

He struggled to his feet, wincing when he put weight on his left leg, and was about to start down the path once more when a sudden, stinging pain thudded against his left shoulder, followed by another further down his back. Eric tried to run, but the weakness in his leg made him stumble to his knees as a third piece of lead shot grazed his ear. His hand flew instinctively to the side of his head and he cried out, against his will, and fought back tears.

"Hold now, pup, or my next shot will crack your skull asplit!"

He clenched his eyes tightly, trying to drive the pain away. Eric felt a warm stickiness in his fingers, but refused to lower his hand and look at the blood he knew he would find there. Instead, he fell to a sitting position and pivoted slowly around to face his tormentor. The boy stood atop the fallen bole of the oak tree, aiming a slingshot at his forehead. His arm was pulled back fully, ready to fire, and if the lead ball contained in the slingshot was of the same weight as those he'd already used, Eric was sure the boast of cracking his skull was no idle one. Still holding his ear, he lowered his head in a sign of surrender.

"That's a good pup," said the boy atop the log, barely winded by the chase. He was at least five years older than Eric, maybe sixteen or seventeen, and jumped down from the log with an agility that said he was no stranger to the rugged terrain of the backwoods. There was something about the older boy that was familiar, Eric thought, but he couldn't quite place him. Perhaps he'd seen him in the village on one of the rare instances McLaren had allowed him to accompany him, or maybe he was a son of one of the servants or groundskeepers at Woodsgate.

He strode casually to where Eric sat, the slingshot never wavering. A grin spread across his face, and Eric noticed the thin beard the boy was attempting to cultivate. The whiskers were very light in color; lighter, in fact, than the long copper-red hair that tumbled unkempt over his collar.

"Paulie! Mobo! Come on around!" There was a thrashing sound from the woods to Eric's left, and presently two more boys appeared at the edge of the trail.

The three of them were dressed in similar clothing: roomy, belted pants of a dark broadcloth fabric, linen shirts with long blousy sleeves, leather lug-soled boots, and vests of leather and heavy canvas. Their clothes showed obvious wear from repeated hiking in the backwoods, but the colorful nylon knapsacks the two newcomers wore appeared new. Each of the three wore a knife sheath on his belt, while the boy with the slingshot also wore a whip coiled at his side.

"Do you know how easy you were to catch?" asked the first boy, slowly releasing the tension on the slingshot. He put the ball into a small sack dangling from his belt and tucked the slingshot itself into a pocket. "I asked you a question," he repeated.

Eric looked up, but did not answer, and noted with satisfaction that his silence had not been taken as fear, but rather as defiance, which seemed to perturb the boy. He nodded sharply to his two companions and they jerked Eric to his feet.

"Cut him, Reid," said the shorter, heavier of the two as he released Eric's left arm and discreetly stepped a few paces behind his leader. "Show him what we think of peepers."

The boy, Reid, laughed and stepped forward. "How about that, now, pup? Did you get an eyeful, and enjoy it?"

Eric had sneaked out of Woodsgate, bypassing the security shielding that surrounded his home, and had spent the better part of the afternoon outside the grounds. He was forbidden to leave the grounds unaccompanied and Master McLaren would be livid when his absence was noticed—again. But any opportunity to ramble through the Kentucky hills, even for a short while, was worth any reprimand the Master might hand out. He had been hiking what he thought was a little-used side path off the main trail when he'd come upon them. He had heard them first, heard the sounds of a woman's high-pitched laughter in a patch of scrub just off a section of the established trail near the village.

Curiosity had drawn him closer and he saw, about a dozen meters distant through a break in the scrub, Reid and his companions—and what they were doing—in a small clearing.

A working whore was with them, one of the women he'd heard about who practiced their trade at the local taverns. She was at least a little intoxicated and seemed to find it difficult to keep from giggling periodically, even as the boys prepared to take their turns with her. She lay naked on a hastily made bed of dry leaves and pine boughs over which she'd spread out her own clothing. Reid unfastened his pants, lowered them to his knees and, not bothering to undress further, climbed on top of the woman, much to her seeming delight.

Eric had watched in fascination and fear of something he *knew* about, both from his formal teachings and boyhood tale-telling, but had never experienced, never seen before.

"Reid! There!" One of the boys pointed at his hiding place in the bushes and all heads turned toward him. He froze, even as Reid scrambled to his feet and quickly, clumsily, refastened his pants.

"Another!" cried the working whore, her voice showing more amusement than annoyance at the interruption. She rolled unsteadily to her side on the makeshift bed, supporting herself on an elbow, and faced Eric. He stared at her, unable to move. "And a young one, at that!" She laughed again, unbalancing herself as she did, and fell once more to her back.

There was a sharp crackling sound as a lead shot whizzed through the leaves at his right, shaking him from his immobility. Even as he turned, he saw that the three were already moving. Only the fact that they hesitated to grab their few belongings gave him a head start. He turned and ran back down the trail in the direction of Woodsgate, the sounds at his back a mixture of angry cries from the boys at his heels and the even angrier cries of the woman, now suddenly aware that her young customers were leaving without paying . . .

"Do you know how easy it was to overtake you?" Reid asked again, standing before him now with knife in hand. He handled the knife casually, even showed off with it by flipping it into the air end over end and snatching it firmly by the handle each time. "It was a simple matter. The trail makes a great curve over the last half-klick." He swept his arm to encompass the woods to his right. "We simply cut across, pup; knowing you'd be slowing here at this tree."

Eric looked up at his tormentor. *Feel free to hide your fear and anger from your enemy,* he recited inwardly, remembering what McLaren had taught him. *But tell the truth about your feelings if it may help you defeat him. Above all, let him know the contempt you feel for him.*

"Three of you, one of me," he said, using every bit of self-discipline he possessed to make the words sound stronger than he actually felt. "Your years of knowledge and experience in the backwoods, against those of a stranger in these parts." He paused, then raised an eyebrow and tried to make his voice sound as sarcastic as possible before adding, "It must have been *very* hard for you."

Reid stared in disbelief, as did his companions, at the twelve-year-old who'd just dared to stand up to him. His smile vanished. "You should be taught," he said, no longer flipping the knife, "not to speak with such disrespect to your elders."

"My elders?" Eric replied, hoping the fear he was beginning to feel didn't show in his voice. He forced a smile and looked directly at Reid. "My elders have more than fuzz on their faces."

One of the other boys—Eric didn't dare take his eyes off Reid to see which one—chuckled under his breath, and Reid cut him off with a sudden, icy stare. He turned back to Eric, approaching him with the knife. "Here's something to think about, pup, next time you decide to spy on us."

Eric wanted to tell them who he was, threaten them with the full might behind his family name, but something deep inside him made him want to see this through on his own. Besides, he realized, they'd probably never believe him anyway. Instead, he stood his ground, hands balled into tight fists at his side. *Wait, wait for the moment,* he thought. *Wait until he is vulnerable—or until there is nothing left to lose.*

Reid lightly ran the back of the blade against Eric's neck and up under his chin, then inserted it—blade edge facing away from his skin—into the collar of Eric's pullover shirt. He slid the knife downward, at an angle, easily slicing the fabric with the obviously razor-sharp edge. Once he'd reached the bottom of the shirt, he returned the knife briefly to Eric's neck, then cut the shirt from his left shoulder down the length of the sleeve before repeating the procedure with the right sleeve. Eric stood motionless, staring straight into Reid's eyes as his shirt fell away. The other two—Mobo and Paulie—laughed aloud as they watched. "Cut him!" Mobo cried again, then they both laughed even harder, urging Reid on.

The breeze played across Eric's bare back and chest and he started to shiver, both from fear and from the chill wind. *Wait . . . wait.*

A sadistic grin beamed from Reid's face as he stuck the knife into the waist of Eric's pants. He sawed at the waistband and thin belt until they finally severed, chuckling as Eric's shirt—which had been tucked into his pants—fell to the ground. Then he quickly ran the knife down the length of the right pants leg. He needed to cut only a few centimeters down the remaining leg before the pants fell away.

Reid laughed aloud and turned to receive the approving laughter of his companions.

In the brief moment his attention was drawn away Eric slapped as hard as he could at Reid's outstretched hand, sending the knife flying into the scrub. The surprised boy turned back just in time to catch nearly the full force of Eric's right elbow as he brought it up forcefully under his chin, causing him to stumble backward, momentarily dazed.

"Come on, bastards!" Eric crouched in a defensive stance when the other two pressed forward—none too surely, having seen what he had just done to Reid—and snapped sharply to each in turn, hands held in fighting position before him whenever either got too close. He knew he couldn't outrun them, especially with the remnants of his pants still dangling from one leg, so he continued to stand his ground hoping to bluff them or, at the least, stall for time until he could think of something else.

Reid staggered to his feet, rubbing tenderly at his jaw, and laughed softly. Eric noticed, however, that he stayed just outside arm's reach even as he seemed to grasp control of his situation.

"Look at this!" he shouted to his friends, pointing. "I do think we've been attacked by a naked man-child." Reid turned and roared in amusement, with the other two quickly joining in the derisive laughter.

Eric let his guard down slightly, taken aback by what Reid was saying. He looked down at himself, naked but for his boots, underwear and the remains of the unsevered portion of his pants hanging in tatters from his left leg, and admitted inwardly just how ridiculous he must have appeared. The reflection took only a moment, but it was enough time for Reid to swing around with his leg, kicking him squarely in the ribs.

His chest felt like it was exploding as he twisted around with the force of the blow and crumpled facedown on the path. Reid was immediately on top of him, forcing the breath out of his lungs. The older boy grabbed his wrists and held them flat against the ground, while at the same time forcing a knee into his back, pinning him helplessly. His ribs ached and Reid's knee in his back hurt like hell, but the pain couldn't match the shame he felt at ignoring his training and letting himself be taken by surprise in this manner. He was glad McLaren was not here now—much less his father—to see how he had failed one of the most basic lessons of self-defense.

"What say you now, pup?" Reid spat, thoroughly enjoying the humiliation he was inflicting. He pulled Eric's wrists backward, pinning them behind his back. Each time he spoke, he twisted his arms higher and higher behind him until Eric thought they might snap. The weight of the knee in his back was so great that Eric could barely draw a breath and he felt himself dizzying; if he couldn't get up soon, he'd surely pass out. "Perhaps this will teach you something more important than respect." He stood up abruptly, and Eric felt a moment's relief spread through his aching limbs.

Reid took the whip from his belt, then played it out and snapped it loudly over his head. "Perhaps this will teach you the meaning of *territory.*" He nodded sharply at his companions, then flicked the whip back and forth as they tied Eric's wrists around the nearest tree.

Eric hung helplessly from the tree, the bark rough against his bare chest, and waited for the whip to strike. He heard them laughing behind him, enjoying every minute of the torment, and tried, unsuccessfully, to look over his shoulder to where Reid stood. There was another sharp *crack!* of the whip and Eric jumped, certain that the next time the whip lashed out would be against his bare back. *Crack!* Again Reid chose not to strike him, and Eric realized what he was doing: More than causing direct pain with the whip itself, Reid wanted to frighten him, terrify him so deeply that he would beg to prevent the inevitable beating. But that was the key, Eric knew. The beating *was* inevitable, but there was no need to give Reid the satisfaction of knowing he was beaten. *Hide your fear, hide your anger; but show your contempt.*

The whip lashed out again, this time actually striking the tree just above his head. Shreds of bark scattered about his hair and shoulders. Eric's eyes closed tightly in fear, but he forced himself to laugh.

Reid stopped, silencing his friends with a wave of his arm, and let the whip hang limply at his side. "What's so funny?" he demanded.

Eric said nothing.

Reid stomped to Eric's side and grabbed a handful of hair, snapping his head back. "I asked you what you were laughing at." He pulled harder, forcing Eric's head to turn in his direction. "Answer me!"

"I was just wondering," Eric replied smoothly, "if you always miss your target."

Incensed, Reid stepped quickly back and let fly with the whip, striking him across his left shoulder. Eric cried out, and tears rolled uncontrollably down his cheeks as the whip struck him a second time, then a third.

For the briefest of moments, Eric thought that the fourth strike was the whip, but as a veritable shower of wood and bark chips fell over him he realized that a part of the tree itself had exploded above him. He opened his eyes and heard yet another blast in his ears, and recognized the sound of an Earther hunting weapon; a shotgun.

"Reid! I'll blow your gods-damned head from your shoulders if you move a muscle!"

The sounds behind him were confusing, and at the same time reassuring: scuffling sounds and fast talking as Reid and the others attempted to deal with whoever it was that had appeared so suddenly; the snort and hooves of a horse, a big one; the *ka-chuck-ka-chuck, clack,* of two more shells being loaded into the chamber of a shotgun.

"Hello!" Eric shouted. "Who's there?" There was no answer.

"Is this the way you have been spending your time, Reid, accosting traveling children?" The horse stomped again and Eric heard the sound of the beast's labored breathing—whoever the newcomer was had come in a hurry. Apparently his pursuers had had a pursuer of their own. There was a pause, and then another heavy sound as the horse leaped the fallen oak, then trotted to where he hung at the tree.

The rider was middle-aged, by Earth standards, and wore clothing that befitted a noble family. He was handsome of face, but wore a troubled expression as their eyes met.

He shook his head as he looked down from his mount. "A mere boy," he said over his shoulder. "And for this you needed help from Fat Mobo and Paulie the Snake?" He reached for the machete at his waist and cut Eric's bonds with a single chop. Eric fell back from the tree immediately, but caught himself before collapsing on the ground. He rubbed his wrists, but pointedly ignored the excruciating pain from the blows he'd just taken from Reid's whip. The stranger looked down at him once more and, apparently assured that he was all right, pulled the reins on his mount and returned his attention to the others.

"I am ashamed," he said simply. The horse snorted again, punctuating his remark as he pulled on the reins and guided the animal closer to Reid and his friends. Eric smiled in satisfaction at the way the two accomplices shied back from the big horse, but noted that Reid stood his ground, unshaken by the horseman's strong words. "Mobo, Paulie—leave. I wish to speak to the brave and manly Reid alone." The two immediately scrambled wordlessly over the oak and rushed back up the trail in the same direction from where the horse had appeared. Reid didn't bother to bid them good-bye, but remained where he stood, glaring at the horseman.

"You should mind your own business, Brendan," he said once his friends had disappeared into the backwoods.

The horse turned slightly as the man slid the shotgun into a saddle holster and smoothly dismounted, landing at Reid's feet. He removed his riding gloves and tucked them into a loop on the saddle, then, in one fluid motion, turned and backhanded Reid, knocking him backward into the trunk of the fallen oak. "You *are* my business," he said.

Reid wiped a bleeding lip with his sleeve and leaped forward, and found himself staring at the knife that had appeared suddenly in Brendan's hand.

"I've taught you nothing," Brendan spat, shaking his head in disgust. Reid stood back and straightened, and it was obvious even from Eric's vantage point that the newcomer's words had hit home, as Reid's anger seemed to drain from him.

"You've taught me much," Reid replied, his voice at once defiant, but more respectful in tone than it had been moments earlier. "But I sometimes fail to see the value in what you've taught."

Brendan nodded. "That much is obvious. But had I been a stranger out to do you harm, and you had attacked—as you did now—out of anger and unarmed, you might now be watching your blood spill onto the ground, and not merely trickling from a cut lip. Would you have seen a value in my lessons then?"

The boy crossed his arms in silence and stared off into the woods.

"And since when have you taken a liking to the torment of those weaker than you?" Brendan pointed to where Eric stood, almost naked, still rubbing sore wrists.

"But we caught him spying on us!"

"Yes, I know," Brendan replied. "I encountered your working whore a kilometer up-trail. It was she who told me what happened and the direction you ran. I came up behind you some minutes ago and followed you here." Eric saw the man smile for the first time since he'd appeared. "If you think I am angry and disappointed, wait until you talk with the whore—"

"I'll probably never see the drunken bitch again," Reid interrupted. "She wasn't that good."

"Perhaps not. But you'll go into town and pay her tavern keeper nonetheless."

Reid started to protest Brendan's decision, but thought better of it, adding in a low voice, "You'll not always be able to tell me what to do, you know."

Brendan casually replaced the knife in the sheath on his belt. If he was offended or concerned by what Reid had said, he didn't show it.

"That's true enough. When you reach eighteen, my obligations to your mother will end and you'll be free to turn your back on House Valtane, although to do so would show even poorer judgment than I've seen you display this day alone." Again, he looked meaningfully at Eric.

The exertion of the chase and the terror of his treatment at

Reid's hands now behind him, Eric felt the cold of the back-woods seeping into his skin. The welts on his back hurt, and he tried to concentrate on the pain as a means of taking his mind off the growing chill. He crossed his arms, covering himself as best he could, and started shivering more intensely than before.

Brendan turned suddenly back to Reid, the look of anger he'd shown earlier once more flashing in his eyes. "Remove your shirt and vest."

Reid's mouth moved wordlessly several times before he finally managed to sputter a single "What?"

"Your shirt and vest; take them off. *Now!*"

He hesitated a moment, but realizing that Brendan was indeed serious, he complied. He removed the vest first, then the shirt, and tossed both into a heap on the ground between them. "Anything else, Master Brendan?" he demanded sarcastically.

Brendan ignored the insult. "For now, no. Get you back to House, where I'll expect you in the exercise room at exactly six o'clock. It seems you need a refresher in hand-to-hand, not to mention manners. Perhaps we can address both at the same time."

Reid stood a moment, unmoving, and stared in unabashed contempt for his teacher. Then, without further discourse, he turned sharply and hopped atop the log. He glanced back once at Eric with a look that said he held him personally responsible for the humiliation he'd just received, then hopped down the other side before disappearing into the backwoods at an unhurried jog.

Apparently satisfied that his young charge was on his way home, Brendan pulled a small nylon container from his saddlebag. The roughly rectangular container sported several pockets and compartments, one of which produced a plastic pouch of antiseptic pads. Brendan tore open one of the pads and daubed it with a gentle and skillful hand on Eric's back. As cold as Eric was beginning to feel, the pad felt even colder where it touched his skin; but there was no stinging and the pain in the welts started to fade almost immediately.

"This will ease the pain and start the healing process, but have these looked at as soon as you get home." He put the used pad into a separate section of the container and returned it to the saddlebag. Retrieving the discarded clothing, he shook them once to remove the leaves, then tossed the bundle to Eric. "The temperature is dropping rapidly, better put these on. I didn't think his pants would fit, or I would have had him leave them as well." He walked over to his horse, which had wandered a few paces away and was nibbling at the long grasses clustered in a small patch off the trail.

Eric wasted no time in tearing away the remnants of his pants and pulling the heavy linen shirt over his head. The welts on his back smarted as the cloth slid over them, but the warmth of the shirt—which hung nearly to his knees—more than made up for any discomfort. He watched his benefactor with interest as he buttoned the collar at his neck and quickly donned the vest. Besides the obvious gratitude he felt for the man Brendan, he was fascinated with what he perceived as an odd mixture of personality traits. It was clear that Reid looked at him in only one way, as his teacher, and Eric had to admit to himself that that was how he looked at his own teacher, Master McLaren. But McLaren *was* one-dimensional, trained as a Master and executing that function flawlessly.

But this man was somehow different. He dealt with his pupil with ease, even when stern brutality was called for, but there was something else about him that Eric could not quite identify. A worldliness, perhaps, or a familiarity with things long past that were missed in his life. Eric knew nothing about this man, but felt himself liking him despite his strangeness. Even now, as Brendan produced an apple from his saddlebag and proceeded to slice it into chunks for his mount, he seemed to exhibit a oneness with the animal, gaining its trust and submission much in the same way he had gained his own.

"Thank you," he said.

Brendan stopped mid-slice on the apple and turned to face him. "So, you do speak, then." He gave the last piece of the apple to the horse, then reached into the saddlebag and pulled out another. "Catch."

Eric snagged the apple easily, and nodded thanks before biting deeply into the fruit. He hadn't realized, until this moment with the tart juices dripping coldly down his chin, just how hungry the activity of the last hour had made him. He finished most of the apple in a few bites, then said, "I've never seen a horse like that. May I . . ."

"Of course." Brendan patted the horse several times as Eric neared to reassure the animal that the small stranger meant no harm. He pointed with the knife at the last bit of apple in Eric's hand. "He'll be your friend for life if you give him that."

Eric approached cautiously, holding the apple out in his palm, and reached up to stroke the horse's head with his other hand. The animal snorted once and reared his head back, but quickly overcame any suspicions it had and eagerly took the treat from Eric's hand. "I've never seen anything like him," he repeated. "He's beautiful."

"You've got a good eye for horses. My Mistress' House has one of the finest privately owned bio-bred farms in Sol system." The man continued stroking the horse's neck in silence as a feeling of awkwardness fell over them. After a moment, Brendan cleared his throat and turned to him. "Are you all right?"

The welts still hurt a good deal, but Eric nodded. "The pain's gone; I'll be fine," he said. He scanned the woods around him, then up at the sky. The cloud cover had thickened and that, combined with the lateness of the day, had caused the back-woods to grow dimmer. "I'd better be getting back."

Brendan followed the boy's upward gaze, then glanced at the timepiece on his wrist. "You may be right. Besides, it looks like rain may be on the way, although it's difficult to be certain in the backwoods." He patted the horse's neck one last time and easily swung himself up into the saddle, then bent down from the saddle and held out his hand. "Climb up, Eric, and I'll give you a ride back to Woodsgate."

Eric had reached up to accept Brendan's hand, but hesitated now and stared in shock. How did this man know him? He studied the man's face, and saw that he apparently regretted having admitted what he knew, or at least wished he'd chosen a better way of admitting it. Taking the horseman's hand in his, he placed his foot in the open stirrup and swung himself up behind the saddle.

They rode in near silence for the next hour; when they spoke it was only to discuss some aspect of the trail or the weather, or to speculate on the type of animal tracks that were visible on the trail itself. They stopped once so Eric could relieve himself, and they took advantage of the break to share the last of the apples from his saddlebag.

They stopped again where the trail crossed the hard-surface access road, with Woodsgate looming vast and foreboding in the gray light at the end of the road. The security cameras had detected their approach, of course, and several armed Imperial guards waited at the open gate. McLaren was there, pacing, as were several of his Master's attendants. Eric thought it odd that McLaren held back. When they were still nearing the gate, Eric had thought he'd seen the Master running forward to greet them or—more likely—to assure his safety. But now he waited with the others. Did McLaren know the horseman? He would have to ask later.

Still several dozen meters distant, Brendan brought the horse to a halt. "This is as far as I go."

Eric swung himself down from the horse and stood looking up at Brendan. "Thank you for your help," he said simply, then turned his back on horse and rider and headed for the gate and the pacing Master.

"I can only apologize for their actions," Brendan called after him, "but I can say this: You handled yourself well back there."

Eric stopped. The guards bristled nervously and tightened their grip on their weapons until he raised a hand, making them relax somewhat, and turned sharply back to face the rider.

"You watched it all, didn't you." It was an accusation, not a question. He stepped closer, his eyes confidently meeting Brendan's. "Why did you wait so long to do something to stop it?"

"For that, I cannot apologize." The horse, apparently nervous at a potential confrontation with the armed guards, snorted impatiently and he patted his neck reassuringly, soothing the animal. "For I am a teacher," he continued, "and you needed to learn an important lesson, Young Prince."

He pulled at the reins, swinging the horse about, and trotted down the road, finally disappearing into the backwoods.

ELEVEN

J avas, Emperor of the Hundred Worlds, stared out over the fog-shrouded Kentucky hills surrounding Woodsgate. He sat on the balcony of his personal suite at the family estate, enjoying the brilliance of the changing colors sweeping the wooded river valley to the southwest, and inhaled deeply of the autumn air. *I stayed away from Earth too long again,* he thought. *I've missed this place . . . I've missed my son.*

Robb McLaren was giving his report, but Javas had paid attention to only half of what his son's Master had been saying.

"Sire?" McLaren asked. The man was well trained, among the finest parenting Masters the Empire could produce, and knew as much about when to intrude upon his Emperor's private thoughts as he did about raising, and teaching, his only child.

Javas turned sharply. "I can't believe you allowed him to slip through the shielding," he snapped, causing the attendant standing at the doorway to jump slightly. "I've checked with security all the way up to Glenney, and he assures me that all shielding was not only in place, but that it had been *doubled* since the last time he slipped out."

"That's true, Sire," McLaren replied, his voice, as always, level and near monotone. Javas often thought that a bomb could go off under his chair while he was speaking and the Master's voice would continue as if nothing had happened. "However, he has become quite skilled at manipulating the security systems—not to mention everything else connected with the main computer. I shouldn't be surprised if the current software of the House systems bears little resemblance to anything of its original programming. He has become that adept."

Javas considered McLaren's words. He looked idly at the Master, and reflected on how much the man reminded him of Montlaven, the tutor that he and his brothers shared when they were growing up at Woodsgate.

Chosen from among the Earthers, as Montlaven had been, McLaren dressed as the Earthers dressed and held many of the same customs and antiquated ideas about natural progress—he did not partake of rejuvenation, for example—and yet Javas seemed to feel a greater understanding of him than he'd ever felt with Montlaven. *Of course*, he reasoned, *I am an adult now, and a parent, and I see those things that only a parent sees. Perhaps I see, and appreciate, things that were invisible to me when I was a child.*

"I suppose I should be grateful, then, that his education in technical matters has exceeded his other pursuits?" He stood, and leaned on the ornate railing of the balcony overlooking the Woodsgate grounds and the Kentucky countryside.

McLaren cleared his throat and stirred uneasily for the first time during this discussion. "Well, uh, I am most impressed by his grasp of technical science, but I . . ."

"Yes?"

The Master paused, then began in a tone that almost conveyed embarrassment. "He is . . . headstrong, stubborn." McLaren looked about nervously, trying to avoid the steady gaze of his Emperor. "If I may be so bold . . . I knew Joseph Montlaven and, as I expected to someday be made Master for your son, we compared notes frequently." He stopped, fidgeted with the cup of coffee on the low table before him. "Neither you nor your brothers were this impetuous. I've never seen a personal drive or determination of will to match Prince Eric's."

"He gets it from his mother."

"But, Sire—" Javas cut him off with a wave of his hand and immersed himself in the pristine beauty of the countryside. He smiled at the news that his son showed the proper strength and incentive to be his heir but, at the same time, he was concerned for the boy's safety. Unlike the cultured, highly civilized life-style of the Moon, where the seat of Empire was located, activities like those in McLaren's report could easily lead to an early death on a rough planet like Earth.

"I understand, Robb," he said. "I'll speak to him of it."

McLaren, aware that the Emperor had just ended this meeting, rose quickly and was escorted from the balcony by the attendant.

Many things had changed at Woodsgate over the years: New buildings had appeared and old ones replaced; interior furnishings and color schemes had gone through countless redesigns; even the stable had been relocated to the other side of the grounds when moving the seat of the Empire required the shuttle landing pad at the estate to be enlarged. Only the garden remained exactly as Javas remembered it from his youth. The Emperor strolled the gently sloping grounds and looked out over the wide expanse of green, the otherwise smooth spread of Kentucky bluegrass dotted here and there by scattered karst. The limestone outcroppings gradually increased in number and size, and finally became a high ridge a hundred meters to the east. There were caves in the outcroppings, and Javas remembered the time his older brothers had taken him along on an underground exploration that had both fascinated and frightened him—much to Montlaven's distress—years earlier. Javas sat on a large outcropping and tried hard to remember exactly how long ago that had been. He had taken no rejuvenations, of course, since he'd become Emperor; but how many times had he renewed before that, and how many years had passed since he'd run these grounds as a child?

"Father!"

Javas turned at the sound and watched his son as he ran down the flagstone path leading from the main house. He'd seen his son as frequently as his schedule and Imperial duties allowed, of course; but the holoconferences held in his personal chamber on the Moon, no matter how lifelike or real they might seem at the time, still could not take the place of actual contact. The boy had grown since he'd last been this physically close to him—when? Spring? Javas shook his head self-consciously and promised himself for perhaps the hundredth time that he would make a stronger effort to return to Woodsgate sooner. Next time.

Eric ran easily, effortlessly, across the grounds with a grace and agility that reminded Javas immediately of Adela. Eric looked much like his father and had inherited much of his physical strength and abilities, but the boy favored his mother in most other respects. His hair was very dark, like Adela's, and his build and features were small for his age. Eric's hands showed his mother's delicate fingers as he waved excitedly in greeting. Above all else, it was his unbound enthusiasm that reminded him most of his mother. Adela de Montgarde, at this moment approaching a planet nearly twenty light-years distant, would be very proud of the son born four years after her departure . . .

"Father!" Eric leaped forward, knocking Javas to the ground. It was a game they had played for years upon greeting each other after a long absence: Eric would jump and attempt to tackle his father, who, more often than not, would eventually allow the boy to topple him to the grass, where they would wrestle until exhausted. As the boy tried now to pin him to the ground, Javas remarked inwardly that Eric had grown even more than he had thought; his compact frame hid greater strength than a casual observer might at first suppose. Flat on his back in the sweet-smelling grass, Javas realized that either the boy was getting a bit too big for this game or he was getting too old.

As Eric almost succeeded in holding him down, Javas pushed firmly—but carefully—with his leg, sending his son flying backward to land on his rump with an audible plop, which ended the impromptu wrestling match with fits of breathless laughter from both of them.

Javas stood, brushing himself off, and extended a hand to help Eric up. They stood a moment and shook hands, and Javas was pleased at the firmness in the boy's grip.

"Hello, Eric. It's good to see you." Javas opened his arms and father embraced son. Over the boy's shoulder, Javas saw McLaren appear briefly on one of the main house's many balconies. It was difficult to be certain from this distance, but it looked like the ever-serious Master had been grinning from ear to ear.

"Welcome home, Father." Eric knew better than to ask how long the Emperor would stay this time.

They talked idly for the better part of the next hour as they walked the grounds of the estate. Eric was deeply involved in what he was learning, and spoke excitedly about how he had progressed in the previous six months. Javas noted with satisfaction that, while the boy discussed his successes with unabashed pride, he did not give in to the obvious temptation that all young boys have to exaggerate; Eric's description of his schooling closely matched that given him earlier in the day by Master McLaren.

The Emperor was proud of his son and regretted the way the boy's smile disappeared when the subject inevitably turned to yesterday's events in the backwoods.

* * *

Eric tossed fitfully, trying unsuccessfully to get to sleep. *No wonder I thought I'd seen him before,* Eric thought. *My brother.*

He lay on his bed, gazing out at the Moon, huge and bright orange, now appearing over the horizon. The color faded and the Moon seemed to shrink in size as it rose. It was quite high in the night sky before Eric finally gave up on sleep, swung his legs over the edge of the bed and went to the computer terminal in the study area occupying the entire far wall of his room.

He rarely used vocal commands, preferring the feeling of intimacy the keyboard gave him. Eric knew of his father's integrator and how it gave him instant access to any Imperial data. Maybe someday he, too, would be so linked; but for now, he felt as one with the computer as his fingers flew over the keys.

Getting out of the educational and informational modes and past the low-level security into the House files was easy; he'd long ago installed enough back doors that the Imperial techs never found them all whenever they upgraded the system. Even when they did find them, he easily installed more. McLaren had spoken to him several times about accessing House systems and playing pranks with some of the routine functions like the sprinklers and clocks, and each time he would promise—with the utmost sincerity, naturally—that he wouldn't access them that way again. With the myriad ways he knew to gain access, it was always an easy promise to keep.

There was no way to access Imperial files from this terminal, of course, but there *were* personal files in the House system: McLaren's, House staff members, his father's; even files belonging to his grandfather. These last, as well as numerous others belonging to deceased family members, had been closed and sealed, and were impossible to open from a terminal. The others, like those belonging to his father and the Master, were "merely" blocked with security codes and passwords. Eric had accessed those files only once, a few years earlier, more as a challenge to see if it was possible than out of curiosity as to their contents, but had reclosed them immediately in respect for his father's privacy. He never attempted to access them again, until now.

It took most of the night to break the security, and once inside Eric hesitated, fingers frozen over the keys. What he was doing was wrong, he knew, but wasn't it just as wrong for his father to have kept secret the facts about his family? Wasn't it wrong to wait for an incident like yesterday's to occur before telling your own son the truth? He stared at the screen for several long minutes, and resolved to stay as much out of his father's private thoughts as possible, but he was determined to learn more about his brother.

He installed a carefully worded worm sequence that would correlate and find only those files containing information about him and his brother, and would then display only those portions of the individual entries that cross-referenced what he wanted to know.

joawe89045—I personally ordered the fertilized ova kept out of her reach, but was unaware that she had duplicated and kept others. She has already hired a surrogate, but Glenney has not yet been able to learn if the woman has been implanted. However, the fact that she has elected to retain the services of a surrogate instead of using an artificial womb tells me much about what she has in mind for the child . . .

joaqp90007—Glenney reports that a healthy baby has been born. I have a son . . .

joacc98172—The boy, Reid, is being reared on Earth. Rihana has purchased a great deal of land adjacent to Somerville, near Woodsgate itself. Damn her! What is she up to . . .

joakl101955—She has engaged Brendan as the boy's Master, but I don't understand why. Bomeer, naturally, expects the worst. Well, at least it will help to consolidate our surveillance efforts . . .

joawe122743—He seems to be very bright and is responding well to his teaching. However, even at five years of age he is already showing signs of being a bully. Glenney reports that many of the townspeople have filed complaints with House Valtane . . .

joawe122745—I have made a decision on the matter . . .

joayy122998—I am informed that the fertilization of the frozen ovum was successful and that the implanted embryo is healthy. I have already given orders that the surrogate will stay at Woodsgate and that the baby will be born there . . .

joabh128732—"Adela, my love, we have a son. His name is Eric, after your father. I regret that I was not able to discuss this with you and hope you will understand my reasons. If not, then perhaps it is your forgiveness that I should hope for . . ."

The sky over the eastern hills was graying when Eric reached the final entry his search program had called up. He rubbed at burning eyes with his cramped fingers and squinted at the last entry.

joatr212665—My sons have met, with undesirable, although predictable, results. I've kept this matter from him for too long and will talk to him later this morning . . .

Eric rubbed his eyes again and slowly backed his way out of his father's files, trying to leave as few footprints as possible. There would be telltales, he knew, and sooner or later his father would discover that he'd accessed the private entries. When it happened, he'd ask for his father's understanding.

Or his forgiveness.

TWELVE

"It's beautiful!" Eric stared, wide-eyed and mouth agape, out the plastiglass window running up the entire wall of his suite. "I don't remember any of this being so fantastic."

"There are other views available, Young Prince," Academician Bomeer said. "Computer! Activate room screen; alternate views, please." The window immediately converted to a holoscreen that showed other vistas of the lunar landscape surrounding the Imperial section of Armelin City. The display cycled through several options: an external view of the enormous Imperial landing bay now receiving incoming traffic; a magnified window-perspective of the new Science and Engineering facility under construction three kilometers to the west; the plastiglass dome of one of the recreational complexes, the lunar-normal gravity inside allowing citizens and vacationers alike to frolic in low-*g* sports. "Simply tell the room system which you prefer."

The original window-aspect reappeared, fascinating Eric more than the others, and he wasted no time in ordering the room system to leave the screen off. He grinned boyishly at how much more sophisticated the room systems were here than at Woodsgate. In fact, although he had been on Luna for several hours, the Prince still had a hard time containing his excitement at virtually everything he saw, heard or experienced. It was obvious to Bomeer that the privilege of coming to the Moon on the occasion of his sixteenth birthday was a welcome present indeed.

Eric turned from the window, tempering his enthusiasm at last, and sat on a long sofa placed in such a manner as to still allow him to glance periodically at the surrounding vista. "Academician Bomeer, will my father be able to break away and spend some time with me?" He pulled his boots off as he spoke, and absently dug his toes into the thick carpeting at his feet. "I was hoping that maybe we could have dinner together tonight, just the two of us."

"I am afraid not." Bomeer selected a chair facing the sofa and sat down, studying the Prince. He had seen Eric nearly ten years earlier when he'd first visited the Moon, then again on a short visit planetside to attend to some of the Emperor's affairs at Woodsgate, but he was simply not prepared for how much the boy had grown. *My God,* he thought as he studied Eric's features. *You truly are your father's son . . . And your mother's.* "The Emperor regrets that he was not able to greet you himself on your arrival, but has asked me to meet with you personally and to see to it that your immediate needs are met in the meantime."

A look of disappointment washed over Eric's face for a moment, but he nodded acceptance. He smiled in understanding at Bomeer and said, "I knew he might be. Oh, well, there's plenty of time. Could you arrange for an escort for me for later? I'd like to see some of the recreational and entertainment facilities here in the Imperial residence, as well as the research labs. Whatever's not restricted, of course."

Bomeer raised an eyebrow, remembering what Javas had said about the boy's prowess with computers.

"Of course. I'll have someone on standby; just give security a call once you have a chance to settle in."

Eric leaned back on the sofa and stretched, working the kinks out of his arms and legs after the lengthy shuttle trip from Earth. "It's probably just as well," he said, yawning. "I think I could use the time to nap out for a while."

"I imagine you are tired," Bomeer replied. "Earthers can do that to you."

Eric raised an eyebrow. "Oh? But I *am* an Earther."

A sudden wave of self-induced shock swept over Bomeer and he stuttered—something he rarely did—in quick apology to his Emperor's son. "Your Highness! I did not mean to imply that—"

Eric laughed, dismissing the academician's unintended insult with a wave of his hand. "Please, you've not offended me." He leaned back into the couch, folding his hands behind his head. "I've heard you hold no great love for Earthers."

"What can I say?" Bomeer shrugged, and chuckled nervously along with the good-natured Prince. "I've not attempted to hide my feelings for Earthers any more than—"

"Any more than you've hidden your feelings for my father's project." Eric's grin broadened mischievously.

"I have known you but a few hours," Bomeer said, cautiously returning Eric's smile, "and already you have caught me off guard; not once, but twice. You not only remind me of your father, but I see a great deal of your grandfather in you as well." Bomeer's estimation of the Prince rose several notches and he stood, spreading his hands wide in open admission as he headed for the door. "In any event, it is my job to express my opinion."

"My father speaks very highly of you for that."

Bomeer stopped, taken somewhat by surprise at this revelation, and turned back to the Prince. "Thank you for saying so."

Eric padded silently across the luxurious carpeting and stood facing the academician. "I've spoken in confidence to you, Academician; maybe you'll return the favor. Tell me: How is my father?"

"He works too hard, he works too long; and he sometimes tries to accomplish too much in a short time." Bomeer paused, taking the measure of the young man before him. "But he is very proud of his son and has been anxiously awaiting your visit for many weeks. Now that you have arrived . . . your father is fine."

Eric extended his hand. "Thank you, Academician."

Bomeer shook hands, then turned for the door, opening the security latch with his thumbprint. "Enjoy your rest. Security will send your escort when you are ready to tour the facilities."

The door slid closed behind Bomeer and, nodding briefly to

the guards posted at each side of the entrance to the Prince's suite, the academician walked briskly down the corridor.

Your son is a fine young man, Javas, he mused. *He will make an excellent Emperor one day.*

Port Director Mila Kaselin lay on her back, her lifeless eyes staring emptily from a crushed and misshapen face into the high reaches of the Imperial landing bay. A portable screen generator had been placed on the floor near her body, the hastily erected shielding now surrounding the controller's station opaqued at its perimeter to hide the gruesome sight Eric stared at now.

Glenney's call had come on his third night on Luna, as he and his father had finally managed to share a private dinner together. His father had left strict orders not to be disturbed, and had even gone so far as to disable the communications page in his dining room system to ensure a quiet evening. But someone had been killed at the port facility, and the Security Chief had thought the situation important enough to warrant interrupting one of the Emperor's all-too-rare family visits. Eric knew what had happened, of course; he had even seen it in Glenney's holoreport showing the grisly scene uncomfortably real—and even more uncomfortably close to the dinner table—and had a good idea of what to expect. Death was no stranger to him than it was to any other sixteen-year-old, but seeing it firsthand was still an experience that caught him more unprepared than he would have liked. Seeing it over the first dinner with his father in nearly eight months hadn't helped.

But then he had insisted on accompanying the Emperor to the scene. "This concerns me," he'd told his father at the conclusion of Glenney's report. "I belong there." But now he had second thoughts about not having waited for him at the table, as his father had suggested.

"She was beaten to death, Sire," Glenney was saying, "plain and simple. Whoever did this overpowered her and knocked her unconscious, and then continued until there was almost nothing left of her." Glenney paused, noting the look on Javas' face as the Emperor knelt before the broken body at his feet. "She, uh . . . Judging from the damage done by the blows, she was probably rendered unconscious almost immediately and didn't suffer through most of this."

Javas stood up rigidly, addressing his Security Chief in a tone that made the usually self-assured Glenney snap to attention. "Is that supposed to diminish what has happened here?" he demanded. The Emperor spun about and walked steadily toward the edge of the circle of shielding. "I want a full report in thirty minutes, Glenney, in my study. Eric!" Glenney's men literally had to scramble to get the shield open fast enough for Javas to pass through without slowing his stride.

Eric hesitated, still transfixed by the body on the floor in front of him. Director Kaselin had personally taken charge of his shuttle when he'd arrived, and she had been the first to greet him when he disembarked the vehicle. He remembered thinking at the time how pretty she was, but he had difficulty now, staring down at her battered corpse, recalling anything at all about what she looked like.

"Eric!" His father had halted several paces on the other side of the shielding and was waiting impatiently with the escort, the look on his face a confused mixture of rage and sorrow. He turned away from the mess and hurriedly joined Javas, who had already resumed walking down the corridor.

They walked the labyrinth of corridors leading to the Emperor's study in wordless silence, the clicking of their boots on the hard surface echoing hollowly as they walked.

Eric had seen his grandfather's study at Woodsgate only once—his father had visited Earth on the occasion of his tenth birthday, and had taken him inside the sealed room to talk about his future role in the Imperial structure—but this room seemed designed to be a mirror image of it. The paneling, the bookshelves filled with as many real books as tapes, the viewscreen, everything.

He took a chair facing the enormous wooden desk and watched his father as he sat heavily behind it. Javas tilted back as fully as the chair would allow, then rubbed his face with the palms of his hands and sighed before tilting the chair forward again and leaning on the desktop. Why was he so troubled by this? To be sure, the person responsible for this horribly cruel murder must be apprehended and punished to the fullest extent of Imperial law; but just as surely his father must have dealt with problems of this severity—and worse—before. Why did this one weigh so heavily upon him? Why, for that matter, had Glenney even felt the necessity of bringing it to his father's attention so quickly?

"Father?"

He looked up, seeming to see Eric in the room for the first time. He rose, opening a set of doors mounted flush into the paneling, and selected a bottle and two glasses from the well-stocked interior. He poured two drinks and replaced the bottle, closing the cabinet so that the doors became virtually invisible in the paneling once more. He handed one of the glasses to him and took the other for himself.

"I'm sorry, Eric," he said. "Not much of a 'happy birthday,' is it?" He regarded the glass in his hand for several moments, then sipped at the contents. Eric sipped tentatively at his own, the smooth brown liquid warming his throat as it went down.

"Who was she?"

His father had been about to lift the glass to his lips again, but stopped, lowering his arm to the desk in front of him and looking squarely into Eric's eyes. "She was a friend." Javas sighed, then pushed abruptly away from the desk. He leaned now against the bookcase, and must have issued a silent command through his integrator, because the viewscreen snapped suddenly to life, displaying a panoramic view of Armelin City. The old construction was obvious from this aerial perspective—older, grayer, more compact with a scattered added-on-later look to many of the domes and modules making up the lunar city—but the Imperial section, occupying fully a third of the image on the viewscreen, appeared as a connected single unit constructed as a fully functioning city unto itself.

"Do you see that, Eric? I built it in ten years. Ten years." Javas paused, sipped at his drink. The picture on the viewscreen expanded as it panned back for a satellite view from many kilometers up. "I didn't know your mother well when we came here from Corinth; we had barely met, once you take into account the inconsistencies of interstellar travel. We spent the entire voyage here in cryosleep, and on arrival we each went about our own tasks—hers to begin the Sun project, mine to establish the seat of Empire here in Sol system while your grandfather was in transit from Corinth. Looking back on it now, I don't think we spoke to each other more than a dozen times over the first five years here.

"My first priority was the landing bay; everything else that was to follow demanded that it be up and running. But more importantly, it had to be running independently—with everything else I had to do, it had to be as nearly self-sufficient as I could make it. Mila Kaselin was one of the first people I assigned here, one of the first I trusted." The screen blanked as his father issued another silent command then crossed back to the desk and sat, still nursing the glass in his hand. "She and I were close, in those early days here."

There was a sudden beeping from the room system; not loud, but it startled Eric all the same. Javas looked to the side for a moment, his brow deeply furrowed, and the beeping stopped, then he continued as if nothing at all had happened to interrupt them. When he faced him again, the hint of an apologetic smile was on his lips.

"But that is only a part of what I'm feeling now." He finished his drink, reaching back to set the glass on a low shelf behind him. "More important than a decades-old memory of what seemed a simpler time when I was only acting Emperor is the fact that someone I've considered untouchable has been murdered." Javas sat up straight in the chair and looked at Eric with an intensity that made him squirm uncomfortably.

"Son, more than twenty years have passed since your grandfather was murdered, and we still do not know who was responsible. Certainly there were many against our goal who plotted to take not only his life but my own as well as your mother's. He who allowed your grandfather to die was pardoned, and he now—well, he is watched." Anger glowed briefly in the Emperor's eyes, frustrated anger fanned by years of fruitless efforts at this one goal.

Eric had never seen his father so disturbed. He set his glass—the drink untouched but for the single sip he'd taken earlier—on the front edge of the desk and pivoted the chair. "And you're afraid," he said, "that those behind my grandfather's death have now renewed their effort to change the leadership of the Empire. And, in doing so, change the Imperial stance involving the project to save the Sun."

"Bomeer was right," he replied. "You are sharper than we give you credit." He took a moment to smile appreciatively at his son. "Yes, then; I believe that the inner workings of the Imperial

structure have been breached." He closed his eyes briefly in a way
Eric had come to associate with his father using his integrator,
then faced the door. "Security Chief Glenney has been waiting
for several minutes; let's hear what he has to say."

The panel door slid aside and Glenney entered, taking a step
inside the room and stopping with the door sliding closed mere
centimeters behind him.

"Sire?" The expression on the man's face showed surprise, and
more than a little concern, at seeing Eric still with his father.

"Be seated. Your report?"

"Sire, as you know, we found—"

"Do *not* tell me what I already know!" The Emperor banged
his fist violently on the desk and glared at his Chief. "A murder
has been committed in one of the highest security areas in the
Imperial section. It goes without saying, therefore, that we have
been breached. It's just as obvious that this was not a random
event, but rather something that has been accomplished over an
extended time, perhaps years. Tell me what I do *not* know."

Glenney paused, a disconcerted gaze shifting from the Emperor to Eric, then back again. He straightened in his chair and
cleared his throat. "We've checked and double-checked the records of anyone who could possibly have had access to the area
where Director Kaselin was working at the time of her death—
Sire, I've personally gone over them, going back more than
twenty years, and have found no discrepancies. This is something
that goes back to your arrival here, someone who has remained
in place since that time and has only now chosen to act." He
glanced at the Prince again.

Eric was immediately on his feet, feeling as though some metallic claw had just wrenched his stomach from him. He ran a
hand through his long, dark hair, then leaned with both hands on
the desk, confronting his father.

"It's me, isn't it?" he burst out. "It's because I'm here that this
has happened. My God, this is *my* fault." He turned away, trying
to hide the shame he felt.

"Sit down, Eric." His father's words were soft, yet firm. He
waited until the Prince was seated, then added, "No, it's not *you*
. . . it's *us.*" Javas stood and came around the desk to stand next
to Eric, then bluntly faced the security man. "Tell him."

"I'm afraid your father is correct, Your Highness," said Glenney, now also on his feet. "The two of you, together, may have been enough of a lure to draw out whoever has been in place for all these years."

Javas reached for his jacket, buttoning it as he demanded, "I want those responsible for this, do you understand me?" Eric watched his father as he spoke, saw how his brow wrinkled and his eyes blinked occasionally as he talked. Even now, as he dealt with this new situation, Eric knew he was mentally issuing dozens of orders, setting perhaps hundreds of things in motion. "What are your recommendations?"

Glenney stood aside and indicated the door. "Sire, there is no proof yet to tie what has happened to a direct threat against yourself or your son, but the timing of this—occurring during Prince Eric's first visit to Luna in nearly ten years—bothers me considerably. I want you out of here. Immediately. I can have anything you need brought down to you later, but I want you off Luna within the hour."

His father, already on his feet, nodded in understanding and fastened the collar of his coat. "I agree."

Fifteen minutes later Eric stood on the apron of the huge landing grid. His father beside him, they stood surrounded by armed Imperial guards as the shuttle *Azalea Dream* went through final preparation for launch.

Eric looked up and allowed his eyes to scan the vast chamber, trying unsuccessfully to pinpoint the spot where they had stood barely more than an hour earlier over the body of the slain Port Director. There were hundreds of personnel moving about the upper reaches of the dome, engaged in jobs Eric could only guess at. He returned his attention to the shuttle, now being prepared for lift-off by Glenney and the port authority staff. Unlike the huge, spherical Imperial fleet shuttles that could ferry a hundred people, the *Azalea Dream* was one of a class of smaller ships, with a capacity of no more than a dozen passengers, that regularly made the quick Earth-Moon run on various Imperial errands. Even so, the small ship was circled by three times the normal amount of technicians and security people as final prep was completed.

"Will you be safe at Woodsgate, Father?" Javas turned to him, the pleased expression on his face confusing Eric. "What is it?" he asked.

"You've just been shown that your life has been threatened, and you ask about my welfare." He shook his head and looked away, but not fast enough that Eric didn't catch a brief glimpse of the shame and regret in his eyes. "When I was your age, I would never have thought in the same terms about my own father if he had been—"

He had been about to say something more but stopped as a single figure broke suddenly away from the group standing at the shuttle ramp and trotted over to where they waited.

"Sire, Young Prince," Glenney said hurriedly, "we're ready to depart. This way, please." He spun about immediately and quickly led the way to the ramp, with Eric and his father, and the accompanying guards, right behind him.

The escort parted when they reached the shuttle, and the ramp extended fully. The two landing techs clattered quickly down from the shuttle and secured the bottom of the ramp, standing immediately aside when finished.

Two of the guards went up the ramp first, and when Glenney indicated that the Emperor should follow, they ascended the ramp quickly, causing the ramp to bounce slightly. Eric started up the ramp next but lost his balance momentarily on the unsteady footing and pitched forward, throwing his hands out before him to brace himself as he fell.

A strong hand grasped his arm, catching him easily before he could complete his fall. Glenney and the nearest guards bristled, but Eric hastily assured them that he was all right, thanks to the quick reflexes of the shuttle landing tech who had broken his fall.

He turned to the tech, a tall, bearded man with dark, feral eyes that flashed when he smiled. "Watch your step, Young Prince."

"Thank you," said Eric. "I will." He scrambled up the ramp and into the shuttle, followed by Glenney and another pair of guards.

The landing techs unsecured the ramp, and followed them inside.

THIRTEEN

Considering the *Azalea Dream* a small shuttle had been a relative observation on Eric's part. Sitting on the landing grid of the huge dome as they waited to board during final prep, the ship had been positively dwarfed by the cavernous facility. And while the *Dream*'s passenger capacity amounted to only a fraction that of the Imperial shuttle that had ferried him to the Moon three days earlier, this so-called hopper shuttle contained a passenger cabin that was both spacious and comfortably appointed with everything from a self-contained entertainment system to a small galley.

There were two rows of plush seats running the length of the cabin, five in each row, and Eric sat across a surprisingly wide aisle from the seat occupied by his father. Each seat had a viewport screen that simulated a window, as well as a program screen recessed into the back of the seat in front of it. The craft had been designed for passenger comfort and it was no surprise that, while there were many hundreds of this class in Imperial use in Sol system, there were many thousands in private service.

Glenney sat in one of the forwardmost seats. He wore a small headset and had swung the seat's program screen from its wall position, and was engaged in busy, quiet conversation, although Eric couldn't tell if he was in contact with the two pilots on the shuttle bridge or the two guards riding with the landing techs in the lower aft deck navigation and landing station. He could have been talking to both or, for that matter, neither. After several minutes of conversation he swung around in his seat, headset still in place, and faced the Emperor.

"We'll depart in a few moments, Sire. Everything has been set up. Other than the Woodsgate staff, few others know that you'll be leaving Armelin City. I've canceled everything that requires your immediate attention, explaining that you'll be spending time with the visiting Prince." His attention was drawn away momentarily as he listened to something in his headset. "A level one quarantine will be instituted on the Imperial section that will begin as soon as we're away."

"Quarantine?" Eric asked, addressing Glenney directly.

The man looked briefly to the Emperor, who nodded.

"Two things occurred the moment Director Kaselin's body was discovered. First, the Imperial section of Armelin City was closed. That is, all vehicular and pedestrian traffic into and out of the section was stopped. Second, a priority computer search going back forty-eight hours was initiated on every door, corridor, workstation or terminal requiring an access code, holocard or thumbprint. That information is correlated with personnel, both on and off duty—" Glenney touched a hand to the earpiece of his headset and turned away a moment to check the program screen.

There was a soft murmuring as the engines went through the start-up cycle, then the slight shudder of the gravity harness engaging, lifting the shuttle off the landing grid. In the viewport Eric saw the grid shrinking below the small ship as it rose; he could have ordered the screen to show an upward vertical perspective, but preferred the view of the landing facility as he waited for the Security Chief to finish.

"We're away, Sire; the harness has been released and we're proceeding under our own power."

"Very good." Javas settled into the comfortable seat and leaned back fully on the headrest, eyes closed. Eric and Glenney both knew that despite appearances, he was far from napping.

Eric paid little attention now to the view as the shuttle entered its transit pattern for Earth, and considered what Glenney had said just before departure.

"So, what the computer's looking for," he began, "is a specific person—or group of people—at a specific place or time. But the level one quarantine?"

"A physical search, Young Prince. In the last hour, every member of security has been stationed throughout the Imperial section. They'll sweep inward, toward the landing bay, physically checking every security checkpoint, every ID, every terminal."

Eric held up a hand, interrupting him. "To what purpose?"

"To what—?" Glenney was startled by the question. "Why, to apprehend whoever is—"

"Don't you think the time has come to stop talking down to

me?" Eric demanded, his face set in a look of grim determination. From the corner of his eye, he saw his father raise an eyebrow, silently observing both himself and Glenney. The Chief's mouth opened and closed several times and he looked to his father, who nodded agreement with his son.

"I know you wish to catch those responsible for the Director's murder," Eric went on. "Only a fool or a child would think otherwise. I am neither. What I want to know is *who* you're looking for." He turned to Javas, now sitting upright in rapt attention to the conversation. "Father, if you have no objections I'd like to see the complete file on what happened today, as well as access to the background files on previous attempts on our family; including those relating to my grandfather's death."

"See that Prince Eric receives access to all the files he's requested," Javas said without hesitation. Glenney was about to protest, but before he could speak the Emperor added, "If it makes you feel better you may enter the necessary codes yourself, then transfer control to him." Glenney turned away, speaking in hushed tones and tapping swiftly at the keys on his program screen. Javas leaned across the aisle, a bemused expression plainly visible on his face. "Oh, and son," he said softly, "thank you for asking for permission this time."

Eric grinned guiltily, rolling his eyes toward the ceiling, and Javas laughed for the first time since they had been interrupted at dinner by Glenney's report. The sound of his father's laughter lifted his spirits, and he wondered if he, too, would find rare times of good humor when he became Emperor.

The Chief stopped in mid-sentence and turned around, obviously bewildered by what was going on behind him. One glance at the expression on the befuddled man's face, however, and Eric couldn't help but join his father in the laughter.

"How soon till we're home?" Eric asked, stretching his cramped legs beneath the seat in front of him.

"Not long, Your Highness," the copilot responded. The communications channel between the bridge and the passenger cabin had been left open during de-orbit so they could hear the progress and description of the landing procedure.

Like most of the hopper shuttles, *Azalea Dream* was fast. There was no way for Eric to have read all the files during the ride to Earth, and when the pilot announced that they were now on final approach to Woodsgate he reluctantly closed the access channel and blanked the program screen. He had learned much from the files. Most of it was as disturbing as it was revealing, but nothing of what he'd read disturbed him as much as the identity of the horseman who had helped him that day in the backwoods. He seemed so different, Eric noted, comparing the memory of that afternoon with what he'd just learned from the files. Was it really possible that the same man who'd shown him kindness that day could really have been responsible for his grandfather's death?

He turned to the viewport and scanned the Kentucky countryside, awash in the deep greens of early July, passing below them. The shuttle made a wide circle, and he saw the town of Somerville pass a few kilometers to the east as they kept the ship over unpopulated forestland until they entered the restricted airspace extending in a five-kilometer radius around the estate. The craft continued its arc, and finally the estate came into view, nestled in the hills west of the town. The Sun was still high in the sky, and here and there a sudden flash reached his eyes as their steady movement caused the angle to be just right to reflect off the surface of an occasional stream or pond.

"Mr. Glenney, would you please see that everyone is secure for pad-down?"

Glenney came down the short aisle, personally inspecting his seat belt as well as his father's, then returned to his own seat and buckled in before turning to the Emperor. "Sire?"

"Anytime."

"We're secure," Glenney said to the copilot. "Proceed with your final approach and landing."

There was only the slightest sensation of movement as the craft came around and began descending at an angle toward the estate. Eric watched the descent without comment, listening to the odd one-sided conversation the pilot and copilot were having with ground control:

"Angle now at sixty-five degrees . . . Thank you, control, will do . . . No, the wind's not a problem at all." There was a pause, and the sound of laughter. *"Right, I'll tell him you said so. If you have us locked in, please confirm our distance . . . Roger that; we're at*

six hundred meters, descending now at a steady five meters per second. Open a gate in the skin at four-sixty."

Eric watched as Woodsgate drew closer in the viewport, and noticed that a large, perfect circle nearly fifty meters in diameter had appeared in the hazy air as they descended. Glenney had mentioned before they left Luna that the estate shielding had been increased to maximum even before the decision to remove them to Earth had been made, but Eric hadn't noticed the fuzzy outline of the dome-shaped shielding until the landing gate had been opened.

"Looking good from our end, control . . . We copy that the skin's open and clear; we'll be inside in ten seconds. Give us a full ten meters clearance, though, before you reclose—" The copilot broke in suddenly, cutting the captain off. *"I'm reading the skin coming back up! Abort landing pro—"*

The entire cabin shook violently and tilted at a crazy angle, throwing Eric against the viewport screen. There was another shudder as what felt like a small detonation came from below, sending the bridge into confused turmoil.

"I don't know, I don't know! A second skin, I think, about a meter above the House shielding . . . What? I'm trying to! What's happening to the harness?"

All movement stopped, and the shuttle hung motionless in the sky as both pilot and copilot jabbered constantly about the ship's condition with ground control. Glenney had unstrapped and was on his hands and knees, climbing the now-sloping floor to the door leading to the bridge, but had no luck pulling it open. Grasping the handle firmly, he ran a hand along a smooth wrinkle in the surface of the bulkhead around the door, realizing that the metal itself had buckled slightly, effectively jamming the door. The internal lights flickered once, then came back on and remained steady, but only static came now from the communications speaker.

"Captain!" Glenney called, but there was no answer from the bridge. He tapped at the headset with his fingers, then switched to another channel. "Navigation, are you there?" He waited a moment, then pulled off the useless headset, letting it slide skittering to the back of the cabin. "Damn!" he spat, then released his grip and slid down the floor to the seats. Using them for support, he leaned between Eric and his father. "Sire, are you both all right?"

"I'm fine," he replied, shaking his dazed head to clear it. "Eric!"

"I'm all right, Father." He dabbed at a trickle of blood at his nose from where he'd banged into the viewport and turned to Glenney. "What happened?"

"I don't know." He looked past Eric at the viewport. Eric and his father both followed his gaze and saw that the outside view was unchanged: They seemed to be motionless, hanging some 450 meters above the estate, with the landing pad plainly visible beneath them. House personnel, Imperial guards and members of the ground landing crew could be seen running on the ground below. "But judging from what the captain was saying before the speaker went out, we seem to be embedded in a second shield of some kind, projected just above the estate's own."

The lights flickered again, and the background hum of the shuttle's systems steadily decreased, then died, leaving the cabin in silence. A red emergency light came on, bathing the three of them in eerie shadows for several tense moments before the main lights returned.

They sat in silence, listening as carefully as they could to several sounds, clearly audible now that the shuttle's main engine had powered down. There was an irregular but steady hammering from aft, in what Eric assumed was the navigation and landing station where the guards and landing techs were. An occasional shouting could be heard from the direction of the bridge, although the words were unintelligible through the thickness of the flooring and bulkheads that separated them. Other sounds assailed them now, the most disconcerting of them being the metallic clangs and pops from the stressed structure of the craft itself.

"I don't like the sound of that," Eric said.

"We may have a worse problem." The tone of his father's words caught his attention immediately and he stared at him. He was sweating, his brow furrowed and eyes squinting in deep concentration. "Glenney, I'm being blocked."

Glenney's eyes widened. "The implants?" he snapped. "Were they damaged in the collision with the shielding?"

"No! They're fine, but they're being blocked or jammed by something."

Eric felt the floor tilt suddenly beneath them. There was a pause, then another lurch and a horrible sound of metal tearing somewhere in the shuttle. The movement stopped with a bone-grinding jerk, the angle of the cabin even steeper than before. Eric glanced at his hands, his fingers white-knuckled on the armrest of the seat, and realized that the ship seemed to be vibrating slightly. He touched the wall above the viewport then, sliding his palm slowly up the surface as it curved into the ceiling, and reached as high as he could without unbuckling his restraints.

It felt like . . . He looked quickly into the viewport, but it seemed the same as before until he picked out an object on the ground and stared at it for several seconds. "We're sliding!"

There was another grinding lurch, then another as the shuttle's weight tore it loose from the shielding, sending it sliding freely down the curving outside surface of the shielding. Eric had just enough time to reflect that the craft slid in a smooth arc, like a snowball would if thrown onto the sun-warmed metal roof of the stables. The sensation of falling was gradual, at first—the *Azalea Dream* had impacted the shielding near its top, where the angle was not as steep—but as it traveled frictionlessly down the side, the angle steepened and they fell faster and faster. A second before impact, at a point where the shielding was nearly vertical to the ground, Eric felt a brief sensation of weightlessness.

FOURTEEN

The *Azalea Dream* had rolled quite a few times before finally coming to rest with the floor remarkably level, tilting to the port side at only a slight angle. Eric had twisted around in his restraints and leaned heavily on the wall, his back flat against the viewport. He sat unmoving for what seemed several minutes, trying to examine his surroundings but finding it difficult to focus his eyes in the dingy shadows cast by the red emergency lighting. It was uncomfortably warm in the cabin, and as he felt droplets of sweat rolling freely down his forehead and beneath his arms, he wondered idly how much time had passed.

There was a groan in front of him as he faced the opposite row of seats, and he struggled to get unbuckled. "Father! Are you all right?" Finally free of the belt, he knelt at the side of Javas' seat, carefully working his father's restraints loose.

"I'm—*ah!*" He pitched forward dizzily once the belt was off and rubbed tenderly at his right biceps. "I'm fine." He pushed himself upright, wincing at the pain in his arm, and looked Eric over with obvious relief that his son had escaped serious injury. "Glenney?"

"He's on the floor," Eric replied, "up front." They both stood carefully, picking their way tentatively over the cushions and galley items that had come loose in the crash, and made their way forward.

That Glenney was dead was immediately clear to both of them. He lay on his back, neck and both arms bent at unnatural angles. His mouth was open, his jaw askew, and a puddle of blood collected beneath him that looked, bathed in the red lighting, more like thick black paint.

"He wasn't strapped in when we broke loose from the shielding," Eric said, remembering how the shuttle had tumbled on impact, tossing the hapless Security Chief violently about the cabin. The floor shuddered as the wreck settled, angling slightly forward, and Eric watched in queasy fascination as Glenney's head rolled to one side and the puddle of blood ran across the floor and up against the forward bulkhead.

"I think we're on the slope on the south side of the grounds," the Emperor said. "We'd better get out of here before we fall the rest of the way down."

Eric agreed and the two of them went immediately to the rear of the cabin where the exit door was located. Through there they would have access to the lower aft deck and the main shuttle hatch, but the door would not budge. The Emperor put a foot on the frame and pulled again, but stopped when the pain in his arm grew too severe. "Here, let me give it a try," Eric said, grabbing the door handle. "Open the access panel and see if turning the release bar manually helps." His father easily popped open a small panel to the left of the door and groped around inside while Eric pulled.

"Wait. Wait a minute." Javas peered inside, trying not to block what little light there was, and reached in once more. "The release bar's in place," he said, puzzled, "but take a look at this and tell me what you think." He pulled his arm out and stood out of Eric's way.

Feeling inside the panel, the Prince grasped the release and turned it several times before giving up and removing his arm. "It spins freely, as if it's not attached to anything."

His father nodded agreement. "That's exactly what I thought. And I don't believe it was damaged in the fall."

Eric, his back to the door, allowed himself to slide to a sitting position on the floor. He was sweating heavily now, and he removed the Imperial dress jacket he'd donned in preparation for the landing. He rolled it into a ball and tossed it the length of the cabin, then leaned his head back against the hard, warm surface of the door. "A second shield projected above the House shielding, effectively sabotaging the shuttle landing. Communications and shuttle systems that should have withstood the initial impact damaged . . . How about your integrator? Is it still being blocked?"

"Let me try—" Javas fell silent as he removed his own jacket and unbuttoned his shirt collar. He folded the jacket once, dropped it to the floor and sat on it as a cushion. A full minute passed before he inhaled deeply and sighed, adding simply, "Yes."

"And now we find . . ." Eric stood, angrily kicking the door squarely in its center. An idea came to him and he pressed his ear to the warm metal, listening carefully for sounds from the other side. He looked around at his feet and found a small pitcher that had been shaken loose from the galley. He banged it sharply against the door four times in quick succession, paused, struck the door four more times, then listened closely again. Nothing. "And now we find that the main exit door has been disabled from the other side. Fairly obvious, isn't it, Father?"

"Yes, I suppose it is," he replied soberly. He sat forward, indicating that Eric should be seated where he was. "Here's what we're up against, then: That door has been sealed, and it appears that everyone in the aft station is either dead or immobilized, so we can't count on their help. My integrator is effectively gone for the time being, so we can't count on getting help that way. For that matter, if someone's gone to the trouble of jamming my implants, it's a fair bet they've already neutralized House communications as well."

Eric crossed his legs as he sat, and leaned forward with his elbows on his knees. *And if no one outside the House knows we've left Luna,* he realized, *then we won't be missed any time soon.* "I've got a feeling that we can't rely on any physical help from inside the grounds, either, if that second shield is still in place."

"And it probably is," his father agreed. "This has all been too well organized for us to assume that the shield has been dissolved. One thing is clear, however: Whoever is responsible for this won't simply assume that we've died in the crash. I imagine they're on their way to us now." He paused, then added, "If they're not already sitting outside, waiting for us, that is." Grasping the back of one of the seats, Javas pulled himself to his feet. He wiped his face and forehead on the back of a shirt sleeve and let out a long, slow breath as he looked around the cabin.

Eric watched as his father grew increasingly uncomfortable in the heat, and noted that his own breath was coming with just as much difficulty. He inhaled deeply, noticing a distinct hot-plastic smell to the air. "It's just as clear that we can't stay in here. With the shuttle systems all down we'll bake sitting here in the sun. Or suffocate."

The craft moved again suddenly, with the floor angling slightly more to the front of the shuttle. The fatigued metal complained loudly, but when the shifting stopped, they both heard a noise that sounded like it was coming from somewhere other than the weakened internal structure itself.

Eric tilted his head, trying to determine the sound's direction. "Up front!" The sudden exclamation caused an odd burning sensation in his throat, making him cough, and he realized that the plastic smell he'd noticed earlier was much heavier than before. His eyes stung and had begun watering freely.

They again stepped carefully down the sloping aisle to the front of the shuttle. Glenney's body had rolled farther, his face turned and now partially hidden beneath some light debris, but several streamers of black blood ran from his body toward the front bulkhead, pooling again where wall met floor. He tried to ignore the sight and concentrated instead on the sounds coming from behind the door leading to the front corridor and flight deck.

There it was, an irregular *thunk-clunk* coming from somewhere forward, perhaps from the cockpit itself. Closer inspection of the door revealed that despite the warped bulkhead that had prevented Glenney from opening it earlier, it was now a few millimeters ajar. Whatever the sound was, Eric reasoned, it may have been there all along and they were only now able to hear it.

"That last movement," the Emperor suggested. He was coughing now, and in the pale red light Eric could see him rubbing his eyes frequently. "It must have stressed the door frame enough to partially free it." Several items had rolled forward, and he quickly grabbed something and banged at the door. "Hello?" He hammered again, but when they listened the irregular sound continued, unchanged.

"Eric, help me pull. If we can—" He coughed violently, gasping for breath. "If we can get this open, we can take the lower corridor from the flight deck to the aft station." His father strained hard on the door handle while Eric curled his fingers under the lip of the door. Pulling together, they managed to open the door another full centimeter. They caught their breath for a moment and pulled again, both of them tumbling backward when the door finally freed itself, letting in a sudden burst of natural sunlight and fresh air. Eric was first on his feet, and hastily opened the door fully, allowing it to rest against the bulkhead where the shuttle's downward angle kept it in place.

He helped his father up, and as soon as they had made their way to the flight deck it became obvious that taking the lower corridor to the exit would not be necessary, as most of the front of the shuttle—nearly the entire cockpit, for that matter—had been torn away in the crash and resultant cartwheeling down the hillside. What was left of the pilot, his body horribly mangled by the jagged metal that had crumpled around him on the way down the hill, was still strapped into his seat. The copilot's chair was missing entirely.

Anxious to be clear of the foul air in the cabin, they moved hurriedly, but carefully, onto the flight deck. There was a brisk breeze, and they inhaled deeply of the untainted air. Although the nose of the *Azalea Dream* was angled downward, the forward end was pointed toward the uphill side, giving them a clear view of the path they had taken down the hill. The ship must have tumbled at least six hundred meters or more down the hillside, and a path of debris and flattened, splintered trees and saplings zigzagged up toward the estate, now hidden among the trees and limestone outcroppings near the top of their fall.

The branches of a downed maple extended into the cockpit, the occasional breeze causing it to hammer *thunk-clunk* against an exposed section of the hull. "Be careful," he said when Eric inched toward the jagged edge of the opening. He nodded back to his father and removed the dead pilot's gloves, surprised at how easily he dealt with death after seeing so much of it in so short a time. He pulled them on and gingerly clambered to a position where he could carefully peer outside.

Debris was everywhere, and there was a faint hissing sound coming from somewhere underneath the wreck, but no sign of movement as far as he could tell anywhere nearby. "I think you were right," he said when he climbed back up to his father in the doorway to the flight deck. "I think we are on the south side of the grounds, but I can't see the House or tell for sure just how far up the side it is. We've got a bit of a climb at best."

"Then we'd better put some distance between us and the shuttle," Javas replied, turning back to the cabin. "But I doubt if we can get into the aft station from the outside. Better see what we can find in here." The air in the cabin had grown even more noxious, and they found that they had to return frequently to the flight deck for air. They scavenged what they could, gathering some food and filling a small flask with what water they were able to coax from the galley dispenser, then retrieved their jackets and stuffed the pockets with anything useful they could find. As a last measure his father hastily examined Glenney's body, turning up two weapons—a concealed knife in a boot sheath, and a pin laser clipped to an inside pocket. Eric knew that neither was particularly deadly, but was grateful that the macabre task of searching Glenney's body had occurred to his father: Both weapons could prove useful if they were forced to spend any amount of time in the backwoods. Back on the flight deck, Javas kept the knife for himself, slipping it into his boot, and handed the laser to him.

The wreck shifted again, and they wasted no further time getting off. Eric still had the pilot's gloves and climbed easily to the ground, then tossed them back up to his father while he surveyed the damaged ship.

The shuttle had come solidly to rest on an exposed outcropping overlooking the entire valley that spread below the royal family's estate. Closer examination showed that despite the unnerving way the wreck had shifted while they were still inside, there had been little danger of it sliding farther. The angle steepened sharply a hundred meters below the outcropping and they couldn't see the river itself, but they could see it reflecting in the sunlight as it meandered through the mountainous Kentucky countryside far to the northwest.

The July air felt pleasantly hot and humid as they examined the crash site, not nearly as stifling as it had been inside the wrecked shuttle. The craft leaked from a dozen places and a thin, smoky haze poured from the exposed cockpit. Whatever was leaking was volatilizing quickly, and must have been connected not only with the hissing that continued from underneath the wreck but with the deteriorating atmosphere inside the shuttle. The hissing diminished in volume as he moved around to the rear of the wreck, enough so that the buzz of grasshoppers in the sunny clearing could easily be heard.

"Father, you'd better take a look at this," Eric called from the back of the now-derelict ship.

Javas came around quickly, staring worriedly at what Eric had found. The main hatch had been opened, but because of the way

the shuttle had come to rest with its nose on the upward angle of
the hill, the opening hung fully two and a half meters over the
limestone and scrub at their feet. There was a good deal of debris
directly below the hatch, almost all of it thrown or fallen from
the opening above. A discarded extinguisher lay several meters
away and fire foam dripped steadily from the lip of the opening.
There was also a good deal of blood on the ground, and bushes
had been flattened as if someone had jumped down from the
hatch. More blood had dripped on the rocks several meters up
the hill, and the direction the vegetation had been flattened indicated that someone had left the clearing in a hurry, going due
north. There still was no movement except the wind, however,
and no sound other than the constant buzz of grasshoppers.

"I think I'm the obvious choice," Eric said, indicating the
opening above their heads. "How's your arm?"

Javas ignored the question and scanned the wreck, frowning.
The smoke pouring from the front of the ship was getting
thicker, and he clearly was not pleased with Eric's offer to go
inside. "Make it a fast look."

His father cupped his hands in front of him and Eric stepped
carefully into the makeshift stirrup they formed. Javas lifted
upward, giving his son the boost he needed to grab onto the edge
of the hatch and scramble up before disappearing inside.

Despite the open hatch, the air was even worse in here than
it had been in the cabin. He looked around quickly and spent
no more than a minute inside, although he wasn't certain if
it was because of the worsening air or the appalling sight that
greeted him.

"Eric!" No sooner had his father called to him than a sharp
metallic clang resounded from the hull of the shuttle.

He returned to the opening and knelt at the edge, lowering a
nylon bag into Javas' upstretched hands. There was another
shot; now at the open hatch, he heard the gunshot itself this time.
Rubbing his eyes, he took several deep breaths, then went back
in for the remainder of what he'd found, tossing down a smaller,
zippered case which his father easily caught. Another shot rico-
cheted loudly off the hull. He sat hurriedly on the lip of the hatch,
his legs dangling, then placed his hands on the edge and swung
around in a smooth motion with his arms to hang briefly from
the opening before dropping the rest of the way to the ground.

"Come on!" he barked as soon as he was down. "Follow me." He slung the nylon bag over his shoulder and started immediately for the cover of the trees at the edge of the outcropping.

His father followed without a word. Several more shots were fired, and while one cut through the scrub and dug into the ground mere meters in front of Eric, none of the projectiles found their mark. Whoever was firing at them was either an incredibly poor marksman, considering how exposed they were out here in the open, or he was deliberately avoiding hitting them in an effort to pin them down at the wreckage. For that reason, if no other, Eric wanted to get his father away from the shuttle as quickly as possible. The shots seemed to originate from the trees at the top of the clearing in the same direction the trail of blood from the shuttle hatch had led.

Once in the sheltering cover of the woods Eric's pace didn't slow, but he looked around him, trying to recognize landmarks and get his bearings. He stomped several hundred meters through the backwoods before finally stopping in an area that, while still angled, had leveled considerably. He looked around again, then pointed to a series of shallow depressions near another outcropping of limestone. The air was much cooler under the canopy of trees, but he refused to allow himself to enjoy it. Not yet. "There. Come on."

There were three sinkholes set into the side of the hill. Dry leaves and branches filled the first two and Eric ignored them and crossed directly to the third: a deeper, rockier hollow set into the side of the landscape. The uphill side was a rocky, nearly vertical wall about five meters high, but the sides and bottom of the depression were mostly moss and ferns covering the gently sloping earth that had filled in the sides and floor of the depression countless years ago. Leaves had piled up at the bottom of this depression, just as at the other two, but an opening was visible at the base of the rocky wall of this sink, the rock surface around the opening moist and covered with moss and lichens. Even though the air in the constant shade of the backwoods was more comfortable than the relentless summer sunshine out in the open, the steady damp breeze issuing from the opening must have been a full ten or fifteen degrees cooler still and felt deliciously refreshing.

On a sign from Eric, both slid carefully to the bottom of the depression. "Do you recognize this, Father?" Eric asked.

He shook his head. "No, I don't think so." The Emperor watched nervously as he dug at the piled leaves at the opening, tossing them behind him like a dog after a favorite bone. "You've been here before, I take it?"

Eric dropped the bag into the enlarged opening, then fell to his knees, pushing the bundle into the darkness in front of him. "Bend low, and watch your head on the ceiling." With that he shoved the bag inside and disappeared in after it.

He crawled forward a short distance, then sat cross-legged on the earthen floor of the chamber once the passageway had widened enough to sit upright. Opening the bag in his lap, he rummaged among its contents as his father, on all fours, crawled up to his side and sat next to him in the cramped passageway.

"Here, take this," he said, handing him a flashlight. He pulled another lamp from the bag and clicked it on, pointing it down the crawlway. "It opens up just around there. Follow me."

They crawled another four or five meters and the passageway opened into a fair-sized room. From where they sat the floor sloped gradually to a long, flat wall on the opposite side. Eric played the flashlight over their surroundings, the narrow beam showing that the room was quite large, its exact boundaries disappearing into the darkness of an even larger cavern to their left. Along the lowest portion of the far wall a tiny rivulet of water trickled musically along the floor, vanishing into a small opening on the right side of the room. Eric took his flashlight and pressed it into the soft earth floor at his feet, allowing the beam of light to reflect off the gray-brown limestone of the ceiling. He extended his hand for his father's light and did the same with it, brightening the underground room considerably. Satisfied that they were secure for the moment, he went into the larger room and returned almost immediately with a small molded box.

"It's still here," he said, sitting back down next to his father. He opened the lid and pulled out a sealed plastic bag containing several stubby candles. There was a narrow ledge in the rock wall at their backs, and Eric dug a handful of the candles out of the bag and placed them, one at a time, on the shelflike ledge. The ledge had been used for this purpose before, and long, frozen rivulets of wax in several different colors and consistencies ran down the face of the wall.

"I'm sorry," he began, his voice echoing hollowly against the rock walls. He removed the pin laser from his coat and lit one of the candles, then replaced the laser in his coat and used the burning candle to light the others. "But I just wanted to get us out of there as quickly as I could."

Javas nodded in the reflected beam of the flashlight, the vapor of his breath floating visibly through the beam in the chilly dampness of the cave, and pulled a galley sandwich from his jacket pocket for each of them before clicking both flashlights off to conserve their charge. "That's fine; I trust your judgment. What did you find inside?"

"They were dead." Eric bit hungrily into the sandwich and washed it down with a long swallow from the flask of water he carried in his jacket, then passed it over. "Both of the guardsmen, and one of the landing techs. The tech must have been unsecured, trying to do something when we were embedded up in the shield, and was probably killed when we hit the ground, like Glenney." He took another bite of the sandwich, chewing slowly.

"And the guards?"

"Still strapped into their seats," he said, swallowing hard. "Their throats were cut."

His father considered the information. "Then the blood on the ground was theirs—"

"No," Eric interrupted, "I don't think so. The other landing tech, the tall one with the beard who caught me by the arm when I stumbled on the ramp, he must have been fairly badly hurt in the crash, too. The medical kit was opened, and there was a lot of blood smeared on it and its contents. Or what was left of them anyway—he used what he needed, then pretty much vandalized the rest. I managed to put together a basic first-aid kit with what was left, though." He indicated the zippered case at his father's side. "I found a few flashlights, some tie-downs and a couple other things we might be able to use."

"And the guards' weapons?"

"Thumb-keyed; useless. Whatever he tried to hit us with back in the clearing must have been hidden on board."

"Pistol of some kind, then, judging from his accuracy, or lack of it. I suppose it's too much to hope that there's a crash kit in that bag?"

Eric shook his head.

"I didn't think so. Either he took it with him or he heaved it over the edge of the outcropping to keep us from getting it. Come to think of it, if he was as badly hurt as you suspect, then he probably couldn't have carried it very far."

Eric reached for the flask of water and said nothing for a moment as he took a long, slow drink. He went to the tiny stream and refilled the flask, then capped it and put it in the bag.

"I'm not so sure he'd have to go that far." He leaned forward and swept the earthen floor smooth in front of him. There were numerous sticks and bits of natural debris near the stream and, using one as a stylus, he drew a rough map of the area.

"We're here," he said, scratching a mark on the floor of the cave. He then drew a straight line, extending it up from the mark. "The grounds are due north about a kilometer—"

"A kilometer!"

Eric nodded soberly, drawing a circle to indicate the main grounds of Woodsgate. "I know. When I recognized the outcropping that stopped the wreck from rolling farther down the hill, I could hardly believe it either. We're lucky to be alive." He continued sketching in the dirt. "The House and grounds are situated at the center of this ridge, here. There are hundreds of kilometers of trails crisscrossing this part of the countryside, but a section of the main trail follows the lower portion of the ridge, completely circling the east, south and west sides of Woodsgate. If we hike straight up to the House, we'll cross it right here." He drew a rough line halfway between the circle and where they were, extending it as he spoke. "The main trail continues to skirt the ridge the House is located on . . . then crosses the access road leading to Woodsgate here . . . and then on into the backwoods on the other side . . . and finally leads east into Somerville."

His father bent over the crude map. "I think I understand what you're getting at. No matter where we would have come down, there was a seventy-five percent chance we'd be within a short distance of the main trail."

"Exactly," Eric agreed. "And my guess is that whoever our friend is working for, they watched the whole thing and are probably on their way out here now, picking him up along the way to lead them to us."

"Then they're probably the *only* ones who saw us go down. One of the observation satellites in LEO will spot the wreckage sooner or later, I suppose, but the chances of us having been spotted when we went down are fairly remote."

Eric nodded in agreement. "And since your integrator is being blocked, the signal from the shuttle's emergency locator is probably being jammed as well."

"If it's even still working," his father added. "That landing tech was pretty thorough."

"Then our best bet is to keep moving, stall for time. Eventually someone will try to raise the House on a routine matter and find it's been cut off and investigate. If we can stay ahead of them until then, we should make it out of this."

His father sighed heavily, then dropped the sandwich wrappers into the opened bag and rose to his feet, careful to avoid bumping his head on the sloping rock ceiling. He rubbed at the stiffness in his arm and surveyed the cave, the light from the row of candles on the wall ledge casting long, unsteady shadows into the larger cavern. "I used to go exploring caves like these with my brothers. There are several of them up above, actually on the House grounds."

"I know. I've been in them."

"And in many others, as well, it seems." He looked down at Eric, smiling. "I never approved of your excursions outside the shielding any more than Master McLaren, but I'm forced to admit I'm grateful for your knowledge of the backwoods."

Eric got up, brushing the seat of his pants with his hands. "I'm not the only one in our family to know these woods." He reached down and retrieved a flashlight from the dirt floor and shined a large circle onto the far wall of the big room to the left. In the center of the circle of light, someone had used a candle flame to smoke several words onto the angled wall. They walked closer to get a better look, and his father stopped cold when he saw what had been written there.

" 'Nicholas,' " Javas read aloud, " 'August 15th, 2409.' " He turned back with a wistful look in his eyes that Eric had never seen before. "My father."

* * *

They took no chances as they climbed, making their way slowly
and carefully through the woods to avoid being detected. Hours
passed and the sun hung low in the sky by the time they reached
the edge of the shielding near the top of the hill. The House
shielding, hazily visible, ended at the edge of the flat portion of
the grounds, but the second shield was considerably wider at its
base than the one on the inside and extended several dozen
meters over the edge of the hill, making it impossible for them to
see what was happening at the House itself.

Gazing upward through the trees, it was easy to see where the
edge of the invisible outer shield was. When it had been activated, several trees had been bisected, neatly clipping branches
and treetops wherever they had come into contact with it. Looking skyward, he could even see several smaller pieces of the
wrecked shuttle still embedded in the upper portion, seemingly
suspended in empty air. Eric squinted at the closest portion of the
shield in front of him and pressed against it with the palms of
both hands. The gas-permeable field felt spongy, yet firm, beneath his fingers. He carefully studied where the shielding met the
ground, looking first one direction then the other into the backwoods, and kicked experimentally at the dirt at its base.

"I think we may be in luck," Eric said.

His father had been perched atop a nearby boulder, keeping a
watchful eye for any signs of pursuit, but quickly jumped down.
"Oh?"

"I think I might be able to get us inside."

The Emperor stared at him in disbelief. "Son, McLaren reported more times than I care to remember about how you
breached the shielding and sneaked out of the grounds. But,
without access to a terminal, how can we . . ."

Eric laughed and clambered down the hillside to stand next to
him. "I have a confession," he said. "I never breached the shielding." He laughed again, shaking his head. "I've never kept a
secret this long. The first time Master caught me outside was not
long after the time I'd reprogrammed a number of the House
systems. When he caught me, he assumed I'd somehow managed
to program an opening, much the same way we do for arriving
and departing shuttles."

Javas hefted the nylon bag, transferring it from one shoulder to the other. "And you didn't."

"No, sir," he replied, remembering. "Oh, I probably could have figured out how to do it, but the shield gate controls are part of House security, and I never dared touch that programming. No, I found a much simpler way. You know the caves on the east side of the garden? There's a small opening near the end of one of them. I enlarged it and pushed the passageway until it made a connection to another cave that exits in a sinkhole well outside the grounds." He pulled the water flask from his pocket and took a quick swallow, then passed it to his father and sat on a nearby log as he continued, smiling broadly.

"I came and went as I pleased, all the while Master McLaren pulled his hair and tried to figure out how I'd reworked the security. He had it reprogrammed several times, even going so far as to call the Security Chief down from Luna one time to—"

Eric halted abruptly, remembering Glenney's face, his jaw and neck smashed as he lay on the floor of the wrecked shuttle. His smile vanished, the memory of a childhood joke on his elders suddenly not quite so funny to him anymore. His father said nothing, neither to chastise him nor to ease the painful thought, and handed the water back. "Anyway," he went on humorlessly, stashing the flask in his pocket, "the connection passes far enough underground that we should be able to get in underneath the shielding; as long as the sinkhole is on the outside of it, that is."

"It's worth a try," his father admitted. "I don't see where we have much choice just now."

They had to drop down from the ridge to make much headway on the rocky terrain and headed around the shielding in a northeasterly direction, being careful to maintain a discreet distance from the trail.

It was dusk when they neared the main access road to the estate. The road was entirely in the open, visible not only from the House but from the opposite direction as well. His father thought it best, and Eric agreed, that they should wait until it was completely dark before attempting to cross the road. They found a sheltered spot and divided the last of the sandwiches from the bag, speculating on what had happened and who might be responsible. Eric had learned a great deal from the files and reports to which Glenney had begrudgingly given him access during the transit from the Moon, and agreed with his father that House Valtane was probably behind this.

"It seems logical," his father was saying. "She was always outside the grasp of even the Emperor, legally speaking. Glenney had suggested on more than one occasion that we go outside the law, but I always refused." The sky had long since grown black, and he cocked his head at the cry of a night bird somewhere in the trees. "I should have listened to him."

They continued talking into the night, but were abruptly interrupted at midnight by a brilliant flash that lit the sky to the east as a magnificent fireball burst into dozens of orange streamers that gradually faded as they fell. A delayed *boom-BOOM-boom* reached their ears, then again as it echoed off the far side of the river valley to the south. They watched the sky above the trees and saw it before it burst this time, as a thin trail of sparks arced upward and exploded at the zenith of its flight. This one exploded three times, each report evenly spaced, each one emitting streamers of different-colored sparks. The sounds, again delayed, drifted across the valley.

"Julyfest," his father said. "I'd forgotten what day this was."

"I was never permitted to attend the fireworks," Eric said softly. "McLaren said it was too dangerous for a Prince to be among an 'uncontrolled environment of ruffians,' as he put it."

His father snorted in the dark. "Yes, Montlaven never permitted me to go either," he said, "and if memory serves, he used pretty much the same words. But it was a magnificent view from the balcony, wasn't it?"

They watched the fireworks, speaking only occasionally. At one point a strong breeze from the east brought the scent of sulfur and black powder, and Eric remembered the odor and felt, just briefly, as if he were a small part of the celebration. Once, on a July night several years earlier, with the last of the fireworks long gone, he had refused to leave the balcony until the thin smoke of the explosions drifted over the estate. The wind had not been right that night, and after the Master had tucked him into bed and retired, he'd sneaked back onto the balcony to wait for the smoke that never came. He remembered that when the Moon rose that night he could see the smoke hanging over the river valley like a fog and wished, neither for the first nor the last time, that he wasn't a prisoner of his family name.

Eric settled back, the odor of fireworks mingled with the backwoods scent of a Kentucky summer still lingering in his nostrils, and fell into a surprisingly restful sleep.

FIFTEEN

A hand shook him steadily, and he woke with a start. "Shhhhh." His father knelt over him, helping him to a sitting position as he shook his head to clear it. He felt damp from sleeping on the ground, and every joint and muscle was cramped and stiff from the cold. He kept silent, and listened carefully in the direction his father pointed, noting that he already had slung the bag over his shoulder. Although the sky was only now beginning to turn gray to the east, the backwoods were already alive with the sounds of morning birds and he had to play close attention to whatever it was that had caught his father's ear.

The main trail ran below them, far enough to remain hidden, yet close enough to hear a horse negotiating that part of the trail that wound around the ridge before ascending to the level of the access road some two hundred meters farther down. They still couldn't see it, but it was plain that the animal had stopped, pawing the ground impatiently, and the beam of a powerful flashlight swept through the trees, followed by another a few meters behind the first—a second horse and rider. Eric crouched lower in the scrub next to his father, certain that the flashlight beams couldn't penetrate their hiding place, and let out a barely audible sigh of relief.

"Listen," his father whispered urgently, extending his arm again. "There; farther down the trail."

He heard it then. "Dogs. Several of them." He remembered the horse ridden by the traitor Brendan and wondered for a moment if the dogs of House Valtane had been as expertly bio-bred as the horses, then quickly concluded that they probably were. "Let's get moving," he said, indicating the wide, open area of the roadway above them. "I think we can make it to the other side before the two horsemen make it up here."

Javas nodded, and without further discussion the two of them made their way as quickly and as quietly as they could to the top of the ridge. They paused at the edge of the bushes, scanning the road in each direction. For security purposes the brush was kept neatly manicured for a distance of twenty to thirty meters on each side of the road, making a fairly wide area where they'd be exposed.

Eric watched the Woodsgate grounds at the end of the road and saw that every light on the estate grounds blazed brightly, and that additional floodlights had been erected on the landing pad and above the main gate, giving them a good picture of what was happening. Dozens of members of the Imperial guard, beefed up by Glenney before the three of them had even left the Moon, patrolled the perimeter. Eric looked closely and realized that a number of the guards appeared to be in the space between the two shields. Apparently a temporary gate had been opened in the House shielding to allow the men to enter the space. He couldn't tell for certain, but judging from all the electronic equipment at their feet and the hand-held metering devices they passed over the inner surface of the second shield, they were still working at trying to breach it. *So close,* he thought, the sight confirming what they'd suspected about the shielding, *and not able to do a thing.*

The entire area was illuminated by several small searchlights that played out over the road and into the surrounding wooded area. Eric was grateful for the additional light that helped them to verify that the road was deserted in both directions, but they would have to take care not to get caught inadvertently in one of the searchlights.

Behind them the dogs grew louder, more frantic, and had certainly picked up their scent by now. They waited nervously for one of the House searchlights to make a last sweep in their direction, then sprinted across the open area. They crossed the wide, mowed shoulder almost immediately and were halfway across the access road itself when his father cried out and stumbled heavily to the pavement.

"Father!" Eric went immediately to his side, helping him unsteadily back onto his feet. His father tried to say something, but suddenly started shaking uncontrollably and couldn't seem to form coherent words. Something hit the pavement just in front of them, sparking brightly as it deflected into the trees and crackled away at an oblique angle through the branches. He stared down the road, expecting that the horses they'd heard had already come around on the trail. There was someone there, just barely visible in the waning darkness. The figure took aim and Eric pulled his father out of the way just as another shot was fired, missing them. Several of the searchlights swung around in their direction and were joined quickly by the beams of a dozen hand-held lights as the guards gathered in a knot at the edge of the shielding.

Eric waved his arms frantically at the guards, trying to make them understand that the additional light was serving only to make them better targets. Another shot echoed in his ears and, not bothering to look where the shot went, he dragged his father toward the shelter of the trees on the opposite side. After a moment, Javas seemed to shake off the disorientation and managed to run several meters, almost halfway to the trees, but then his legs and arms twitched spasmodically and he crumpled once more to the ground.

He pushed himself on unsteady knees, his head jerking uncontrollably from side to side. "N-n-n-no . . . Er-ic!" A painful grimace showed plainly on his face as he forced each word through clenched teeth. "R-r-run!"

"What is it? Father!" Eric struggled to drag him the rest of the way into the scrub, where yet again he managed to stand up on his own. His face was ashen, but the painful look had disappeared for the moment. He gripped at his right shoulder, and in the glowing dawn light Eric saw blood oozing between the clenched fingers.

"Eric, which way?" He panted desperately, but was speaking clearly now.

"There, but I'm not sure how far!" Eric hastily surveyed their surroundings. The landscape sloped steadily away from the level of the access road, and they were in the bottom of a small depression. "You stay here, I'll lead them to the east. I can get to the main trail in a few minutes, and once there I can run toward the town. Stay down and you should be—"

"No!" he yelled, nearly at the top of his lungs, silencing Eric. He turned, pointing his uninjured arm in the direction they'd just come. "Listen! Do you hear them?" The dogs were closer now; it would be a matter of minutes before they caught up with them if they didn't start moving soon. "They'll follow you right to the trail, after they've already found me. No; you've got to make a run for the cave, get inside the grounds."

The backwoods brightened rapidly now, giving him a better feel for their location in relation to the cave. "Come on," he said, pulling Javas' left arm around his shoulder to support him. "I think we can both make it."

"All right." He started moving. "But promise me you'll— *unnh!*" His father's eyes rolled back and he jerked repeatedly again. Eric held his father to keep him from falling, powerless to ease his pain as he felt the muscles contracting in tiny, regular seizures beneath the man's jacket. Saliva frothed through gritted teeth as five, eight, ten times he stiffened before the seizures stopped, leaving him weak and pale again. "All right, I—I think I'll be . . . I think I'll be able to run for a minute."

Eric didn't hesitate, grateful only that whatever it was had passed. With Eric still supporting his father's weight, the two of them made their way carefully through the backwoods in the direction he was certain would take them to the cave entrance. They made it out of the depression and came across a little-used hunting trail going in roughly the direction he remembered. The trail was a mixed blessing: The surer footing would enable them to pick up their own pace as they ran; but it also meant that there was a greater danger of the horses catching up with them, which would not be the case on the uneven terrain off the trail. Eric opted for speed and they had just begun moving again as the next set of seizures hit, crippling his father just as they had before.

"My God, what *is* it?" Eric felt tears of angry frustration run down his cheeks at his own helplessness to do anything. "What's wrong?" He held his father tightly in his arms, stroking the back of his head until the seizures—as before, exactly ten of them—

passed and he sat up, dazed and disoriented. "What is it?" Eric asked again.

His father panted heavily, increasingly exhausted by each successive bout with the seizures, and tore at his jacket to get it off, then used Glenney's knife to cut the blood-soaked sleeve of his shirt away, exposing the surprisingly small but deep wound in his upper arm. "It's what they shot me with," he gasped, feeling where the skin had been penetrated. "A charged projectile of some kind, timed to send a series of electric shocks directly into my nervous system." He looked at Eric and handed him the knife. "You've got to get it out. I don't know how many more times I can take it and keep on going."

Eric wiped the blood away from the wound and examined it closely, pressing gently where the projectile had entered. His father gasped painfully. "It's deep, Father. I'm not sure I can—" He jumped to his feet, listening carefully. They had put some distance between themselves and the dogs in the last several minutes, or maybe the animals had momentarily lost the scent, but the barking grew closer again.

"Eric, there's no time! Go—*unnh!*" He fell backward to the ground, his back arching as the first of the seizures went through him.

Now! Eric thought, and in desperation pulled the pin laser from his jacket pocket. He fell on top of his father, pinning his chest with one knee while holding his arm firmly to the ground with the other. His father's body spasmed a third time, then a fourth. Gripping the arm with his left hand, he thumbed the safety on the pen-sized laser with his right and jammed it into the wound. A fifth spasm. The fresh blood that oozed from around the inserted laser was slippery and he lost his grip momentarily as the muscles contracted again, jerking the arm powerfully. Eric struggled to steady the arm and made sure the laser was into the wound as far as it would go. He looked at his father's face, his eyes glassy and staring, and realized when he saw the saliva frothing pinkly at the corners of his mouth that he must have bitten his tongue or lip.

"Father, this is all my fault," he sobbed, even though he knew his words fell on unhearing ears. "I'm so sorry!"

There was another seizure, the sixth, and Eric thumbed the

activator on the pin laser, holding the button down to keep the tiny beam firing steadily. There was a horrible sizzling that wrenched his stomach, and tiny curls of foul-smelling smoke poured from the edges of the wound. He closed his eyes at the sight and fought back the wave of nausea sweeping over him, but he kept holding the activator switch until he felt a sudden popping beneath his fingers, followed by his father's single piercing scream of pain. He released the button and immediately pulled the laser out of the partially cauterized wound.

His father went limp, the violent muscle contractions halting in mid-seizure. The glassiness disappeared from his eyes and he sat up shakily, his face ghostly white. Eric helped him try to stand, but Javas fell weakly to his hands and knees, his stomach heaving. He gasped several times, then rose once more to his knees, catching his breath. The color was beginning to return to his face and he looked up at Eric, a weak smile spreading across his face.

"Th-thank you, son." He extended his left hand and allowed Eric to help him to his feet, then held onto his upper arm, the wound now barely bleeding.

"Are you all right? Can you walk?"

He nodded tiredly and started moving, slowly at first, one foot plodding ahead of the other as Eric helped support his weight. He regained his strength quickly as they traveled, but Eric realized that they'd lost too much time and looked desperately for landmarks. The dogs would not be far behind them now.

There they are . . . There was a great deal of karst here, but two large chunks of limestone—one on each side of the path—stood out among the outcroppings scattered throughout the woods. From there it was just another half kilometer to the cave.

They hurried through the opening between the two rocks, but had barely cleared them when the first of the dogs came up from behind. Eric whirled to meet them, the pin laser in hand, but the animal did not attack as he'd expected. His father joined him at his side, holding the knife well out in front of him, but still the dog hung back.

The dog was unlike any Eric had seen. It bore a resemblance, in build and coloring, to a Doberman; but the legs were much longer and thinner and ended in flat, wide paws perfectly suited for speed in the unsure footing of the backwoods. A second dog appeared, followed immediately by a third. Eric noticed that, unlike the baying dogs still in the distance, these animals hadn't made a sound and reasoned that they had been bio-bred for speed and stealth, and trained to keep their quarry from moving until the slower, noisier dogs—and their masters—caught up.

The lead dog growled, its head lowered and unmoving but its eyes darting back and forth between the two of them. Eric raised the pin laser, and all three animals oriented on the sudden movement as Eric thumbed the switch and fired on the one in the center. The dog was beyond the effective focal length of the laser, unfortunately, and it did little more than singe a spot on its short black fur, but the lead dog seemed aware of the weapon, what it was and what it could do, and kept a discreet distance from Eric as the other two animals slowly moved to either side as if to encircle them like some wild prey—which, it occurred to Eric, was exactly what they were.

"Don't move," said a voice behind them, and both Eric and his father froze. The dogs growled louder, clearly unsettled by the newcomer, who walked briskly to stand between the two men, the barrel of his shotgun pointed at the dogs. Eric continued to keep the pin laser trained on the dog nearest him, but from the corner of his eye saw that his father's mouth had dropped when he recognized who the man was.

"Brendan—"

"Sire, reach behind me. Tucked into my belt is a revolver. *Slowly!* Do you have it? Now, aim it carefully at the animal on your right, I'll take the other two. Prince Eric, don't move . . ."

Brendan waited until the Emperor dropped the knife into his boot to better handle the revolver with his uninjured arm, then fired over Eric's shoulder, catching the dog on the left squarely in the face, nearly severing the head from its body. He brought the gun around and shot the lead dog a split second before his father fired at the remaining animal on the far right, bringing it down.

Brendan paused a few seconds to be sure they were dead, then in one smooth motion slipped the shotgun over his shoulder and into a holster mounted on the side of the backpack he wore. He pulled a small vial from one of the side pockets on the pack and quickly sprinkled its contents, a grainy black powder, on the ground and around each of the dead animals. "If the other dogs come this way, they won't be able to track us once they've inhaled some of that."

"Poison?" Eric asked.

"No, nothing so exotic; or cruel, for that matter," he said, already turning away from the grisly scene. "It's ordinary pepper." He took several steps into the brush before Javas stopped him.

"Wait, murderer."

The icy cold tone of his father's voice caused a sick, empty feeling in the pit of his stomach, and as he spun to face him he saw that he now had the gun leveled steadily at Brendan. The man halted mid-stride, then sighed heavily and crunched almost unconcernedly back through the fallen leaves and branches to stand before the Emperor.

"What would you have of me, Sire?" he asked simply, his arms spread at his side. "Shall I stand before that tree, so that you may play the role of executioner? Or will you permit me to treat your wound and lead you, and your son, to safety?"

"I'm not so sure I would mind seeing your blood mingled with that of these other animals," Javas replied, nodding at the carcasses of the three dogs. "And I don't need your help to reach safety."

"Oh?" asked Brendan. "With your integrator still blocked?"

His father's eyes widened in stunned surprise at the admission. How had he known?

Brendan cocked his head in the direction of the road. "Have you wondered why they haven't caught up with you?"

Javas looked at Eric, clearly puzzled as to what the man was suggesting, and lowered the revolver slightly.

Eric listened carefully. The dogs still barked in the distance, but it was clear that they were not coming any closer. "They're no longer following us," he said.

"There is no need for them to be," he responded, pointing at his father's injured arm. "They didn't expect you to get very far. The purpose of the horsemen and dogs was to drive you in this direction, keep you from doubling back to the road until the rest of them came around the estate—much more quietly—from the other side." He gazed up the path in the same direction the cave lay. "They're not far, Sire. It should only be a matter of minutes before they reach this point, which"—Brendan looked back to

Javas, an eyebrow raised—"doesn't leave you much time, does it, to make a choice?"

Javas lowered the gun the rest of the way and tucked it into his belt. "Let's go, then."

Brendan turned his back to them without a word, and stepped into the brush in the same direction he'd started a few minutes earlier.

Can I trust you? Eric wondered, trying to sort out his feelings for Brendan. *Surely you're aware of how much my father hates you, and yet, you knew he wouldn't fire the weapon; you knew he'd trust you to lead us to safety. How can you be so sure of human nature? Are you really the traitor you've been painted to be?* "Just a moment, I know of a—" Eric began, unsure of how much to reveal. "I know of a place of safety, less than a kilometer up this path. Can we make it that far before they reach us?"

Brendan scanned the woods around him, listening carefully for several moments before shaking his head. "I don't think so. But we can make good time through this section of the backwoods here," he said, waving his arm to the east. "We'll stay clear of the main trail, but I think we can join one of the secondary trail systems far enough down that we can get to a comm facility before they realize we've left the area." He looked from Javas to Eric, then back to his father and added, his voice softer, "How is your arm, Sire? Will you be able to travel for a while before I take a look at it?"

"I think so." He nodded in the direction Brendan had indicated. "This way, then?"

The three of them headed into the backwoods, tramping through the brush and speaking only occasionally to one another. Because of the relentless thickness of the undergrowth, their progress was slow, and Brendan was forced to stop more frequently than he would have liked to check their direction and compare notes with Eric on their surroundings. His father had said nothing at all, although Eric couldn't be sure if his silence was due to his contempt for Brendan, or because of the pain he must be suffering. He cradled his arm constantly as he walked, holding it close in to his chest, and began sweating profusely with the effort of the hike. He held up the pace well, however, and they managed to cover a good deal of terrain before Brendan insisted on stopping long enough to tend to his wound.

"How did you know my integrator was being blocked?" his father asked matter-of-factly as Brendan finished bandaging his arm. Although there was little emotion in his words, it marked the first time the Emperor had addressed him directly since their confrontation back at the path.

"When I was your father's personal medical attendant— How does that feel? Is it too tight?" Javas shook his head. "My implants were linked directly to his integrator," he continued, "at exactly the same wavelength. Everything I did for his care—to stabilize medication levels, adjust his intensive-care equipment, even simply to monitor his condition—I channeled through him. When he died—"

The Emperor pulled his arm away suddenly, a look of cold anger sweeping across his features, and appeared about to say something but instead stared out through the trees.

Brendan shrugged, making no attempt to defend himself from Javas' silent accusation, and began collecting his things, replacing them carefully, but hurriedly, in the medical kit as he spoke. "When he died, my implants became inactive. I could no longer access the Imperial systems any more than I could his medical files. But my implants are still there, still intact." He closed the kit and stashed it in the backpack, then slipped it back on. "We'd better get moving."

"Your implants are still functional?" Eric asked as he fell into step behind the other two.

"They are, Young Prince, and I am constantly aware of their presence, but they were tuned to operate only through your grandfather. Yesterday afternoon, at almost the exact moment your shuttle approached, I sensed a numbness in my head as if they had suddenly gone inoperative. There's some kind of jamming signal covering this area"—he swept his arm around him to take in the entire backwoods—"like a heavy blanket."

His father stopped in his tracks. "You were near the House when we crashed?" he asked suspiciously. "You've not been in service to House Valtane for nearly three years. Why were you in the vicinity?"

"Your intelligence information is very good. I did leave House Valtane when Reid reached eighteen." Brendan kept his pace going, not bothering to turn back as he answered. "I live in the backwoods—I'm taking you to my home now."

His father was about to ask another question, but at the mention of his brother's name Javas fell silent once again. They continued on, finally reaching a narrow trail where their pace increased considerably on the smooth, growth-free surface. Sure of his surroundings now, Brendan no longer needed to reorient himself and they stopped only twice: once to check the dressing on Javas' arm, and again when the sun was directly overhead.

Twenty-four hours, Eric thought, gazing up at the bright shafts of sunlight filtering down through the trees, *with no sign of a search.* Either there had been no occasion for anyone on the outside to contact Woodsgate, or—was it possible that contact had been attempted, and intercepted by whoever was responsible for wrecking the shuttle? Routine contact with the Imperial estate may have been met with faked responses, arousing no suspicion.

"I live just over this next ridge," Brendan was saying, indicating a low, thickly wooded rise up ahead, then extended his arm to the right. "We're paralleling the main trail right now, a little more than two hundred meters due south of here."

Brendan's house was easily visible once they cleared the rise, nestled between the ridge they'd just crossed and a longer, higher one that rose steadily to the north. Like most things on Earth, it was a mixture of Old World construction and modern technology. The main part of the house had been fashioned from brightly colored prefabricated panels and featured a wide, domed roof with large plastiglass skylights. A long extension made of logs—from the surrounding woods, Eric guessed—had been added, and consisted of a combination storage building or workshop and a small stable. There was a portable fusion generator at one side of the prefabbed section that supplied all the dwelling's energy needs, and a receiving dish mounted on the roof. It was larger than Eric had expected, and neatly designed and constructed, the combination of plastic and wood not at all unpleasant to his eye.

Brendan let out a long, sharp whistle as they approached the house. The brush and smaller trees had been cleared in a wide circle around the house and he whistled again when they neared the edge of the grassy area a few dozen meters from the stable.

Not quite in the open, Brendan stopped abruptly and motioned them back with his hand. "Get down," he hissed, dropping to one knee at the same time he slid the shotgun out of his holster and thumbed the safety off. Eric and his father drew their own weapons and remained in the thicker portion of the scrub just outside the cleared yard. "Stay here." He sprinted across the yard, stopping briefly behind the cover of a thick tree before carefully crossing the remaining distance to the entrance of the log structure. The door was made in two parts that opened separately, one above the other. The top door was open and he crouched silently in front of the closed lower section, listening carefully for several moments before easing the bottom door ajar and slipping inside.

As his father kept his eyes trained on the house itself, Eric studied their surroundings. There was a well-worn narrow path on the far side of the property, below the house, that disappeared through the woods in a southeasterly direction, and Eric assumed it led to the main trail. He made a mental note of its location in case Brendan ran into trouble and the two of them had to make a run of it. Minutes passed uncomfortably and Eric was sure that something had happened to him when he appeared, oddly enough, at the front door of the prefabbed portion of the house. He came out onto the porch and looked nervously around, then sprinted back to their hiding place in the scrub.

"They've been here already."

"Who's been here?" Javas demanded.

Brendan stared at the Emperor, his voice deadly serious. "Your son, and his . . . people. They've completely ransacked my home. I tried to find some additional weapons but they were very thorough about it. My comm screen, most of my medical gear, everything. My horse—" His face twisted in a mixture of rage and sorrow, and he checked the load on the shotgun and gripped it so tightly in his hands that his knuckles went white. He started fidgeting nervously, the pitch of his voice rising as he continued. "The bastards didn't even kill him cleanly. They cut his throat and let him bleed to death in his stall." He scanned the area again, his breath coming in quick gasps. "I—I can't, won't, let it happen again! We've got to get you out of here, find a comm station."

Cut its throat? Eric remarked inwardly. *The guards on the shuttle had their throats—*

"What are you getting at?" his father demanded. "You can't let *what* happen again?"

He didn't answer, but continued looking almost frantically around at their surroundings for any sign of movement. Eric watched Brendan for several moments and studied the look of fear in his eyes, trying to identify something there that was more than simply being afraid for one's life. *I've seen that look before,* he suddenly realized. Glenney's face had had the same fearful expression when they were caught in the shielding before the shuttle had crashed. His father's eyes had flashed the same terrified visage, if only momentarily, back on Luna when it seemed that an attempt was being made on their lives. Not a fear of death itself or even of impending disaster, but a fear of being totally helpless to prevent something from happening. For Glenney, it was the knowledge that he was failing in his only duty, that of protecting him and the Emperor. His father must have felt the same way about him when the threat first appeared. But in Brendan's case—

"Let *what* happen again?" his father repeated, grasping him by the sleeve. He jerked Brendan around angrily, nearly unbalancing him, forcing him to look directly into his face. "Answer me!"

The sudden confrontation with his father seemed to snap Brendan out of his building panic. His eyes lost some of their wildness and he made himself calm down, swallowing audibly in an attempt to slow his breathing. He relaxed his grip on the shotgun and reached an unsteady hand into one of his pockets, then extended his outstretched palm. "Sire, does this look familiar?" he asked. There was more than a hint of shame in his voice.

All traces of anger, and a good deal of the color, drained instantly from his father's face when he saw the object—a simple gold bracelet—in Brendan's hand. The Emperor picked it up carefully, as if it were red-hot, and examined it wordlessly, a troubled frown spreading across his lips. As he turned it over in his hand, the shiny metal reflected the occasional ray of direct sunshine that managed to sift down through the trees. Part of its gleaming surface was obscured with a good deal of dried blood, but on one side Eric could just make out what appeared to be a delicately ornate engraving of a majestic bird, rising from flames.

SIXTEEN

"**M**y God," Eric said, almost under his breath, "is that what I think it is? Father, Glenney's security reports—they contained a description of this bracelet, connecting it to the group responsible for my grandfather's death. Surely they've not reorganized to fight the Sun project?"

Javas' lips drew into a tight line as he stared at the object. "Where did this come from?" he asked quietly, his eyes not moving from the bracelet in his hand.

By this point, Brendan had regained most of his self-control. He continued to warily survey their surroundings, and it was clear to Eric that his concerns dealt not only with those who had apparently been here but also with finding a clear means of escape. "Sire, I found it on my dining table, a spot of dried blood beneath it. He placed it on my table himself, his hands still dripping, after killing my horse."

"*Who* did?" the Emperor demanded. His father could contain himself no more, and gripped the bracelet so tightly that Eric thought he saw it beginning to flatten in his hand.

Brendan lowered his head, his words a whisper. "His name is Johnson, Sire. He was, is, the leader of those on Earth who would end your father's dream to save the Sun. He has no other goal in life but to stop this project. The man is absolutely brutal, bloodthirsty in every way, and thinks nothing of sacrificing others to achieve his ends."

The Emperor turned away, his eyes reaching skyward. Eric had never seen his father so torn with emotion. He shook his head slowly, speaking under his breath. "All those in the landing bay. Mila. Glenney. How many others?"

There was an uncomfortable pause before Brendan added, "Your father."

The Emperor lowered his head slowly and faced the two of them. Something passed then between Brendan and his father: a look, a nod, the tiniest raising of an eyebrow. His father sighed heavily, wearily. "And this man is allied with my—with Reid Valtane?"

"It would be more accurate to say that Reid Valtane is a product of this man."

They had remained still, talking quietly long enough that the natural sounds of the backwoods had returned around them as they spoke. But a sudden flurry of birds through the treetops caught their attention just seconds before they heard the horses approaching over the ridge on the northern side of the house.

There were three of them, and they rode swiftly, noisily, down the ridge in their direction with weapons waving above their heads. They were still at the crest of the the heavily wooded ridge, and since they were riding through the thickest part of the backwoods undergrowth it would be several moments before they reached the clearing; but even at this distance Eric could hear them laughing, already enjoying the chase.

"Come on! This way!" Brendan was immediately on his feet, already moving to the south, down the gradual incline leading to the main trail. His father pocketed the bracelet and turned to follow, calling to Eric to do the same.

"I'm right behind you," he yelled. He jammed the pin laser through the ever-present layer of dead leaves and flicked it on, then tamped it the rest of the way into the moist dirt underneath, hoping silently that one of their pursuers was directly above it when it overloaded.

The three of them ran as fast as they could through the underbrush, trying to reach the main trail. While the horses could easily outrun them on the trail, they were better able to negotiate the underbrush and downed branches and seemed to be making some headway. Since Brendan was leading them through the underbrush, Eric assumed that the path he'd seen earlier must not have been as direct a way to get to the trail as the way they were going. Still, if the horsemen took the path, the surer footing for their animals might lead them there before them, even if it was a slightly longer way to go. He slowed as he ran, looking over his shoulder, and saw that the trio was following them in nearly a straight line. *Good,* he thought, crossing his fingers, *right over the laser. Now, if only the timing is right.*

It wasn't; not quite, anyway. The horses had reached the clearing and immediately picked up speed, heading for the exact route they'd taken through the scrub—looking back, he could see the ferns and brush broken and matted by their passage, marking clearly the way they'd gone—and the front rider was still several meters away from where they'd been hiding when the laser reached overload. Had the timing been better and the horse directly above when it blew, it might have done serious injury to both horse and rider. As it was, however, the horse reared back, throwing the rider to the ground. His companions had been following closely enough that their horses also broke stride and milled about in frightened confusion as the rider who had been thrown remounted. Having lost their advantage of surprise, the riders circled each other, talking rapidly among themselves, and split up, one galloping away toward the path, the other two continuing the way they had run through the underbrush. Eric nearly laughed aloud at how well his plan had worked, good timing or no. In any event, their lead had increased tremendously, although Eric now realized that he felt suddenly naked without the laser.

The terrain became considerably steeper, and they were forced to continue their escape in a combination of running-sliding-running the last several meters before reaching the trail itself. They stood panting, trying to catch their breath, and considered their options.

"The one who took the path will most certainly turn back this way," Brendan gasped. "The other two will be slower, especially on the steeper parts we just came down. If we turn west, back toward Woodsgate, we'll have all three of them behind us; but if we turn east, toward town, we'll have but one opponent . . ."

The words hung in the air only a few seconds before his father flipped open the chamber on the revolver to check the load, then deftly snapped it closed again. "I understand. Let's go."

They ran quietly to the east, listening carefully for the horse they knew would soon be coming their way. They had covered only a few hundred meters when—although they could not yet see him coming from around the curve of the trail—they heard the hoofbeats echoing though the backwoods and jumped for cover on either side of the trail. Brendan and his father fired simultaneously when he rounded the curve, the combined blasts of the shotgun and revolver sending the rider literally flying out of the saddle.

The two older men went into action immediately, and Eric was amazed at how they worked together, doing what needed to be done with only a few words spoken between them. While his father dragged the downed rider into the growth at the side of the trail, Brendan tried to retrieve the horse, but had little success with the terrified animal. Instead, he slapped it on the rear and sent it running down the trail to the west in hopes that it might slow down any pursuit from that direction. With luck, the frightened animal would keep going down the trail and the two horsemen who had followed their path through the underbrush would see its hoofprints in the soft, packed earth and follow in the wrong direction. Eric hurried to his father, who knelt at the dead rider's side, and recognized the overweight man instantly as the one his brother had called Mobo.

Brendan came back to them with another shotgun, a single-barrel model, pulled from the saddle holster of the horse before he set the animal free. "Have you ever fired one of these?" he asked, tossing it to Eric.

Eric hefted the weapon in his hands, testing its weight, and allowed his fingers to explore the trigger housing. "No, not one like this."

"It's loaded, and it's easy to shoot. Just point it in the right direction, like a laser—oh, nice bit of work back there with the pin laser, by the way." Was that just the hint of a smile on his lips? "Let's move." As before, Brendan led the way.

The three of them continued running, stopping only briefly when they realized that the riderless horse must have indeed led the other two to the west. They shared the remainder of the water in the flask, then started off again, at an easy jog to conserve their strength, toward Somerville.

They had covered maybe two kilometers when the trail began to look familiar to Eric. He'd been here before, a number of times, and he tried to remember landmarks and potential side trails in case the need arose. He had dropped back behind the others, scanning their current location, and was visually separated from them around a curve in the trail when he heard a sudden gasp in front of him.

"Father!" He rushed forward, instantly recognizing the location as the same clearing where his brother had accosted him four years earlier. The downed oak was there, unchanged, the rough-

hewn steps in its side just as he remembered them. Brendan and
his father had been about to climb over it when they ran into a
shield of some kind. They hung suspended in the clearing, their
feet several centimeters above the ground as they struggled to
free themselves from—what? It looked like they were caught in
some invisible spiderweb as they groped and thrashed, almost in
slow motion, against an unseen wall in front of them. Whenever
their feet scraped the ground, they kicked up leaves and dirt that
instantly became mired in whatever was holding them. Eric
raised the shotgun, looking frantically for a target, and was
nudged in the back by something. He whirled around and felt
himself instantly mired in a thickness of air that seemed to hold
him solidly. The more he struggled, the thicker the air became
and the harder it seemed to be able to move at all. He lost his grip
on the shotgun and stared incredulously as it floated in the air
next to him, just out of his reach. He tried not to resist it, relaxing
his arms and legs in an attempt to free himself by moving slowly,
but to no avail.

"Well, what have we here?" a deep, booming voice asked. He
heard the man's boots scuffing across the bark of the downed oak
tree behind him, then rustling through the dry leaves on the
ground, and struggled desperately to turn around, trying to face
the speaker. "Why, it looks like the former Master of House
Valtane." His commanding voice lilted sarcastically as he spoke
to Brendan. "And look who you've brought me: Javas, son of
Nicholas, Emperor of the Hundred Worlds."

It was apparent that his father and Brendan were still held
helpless by the section of the force field behind him, but it
sounded like the newcomer was somehow walking freely about
them. *This isn't one large field,* Eric reasoned, *but single fields
around each of us.* He struggled again, but managed only to turn
his head a few centimeters. He might not have bothered because
the newcomer walked to him next, circling him as if there was
nothing there to hamper him. It was him—the tall, bearded man
who had caught him as he fell on the shuttle ramp back on Luna.
The man Brendan had called Johnson. There was a long plastiskin bandage running down his neck and into the open collar of
his shirt, and he walked with a slight limp from the injuries he'd
received in the shuttle crash the previous day. It was just as
obvious, as evidenced by how well he seemed to be getting

around, that he'd received a good deal of advanced medical attention. From the physicians at House Valtane, no doubt. He had no weapon that he could see, but held a small, flat object in his right hand.

"Prince Eric, I've been watching your development for some time. It's good to make your acquaintance in less formal circumstances than our brief encounter on the Moon." He walked up to Eric's shotgun and ran the thing in his hand around the perimeter of the gun, then plucked it effortlessly out of the air, adding it to the weapons he must have taken in a similar manner from the others. He slipped the controller device into his shirt pocket.

Eric was furious and tried to speak, but found that although his breathing seemed normal, he couldn't utter a sound.

"Save your breath, Young Prince," Johnson said, "you should have but a short wait." He turned away, walking out of sight behind him once more. Eric heard a brief bit of static, then, "They turned to the east, Lord. I have them."

He had felt trapped, helpless, before—at this exact spot, in fact—but for the first time in his life, he felt abject humiliation. He struggled again, uselessly, more out of anger at his situation than from any hope that he might actually break the grip of the field holding him. He concentrated on the sounds behind him: He could hear the occasional struggling of his father and Brendan as their feet would contact the ground and scoop through the leaves below them. Johnson stacked the weapons out of reach, then unfastened a pack or bag of some kind and removed a canteen, the loud slurping unmistakable. From time to time a bird called somewhere in the backwoods, and at one point he thought he heard the trilling of a raccoon, which disappeared immediately at the sound of approaching hoofbeats.

Hanging as he was, facing down the trail, he was the first to see the riders when they rounded the curve of the trail. There were three of them, their horses as magnificent as the one he'd seen Brendan riding when they first met at this place. They led a fourth horse, Mobo's body draped over it, his arms and legs dangling grotesquely over the animal's flanks.

He'd never seen one of the riders before, but he recognized the one leading Mobo's horse as his brother's friend Paulie. The man's eyes were filled with anger and hatred as he stared at him and, although he obviously held him responsible for what had happened to his companion, he didn't speak. He led his animal to a grassy area on the side of the clearing, followed by the dead man's horse and the other rider, leaving only the leader's horse on the trail proper. The rider gracefully alighted on the ground, allowing his mount to follow the others to the grass.

It was his brother. Reid had been bigger than Eric four years ago, but now he virtually dwarfed him. His muscular build and physical features closely matched his father's. His thin beard was gone, and his copper-colored hair had lightened, and he looked even more like his father than he had remembered from their first meeting. In fact, where he had merely looked familiar to him when they had first met, it would now be apparent to even a casual observer that the Emperor and Reid were father and son. Eric wondered idly if anyone would ever make the same assumption about himself.

Reid stood silently before him for several moments, then circled around to examine the others.

"Father," he heard him say, a sarcastic chuckle underlying his words, "how nice it is to see you again for the first time. And Master; you, too, are looking well." His brother laughed aloud, then walked to a point where Eric could just see him if he strained his neck enough. Reid shook his head in mock sadness at the sight before him. "Is this any way to treat the Emperor of the Hundred Worlds, and his Crown Prince? Johnson!"

He held out his hand, deftly catching the controller that Johnson tossed to him. "Cover them with . . ." A sudden thought occurred to him, and he laughed again. "Use the Master's own shotgun." There was a sharp, metallic sound as Johnson broke the magazine and checked the load, then walked to stand next to Reid. Satisfied that Johnson had a clear field of fire that included all three of them, Reid held the controller before him.

Eric fell suddenly, losing his balance as his feet hit the ground. His father and Brendan had both managed to stay upright when the field released. Eric scrambled quickly to his feet; too quickly, causing Johnson to swing the shotgun immediately in his direction.

"Sit down," he ordered, punctuating the remark with the shotgun, "cross-legged. All three of you."

"Paulie! David!" Reid called over his shoulder. "Take Mobo back to the House."

"And one of you fetch my horse before you leave," added Johnson, tilting his head behind him. "You'll find him tied a few meters down-trail."

The one identified as David scrambled over the oak and disappeared, while Paulie came forward and said something under his breath to Reid, who smiled wickedly and nodded in Eric's direction. Paulie crossed quickly to him and hit him full in the face with his fist, knocking him backward on the ground. "He told you to sit down," Paulie said emotionlessly. Eric wanted to throttle him, but staring up the barrels of the shotgun trained squarely on him, he fought back his anger and quietly sat upright, crossing his legs as ordered.

Hide your anger; hide your fear. Show your contempt. "That's it?" he asked, wiping at his bleeding lip. "I would have thought that with a weapon trained over your shoulder to back you up, your bravery would have been such that you could have delivered a better blow than that."

Paulie lunged forward, but Reid restrained him with an outstretched arm. "Forget it," he said, his voice and commanding delivery immediately reminding Eric of Johnson's way of speaking. His brother had obviously picked up a number of the bearded man's strengths. "Now get moving, both of you." Paulie opened his mouth as if to argue, then thought better of it and crossed wordlessly to his mount and, with David rejoining him, led Mobo's horse into the underbrush to clear the downed oak before disappearing on the eastern portion of the trail.

Reid waited until the sounds of their horses faded away into the backwoods before speaking. *"Father,* it has been such a long time, and we have such a short time left to us."

"Time for what, *son?"* the Emperor asked, looking up from his place on the ground.

"Why, to get to know each other before I kill you, of course."

Brendan stirred uneasily at the remark, but held his tongue.

"That's what this is all about, then? Your mother's attempt to put her bastard son on the throne?"

Reid chuckled at the insult. "I'm no bastard. I was born according to the old ways of a natural womb, on Earth, as mandated by Imperial law and custom. As the only living heir to the throne, there won't even be a question raised as to the validity of my claim, once your bodies are discovered aboard the wreckage of the shuttle and the news of your tragic deaths reaches Armelin City."

"And you think you'll get away with this?" Eric demanded. "You think no one will connect House Valtane to this?"

"And why should they, little brother?" he asked, crossing in front of him. "You'll be the victims of a desperate attempt by the Sarpan to defend themselves." He held the controller up between thumb and forefinger. "See this? It's an integrated unit that controls not only the shielding in place over your palatial home, but the sticky field Johnson used to snare the three of you. There are hundreds of types of shield technology in use in the Empire, but the shield over Woodsgate has undoubtedly been analyzed from the inside, and its origin will be directly traced back to the Sarpan. Just as the nerve slug I shot you with this morning will match the Sarpan gun we've planted in the wreckage."

"Sarpan?" His father gripped the bandage on his arm and stared in disbelief at Reid's statement. "Your mother has made a deal with the aliens?"

Reid shrugged. "One finds allegiance where one can."

"Yeah," snorted Eric, nodding disgustedly in Johnson's direction. "That much is painfully clear."

"Yes," agreed Johnson, his feral eyes narrowing at Eric, "but sometimes the allegiance can truly be of mutual benefit to all parties concerned." He walked to the fallen oak and sat, the barrel of the shotgun still trained on the three of them. "The frogs feel threatened by your blasphemous project to alter the Sun's natural course. They don't understand your efforts and see only an Imperial expansion that brings humans closer to Sarpan space. They were more than happy to lend assistance to House Valtane, knowing that the final determination will show them to have acted only out of fear for their own existence."

"Such a horrible misunderstanding," Reid added with mock sincerity. "Of course, when I'm made Emperor I will do all I can to smooth relations with the Sarpan Realm . . . even if it means dismantling the project."

"But you can't!" His father moved forward in anger, checking himself abruptly when Johnson jumped to his feet.

"Oh? Once word spreads through the Empire that a major confrontation with the Sarpan Realm can be resolved as simply as postponing an effort that few members of the Hundred Worlds really understood anyway . . . In another twenty-five or thirty years, the urgency of this stupid project begun by Emperor Nicholas and the Grisian scientist will no longer be as keenly felt. I'll see to it."

"I've studied the data," Eric interjected. "My mother's conclusions are valid."

"It doesn't really matter, does it?" he shot back, "since I could not possibly care less about pursuing your mother's work."

"You disgust me, Reid," Brendan put in, speaking for the first time since their capture. He looked at Johnson, adding, "To think I played any part in his upbringing, in the name of a debt to House Valtane."

Johnson laughed, truly amused at Brendan's words, his booming voice echoing through the trees. "I would think you'd be getting comfortable with being used by now." Two steps and Johnson stood before him, his enormous frame towering over the former Master. "Beginning with Emperor Nicholas, you've made a life's work of being a puppet, after all."

Brendan leaped for Johnson's gun, but the man must have been expecting the move and neatly sidestepped the attack, bringing the butt of the shotgun up brutally under Brendan's chin. His father moved to catch Brendan as he fell, but caught the toe of Reid's boot in his stomach for his trouble and fell back gasping on the ground. "Stay out of this, *Father.*" He spat the word like a curse.

Eric sat rooted, keeping his anger and concern in check as best he could. He wanted to go to his father's side, but knew that Johnson—or his brother—would love for him to try, and held himself back. *Wait, wait.*

His father seemed all right, but winded by the blow to his stomach. Brendan lay on the ground moaning, Johnson standing menacingly above him. Waiting, it seemed, for something. As he studied the man's face, the pure meanness behind the wolflike eyes, he saw that Johnson had intentionally goaded Brendan into attacking him out of some perverted sense of pleasure. The two men fully intended to kill them, that was apparent, but Eric realized that he and his father would be kept alive long enough to be marched back to the shuttle. Brendan, on the other hand, would most certainly be killed here, now, his body discarded in the backwoods.

He shifted his gaze to Reid and saw that he was enjoying Johnson's torment of the former Master as much as the Earthman was. The resemblance to his father was merely physical, after all. Any influence Brendan may have had in his upbringing had been completely outweighed by whatever conditioning Johnson had exerted. Brendan managed to sit up groggily, and Eric saw that Johnson was readying to strike him again.

"What do you mean 'used'?" Eric asked quickly, trying to forestall another blow and play for time.

Almost instantly, his father picked up on what he was attempting. "Brendan, what's he talking about?"

Johnson stood back and looked over his shoulder at Reid, then said, "Go ahead. Tell him."

Brendan massaged his jaw and was still wavering from the blow he'd taken. "Go to hell," he croaked, not even bothering to raise his head.

Johnson kicked him savagely, sending him writhing to the ground once more. His father had managed to edge closer and reached out to Brendan, but Johnson smacked the barrel of the shotgun sharply against the side of his head, forcing him back. "Do it, just do it!" he yelled, roughly prodding his father in the face with the gun. "I'll drag your gods-damned corpse back to the shuttle myself—"

"Enough!" Reid grabbed the man's shoulder, restraining him. Johnson stood aside, but kept the gun leveled. "The Sarpan don't use shotguns," he reminded him, then leaned into his father's face. "But don't think I won't kill you here, myself, if it comes to it. It would be more trouble, but we could make a shotgun wound look like a crash injury." He straightened and suddenly kicked his father forcefully in the ribs, knocking him on his back.

Eric marveled at how well his brother was playing this out. He had stood back and studied the three of them while Johnson worked on them, both physically and emotionally, intervening only when it seemed necessary to avoid having his plans altered. He paced a few meters away, turning back to address them.

"What Brendan is now realizing," he began, raising an eyebrow, "and what he seems too ashamed to admit, is that he's the reason we caught you so easily." He walked in a wide circle around them, concentrating his gaze on Brendan as he spoke. "His implants may be inactive, but my mother has monitored them for years. You didn't know that, did you, Master? We've watched you, followed you, traced your steps since I was a boy. Then, after you left our service three years ago, we still knew every move you made. Knew of your hovel in the woods, and how you've shadowed our House as well as the Imperial residence. We tracked you easily once you met up with my father and brother, and it was simplicity itself to set up a trap at your home. Were you so naive as to think you could prevent the inevitable?"

His father sat up again, wincing with the movement—the blows he'd taken, along with his injured arm, were beginning to take a heavy toll upon him. Eric saw fresh blood oozing slowly down the man's wrist and realized that his wound had reopened and was once again bleeding freely. "Why, Brendan?" His words came weakly, his voice rasping. "I asked you before why you stayed here, in the backwoods, and you never answered."

"I sought . . ." Brendan coughed, wiped a bit of blood from his lips. "I sought to serve you, Sire, to make up for—" He stopped, looked apologetically to Javas. "I wanted only to watch them. They hated you, that was plain. Their plans had been thwarted by your father, their numbers reduced when they were systematically rounded up after his death. I had hoped to be able to watch them, perhaps somehow warn you if the resistance to your regime mounted once more. But instead . . ." He hung his head in shame, his voice shaking as he whispered, "Instead, I've betrayed your House once again."

His father started to speak, obviously confused by what he was hearing.

"You still don't get it, do you?" Reid came forward, grasping the lapels of the Emperor's jacket. "The Master has been stupidly loyal to the Empire all along." He released his hold on the jacket, letting Javas fall heavily to the ground.

"We've wasted enough time here, Lord," Johnson said.

"You're right," Reid agreed, turning for his horse. "On your feet."

A satisfied smile spread over Johnson's features and he raised the shotgun toward Brendan's face as everything seemed to happen at once.

"No!" Eric tried to stand, desperate to do something but knowing he was too far to the side. His call distracted the gunman, however, allowing his father the split second he needed to leap sideways in an attempt to reach Johnson. He managed to deflect the gun enough that when it discharged, only a small portion of the blast caught Brendan in his left shoulder and upper chest. The force of the blast sent him flying backward into the scrub at the edge of the trail. At the same time, Javas kicked upward, knocking the gun aside but not with enough strength to dislodge it from Johnson's grip.

"Damn your interference!" With Brendan groaning in agony on the ground below him, Johnson turned to where his father staggered upright. He flipped the shotgun around, smashing the butt end into his face with a horrible, audible crunch.

Not caring if a second blast came his way, Eric sprang to his father's side. He was bleeding heavily from a deep purple-red gash that ran several centimeters in length, and his eye was already swelling shut over his flattened cheekbone. He was still conscious, barely, and gasped for breath as Eric cradled him in his lap. Johnson stood over them, his feral eyes glowing with rage, the twin barrels of the shotgun pointed directly at them.

Reid had come forward and held the controller out in front of him, but lowered it again when he saw that all resistance had stopped. "Finish the Master."

"Very well, Lord." The sudden anger drained from Johnson as he turned away reluctantly and crossed the trail to where Brendan lay in the underbrush.

"Eric," the Emperor gasped, "my boot."

The knife! Eric reached down his father's side and into his boot. In one fluid movement he drew the blade from its sheath and flung it at Johnson.

The blade found its mark just below the man's beard and he fell to his knees, his breath coming in tortured, gurgling wheezes. Still on his knees, he turned to Eric. Where before, his eyes had reflected the cunning and ruthlessness of a savage predator, now they glowed only with the fear of trapped prey. He fell forward on top of the shotgun, the life spilling out of him into the scrub.

Not taking the time to look behind him, Eric made a dash for the weapon, yanking it forcibly from beneath Johnson's still body. He spun around, aiming the gun at his brother, now the only other person still on his feet. Reid stood only a few meters away, unmoving, with the controller held out before him. His face was unreadable. Behind him, he heard Brendan groaning; before him, his father lay panting on the ground.

"What do you care about the Master?" Reid asked confidently. "He's a traitor to your House."

Where is it? Eric wondered. Without taking his eyes from Reid and keeping the shotgun pointed straight ahead, he moved forward slowly, kicking up some leaves experimentally, hoping to find the sticky field.

"If our father were not bound by his promise to our grandfather, he would surely have killed him himself." Reid ran a hand through his long hair almost nonchalantly as he spoke, and seemed untroubled by all that had happened. It was clear that Johnson meant nothing to him, and had only served as a means to an end; Reid would probably have ordered his death himself once he'd achieved his goals.

Eric edged closer, Reid's hand following his every movement. The sticky field was certainly somewhere between him and his brother, he reasoned, but other questions raced through his head: Is it movable? Can he direct it? Enlarge it? Contract it around him? How high is it, and does it extend all the way to the ground below him? Can the shotgun penetrate it?

"You know, Eric," his brother said, using his name for the first time, "I'm quite impressed by how well you've handled yourself."

He felt a sudden pressure at his back and turned slightly before he fought off the urge to whip around. He stopped moving forward and stepped to the side, but found that he was mired as before, unable to move. He froze, the shotgun thrust out before him, and tried not to entangle himself in the rapidly enveloping field any more deeply than he already had. The field at his back was cold against his skin—he hadn't noticed that before when he'd struggled with it. He remained motionless, but hopes of not becoming helplessly stuck melted as he felt the chilling sweep of the Sarpan field cover his body, sweeping around from behind him in a split second to hold him fast, leaving him little more than a statue. He kicked his foot and stirred up dust that caught in the field around him as it floated upward. The field seemed to be tightly focused on him, wrapping around him like a cocoon.

Seeing that he was now held securely by the sticky field, Reid stopped his banter and slipped the controller into his shirt pocket, then crossed to where his father lay on the ground, checking his condition. Javas appeared to be all right for the moment, but from Eric's vantage point he seemed to lapse in and out of consciousness. Standing again, Reid strode casually up to where he was being held tight in the field's grip and stood mockingly at his side.

He tried to speak, in vain, and managed only to frown up at his tormentor. *Show your contempt.*

"It was stupid of you to fight me, Eric," Reid said, leaning so close that he could feel his brother's breath on his face. "Look at you: You take more after your scientist mother than the Emperor. I'm stronger, more suited for rule than you could ever be." He started to say something else, but a sudden rustle from the underbrush caught his attention and he turned away for a moment. The rustling stopped, and was replaced by Brendan's groaning as the man fell back into the scrub once more. "Pathetic. The Master is trying to help you, still trying to prove to you that he's no traitor. Since you've managed to kill Johnson, I'll take care of this last chore myself."

He went to the fallen oak where the guns had been piled, and picked up both of the weapons Johnson had confiscated from them. "I recognize Mobo's gun," he said, leaning it against the oak, then picked up the revolver. "This one must belong to the Master. I believe I'll use it to kill him."

Wait, wait.

"No, don't do it . . ." His father had managed to raise himself up on one elbow, but was helpless to intervene as Reid approached the trail. Eric waited until his brother was almost in front of him, then with every bit of strength he possessed pushed the gun forward and watched as the dust delineating the edge of the field stretched, then snapped back closer to his body. The moment the chamber cleared the edge of the field, he squeezed the trigger.

Reid was barely a meter in front of him when he fired, and the full blast of the shotgun threw his brother forcefully against the oak. Eric felt the sticky field dissolve around him almost instantly, and he hit the ground and rolled to the side in the event Reid tried to respond with the revolver. He needn't have bothered. Reid, his chest blown nearly away, was dead before he hit the tree. His head lolling to one side, his brother's body leaned in an almost natural position against the oak. Eric swallowed hard as he stared at the gaping hole in Reid's chest, and saw that bits and pieces of the controller electronics were scattered amid the blood.

Eric turned away. "Father, are you all right?" he asked, supporting his shoulders.

"I'll be fine. Help me up." He weaved unsteadily as Eric helped him to his feet, but kept his balance.

Together the two of them went to Brendan. They removed his backpack in an attempt to make him as comfortable as possible. Eric rummaged through the backpack until he found the medical kit and dressed the Master's wounds as best he could, but it was clear to both of them that the injuries were even more severe than he had thought; he'd lost too much blood.

"The shield controller was destroyed," Eric said, trying to keep Brendan alert. He removed his jacket and made a pillow for him; his father's jacket was already draped over him. "If he was telling the truth about it being an integrated control, then the shield on the House should be down, too. Lie still; we'll have help soon."

Brendan ignored the hopeful remark and addressed his father. "Sire . . . Your integrator . . . ?" He coughed again, spitting blood. He seemed to grow weaker, his skin more pallid by the minute.

The Emperor shook his head. "No, it's still out. But they'll be searching the woods any time now with body heat scans. Hang on, Brendan." He looked around, hoping to spot some sign of impending rescue, but Brendan's hand on his arm drew his attention.

"Sire . . . Your father . . ."

"Shhhh. Don't talk."

"No." Eric felt Brendan shivering beneath his touch, saw his lips quivering as he spoke. Brendan's eyes grew glassy, but stared desperately into his father's face as he tried to sit. "I didn't kill him."

His father stiffened. "I think I know that now."

"He was already dying. We . . . we even had to keep him in cryosleep for . . . most of the journey here." Brendan released his grip on Javas' arm and fell back against Eric's rolled jacket, catching his breath before going on. "He hid it from me . . . hid it from all of us with his integrator. Johnson's . . . people would have murdered him, but he beat them to it . . . knowing that the public spectacle of his death would result in an intensive . . . effort to find his killers . . ."

"And gain immediate support for the project," Javas finished for him. "He gave you the bracelet, didn't he, using you as the bait Glenney needed to hunt down Johnson's people."

Brendan nodded almost imperceptibly at the burden that had just been lifted from him. As he died, the hint of a smile appeared at the corners of his mouth.

There was a humming vibration above their heads and Eric looked upward at the hovercraft skimming the treetops, recognizing it by its markings as one of the short-range hoppers kept at the House. The craft slowed as it passed over their location, then circled around and reoriented over the clearing as it prepared to land.

His father hadn't moved, and remained staring at Brendan's body, his eyes moist.

"You've done something few can do, my friend," he said softly, his words nearly lost in the increasing whine of the descending hovercraft. "You've given your life twice for your Emperor."

The day had begun with a beautiful summer sunrise over the green Kentucky hills to the east. It was still early, and Eric and his father strolled the grounds on what was to be their last morning together before the Emperor returned to the Moon. In the two days that had passed since returning to Woodsgate, his father's wounds had been quick-healed, and only a slight shininess of plastiskin remained on his cheek where the bone structure of his face had been rebuilt. In a few days more even that would be gone, and with it, all physical traces of their ordeal.

"I'll tell you something else," his father was saying. He'd stopped to make a point, and Eric let his eyes roam the garden as he spoke. He felt a strong, humid breeze from the south and already felt warm in his formal Imperial jacket. Today would be hot, he knew. "In many ways, I don't really miss it. Without my integrator, I've been more at peace with myself than I have in years." He chuckled to himself, then added, "Of course, once they've reactivated the circuitry I'm sure I'll wonder how I ever got along without it."

"What about House Valtane?"

Eric's blunt question took his father by surprise, and he resumed walking before answering. "I don't know. I'm forced to admit that she's covered her tracks well. We've been able to find little, if any, ties to the Sarpan other than the most innocuous of trade agreements. She apparently has no interest whatever in the project, other than how it might affect her personal gain, and merely used the zealousness of Johnson and his people to get to us. Without their leader to guide them, it's becoming ridiculously easy to round up what's left of them."

"There will still be resistance, I suppose."

His father sighed. "Yes, I suppose there will. But nothing as fanatical—or as fatalistic—as Johnson's group. They were the only serious threat." Javas looked away again and cleared his throat. He was clearly uneasy about something. He took a deep breath, then said, "Eric . . . has Master McLaren told you of the test of courage that is given to each heir to the Empire upon his reaching manhood?"

Eric felt his heart race suddenly, but hid his true feelings as best he could. "He's not yet spoken of it to me, not directly anyway; but yes, I know of it."

His father nodded in understanding. "Do you know that my oldest brother failed?"

A whisper: "Yes."

Javas sighed again. "I can't guess how much you know about what happened, but accept that the test is the final determination of a man's fitness to rule. To fail the test proves cowardice, which is punishable by death—instantly and without question—at the hands of a member of the House of Arman. Only he can set the conditions of the test; only he can be the judge in this. It is tradition, and cannot, *will* not, be broken."

Javas paused, and stared off into the distance where a flock of game birds was clearing a rise at the edge of the estate grounds. "Eric, officially speaking, your test would still be many years away. However, I can conceive of no test that would prove your courage more than the ordeal you've just gone through. There will be no need to test you further." He smiled then and held out his hand. "You've made me proud, in more ways than you can imagine."

Eric was about to reply, but was interrupted by a sudden, steady whine behind them as the shuttle prepared for takeoff, and the two men turned back to the front of the House. McLaren stood waiting at the edge of the shuttle pad, hands clasped behind his back and a dour expression on his face. *Things truly are back to normal,* Eric mused as they neared.

The head of House security sprinted up to them, bowing his head nervously. "Sire, your shuttle is ready to depart."

The Emperor nodded to dismiss him, and when he was out of earshot, said, "I've got a feeling it will be a long time, if ever, before Imperial security is the same again."

"Good." Eric turned to his father, and extended his hand in farewell.

"Good-bye, Eric," the Emperor said, shaking his hand firmly before turning for the shuttle.

"Father?" Eric said suddenly, stopping him. "I'm proud to be your son."

His father raised his hand to the waiting security personnel at the shuttle to signal that he was coming and turned back to Eric. "I fought your grandfather for so many years," he said, shaking his head sadly. "I never told him how proud I was of him until he was an old man, almost too late. Thank you for not making me wait as long." The Emperor smiled warmly, then headed for the waiting shuttle.

Eric watched as the craft lifted off and passed through the shielding. It circled the grounds once, then disappeared through the clouds.

. . . there are a few physical differences, as well. Due to the gravity of 1.2 g, most native Pallatins are shorter in stature than human standard. Further, after three centuries their eyes are larger to better utilize the dimmer light emitted by their K-2 sun. The eyes have been described as very expressive and are, to the keen observer, a key indicator of their emotions at any given moment . . .

Eric found it difficult to sleep that night, and sat idly fingering the keys of the terminal at his study desk. He was only half reading the screen and tapped at the keys to bring up a different file. The readout on the flatscreen display showed a green planet, slightly larger than Earth, turning slowly as a description of the world scrolled by beneath it.

Pallatin, it read. *Star type: K-2. Distance: 16.5 light-years. Colony established: 2321. Economy: Ship construction, heavy and light industrial, bioengineering, literature . . .*

Sixteen and a half light-years. He did a quick mental calculation—at top speed, Dr. Adela de Montgarde was probably arriving at Pallatin just about now. Or perhaps she had even concluded her business there and was now on her way home. In any event, she certainly would know by now that she had a son, waiting on Earth.

Eric had never felt a closeness to his absent mother, had never felt a need to contact her. Besides, he'd reasoned, the distances made the relevancy of any message he might send pointless. The events of the past week, however, had made him rethink his reasoning.

It would still take several years for the message to reach her; in fact, it would probably be intercepted on the return trip. It didn't really matter, though, as she would most likely be in cryosleep when the message was received. It would greet her upon her awakening when she reentered Sol system, as would each of the periodic recordings that would follow this one.

He tapped the keyboard lightly and the display disappeared, then quickly keyboarded the sequence to set up a holographic recording. Soft lighting came up around the flatscreen as the system prepared to record, and a low chiming told him when it was ready.

"Record." The glow changed subtly as the recording process started.

"Hello, Mother," he began. "Let me tell you about myself."

PART FOUR

TO REAP THE WHIRLWIND

SEVENTEEN

*T*he Old Man is talking to his son, Amasee Niles thought as he watched the huge moon rise. It glowed a brilliant orange, matching the dying glow of Pallatin's K-2 star. With the sky not yet dark, it looked as though there were two suns in the sky: a brighter, sinking one in the west; another, seemingly only slightly dimmer, climbing the eastern sky. He smiled, remembering the children's tale his mother used to tell him on those occasions when the moon's orbit was just right and both objects were in the sky at the same time.

"The sun doesn't go down until the moon rises," she had told him, just as countless other mothers had told countless other children. And like those others, he had listened wide-eyed and believing. "He waits there, seeming to hang forever on the horizon until his son appears. For a while, when they're in the sky at the same time, he tells his son of his day: what happened on the world below him and what the little people were doing. He tells him to look after the little people, and sometimes . . ." She had paused then, he remembered, and lowered her voice as if imparting a secret meant only for him. "Sometimes, he picks out one little boy or girl and tells the moon to be especially watchful over that one, and to bring good luck. And do you know how to tell if you're the one? Well, you keep watching the moon and think good thoughts, and if your thoughts are good enough and you look very closely, you'll see him wink at you. Just at you and nobody else."

He remembered lying awake that night as long as he could, staring at the moon, hoping the big face he imagined there would wink just for him. And again the next time the orbit brought it to the same position two months later, and the next. But he always fell asleep.

How many years ago was that? he wondered, surprised at how well he remembered it all. He gazed steadily at the moon, nearly half the size of Pallatin itself. Rugged craters covered its surface and many of them could be easily identified without a telescope, but for just the briefest of moments he tried to imagine the face he remembered from childhood. He squinted and stared, and for a second his mind let go of the reality that what he saw was merely a pattern of craters and mountains, and he thought he saw the face. But then the rational part of his mind intruded once more, and the pattern became just ordinary empty craters again.

Amasee Niles stood at the lower edge of his farm, leaning forward on his elbows on the low strand-metal fence that circled his property, and gazed quietly at the rugged landscape spreading out below his homestead. He'd located the house halfway up a gently sloping ridge, and from where he stood he could see the entire countryside to the east for dozens of kilometers. The bare, exposed sheets of gray rock that had been thrust violently upward in the Big Quake stood out sharply against the soft green of the surrounding grassland. Here and there the hardy bioengineered grasses had managed to establish a foothold on the bare rock, and even at this distance Amasee could pick out several spots of green among the now-silent gray slabs.

He looked closely, trying hard to pick out the site of the original Westland colony, but the surface features had changed so much, so drastically, that the location of the once-familiar landmark—a scattering of small houses, civic buildings and meeting hall surrounding a circular town green—was impossible to spot. Even the cracked and broken concrete of the obsolete landing strip, the largest structure there, was nowhere to be found. He gave up with a troubled shake of his head. The main city of Dannen, reestablished several kilometers to the west more than two hundred years ago, had experienced severe damage; thousands had been left homeless and many had been hurt, but there was, miraculously, no loss of life caused by the earthquake almost twenty years earlier. But at first light following the tremors the residents were stunned to find that Pallatin's original settlement of Dannen's Down, maintained and preserved as an historical village, had disappeared, swallowed whole by the turbulent ground. The loss of life was minor in number—only the live-in caretakers and historical roleplayers signed on for the season were in residence when it hit—but devastating in its completeness. His sister Katie, her twin sons, Zack and Toma, and twenty others; all friends, all gone, killed in minutes as Pallatin's restless geology reached up and took them inside.

Twenty-three people, he thought, reminding himself for the hundredth time that Dannen had been lucky. Although few were killed in the eastern portion of Pallatin's only major continent, nearly three thousand people had died throughout Westland; Chesterton, less than twenty kilometers to the north, had suffered more than two hundred deaths—almost a fourth of its population—and other settlements, ranging in size from small towns to major trading and industrial centers, had all experienced losses far greater in proportion to their population than had Dannen. *So why do these twenty-three haunt me?*

He heard a rustling in the tall grass behind him and recognized Marabell by her gait. Without turning around, he said, "I know, I know; I'm going to be late if I don't leave before sunset."

There was a soft, high-pitched chuckle behind him and he felt delicate hands slip around his waist. She leaned her head softly against his back, and as an early evening breeze came up behind them it brought the scent of lilacs to him. Without looking, he knew that Marabell had picked a handful of the fragrant flowers from the bushes behind the house.

"You probably thought I was sneaking up on you again, didn't you?" Her voice was light, although behind her teasing lay an understanding that her husband was troubled.

"And weren't you?" he asked, laughing. He turned around in her embrace, leaning backward against the fence, and pulled her to him. He held her silently for a moment, staring over her shoulder at the house. The kitchen lights glowed warmly. Clint was nowhere to be seen, but their youngest son, Thad, occupied himself happily on a play set beneath the iron oaks to one side of the house. "Where's Clint?" he asked. "I was hoping to see him before I left."

She smiled up into his eyes. "Am, he's eighteen. Where do think he'd be about now?"

"The Anderston girl again?"

"Not 'again,' Am; *still.* You refuse to see him growing up, don't you?" As before, her words were light and airy.

Amasee ran a hand through his wife's long brown hair, stroking idly down the length of it as it fell over her shoulders and down her back, unintentionally dislodging the lilacs she'd tucked behind one ear. The huge orange ball that was Dannen's Star hung low on the horizon, and the oblique rays of the evening light glinted hazily through her sweet-smelling hair.

"Can't blame me there, can you?" He shrugged, reaching for the fallen lilacs. "I'm in no hurry to admit my advancing age. Any more than you're ready to admit that you're about to lose your eldest son . . . old woman." He brought the flowers to his nose, pretending to hide the mischievous grin spreading across his face.

"Who are you calling an old woman!" She pulled back in mock protest and jabbed him playfully in the ribs. They both laughed and held each other briefly before he turned to lean on the fence and stare out again over the darkening landscape. Already the first stars were beginning to appear and it was getting more difficult to distinguish the green grass from the angry gray rocks in the distance. Marabell embraced him from behind, and he reveled at how good her arms felt around him.

"I wish I was just a farmer again," he said finally. "I wish I didn't have to leave you."

"Then don't," she replied simply. "Stay home and take care of us." Her arms tightened around his waist and for a moment he considered giving in to what they both wanted: for him to quit, and devote himself to his family.

"No." He sighed heavily in resignation. "I can't." He shifted his gaze skyward, searching for the right grouping among the early stars, then extended an arm to a point just above the eastern horizon. "The Westland Congress has only four weeks of Joint Dominion with Eastland left before that starship will be here, in orbit around Pallatin. Oh, did I tell you we can see the *Levant* now? They're in full deceleration and we've been able to spot the flare."

She moved to his side, her right arm still around his waist, and followed his gaze into the night sky. "I hate them." Marabell's voice was a whisper.

He smiled. "You don't even know them."

They walked silently, hand in hand, back to the house where Amasee picked up Thad, tossing him gleefully into the air several times before giving him a hug and good-bye kiss.

"When you coming home, Daddy?" he asked.

"I'll be back next week, but only for a few days before I have to go again."

The boy considered the information, accepted it and turned back to the play set. "I'll wave from the top!" he called over his shoulder, then proceeded to scramble up the narrow bars of the play set until reaching a small, enclosed platform above the swings. "All right! I'm ready, Daddy!"

"Just a minute," Amasee called out, then turned back to his wife. They embraced a last time and kissed softly before walking together to the car. He lifted the door, glancing at the suitcase he'd tossed into the backseat earlier, and got in. There was a catch-all on the console between the seats and he carefully set the lilacs in it. "I'll call when I get to the capital."

She nodded and stood back from the car as he swung the door down and started the engine, the soft whine of the electric motor fading in intensity as the flywheel came up to speed. Amasee pulled the car slowly down the gravel drive that led to the main road to the city, careful to remember to wave to Thad, and flashed his lights in a silent good-bye to Marabell.

The main road was hardtop, and he accelerated rapidly on the smooth pavement. Darkness was closing in quickly now, and he dialed the car's headlights to their highest setting until he reached the connecting ramp to the intercity highway. Built shortly after the Quake, the new road was a straight throughway to the shuttle station on the south side of Dannen.

As he pulled the car into the leftmost lane, a chime sounded and an accompanying light blinked on the dashboard indicating that the magnetic guidance strips embedded in the road had linked to the car's system. "Dannen Station," he said aloud, "northbound terminal." He squeezed the steering wheel twice, locking the car into road guidance, and leaned back into the seat. The car accelerated smoothly.

It would take nearly an hour to get to the station and he

thought about napping, realizing that he'd get little rest once he arrived at the capital, but instead watched the cars in the noncontrol section of roadway at his right as they sped past the windows. When the glow of Dannen Station appeared through the windshield, still two kilometers distant, he idly watched the red and white lights of aircraft coming and going from the facility. Most were simple air traffic, but at one point he recognized the lights and exhaust signature of a spaceplane. Even at this distance the white-hot exhaust almost hurt to look at. As the spaceplane's trajectory became more vertical, the windshield vibrated and he felt the rolling thunder of the rocket motors kick in as the air-breathing jet engines shut down. It receded rapidly into the sky, but the night was cloudless and he was able to follow the pinpoints of its exhaust as they dwindled on its way into orbit.

He glanced at the clock on the dash. *Right on time,* he thought. The plane was the daily shuttle ferrying personnel and supplies to a starship in orbit, a very special ship. The *Thunder Child* was among the fastest class of starships Pallatin constructed, but its mission would be diplomatic, not exploratory. The diplomacy carried aboard her was backed with more than diplomats, however: Instead of the latest scientific equipment Pallatin's researchers could devise, the ship fairly bristled with weaponry. In less than three weeks it would leave orbit to meet the Imperial starship that even now was decelerating toward Pallatin.

Amasee Niles, as Speaker of the Westland Congress—together with his Eastland counterpart—would be aboard the *Thunder Child* when it left.

He followed the lights until they grew too dim to see, then, squeezing the steering wheel twice to disengage the road link, pulled the car back into the manual lane. The automatic system would have taken him directly into the terminal, but he felt the sudden need to *do* something, anything, to keep his hands—and his mind—occupied. Despite his best efforts, however, one thought forced itself upon him, against his will, just as it had time and again in the last months of final preparation for the starship's coming:

Yes, I hate them, too.

Javas' message string was different from the many thousands that awaited Adela when, still a month away from Pallatin, she awoke from nearly twenty years of cryosleep. She had put through a worm program, of course, to sort and categorize each of the strings according to importance, subject matter, timeliness and any of dozens of other criteria that would allow her to better handle the sheer mass of information demanding her attention. Many didn't need to be addressed for some time, and could wait in a holding file until later. Messages that did not require her personal attention at all, according to the explicit criteria she'd encoded into the worm, were rerouted automatically to other members of her project team. It was their job—indeed, their whole reason for accompanying her on this trip—to handle the items related to her work while she was involved in the diplomacy of the mission or while she was in cryosleep. Still other messages had been outdated years ago and were simply purged from the waiting queue entirely.

It was the queue coded as "personal" that concerned her now, and even among them the worm program had arranged all the strings in order of importance. Except one. The worm had kicked the string to the top of the queue against the criteria that she'd carefully emplaced: her own programming superseded by Imperial code.

Adela de Montgarde stirred uneasily in her chair, experiencing both anxious anticipation to view the holo from Javas, and dread as to its contents. Why had he separated this string from the others? There were several other personal message strings from him; why had this one been given imperative-to-read-first status?

"System." Her voice was soft in the confines of her private suite aboard the huge ship, and it carried with it a tone she didn't much care for, a tone that told more about her feelings just now than she wanted to admit to herself.

"Ma'am?" the room system responded. The nondescript efficiency of the voice, different from the softly feminine voice of the system back on Luna, was at once annoying and reassuring.

"Please put a code one interrupt on all incoming messages until further notice." There was a confirming chirp from the system, indicating that she wouldn't be disturbed for anything short of a shipwide emergency. "Display personal string one-A, message one." The corner of the room brightened, changing into what she recognized as Javas' study at the family estate on Earth. He sat in one of the leather chairs before his old wooden desk.

The large double doors behind him had been opened, and she could see the rolling Kentucky hillside spreading majestically into the distance. He looked worn, older, and she found it necessary to remind herself that this recording had been made only a few years after her departure from Sol system. *How much older must he look now?* she wondered as the sixteen-year-old recording coalesced before her. She wished, not for the first time, that she could have stayed behind at his side.

Her attention had been immediately, emotionally, drawn to his face when the image appeared, and it wasn't until he shifted slightly in the chair before speaking that she became aware of the compact, blanket-wrapped bundle in his arms. One corner of the receiving blanket had been pulled aside, revealing a tiny, peaceful face. The infant was asleep, its fresh, pink features appearing incongruously small in the man's strong arms. A thick mass of dark hair, in a shade that closely matched her own, stood out in marked contrast to Javas' blond hair.

But Adela could see—perhaps in the man's eyes or in the way his arms seemed to naturally enfold the baby in his arms—that the two were connected, bonded in a way that she was not. Bonded in a way she could only long to experience.

"Adela, my love, we have a son. His name is Eric, after your father. I regret that I was not able to discuss this with you and hope you will understand my reasons. If not, then perhaps it is your forgiveness that I . . ."

"Pause." Adela stared in fascination at the frozen image before her, unable even to determine exactly what she was feeling at this moment. She hadn't known what to expect of this string, but was this news more, or less, disturbing; more, or less, surprising than anything she could have anticipated? Was she angry with him for having done this, or joyful for the miracle that had produced this small part of herself, this proof of the love she felt for a man more than sixteen years distant in space, and forty years distant in time itself? Adela shook her head in frustrated confusion, pushing any decision she might make concerning her feelings away for now—much in the same way the worm had pushed the nonimmediate messages further and further down the queue for later consideration. There was one thing, however, of which she was certain: The child was beautiful.

She opened her mouth to speak, to restart the playback, and

was shocked at the croaked whisper that came out. The room system itself had not been able to pick up the word, and beeped in confusion. Adela cleared her throat.

"Resume playback, please."

". . . should hope for," he said, finishing the sentence begun earlier. He stirred again in the chair, distracted from the recorder lens as a tiny arm came up from the blanket. The infant had been awakened by his father's voice, she saw, and the little eyes blinked at the bright light streaming through the double doors into the Emperor's study. The baby didn't seem pleased, and wrinkled his brow in dislike at the intrusion into whatever thoughts had been going through its dreams, but did not cry. Javas stood, cradling the bundle protectively in his strong arms as he almost imperceptibly rocked the infant. "I won't go into my reasons just now; I'll save the lengthy explanation for the following recording in this string. But I wanted . . . to share this with you first." He stood there for several moments, trying to think of something else to add and, although he looked as though he were about to say something, stopped when a tiny hand reached out and grazed his cheek. Whatever he was going to say was instantly lost as he smiled and lowered his eyes to the infant before silently commanding the recording to end. The image dimmed, then faded from view.

"Shall I display the next message, ma'am?"

Adela didn't answer at first, and sat staring quietly at the now-dark corner of the room. She had discussed this possibility with Javas before leaving for Pallatin and had accepted, at the time, the implications. *So why can't I tell what I'm feeling right now?* she wondered, and fell heavily back into the cushioning firmness of the chair. The gravity in her quarters—as in the quarters of nearly everyone on the ship who'd be visiting the planet—had been set to Pallatin-normal, allowing her an opportunity to adjust to the 1.2 g environment below. Her day was only half begun, and already she felt exhausted.

"Shall I display the next message, ma'am?" the system repeated.

"Uh, no," she replied. "Replay previous recording."

The corner glowed again as the message began once more. She let it play through till the end, waiting for the moment when Javas had stood just before ending the recording. "Pause, and mark." The image froze. "Resume." The playback restarted, and continued through his silent command to end the recording. "Pause, and mark," she repeated just before the image began to fade. "System. Edit, please."

"Ready."

"Loop and smooth the marked segment, please."

"Ready."

"Playback."

The computer had edited the recording, smoothly blending Javas' movements from the moment where he smiled and turned his eyes to the infant and the end of the recording itself, looping the segment into one continuous image.

She rose then and approached the holographic projection before her, stopping mere centimeters from the lifelike image as she looked into the infant's face. She wanted more than anything to hold, to touch her son and would have gladly given up the entire project and her role in it for just a moment alone with Javas and their child. She reached out, her fingers passing through the image, and noticed something she hadn't seen from her previous vantage point when she'd first viewed the recording: A happy, toothless smile had spread over the baby's face as it stared up into Javas' eyes. Adela stepped through the image itself and looked down into the baby's face from almost the same angle Javas had when he'd made the recording sixteen years earlier.

Although she knew better, she tried to force from her mind the fact that the baby seemingly looking up at her was now, at this exact moment back on Earth, a young adult.

"Eric," she whispered, and felt the corners of her mouth turn up in the beginnings of a smile that quickly broadened of its own accord into a joyous grin.

EIGHTEEN

Commander Montero, captain of the Imperial starship *Levant*, droned on, giving his delivery of the required precontact briefing as much excitement as he did most of his lectures. Which was to say that a schoolboy's recitation of a memorized spelling list would contain more spark. Even the constantly changing images on the holoscreen behind him failed to enliven the briefing. The boredom hanging like a dark cloud over the room was compounded by the fact that virtually everything Montero said came from the mission data stick that everyone attending the briefing had already been required to review anyway. With only a week to go before the rendezvous with the Pallatin ship, even the busiest member of the mission would have had time to read the file. Twice.

Only a few of those in the room were actually part of the ship's crew; most of the members of the diplomatic contact team were nonmilitary personnel, like Adela, and had little experience with the details and rigors of a military briefing. Although a few questions were asked and some clarifications were made to the contents of the data stick, most of the information was being given only because protocol required that a formal briefing be held.

There were more than fifty seats in the briefing room, nearly all of them filled, making it somewhat easier for those who had only recently come out of cryosleep to take the opportunity to nod off if they slouched in their seats just right and hid behind those in front of them. Adela scanned the rows around her, easily picking out several people who couldn't have been out of the tank more than a few days, and wondered idly if she looked that bad when she came out of cryo. *May as well get used to it,* she thought, nudging the person next to her with an elbow to quiet his snoring. *When this project is finally over, I'll have logged more years of cryosleep than everyone in this room—maybe even the ship—combined.* It wasn't a pleasant thought, realizing that she would outlive most of the people in the briefing room. But with only a few exceptions, these people here were strangers and meant little to her, but for the important role they might play in the mission to Pallatin. And *that* realization disturbed her even more. *Just when did I stop caring about other people?* She lowered her head and sighed loudly enough that those around her might have heard if the crewman next to her hadn't started snoring again.

The real reason for her feelings was clear, she knew, and had been for some time. It wasn't that she cared less for others, it was that she cared more for something else: the project itself. It wasn't more important than her life; it *was* her life. After all, isn't that why Rihana Valtane's words still echoed in her mind as clearly as they had that day in her office back on Luna some twenty-odd years earlier? "You will lose him, you know," Rihana had said, "just as I did."

Even now, Adela saw the woman's wicked smile, heard the amused satisfaction that laughed silently at her from behind the truth in Rihana's words: When the Pallatin problem was resolved and she returned to Earth, Javas would be more than forty years older than when she left. Eric would be a grown man. And after the next period of cryosleep? And the next? *Damn you,* she cried out silently. *God damn you for being right.* Adela felt her lips tighten and noticed that her hands had balled into fists in her lap.

She forced herself to calm down, pushed the thoughts of losing Javas and Eric out of her mind and concentrated instead on Montero's lecture.

". . . the major landmass is divided longitudinally by an enormous fault system," he was saying, absently pulling on one corner of his thick brown moustache, "consisting of high ridges thrust up through the planetary crust and deep canyons stretching hundreds of kilometers. As on the rest of the planet, this fault system is very active, and weekly, even daily, tremors are not uncommon. The entire planet is highly active tectonically, a condition caused by the planet's relatively young age, as well as its higher gravity and vast amounts of heavy metal deposits. According to Imperial records, there has been some effort by the citizens of the eastern portion of the continent to reconfigure the entire planet's coordinate system based on this fault line, making it, in effect, longitude zero, which would add an emotional and psychological division to the continent as well. It is not surprising that the Eastland natives are the most adamant about not wishing to cooperate with the Empire. The natives call this major fault 'Arroyo,' and many of their location names are based on the given fault name even when the intent seems to refer instead to the proper longitude. Terms and phrases like 'dawnside Arroyo' and 'one hundred kilometers west Arroyo' are quite common, although the actual significance of the name itself is unclear. The major cities are separated—"

"Is there water in this fault system?" Adela called out. She wasn't sure why she had felt the need to speak up just now. Perhaps it was the lingering anger from her thoughts of Rihana Valtane moments before. Or the cavalier attitude with which Montero seemed to view their entire purpose here. More likely, the underlying reason was a combination of both.

Commander Montero stared open-mouthed at her, the look on his face frozen somewhere between surprised anger at being interrupted and frantic indecision at not being able to answer her question. It didn't help that everyone in the room not asleep was now staring at him, waiting for him to respond to the Emperor's chosen representative. He forced a smile, then, "Say again?"

Adela leaned back in her seat and felt everyone shift their attention back to her. "The fault system. Does water periodically fill portions of it?" Ignoring the stares of the others at the briefing, she crossed her arms and waited for him to reply.

"Well . . . They, uh . . ." Montero keyed the info screen mounted in his podium, searching for the information. It took a few moments before he found what he was looking for. "Our reports indicate that portions of the fault do hydrate from time to time." Another pause as he read. "As the edges of the major plates running the length of the fault rise and fall with tectonic activity, both the northern and southern seas occasionally flood into the depression caused by the seismic tremors. According to what we've been able to glean from our probing of their libraries, the fault has, on two occasions since Pallatin was colonized, been a continuous waterway from the Grande Sea on the north to the Gulf of Caldonia to the south. Although subsequent activity drained most of the water after each occurrence."

"That's almost exactly what the word means." Several of those attending pivoted and gazed at her with renewed interest and she addressed them, rather than Montero, as she spoke. "It's an Old Earth term from an area of the North American continent called American Southwest. It refers to a gully or trench that, while normally dry, occasionally fills with water."

Montero cleared his throat loudly. "Thank you, Dr. Montgarde." There was just the hint of sarcasm behind his gratitude.

Adela had to remind herself as she listened to Montero resume his rote delivery that the experienced Imperial officer had been hand-chosen by Supreme Commander Fain for his military and spacing abilities, and not his outgoing personality.

"As I started to say before, the cities are widely separated. The more densely settled population centers, those with populations ranging from twenty-five thousand on up to four hundred thousand, are frequently surrounded by smaller communities—mostly agricultural or light industry in nature—that continue to spring up as the population spreads out. However, most of these main 'hub cities' are separated from each other by many hundreds of kilometers, and are sometimes connected by a single main road or air traffic only. This is not unusual. In fact, we've seen that on many colony worlds it takes centuries for the open spaces between population centers to 'fill up,' for lack of a better word."

"That's not always true," Adela put in. "They don't always 'fill up.' How about Australia?" Again, all eyes turned to her.

Again, Montero's face reddened, but more in mild impatience this time than in frustration. "How about where?"

She stood, addressing the room at large. "Australia is a continent in the southern hemisphere of Earth, settled and colonized much the same way we bring planets into the Hundred Worlds. But most of Australia has an incredibly harsh environment, and although many of its cities became metropolises they still were separated by tremendous distances with little between them even at the height of its population in the late twenty-third century. Pallatin is the same; although you're beginning to see individual settlements in the intervening spaces between centers, the rough environment here—the hot summers and almost constant seismic activity—will most likely keep this world on the same level as Australia. I doubt seriously that Pallatin will ever 'fill up.' "

Montero's jaw tightened as if he were gritting his teeth, which he probably was. He was aware of her place of importance, not only to the mission but to the Emperor himself, and he spoke in carefully modulated tones as he addressed Adela. "I fail to see what Old Earth history has to do with our current mission here."

Adela had enjoyed baiting him, prodding at his pompous nature, but every bit of pleasure drained from her at the remark. "Commander Montero, everything we do here relates to Earth. Our whole purpose for *being* here is because of Earth's importance." She retook her seat before continuing, taking in the others in the briefing room as she went on. "The more all of us know about Earth, the better the chances of our success here. Everything I've talked about is available in the ship's files, of course, easily accessible to anyone with an interest in learning more. In fact, I'll be happy to give the code numbers for the files to anyone who—"

"Dr. Montgarde—" The sudden timbre of his voice silenced her immediately, and several of the uniformed people around her instantly—if not involuntarily—sat straighter in their chairs. It was obvious that while Montero may not enjoy protocol-required briefings, he still was in command aboard the ship. "Not everyone on board this ship is as convinced at the necessity of saving your precious Earth as you." He lowered his gaze on her, one eyebrow arched, and a look in his eyes told her more than his words that he was here because he was ordered to be. It became clear to Adela that his interests concerned forcing Pallatin back into line as a member of the Hundred Worlds, and not as a means of furthering the project.

She leaned back in her seat and tried to read the faces on those around her. Who among them agreed with Montero, and who believed that Emperor Nicholas' dream was a worthy goal? She had no way of telling, but decided that until she found out just who was on her side it might be better not to antagonize Montero further.

"The politics of the two halves of the continent," he went on as if nothing had happened, "seem as ideologically divided as their geography. Those in Eastland remain as uncooperative as they were at the time of Emperor Nicholas' address. Those in Westland, however, appear to be leaning toward a normalization of relations with the Hundred Worlds. This, after our long voyage, is a pleasant surprise . . ." He continued his briefing, taking questions as they came, until finishing up a half hour later.

Leaving the holoscreen set on a view of the planet itself, he dismissed the meeting. The uniformed members of the team snapped smartly to attention as he left the room without a word, either to her or to anyone else.

Several people asked politely for the code numbers for the Old Earth history files before they left. As she spoke briefly to them, Adela got the impression that many of the contact team cared no more for Montero or his ways than she did, although she had spent so little time out of the tank on this trip that she hadn't gotten to know any of them well enough that they actually said anything specific to her in that regard. As to how the crew members scattered around the briefing room felt about their commanding officer, she could only guess.

A chime sounded, indicating that the ship's mess had opened, and the room cleared quickly. As she made her way to the starboard corridor a uniformed crewman approached her. Not unhandsome, he was of medium build with dark, almost black skin, brown eyes that peered intensely out from beneath a thick, low brow, and wavy black hair that, like many of his crewmates, was pulled back and tied into a short ponytail that just touched the high collar of his uniform. The tabs on his collar indicated that he was a Lieutenant. He appeared to be in his mid-thirties— but then, so did she. "Dr. Montgarde, may I walk with you for a few minutes?"

She knew little about him, other than the fact that he was a specialist in Imperial law, and that he had spent only half the trip in cryosleep. She had met him at one of the pre-embarkation meetings, but had spoken to him only momentarily and couldn't remember his name. "Certainly. Lieutenant . . . ?"

"Woorunmarra."

"Lieutenant Woorunmarra, of course. I'm sorry. I'm usually better at names."

"Don't apologize," he said, smiling, flashing very white teeth, "it's not an easy one to remember." As he spoke, she tried to place the odd accent. She'd heard many accents in the last several decades as she traveled from planet to planet among the Hundred Worlds since the beginning of the project. But this one seemed stranger than most: harsh, guttural, and yet, each word perfectly formed and melodically enunciated. "I wanted to thank you, back there," he went on, nodding over his shoulder in the direction of the briefing room.

"Thank me?" Adela responded, not understanding. "Thank me for what?"

"Perhaps I should explain. I'm an Earther. I signed on with the Imperial forces when the Empire began its resettlement on Luna." He stopped, looked at her. "Not everyone on Earth is against the Emperor's plan. I wanted to do what I could to help, if only in a small way, so I enlisted." They resumed walking, taking the corridor leading to the officer's mess.

"But what did I do that—"

He silenced her with a raised hand. "You know Earth, spoke well of her." He stopped, a smile spreading across his face. "And you spoke of my homeland as though you knew it."

"Homeland . . . You're from Australia?"

"I am Aborigine. My people, the Arunta, are among the oldest civilizations on Earth, and the only people who remain unchanged."

"Unchanged?" Adela looked at him dubiously, and without talking down to him, said in a friendly tone of voice, "You're an officer aboard one of the Empire's fastest starships, approaching a planet sixteen and a half light-years away from Australia. I'd say that qualifies as change."

The Lieutenant smiled again, the sound of his laughter as melodic as his words. "You take the word too literally, Dr. Montgarde. I speak of not changin' *here*"—he lightly touched his forehead—"and *here.*" He placed the palm of his hand over his heart. "While Earth grew, and her population went out, first to the solar system and then the stars, her people became different. Their values, their lives. Sometimes, I think their very souls changed. But it was different for us. In the outback, our lives continued as they always did. The family group was always central. The land. The sky. All a part of the Dream Lines and at the heart of who we are. Do you understand?"

"I think so." They reached the entrance to the officer's mess and stood to one side of the doorway as they spoke. There was little traffic in the corridor now; the two of them had taken their time and most of the officers were already inside.

"But then the world changed back," he said, tilting his head.

There was a distant look on his face, as though his eyes were watching the scene he described so very far away. "Most of Earth's people left, and those who remained returned to many of the same old values the Aborigine tribes never abandoned."

"I've studied Earth a great deal," Adela said, "but you're obviously much more than a simple tribesman."

"Ah, that." Again he laughed. There was a long, cushioned seating area that ran for ten meters on each side of the mess entrance and he indicated they should sit.

He seemed so at ease with himself, so satisfied with his life. Further, his pleasant manner was infectious, and she found herself finally letting go of the anger and frustration she had felt at the briefing.

"Many of my people are educated; many are not. It's an individual decision. But understand something: Even those who go away from the tribe for very long periods of time return to the outback unchanged. After my graduation from the University at Canberra, I returned home and it was as if I'd never left. My belongin's and city clothing put away, I was in the bush hunting turkey and roo with my brothers within an hour after my arrival. Even though my brothers could barely read and write, it was as if there were no differences among us in the outback. In our home."

"I would love to see your home one day."

He looked at her, his head cocked to one side, and nodded. "Yes. I think you'd like it." He looked away suddenly, his features at once serious. "We have a legend that tells of those who protect us. It is said that they're responsible for keepin' my people whole, and that they'll be with us in the Dream Time, to keep us as one in the time of fire. We called them the Sky Heroes."

Adela was fascinated by his tale and motioned for him to continue.

"It is well known, even among many of my people, what will happen to the Sun—we have the broadcasts from the nets—but it is foretold that the Sky Heroes will protect our way of life."

"Is this a . . ." She hesitated, not wanting to offend him. "Is this a religion, a matter of faith?"

He turned to her again, his face less serious. "For many Aborigine, yes. For others, it's only legend and campfire stories for the young. For me?" He smiled and shrugged his shoulders. "Who knows where legend stops and fact begins, ay? But ask yourself somethin': Who's goin' to stop the Sun from dying? Who's goin' to stop the great fire?"

"I'm afraid I don't follow you."

He took one of her hands in his. The skin of his hands was rough and calloused, but his touch was warm, strong. "You are. Your scientists, your star captains, your mighty ships. Come to Earth to help us remain whole."

Adela nodded in understanding. "We are the Sky Heroes," she said softly, feeling not a little embarrassment. "Thank you for sharing this with me."

Again he shrugged, and released her hand. "To be honest, I needed to share it with someone. You see, many of those in my settlement—who believe the old legends—feel that I've gone to join the Sky Heroes, that I've become one of them. Most know I'm on a starship, that it's nothin' more than an extension of the same technology that gives us refrigerators, electric lights and communication. But the others— It's a big responsibility for me."

Yes, she thought. *It is a very big responsibility.*

Amasee Niles stood outside Kip Salera's cabin, contemplating whether the course he was about to pursue would violate Dominion protocol. No, that wasn't true, he reminded himself—he already *knew* that meeting Salera in an unofficial capacity in this manner was a breach of procedure.

Despite his best efforts, they had barely spoken since *Thunder Child* had left Pallatin, and on the rare occasion when they did talk directly to one another it was only with the most officious manner during meals or briefings where others were present. But with only days remaining before their rendezvous with the Imperial ship, Amasee felt the need to try to establish at least some small amount of personal rapport with the Eastland representative.

He cleared his throat, the sound echoing softly in the deserted passageway, and rapped on the door.

"It's open, Niles," came a muffled reply from inside. "Come in."

The door slid open, revealing a comfortable stateroom that

was—although oddly mirror-imaged—identical in both design and furnishings to his own quarters on the port side of the ship. Salera was at his desk on the far side of the room, his back to him, and made a point of ignoring Amasee as he shuffled several folders and data sticks into a zippered case. The desk was next to the bed, and Amasee could see more than a few identical folders scattered over the bedspread. The door closed behind him, and he waited patiently inside the doorway for the man to finish before speaking.

"Be with you in a moment, Niles," he said, still without turning. Salera leaned the case against the side of the desk, then pivoted about in the chair and proceeded to gather the folders from the bed, stacking them one atop the other in a growing pile placed to one corner of the desk. He glanced up once as he reached for a folder on the side of the bed opposite him, meeting Amasee's eyes for the first time since he'd entered. "Where are my manners? Please, be seated." He nodded to a seating group on the other side of the stateroom and continued stacking, selecting each folder one by one in accordance with whatever order of importance he was assigning them.

"You knew it was me." In spite of the heavy sarcasm obvious in Salera's comment about manners—and in spite of the distrust and misgivings he felt for his Dominion counterpart—Amasee kept his own delivery light and noncommittal.

"I expected you, you know. You Westlanders are nothing if not predictable." He finished his stacking and, picking up a tall glass from the desk, sat in the sofa across from Amasee. He took a long drink from the glass, rattling ice cubes as he lowered it, and made no offer of a similar refreshment to his guest. "Besides, you knocked on the door, instead of ringing. Your Westland farmer's habits seem very hard to break."

Amasee shrugged, ignoring the remark. Since becoming a Dominion representative, he had grown used to the ridicule often directed at Westland traditions. Even small customs like knocking, considered a simple act of politeness at home, seemed to delight Salera and his fellow representatives to the Joint Dominion.

"Anyway," Salera went on, "I would have been disappointed had you not made an attempt to influence me before our meeting with the invaders."

Amasee bristled at the word but, knowing that the Eastlander was making an obvious attempt to get under his skin, controlled his response. "I don't like that term," he said carefully, "any more than our respective Congresses do."

"But then, we are not meeting in Joint Dominion, are we?" Salera finished his drink, never taking his eyes off him, and leaned back in the sofa. He hung his arm over the armrest, swirling the ice annoyingly around the bottom of the glass dangling loosely in his fingertips. "And if I prefer, in the privacy of my own room, to speak of these Imperial 'diplomats' as I feel they really are, then what difference does it make what words I use?" He paused a beat, then let all traces of amused sarcasm disappear as he added, "Unless, of course, you wish to declare an official inter-Congress meeting between us. If that is your intention, farmer, then our recorders should be summoned from their respective cabins, and remain present for as long as we have anything important to say to one another." Salera sat motionless, head tilted questioningly, and waited. "Shall I call them?"

This is a waste of time, Amasee thought, *and this man is a fool.* The other man could read the anger on his face, he knew, and he opened his mouth to speak, but thought better of it and swallowed hard, forcing his anger down and carefully choosing his next words.

"No. It's not necessary to call them." He crossed his legs, assuming a relaxed pose, and noted with a bit of surprise that he felt better, less agitated, now that their initial hostilities were in the open. "I intend to consider anything we say to each other in this room off the record."

"I thought so." He rose, crossing to the stateroom's wet bar. "Since this appears to be a purely social call, then, perhaps I should be a bit more sociable. May I offer you something?"

Amasee nodded, and the two chatted idly for the minute or two it took for him to prepare the drinks. They talked of nothing consequential, limiting their discussion to mundane banter—living arrangements on the ship, the quality of the food, speculation on the evening's entertainment programming—and Amasee noticed that Salera's manner changed slightly as they spoke, as if the Eastlander had also been hoping for an opportunity to meet in private. Their mutual animosity remained, but was, for the moment, being set aside by unspoken agreement between them.

"I'm not here to attempt to change your mind," Amasee began once Salera returned to his place on the sofa. "We both know that would be a pointless waste of time. However, I feel it is absolutely imperative that the Imperial"—he hesitated, not wanting to use a word the other might consider an attempt at agitation—"representatives be allowed to attend a session of Joint Dominion without undue influence. From either of us."

"Meaning?"

"You know exactly what I mean, Kip! We can't afford to antagonize them at this point."

"I disagree. It matters little to me if they feel antagonized. They already know how we feel about their interference. Have for years. What possible difference could it make to reaffirm our beliefs?"

Amasee nodded, granting at least part of the point he had tried to make. "Yes, but that knowledge is outdated by decades, and you know it. Things have changed on Pallatin, attitudes have changed, just in the time it's taken them to travel here from Sol."

"Maybe attitudes have changed in the Westland Congress," Salera said, "but not in ours, as you discovered in Joint Dominion. We still want no part of the Hundred Worlds, and frankly, I intend to remind them of that fact as soon as we rendezvous with their starship." He sat back, as determined in his decision as Amasee himself was.

Amasee nodded again, smiling in resignation at their mutual obstinance. "I expected as much." He sighed heavily, setting his glass down on the end table, then leaned forward on his knees and clasped his hands before him. He regarded his counterpart with a look of deadly seriousness, adding, "However, please understand that if you do, I've been authorized by my Congress to pledge full, immediate allegiance to the Hundred Worlds on the spot."

Salera's eyes widened in surprised shock as he realized the implications. "But the Westland Congress never discussed this with us in Joint Dominion!" he sputtered, instantly on his feet. "We agreed, *voted,* that any decision to accept the Empire would be made on a planetwide basis!"

"I know." Amasee lowered his head, his voice taking on a

matter-of-fact tone. "We never welcomed Imperial intervention any more than Eastland has, but we've always had doubts about severing Pallatin completely from the Empire because of the genetic aspects of a total separation. That's even more important now that drift has been proven. We need to check the rate of drift or we won't be able to map the code; and without the mapping, we leave ourselves wide open to new disease."

Salera shook his head. "We considered that and rejected it. Any drift that is likely to occur is insignificant."

"Maybe so, and maybe the threat is more imagined than real. But there's a vastly simpler reason for staying in the Hundred Worlds." He stood, paced the room nervously before continuing. "We changed, Kip, after the Quake; we've been trying to tell you people that for years. Without your help, Westland might never have been able to rebuild, much less advance. It could not have been done alone. We realize now that Pallatin needs the Empire, just as we needed Eastland after the Quake." He stopped pacing and turned to the Eastlander.

Salera stared impassively at him, his face an unrevealing mask. His initial shock and anger at Amasee's threat were obviously gone, but he kept well hidden whatever feelings were going through him now. "Big words from someone who wasn't even here when the Quake hit," he said emotionlessly.

There had been no background noise in the room—no music, no information feed, nothing—but the cabin seemed to fall into an even colder silence at the man's words. Salera stared into his eyes, and although he had certainly meant what he'd said, behind the cold stare was a look of regret at having said it.

"Am . . . I'm sorry, that was uncalled-for."

"No," Amasee replied, surprised at himself that he felt no anger at the remark. He dug his hands deep into his pockets and approached the other man. "No, you're right. But the fact remains that Westland has come to this decision, and that I've been authorized to ally with the Empire if you attempt in any way to antagonize or threaten the Imperial representatives before they've had a chance to appear in Joint Dominion."

He left the threat hanging there, unchallenged, and both men knew the unofficial meeting had come to an end. Salera turned wordlessly and Amasee followed him to the door, but stopped when the man looked back at him before opening it.

"They're only one starship," he said, almost pleading. "Together, standing as one, Pallatin might have turned them away."

"Maybe," Amasee agreed. "But our philosophies are still too different, yours and ours, and once the Imperial threat was gone we would have drawn even further apart than we are now. And Pallatin would ultimately fall."

Amasee reached past Salera and thumbed the control switch in the doorjamb, and silently left the stateroom.

NINETEEN

B y agreement—reached more through mutual distrust than diplomacy—the two ships came to a halt at the outside limit of their immediate firing range, full shields raised, and remained dead in space until boarding parties could be exchanged.

The Imperial party was immediately outnumbered and disarmed by the security forces aboard *Thunder Child* the moment they disembarked their transfer shuttle. The Imperial forces put up no resistance whatever, nor had they been ordered to.

Meanwhile, aboard the Imperial starship, the boarding party from the Pallatin ship was similarly received the instant their shuttle docked and the mating seal opened. No resistance was offered by the Pallatins, no overt force used by the starship crew.

Pallatin's level of shield technology, laughably inferior to the Empire's, might have allowed the *Levant* to easily blast the colonial ship from space, and the rumor that Commander Montero might do just that as a demonstration of Imperial force had been circulating among the crew for days. Surely an overt display of Imperial power would bring the upstart colony into line, they thought, followed by an immediate turnaround for home. But then, suppose the advancing ship was little more than an enormous explosive device with only enough crew and thrust to get it into position, waiting for just such a response from the Empire?

Likewise, the *Thunder Child* might manage to destroy the larger Imperial visitor, or disable it in space. More than a few of the passengers aboard her thought longingly of the possibility, thinking that such an action would say *"Leave us alone"* more loudly than any words. Of course, there was no way to tell that this envoy from the Hundred Worlds was not intended as a decoy ship, with the genuine—fully armed—Imperial starship following a light-month behind the first.

The inspection took nearly two days. While the true extent of the firepower of each ship was kept from the respective boarding parties, each captain was ultimately assured that the opposite vessel was what it had been purported to be.

Finally, satisfied that the other was responding honestly, each captain ordered his boarding party to return.

Another full day passed, technicians from each ship carefully monitoring the other for the slightest movement or hint of aggression, while debriefing of the boarding parties took place.

Still another day passed as diplomatic discussions and agreements were conducted between the commanding officers of each ship. Then yet another as final preparations were made.

A week after they met in space, the *Levant* and *Thunder Child* finally turned toward Pallatin on a heading that would carry them into orbital insertion.

Commander Montero breathed a sigh of relief once they were safely, and without incident, under way. But somewhere deep in the back of his mind was just the slightest disappointment that the entire matter might have been settled at their first meeting, sending a resounding message to every one of the frontier worlds that to go against the Empire was a useless gesture. Fain had given him the authority, after all, to act as he saw best. Montero pushed the nagging thought out of his mind.

He had no way of knowing, of course, that the captain of the *Thunder Child* felt almost exactly the same conflicting mixture of relief—and regret—that he did.

TWENTY

"**P**allatin is not the same world it was," said the man who had identified himself as Niles. "We ask only that you meet with us in Joint Dominion before deciding on a course of action that would, of necessity, be based on outdated information."

Montero sat straight in his chair, as he had throughout this meeting, and nodded pensively. "I am willing to listen." His demeanor was considerably different from that shown at the several briefings that had taken place in the four weeks since Adela had come out of cryosleep. In those lectures, he was merely dictating a list of facts to bored personnel as a simple act of shipboard protocol. Here, however, there was something at stake, not only for the sake of the successful completion of the mission, but it was clear to Adela that there was a certain amount of personal pride connected to the seriousness with which he conducted himself at this meeting with the Pallatin representatives. His lack of communication skills at briefings was more than counterbalanced by the adept nature in which he handled the diplomatic needs of his command.

Adela herself had little role to play during this session. Although she was nominally Emperor Javas' official Imperial representative, it was Montero who had jurisdiction here—and the final decision as to their next course of action. Her opportunity to speak would come later, she knew, so she sat quietly, taking in everything she could about the two men from the planet below them. They, along with Captain Thommas of the *Thunder Child,* had called for this informal meeting to take place once they'd established orbit around the planet. The three Pallatins sat at one end of the long conference table while Montero; Nelon, his First Officer; a representative of the Imperial Council of Academicians named Yuleeva; and Lieutenant Billy Woorunmarra sat with her at the other. Like her, the others remained silent unless asked by Montero for their input.

"What my esteemed counterpart is saying is quite true." Representative Salera, Speaker of the Eastland Congress, smiled warmly, glancing in polite deference to the man sitting next to him at the table. "The Quake not only caused major damage to a large portion of the infrastructure west of Arroyo, but several of the shipyards were affected, some extensively. Notably, the facilities at Blankensport, Taw and South Passage remain closed to this day; others, including two Eastland yards closest to the epicenter, are still not operating at full capacity."

Representative Niles nodded in agreement. "It has become necessary to cut back or delay delivery on several contracts. Other contracts have been withdrawn, with customers applying to suppliers on other worlds." The Speaker of the Westland Congress shrugged, extending his palms outward on the tabletop. "You see, Commander Montero, so much has changed since you left Sol for Pallatin. While my world's representatives originally refused all cooperation at the time your project was originally announced—openly denounced the Hundred Worlds, in fact—our circumstances have changed such that it is now a matter of extreme impracticality, rather than mere defiance, that makes honoring the requests made by the Emperor so many years ago a difficult task for us."

"Am I to understand, then," asked Montero simply, "that the Joint Dominion of Pallatin no longer opposes the Emperor of the Hundred Worlds?" His hands before him on the table, he leaned forward on his elbows and looked into the face of each of the men in turn.

Adela followed his gaze, attempting to read on their faces what wasn't being said aloud. Captain Thommas remained impassive, as he had throughout the discussion; clearly his duty was to convey and escort the two official planetary representatives, leaving all matters of diplomacy to them, and he made no attempt to offer anything in response to Montero's question. Speaker Niles, likewise, did not reply immediately, but turned instead to his counterpart. Salera, however, was visibly agitated by Montero's blunt query. His large eyes widened, darting occasionally to his two companions, and he seemed to wrestle with a response. Adela noted that Montero missed none of it, and raised her respect for the Commander as he waited patiently for an answer. Salera opened his mouth to speak, but hesitated, then started to reply when Speaker Niles interrupted.

"While it is true that Speaker Salera and I represent the Joint Dominion, I think I speak for both of us when I say that we would prefer not to influence you with our own opinions at this time."

Salera seemed at once unburdened by the remark, and the look of anxiety in his expressive eyes disappeared immediately. "I agree with Speaker Niles' assessment of the situation." He leaned back in his chair and addressed Montero directly. "It would be better, if you agree to accept our invitation to attend Joint Dominion, that you come with no biases caused by anything we might say." He looked questioningly at his counterpart, an eyebrow raised as if to ask, "Was that satisfactory?"

Representative Niles nodded politely, looking unmistakably pleased at what the other man had said.

Montero smiled in understanding. "I concur. For my part, I am willing to keep an open mind in this." He stood, signaling that the meeting had concluded, and added, "Captain Thommas, Speaker Salera, Speaker Niles; thank you for your time and your candid remarks concerning the status of Pallatin in relation to the rest of the Hundred Worlds. I await your formal invitation." He smiled again, then bowed slightly.

They returned the formal gesture and left immediately. Montero spoke briefly to the academician before dismissing him, then said a few words to his officers, who followed him out of the room. They didn't go far, however, and stood talking just outside the open door.

Adela paid little attention to them, her thoughts still on the discussion just concluded.

They were fascinating men.

It was obvious to Adela by the way they had spoken to one another that there was no love lost between the two representatives, but each radiated a strength and comradeship—even in those subject areas in which they clearly disagreed—that displayed a great sense of both pride and honor at what Pallatin had accomplished. If the rest of their people were as strong-willed as were these two, even in disagreement, then the mission to gain Pallatin's support would not be as simple a matter as using force.

What was it Speaker Salera wasn't saying? she wondered. Something had passed between the two of them at the conclusion of the meeting, Adela knew, but what? It was obvious to her, and certainly to Montero as well, that he was holding something back.

She was no closer to figuring out what it was an hour later when, back in her cabin, her thoughts were disturbed by the door chime.

"Yes?" she called, activating the room system. "Who is it?"

"Only me, Doctor." She recognized Lieutenant Woorunmarra's melodic voice. "May I talk to you?"

"Open." She crossed the short distance to the door, picking up a notepad from her desk, and extended her hand as she welcomed the officer in and led him to the seating area. "Please, feel at home."

"Thank you." He looked enviously around at the comfortable suite with an appreciative look common to military personnel more used to spartan living quarters, and nodded his approval. "We've received formal invitation to attend a session of Joint Dominion, and Commander Montero has accepted."

"That's excellent! When?"

"In three days, ship's time."

She opened the pad and quickly keyed in the information. "They didn't waste much time, did they?"

"No, but I'm not really that surprised. The session must've been planned for weeks to coincide with our arrival. No doubt they merely needed only to relay our willingness to join them before makin' it official."

It made sense. Why else would they have been so confident that setting up a Joint Dominion could be handled as quickly as they'd indicated? "I'll need every bit of the time to get ready," she said, still tapping notes into the pad. "Although I'll be able to let some of the others handle a few of—"

"There's something else," he interrupted, his voice uncharacteristically somber. "I'm the only member of the diplomatic team who's to attend the session."

Her fingers froze over the keys of the notepad and she was about to protest, but he held up a hand before she could speak.

"I'll be accompanied by several members of the ship's security, politely and discreetly armed, of course; but Commander Montero feels that, in the interests of safety, no other essential contact personnel should go down at this time."

"Safety!" she burst out, unable to hold back her anger, and was on her feet immediately. "Safety from what? System!"

"Ma'am?"

Adela stood facing the holo display area in the corner of the room, her back to the young officer. "I want to talk to Commander Montero, right now."

There was a confirming chirp as the room system complied. She looked over her shoulder and stared wordlessly at the Lieutenant for several moments and, literally too angry to speak to him just then, turned away again and entered a few more notes into the pad before slapping the cover closed. Woorunmarra started to say something, but apparently thought better of it and settled back quietly and waited as the call was put through.

There was another chirp as the system responded, and Adela faced the corner, expecting it to brighten with the glow of the holo. It did not, and Adela felt the anger rise anew within her.

"Ma'am? Commander Montero requests that—"

"System," she said forcefully, cutting off the response. "Put it through again."

"I'm sorry, ma'am," the room system responded, sounding efficiently anything but apologetic, "your last command had been disallowed by executive order of the Commander until delivery of current message. Will you accept?"

Damn him, she thought, sighing in frustration. "Yes! I'll accept."

"Commander Montero requests that you and Lieutenant Woorunmarra meet with him personally. He'll be waiting in his starboard office on the command deck, and will expect your arrival in fifteen minutes."

Adela turned and went back to sit across from Woorunmarra, calling back over her shoulder, "Tell Commander Montero we're on our way." She looked at him, studying his features, and couldn't decide if she was mad at him or not.

"Well, now," he chuckled. "If I didn't know better, I'd swear he was expecting your call."

"The movements are taking place here, here and here."

As First Officer Nelon spoke, Adela saw a glowing red dot appeared at each of the points he described on the projected representation of Pallatin hanging in the air next to him. A dozen such marks were already scattered on the surface of the projection, most of them located in the Eastland portion of the continent.

"And here," Nelon went on, "are the locations where we've detected fluctuations in power consumption and routing." A series of pulsing yellow circles appeared, interconnected by thin yellow lines. Again, most of the activity appeared in the major cities of the east and along the eastern edge of the Arroyo fault.

Montero sat behind the desk, hands steepled against his chin, and frowned in displeasure at what he was hearing. She and Woorunmarra occupied two of the chairs placed opposite the desk, the angle just right that Adela could see the Commander's displeased reflection in the smooth plastic surface of the desktop.

"We've been holographing the surface of the planet for weeks, of course," Montero put in. "But the activity you see up there has been taking place for only the last few days, beginning first in the east. Westland has begun to respond in a similar manner, as you can see, to whatever is happening down there. We don't know what the significance is, or if there's any reason to suspect a hostile intent directed at us."

"Nothin' at all on the air?" asked Woorunmarra of the First Officer.

Nelon glanced once at Montero, who nodded for him to continue. "We've monitored all their broadcasts, both public and private—we have been, in fact, since long before we were close enough to get these readings here—but there's been nothing said of this."

Adela swiveled in her chair and indicated the marks on the holo. "No hint in the broadcasts what any of this might be about?"

"Well, there's been a great deal of talk about our coming, as you might expect. Not all of it complimentary to the Hundred Worlds, either." Nelon shook his head in frustration and swept an arm through the projection. "But nothing that seems related to any of this. Either this is something that's so normal there's no reason to broadcast it, or they want to keep it from us as long as they can."

Adela stood, nearing the projection for a better look, and studied the locations of the overlaid lines and marked spots on the globe. There were far more on the eastern continental mass, with the power readings radiating in logical sequences from point to point. On the western side, the markings were much more random and interspersed, as though being done in a hurry. After several moments she turned back, addressing no one in particular. "Maybe it's not us they're trying to keep this from."

The room was silent for several moments as Adela's suggestion was considered. Finally Montero nodded thoughtfully, stroking his moustache with the tips of his thumb and index finger. "It makes sense. That would explain why the readings appeared in the east first, followed later by similar activity in the west. Monitoring satellites operated from the spaceport in Dannen must have picked up the same readings at about the same time we did, and are only now responding to whatever is happening. It might also explain why both Speakers were so vague when we contacted them and asked what was going on down there. Obviously neither is fully aware of what the other is up to." Montero paused. "I think it's just as obvious that our real adversary here is Eastland." He turned to his First Officer. "Thank you, Nelon. Keep monitoring the movements and power readings, and let me know if any significant changes in the numbers occur." Nelon snapped stiffly to attention, nodded curtly and exited the room, leaving the three of them alone.

"Do you understand now," Montero asked Adela, "why I've limited the size of the delegation to the Joint Dominion?"

Adela looked squarely at him and considered her words judiciously. Where just a short time earlier she might have willingly let her anger at his decision speak for her, Nelon's presentation of what was happening on the planet below told both her and Woorunmarra that Montero had truly made his decision based on honest fear for their safety.

"Yes, I do understand your concerns, Commander; but I have been chosen by Emperor Javas himself to represent the Hundred Worlds in this matter. He and I both knew the risks involved before we set out from Sol. Admittedly, with this new information there may be more of a threat hidden here than any of us thought; but I accepted the risks, as did he, and am perfectly willing to go through with my part. Can you do any less?"

Woorunmarra cleared his throat. "If I may speak?" Montero was clearly prepared to listen to their arguments, and motioned for him to go on. "I'm afraid I have to agree with Dr. Montgarde. It's well known now throughout the Hundred Worlds that the project has begun and that she plays the most important role in its successful completion. With that comes the knowledge that the Emperor—represented by you and the full power of the weaponry on this starship—would most certainly punish any world responsible for harmin' her. For this very reason, Dr. Montgarde would probably be the safest member of the diplomatic team while on the planet."

"That's probably true," Montero agreed, "but it is no less true that if something *were* to happen to Dr. Montgarde while she was planetside, the project might be irreparably set back." He turned to Adela, raising an eyebrow. "Are you prepared to accept that risk, Doctor?"

Adela smiled. "Perhaps my actual importance has been exaggerated a bit, for the sake of good public relations." The Commander's brow furrowed momentarily, and a puzzled look swept over his features. "What I mean is that I am not entirely indispensable to the project. Everything I've researched—the formulae, the equations, the resources and needs—is a matter of Imperial record." She sighed heavily as she realized the implications of what she was saying. She knew it was true, but had never admitted it to herself. "It's true that I am the driving force behind the project and that the progress of the preparatory research and development of ships and materials might be slowed down somewhat by my absence. However, the project has almost taken on a life of its own. Most of the Hundred Worlds have embraced our efforts as a way of revitalizing themselves and their economies. The scientific community within the Empire is already seeing benefits and new discoveries from the early research."

She paused, allowing her smile to return before adding, "Even Commander Fain sees the advantages to be gained in increased fleet strength."

Montero looked from her to Woorunmarra, then back to her again. "Go on."

"Commander, half of my work—the original research, and convincing Emperor Nicholas of its worthiness—is finished. The other half won't take place until very near the end of the project many generations from now. The most important thing I can do now is to represent the project and smooth its forward motion, to convince those still uncertain of its validity." She stood and approached the holographic image of Pallatin. In the time they'd spoken, additional lines of power routing had appeared, further crisscrossing the planet's surface. "Don't you see? If I'm to be excluded from the legitimate diplomatic functions of this mission, then I fail to understand why I'm here at all. I might as well get back in the tank and sleep until my scientific abilities are required."

Clearly weakening, Montero rubbed tiredly at his temples as he addressed her. "You are an integral part of my duties here, Dr. Montgarde, I won't—*can't* deny it. But you are also the single most important aspect of the reason behind our mission here. I've made no secret of my doubts for this plan to save Earth's Sun. But then again, were it not for your project, the opportunity to bring some of the more recalcitrant members of the Hundred Worlds into line might never have arisen. For that I am truly grateful. And who knows? Perhaps this idea that has so captured Emperor Javas and Commander Fain is a worthy goal after all. If that is so, then we all win. Please, be seated."

Adela returned to her chair, glancing once at Woorunmarra, who couldn't hide the look of approval on his dark features and made no attempt to do so.

"Did you know that I met with the Emperor before we left?" he asked, his face glowing pleasantly with the memory. "I've never been nervous or frightened of anything since joining the Imperial Forces. Until then. He and Commander Fain wanted to speak to me personally before the *Levant* set out, to tell me how important it was that this mission be successful. They told me I was to do anything, make any decision that I felt would increase our chances of a favorable outcome. But the Emperor also told me to trust your judgment, Doctor. Now, why do you suppose he said that?"

Adela had no answer for the rhetorical question and waited silently for him to continue.

"Very well," he said at last. "You will accompany Lieutenant Woorunmarra to the Joint Dominion." He stood and extended his hand, first to her, then Woorunmarra.

"Good luck to both of you."

TWENTY-ONE

The chamber was filled to capacity, although Adela didn't actually find it necessary to look for empty seats to prove it. The sound level alone told her that there could not possibly be room for more people in here. The Dominion chamber had been designed along the lines of an amphitheater or lecture hall: a circular arrangement of comfortable seats placed at long, curved tables tiered row upon row. At each seat, the light of a shaded lamp reflected off a flat-panel keypad mounted flush in the tabletop before every representative. A long, steep set of steps bisected the circle of seats, with the representatives from districts in Eastland seated on one side, while those from Westland occupied the seats on the other. Behind her, mounted on the curved wall, was a tally board listing the names of each of the representatives; all the names glowed softly on the board and were divided, with those from Westland listed in order according to their numerical district on the left side, while the representatives from Eastland were on the right.

Adela let her eyes scan up the inclining rows to where a double balcony of spectators, similarly divided, overlooked the proceedings in the chamber. Those seated there were every bit as animated as the representatives below them. At each doorway, at the top and bottom of the steps, and at the end of every tenth row, a Dominion security officer stood and watched the unruly crowd with nervous eyes. The entire thing reminded her of the Grisian Parliament, although her homeworld had nothing that compared with this huge chamber and, more importantly, had never seen this much turmoil and disagreement during a parliamentary session.

Her prepared address before the Joint Dominion had been well received at first, or rather, it had been well received from the Westland side of the chamber. The Eastland representatives had listened to her politely, but silently, for the most part, and it wasn't until the floor had been opened for questions that the real pandemonium had set in. Members of both sides of the chamber

were shouting and arguing not only with those on the other side
but among themselves as well. Several were on their feet as they
demonstrated, and it seemed that actual physical confrontation
might be imminent at several spots in the big room. If the disorder in the chamber was any indication, her address had been
entirely wasted on them.

The two Speakers, seated with several Dominion officials at a
long table on the dais directly below the podium where she now
stood, were making futile attempts to restore order. Each banged
gavels and shouted at the Dominion members in the seats nearest
them.

This is hopeless, Adela thought disgustedly. *Totally and irre-
trievably hopeless.* She found Woorunmarra in the assembly,
flanked by several Imperial guards in the guest seating area, and
saw that the feelings of failure that were now going through her
were also reflected in him. The dark features that so effortlessly
beamed his very thoughts when happy, expressed, she was sorry
to discover, unhappiness even more effectively. Her lips drew
into a tight line and she shook her head in frustration. He nodded
back, indicating that he understood.

A movement below her caught her attention. Speaker Niles
had leaned to his Eastland counterpart and was discussing something with him, and even though he had to shout for the man to
hear, she still wasn't able to make out what he was saying over
the din. The two spoke animatedly for several minutes, seeming
to be in nearly as strong a state of disagreement as the chamber
at large, before Salera gave an assenting wave of his arm.

Niles leaned forward and shouted into the microphone. "This
chamber will come to order or it will be cleared!" He hammered
the gavel on its strike plate several times as he shouted. "This
session will be terminated and the chamber cleared!" It was
necessary for him to make the threat repeatedly before it seemed
that the noise finally began to subside. Just as the uproar had
begun in the lower portions of the chamber before spreading up
through the spectator galleries, so now did the slow wave of
quieting. Speaker Niles continued to hammer away with the
gavel until everyone returned to their seats and all that was left
in the chamber was a heavy, constant murmuring.

"Members of the Joint Dominion, your attention. If there is a
further outburst similar to the one just concluded, we will declare

this Dominion terminated." He looked to his side, and Speaker Salera leaned forward.

"Speaker Niles of Dannen is correct. While I am hesitant to bring these important proceedings to a halt, and while I am on record as being in opposition to the Speaker's position as it regards the requests made of us by the Emperor's representative, I am forced to agree that disorder in this chamber cannot be tolerated."

The murmur decreased further.

"Very well," said Niles. "These proceedings will resume from the point at which they were interrupted. Speaker Salera?" He placed the gavel on the table and leaned back in the chair.

"Thank you," Salera said, standing to address the chamber. "There was a question on the floor from Eastland Representative Blakert of Stannary. Representative, the floor is yours; would you please restate the question?" Salera indicated a man in the fourth row and nodded his head reassuringly to him. Even from her vantage point behind Salera, Adela could tell that something passed between the Eastland Speaker and his representative, some silent message or agreement that she couldn't understand.

In the fourth row, a man stood and faced Adela. "Since the Empire is asking Pallatin to participate in this project on a planetwide basis," he began, "requiring a united statement issued by the Joint Dominion before taking any action against us, what would be the Imperial response if no statement were to be issued?"

What's he getting at? Adela wondered. She saw that most of the people in the chamber grew nervous at his question. Speaker Niles stared at Salera, a deadly, questioning expression plain on his face. The sound of whispering among the representatives reached her ears.

"I'm afraid that I was prepared only for your scientific and technical questions regarding the project to save Earth's Sun," she replied. "Your question steps into the area of legalities and colonial protocol, and I'd like to defer your question to Lieutenant Woorunmarra, who has accompanied me here today. The Lieutenant is here to interpret the legal aspects of our dealings with your government, and reports directly to Commander Montero aboard the *Levant*."

Both Niles and Salera, almost in unison, said, "No objec-

tions." Speaker Niles motioned for him to approach, and he
joined Adela on the podium.

Woorunmarra spoke directly to the man without hesitation.
"Am I to understand, Representative Blakert, that a joint statement might be delayed, for reasons beyond the control of the
Joint Dominion?" He had obviously studied the protocol of the
colony's governmental procedure, and Adela was impressed with
the way he presented himself. When he spoke, he spoke in an
official manner, and she was surprised to hear that nearly all
traces of the accent and speaking patterns to which she'd become
accustomed had vanished. She was not the only one impressed,
it seemed; both Speakers had turned to listen to him as he responded to the question and they, too, seemed taken with him.

"No, Lieutenant." Blakert paused and regarded the Speaker
for his Congress. Salera nodded slowly for him to continue. "I
am asking what the Imperial response would be if the two Congresses could not agree to issue a joint statement."

Woorunmarra considered the question for a moment before
replying. "If lengthy debate on the wording of a joint statement
were to continue, Commander Montero, as the official liaison for
the Emperor, would take no overt action against the people of
Pallatin—unless a direct attack were made against the Imperial
vessel *Levant* or against any member of her crew—until such
time as a vote was taken in Joint Dominion, and a statement
issued."

"And if no such statement was forthcoming, Lieutenant . . . ?"
The man appeared to try to remember the pronunciation of the
Lieutenant's aboriginal family name, but gave up. "What would
be the Imperial response?"

There was a sudden increase in the background chatter among
those in the chamber at the question, and Speaker Niles was
forced to retrieve the gavel from its resting place and strike it
firmly a few times to restore order. When relative quiet had
returned, he turned to the podium to indicate that the Lieutenant
could continue. When he did, Adela saw the worried look on his
face, the undisguised fear in his eyes.

"There would be no overt response," Woorunmarra said levelly. The man remained standing, looking pleased at the answer
until he added, "Initially."

"Initially, sir?" Blakert replied.

"It is a point of Imperial law and custom, as I'm sure you are fully aware, Representative Blakert, that the Empire would not wish to interfere with, nor make demands of, a member world that is not united in its dealings with the Empire. However, just as Commander Montero has been given the authority—by Emperor Javas himself—to determine the best course of action to take should the Joint Dominion issue a united statement against the Empire; so, too, has he been given the authority to deal with Pallatin, as he determines best, should there be a total lack of cooperation. The decision would be his to make, at such time as he sees fit to make it, and would be backed up by the full might of the Hundred Worlds."

"May I ask a question of the Eastland Representative?" inquired Niles, then waited. Dominion rules of order required the permission of the Eastland Speaker before he could directly address or interrogate a representative of the opposite Congress who had been granted the floor. Salera seemed about to refuse, but apparently thought better of it and motioned for Niles to proceed.

"Why would no joint statement be issued?" he asked bluntly. His voice carried with it a tone of challenge, it seemed to Adela, but at the same time clearly expressing that he already knew the answer. "The debate here will most certainly be both heated and lengthy, as our discussions proved during the weeks we awaited the arrival of the Imperial starship, but the question may be called at virtually any time."

Most of the whispering in the Dominion chamber faded quickly away as members of both Congresses turned their complete attention to the confrontation forming between the Westland Speaker and Eastland representative. For the first time since he'd gotten up to address the Speaker, Blakert grew openly nervous. He seemed to be having trouble finding something to do with his hands, and his eyes darted from Niles to Salera and back again.

"Representative Blakert?"

"It's true that at any point in the debate the question may be called," the man said finally. "But that would only apply if a Joint Dominion were in session . . . indeed, if a Dominion still existed." He paused, and the whispers increased to fill in the gap as he regarded Woorunmarra once more, asking, "Legally speaking, Lieutenant, based on what you said a few minutes ago, the Empire of the Hundred Worlds would not interfere if a condition were to arise that prevented a united statement to be issued. Would that consideration also cover a condition under which the Dominion were to, for whatever reason, be dissolved?"

The chamber exploded in raucous cries and shouted accusations from the Westland Congress, forcing Niles to again use the gavel repeatedly. It took several minutes for the noise to subside, and as Woorunmarra awaited an opportunity to answer, Adela saw Speaker Niles turn to Salera, his eyes wide with anger. Still pounding the gavel with his right hand, he covered his microphone with his left, shouting more in rage than to be heard.

"Bastard!" she heard him exclaim. She regarded Woorunmarra at her side, and it was clear from the look on his face that he could also hear what the man was saying. "You set this up all along, didn't you?"

Salera cupped his hand over his own microphone. "We need to stay together if we're to defy the Empire, Am!"

"We must stay together, yes; but not in defiance of the Hundred Worlds! We need them as much as we need each other!"

"It's your choice, Am," he said, lowering his voice as the room began to settle. "We can dissolve the Dominion. We've got the votes to do it."

Niles shrank back in horror at what Salera was suggesting and, as order returned to the chamber, lay the gavel on its side in front of him. Without turning, he indicated for Woorunmarra to reply to the question.

"Representative Blakert, if at any time during our visit the Dominion should be dissolved, no action would be taken until such time as a resolution to the difficulties between the two Congresses were to be reached. We would offer whatever assistance and mediation we could, at Pallatin's request, to resolve the differences between you." There was a heightened buzz at this, but he quickly continued before disorder could spread through the chamber. "I must caution you, however—this applies to dealings with member worlds under normal circumstances. Our reason for being here in the first place stems from Pallatin's refusal to cooperate with the Hundred Worlds and, obviously, the situation could be called anything *but* normal circumstances. With that in mind, let me restate that Commander Montero has the ultimate authority here, and will act as he sees fit for the general welfare of the Empire. Does that answer your question?"

"Yes, sir, it does." Blakert looked solemnly at the faces of his co-representatives seated nearest him. All were silent, waiting for him to continue.

Woorunmarra leaned to Adela and spoke softly in her ear. "You know what they're doin', don't you?"

"Speaker Niles was right," she whispered back, guessing what he was getting at. "This whole thing, this whole session and our part in it, was nothing but an elaborate setup."

He nodded agreement and seemed about to add something, but stopped when Blakert spoke up again.

"Speakers, my fellow Representatives to the Ninety-second Dominion, citizens of Pallatin," he began. The chamber was hushed, expectant, and he pivoted about slowly as he addressed the attendees, allowing his gaze to sweep over the crowd before turning back to face Salera and Niles. "I move that the Eastland Congress call for a vote of secession."

There was, surprisingly, less reaction than Adela had expected; a steady murmuring spread quickly through the rows and galleries, but there was not the total outburst of emotion that she had imagined would occur. Speaker Niles sat unmoving, apparently resigned to the inevitable outcome of what was happening, his hands steepled over his lips. He stared at the representative, still standing before the dais, and refused to even acknowledge the presence of the Speaker sitting next to him. For his part, Salera seemed no more comfortable with his own closeness to his Westland counterpart. She studied Niles' face as best she could from her vantage point behind and to one side of him; where unbridled rage had been a few moments earlier, his face now reflected what she could only describe as sorrow. Adela knew enough about the political structure of Pallatin's Dominion form of government to know that he was powerless to stop the inter-Congress vote that had just been requested.

Blakert, in what now seemed an obviously planned—if not actually rehearsed—procedure, turned to another representative seated in the row behind him. The woman stood without hesitation and faced the dais. "Speaker Salera, Hauley township seconds the call for a vote of secession."

"A vote has been called and seconded." Behind Adela, the left

side of the enormous tally board went dark, the names of the
Westland representatives fading immediately from view. It
would stand to reason that the table keypads had been activated
as well. Salera stood, still avoiding Niles' eyes. "Representative
Blakert, please state the question."

"Thank you, Speaker Salera." Blakert smiled uneasily as he
regarded those seated around him. "Let this question stand:
Shall Eastland withdraw from the Dominion of Pallatin?" He
retook his seat and thumbed his choice into the keypad to officially begin the voting process, and a corresponding red light
glowed in the "yes" column by his name on the board. The
woman who had seconded the call voted next; another red light
blinked on. The voting under way, a low, steady chatter returned
to the chamber. While Adela and Woorunmarra watched, the
board quickly became dappled with glowing lights as the rest of
the Eastland Congress voted.

Although both Speakers had smaller versions of the tally
board mounted into the tabletops before them, Salera had swiveled his chair around to watch the big board as the votes came
in. He nodded approvingly as the board filled up, but behind his
confident expression lay something else, Adela noted. Another
red light came on next to a name near the bottom of the board,
and their eyes met for several seconds, confirming her suspicions.
His large eyes radiated a sense of worry and foreboding, a visible
sense of apprehension that plainly told her he was hoping they
were doing the right thing.

Salera stood and leaned over the podium, speaking to both of
them directly. "It might be better," he said quietly, getting
quickly to the point, "if the two of you waited in the guest area."
He indicated the gallery where she and Woorunmarra had been
seated prior to addressing the chamber.

Adela saw that the Imperial guards were already on their feet,
nervously watching the chamber, and that even now a pair of
them was approaching the dais to escort them back to the gallery. "You may be right."

Salera bowed his head slightly and stood aside, allowing them
to pass down the short set of steps leading to the floor. As they
crossed in front of him, Salera put his hand on Woorunmarra's
arm, stopping him. "Please inform your Commander that I'll

speak with him as soon as I can. I'm sorry it had to come to this, Lieutenant."

The Imperial officer paused as he considered his response carefully. "Let us hope," he said levelly, "that we are not all a lot sorrier before this is finished." He turned away abruptly and led Adela to the floor, where the guards fell dutifully into step on either side of them.

It didn't take long for the voting to be completed. A glance at the tally board showed that, while a handful of the Eastlanders had abstained, there were no dissenting votes. Again, Adela was convinced that the secession vote had been planned in advance.

"He knew he would win."

"Of course he did," Woorunmarra agreed, pointing to the board. "Or he'd've never made the attempt. Look there, he's even managed to talk the few members who were against the move to abstain, making the secession vote unanimous." He allowed the hint of a smile to form at the corners of his lips, adding, "Which is why I wish you outranked me."

She raised a puzzled eyebrow. "Why is that?"

"So that you would be the one to tell Montero."

Adela couldn't help laughing aloud and pretended not to see the guard seated next to her turn a sudden curious eye in her direction. *Thank you,* Adela thought, *for bringing a moment's laughter to this hopeless situation.*

The hammering of a gavel cut obtrusively into their brief conversation, and they returned their attention to the dais as the constant background of talking decreased in intensity.

"May I have your attention?" While Salera waited for order to return he spoke a few words to one of the officials seated at his left. The man nodded curtly and rose, quickly descending the steps and exiting the chamber. "The vote is unanimous," he said simply once the official had left. "As of this date, Eastland is no longer a part of the Dominion of Pallatin."

Again, Adela was surprised by the response. There was no outburst, no shouting by those in attendance. From here and there an occasional whisper reached her ears, but that was the exception. Nearly everyone else—on both sides of the chamber—waited in stunned silence for the Eastland Speaker to continue.

He coughed softly to clear his throat, and took a sip from the

water glass on the table. Niles sat impassively, staring at him.
Salera glanced at him once as he set the glass down. "Within the
next two days, all persons not citizens of Eastland must leave
the—" He stopped, apparently realizing that the word he was
about to use was incorrect. "Must leave our country." It was
clear to Adela that even though he had been prepared for this
moment, the word still felt strange and unfamiliar to him. "I
have given orders that no representative or citizen of Westland
in the process of leaving is to be harassed or interfered with in
any way. Anyone doing so will be dealt with severely. On this,
you have my word."

Adela and Woorunmarra watched the crowd and noted that
the spectators in the upper galleries, unnoticed by those in the
lower rows, were already being cleared from the chamber by the
security personnel. Those in the Eastland section talked quietly
among themselves, while on the Westland side the representatives looked back and forth to one another. There was no panic,
no outcry, but rather an overwhelming air of subdued shock and
confusion over what to do next. Most kept their attention on the
dais, waiting for some direction from Speaker Niles.

"With utmost respect," Salera concluded, "I must now ask
that all citizens of Westland please leave this chamber." He lay
the gavel on the table and turned to Niles, extending his hand.
"I'm sorry, Am."

Niles stood slowly and, ignoring the Speaker's hand, addressed the now-silent chamber.

"Members of the Ninety-second Dominion . . ." His voice was
strong, and carried with it much more authority than had Salera's. Adela's respect for the man doubled at how well he handled himself in the face of defeat—a defeat for which he had been
set up with no possible course of action he could have taken to
stop it.

"More has happened here today than the dissolution of a
governing body," he began. "Today we divided a world. However, simply dissolving the governing bonds between us will not
serve to make us a different people, as Speaker Salera might wish.
Have we not, after all, always been a diverse world, with different
ideals and goals, different lives and pleasures? Different pains
and—different losses?" He paused, staring down at the gavel in
his hands.

"Pallatin has always been a harsh, unforgiving place. Those who came first, who began the taming of our home, did so by beating the incredible odds working against them, and they did it as one world, with little help from any of the hundred others. But because of their unity of purpose, they succeeded in spite of the inattention of others. And it is with a similar attitude that many here now view outside intervention from those same Hundred Worlds in their time of need.

"It's true that we in the west are a different people now from those here in the east. And now that you've had an opportunity to see the representatives from the Empire, I'm sure you realize just how vastly different we have become from those on other worlds. But we are still one people, with a common need that overshadows all else . . ." Niles paused again, leaned forward on the table, then resumed speaking in a tone much louder than before. "Pallatin is still a harsh world, and we need each other to control it, to keep the angry forces within her docile—to keep her a home. I am saddened that Speaker Salera and the representatives of the Eastland Congress, in their efforts to prevent outside interference from creeping into our way of life, have failed to realize that neither body can do it alone."

He stopped and allowed his eyes to scan the assemblage before him, pausing so long that for a moment Adela thought he might be looking into the eyes of each individual member in turn. Finally he sighed deeply, his eyes lowered to the gavel in his hands once more. He turned it over in his hands as if studying it, then looked up to the assembly, addressing this time only one side of the large room.

"Members of the Westland Congress, we are no longer welcome here. Let us return home." He took one last look at Salera, then dropped the gavel to the table. It clattered noisily across the polished surface before falling to the carpeted floor.

The Speaker immediately left the dais and neither looked back nor spoke to anyone as he made his way to the floor and walked briskly from the chamber.

TWENTY-TWO

T he viewer in Speaker Niles' office at the Westland capital
was a flatscreen. Not that holographic technology was
unavailable in Westland, it was; but the decision to install
the more simple flatscreen display was apparently a matter of
choice on the part of Niles himself. Simplicity seemed to be the
way of life for the Speaker, just as it was for the Westlanders in
general. Normally Adela would have missed being able to see the
small nuances in facial expressions and body language afforded
by a hologram, but she found that in this discussion the additional clues to mood, motive and inner thoughts were unnecessary: It was abundantly clear what was going through the mind
of everyone taking part in this briefing session.

"Speaker Salera kept his word," Montero was saying to Woorunmarra. "He contacted me about an hour ago, at about the
same time you arrived there in Newcastle."

Adela watched the Commander as he spoke, and realized that
even a life-sized holograph could not have more clearly shown
how deeply disturbed he was at how quickly the situation here on
Pallatin had soured. Any doubts she might have had were erased
by the presence of several key members of the *Levant*'s crew
seated with Montero. First Officer Nelon was there, of course, as
was Woorunmarra's shipside counterpart. But also in attendance
was the *Levant*'s Weapons Master, Kyovska, and several of his
lieutenants. It was obvious that Montero, while loath to use force
here, was still keeping his options open.

So, apparently, was the Westland Congress. Invited by
Speaker Niles to sit in on this briefing were other Westland
representatives, as well as several uniformed men and women
who had been introduced as top officers of the Congressional
Guard, the equivalent of a national armed force. Now that Westland had thrown its allegiance to the Hundred Worlds, briefings
of this type would most likely become commonplace.

"Did he give any indication at all as to which pressure taps are
involved?" Woorunmarra asked, catching her attention.

"That's just it; he's told us every one of them, as well as detailing their locations." Montero shook his head in frustration. "I suppose he could be lying about some of them, but most match up with the surface scanning we've done. The troop movements and power routing we've been able to detect coincide with the information he's given us."

"I'd be willing to bet he's telling the truth," Adela put in. "It's clear he doesn't want to use force, and he's hoping that by letting us know just how firmly in place he is, we'll avoid a confrontation in those key areas."

"Speaker?" asked one of the uniformed men. His rank insignia identified him as a General. He waited until Niles nodded for him to continue before addressing Montero. "Commander, can you download that information to us? We've received a similar communiqué from Eastland regarding the locations and would like to run a cross-check on them."

"Of course."

The General spoke briefly to the officer seated next to him and waited while he keyed several commands into a portable keypad. In the lower right corner of the flatscreen the words "receive mode ready" appeared.

Montero's image faded, replaced by that of a wide-scale map of the planet's near hemisphere. The image zoomed in on Pallatin's major continent, centering on the entire length of the Arroyo fault. With the fault itself running from the top to the bottom of the screen, it was easy to see several hundred kilometers to either side of the fault line. The map had obviously been extracted from somewhere in the middle of Salera's communication with Montero, and his voice was running beneath the visual.

". . . understand that none of this pleases me. We had hoped that Westland would support us and saved this as a last resort. Please note that in addition to the eighty-six tap stations directly adjacent to Arroyo, we . . ." There was a pause as Salera lowered his voice, taking on an almost apologetic tone. "We also hold five control stations on Westland soil." Niles was on his feet at this, as was the General and one of the other representatives—Carolane Pence, Adela remembered from the introductions—although whether they had risen in shock or merely to get a closer look at the map, Adela couldn't tell. Their faces remained impassive.

Five dots on the western side came suddenly to life at the far northern end of the fault, their orange glow matching those scattered along the length of the eastern side. The five were located almost directly on the fault line itself and were grouped so close together that at first glance they appeared to be a single station.

"Commander, can you freeze the image?" Niles asked, then turned to the General. "Can we get an identification on these stations?" The General started to ask the officer with the keypad to cross-reference the location, but was interrupted by Representative Pence.

"We don't need to," she said, retaking her seat. "It's the Leeper grouping, extreme northeast corner of my district."

Niles smiled a thank-you and asked Montero to resume the playback. The map zoomed in on the five stations, showing the area in greater detail. They were arranged in a nearly perfect line running parallel to the edge of the fault, the scale indicator at the top edge of the map showing them to be just under a kilometer apart from each other.

"Please believe me," Salera's voice went on, "when I say that we aim to keep control of these stations; do not force our hand on this. And please, Commander—understand that, while we would be hesitant to use them, we are prepared to do just that."

The playback of the segment stopped and faded, and Montero once more stared out from the screen, the look of troubled frustration on his face no less apparent than before. "Speaker, may I ask the significance of the, uh, 'Leeper grouping,' as you referred to it?"

Niles hesitated. He had been most cooperative since the dissolution vote at Dominion, but it seemed that he was still not entirely comfortable with this new alliance with the Imperial Commander.

"Speaker Niles," Adela said calmly, "we can't help you if we're not fully informed."

He shot a sidelong glance at her, concern showing in his eyes, then softened as he smiled, nodding in acceptance. "You're right, I know that, but . . . understand that it was not all that many years ago that I, too, would have considered you an invader to our world."

"And what changed your mind?"

Niles shook his head. "It's not important right now." He opened a desk drawer and removed a light pen, then approached the screen, saying, "Commander, can you put the map back up, please?" In a matter of seconds the map returned, still at the zoomed-in shot where it had cut off before. "Pull back, please, to show the full length of Arroyo. Thank you." He activated the light pen and circled the Leeper grouping, then drew a line to another set of similarly arranged orange dots that appeared on the opposite side of the fault, slightly south of the first, and encircled them as well.

"Commander, the isolated stations that you see highlighted along the length of Arroyo and throughout both sides of the continent act as individual pressure taps, bleeding off tectonic stresses as they occur in the areas in which they're located. They operate independently of one another, but act to reinforce the main controls we have over plate activity along Arroyo itself. But the Leeper grouping, unlike the individual stations, functions as a single control station, a combination pressure-tap and monitor/relay station specifically designed to work in concert with a matched control grouping on the opposite side. Look here." He drew circles around a dozen more such groupings on the eastern side. "These are all tied in to matching stations on this side," he went on, extending lines across the fault to the corresponding groupings. "We've heard from most of them and, as you might expect, they've been disconnected from their counterparts on the eastern side. If you could give me the close-up of Leeper again?"

The scene zoomed in, close enough that surface details and the actual fault could be discerned in the overhead view. Using the light pen, he traced a series of concentric circles around the Leeper grouping, then another series around its counterpart on the eastern side, giving the appearance of ripples spreading away from two stones dropped a few meters apart into a still lake. "Each of these groupings is connected to a network of smaller, unmanned taps located along these lines." Niles marked several X's on each of the rings as he spoke. "Responding to whatever tectonic activity occurs in the region of a control grouping, signals are sent to these unmanned taps—and, if needed, to the larger isolated pressure stations—to relieve or apply stress, effectively controlling major earthquake activity." He returned to his desk, dropping the light pen on the desktop as he sat, adding,

"This latest information explains why we haven't been able to contact Leeper."

Montero appeared on the screen. He sat in silent thought for several moments, pulling absently at one corner of his moustache, then leaned aside and said something to Nelon. The First Officer in turn spoke to the Weapons Master, and the two of them left the room.

"I'll be blunt, Speaker," he finally offered, "and I'll be thankful for your candid response. Just how much control do they have at this point?"

Adela was surprised to see the hint of a smile appear briefly on Niles' lips. "I appreciate your straightforward manner, Commander." He leaned forward on the desk, steepling his hands in front of his face in a gesture Adela had come to recognize as one of his mannerisms. "If Salera controls the Leeper grouping, and there's no reason at this time to assume he does not, then Westland is in serious danger. Very serious danger." Niles picked up a handset from the comm terminal on the desk and spoke briefly into it, then set it back in its holder before going on. "Understand that the pressure-tap system is designed to work on a continentwide basis to control fault activity. There are constant tremors, especially in the interior regions nearest Arroyo, but there has not been a major earthquake in more than a decade because of the success of the tap system."

There was an insistent beeping from the comm terminal, and Niles picked up the handset once more, telling whoever was on the other end, "Stand by," loudly enough that he could be heard by everyone in the room. "I'm going to have a playback put up showing how the system works from a recording made two years ago." He spoke into the handset and a different overhead view of Pallatin appeared on the flatscreen. This one was similar to the other, but an overlay clearly showed the entire system of pressure-tap stations in both halves of the continent. "The unmanned taps are highlighted in blue, the individual manned stations in green, and the control groupings are in yellow. That's Leeper there at the top left of Arroyo. When I start playback, the tectonic pressure forces will appear as a growing red area on the overlay." Then, into the handset: "Go ahead."

Nothing seemed to happen at first, but as they looked, a red stain widened and spread out from the upper half of the fault, extending several hundred kilometers in the most actively affected portions of the fault. Parts of the fault itself where the stain spread out the farthest glowed so brightly that it looked like a river of fire bisecting the continent.

"Does this show the extent of the earthquake itself?" Adela asked.

"No, Dr. Montgarde. This is the pressure building up over several months that you're seeing right now. You're correct, however, in assuming that the red area shows the pattern of tremors that would occur if the process played itself out. Watch, though, as the tap stations come on-line."

The red glow spread farther, extending more to the western side of the fault. The groupings visibly activated first, glowing intensely in the worst areas of the pressure buildup. As they watched, spiderweb lines traced out from the groupings to the concentric rings of unmanned stations surrounding them. From a pairing of control stations located not quite a third of the way from the top of the fault, a series of bolder yellow lines snaked out to larger, manned stations centered in a particularly bright red area on the Westland side, and from these more threadlike circles expanded around them. Another set of yellow lines shot out to a second manned station in Westland, slightly above and to the right of the first, and repeated the series of expanding rings around it. A control pairing three down from the other that had activated suddenly glowed. As before, the yellow lines traced a delicate pattern of circles and lines leading to yet another spot on the Westland side, then again to one on the eastern edge of the fault.

Adela almost thought the lacy patterns beautiful, but found it necessary to remind herself of the amount of destructive fury she was looking at. She watched in awestruck fascination as more control pairings activated and lines arced out again and again across the landmass, until finally it became clear that the red glow had begun to diminish in several spots on the overlay.

The glowing area faded, the circles dimming in a backward-leading dance to their originating stations. As if draining water from a basin, the red disappeared along the direction of the stations that had activated until at last only the control groupings themselves still remained lighted. The overlay darkened, the line of control groupings tracing the length of the fault like a brilliant chain of diamonds. Finally even they winked out one by one. Speaker Niles spoke briefly into the handset, and the map and overlay disappeared, showing Montero and the others aboard *Levant*. Sometime during the playback, or perhaps just before it started, First Officer Nelon and the Weapons Master had returned.

"Impressive." The Commander was clearly affected by what he had just seen, and sat straighter in his chair as he soberly addressed Niles. "Shall I assume that now that Eastland has taken full control of all stations on the eastern side of the fault, these would be inaccessible to you should further tectonic activity occur?"

Niles nodded silently.

"But you would still have *some* control over pressure buildups, wouldn't you?"

Niles sighed heavily and rubbed his face with both hands. "That's true; but it wouldn't be enough in the event of a major movement like the one on the recording. That would require the combined efforts of stations on both sides of the fault to equalize pressure."

"But that's crazy!" Adela interrupted, barely able to believe what she was hearing. "If another earthquake like that occurred they'd be putting themselves in danger."

"My thought exactly," Woorunmarra agreed.

"Not entirely." Niles shrugged unhappily, turning his attention away from the flatscreen. "They have the entire system east of Arroyo, intact. And they control Leeper. Through Leeper, they can link into the control groupings on our side."

Woorunmarra nodded slowly in understanding. "I think I see now. If a pressure buildup threatens them, through the Leeper grouping they can override into your system and use it in tandem to bleed off the pressures that affect the area east of Arroyo much the same way as in the recording we just saw." He paused, lowering his eyes. "On the other hand, if they monitor a pressure buildup that looks like it'll have the greatest impact on the west . . ."

"They activate the eastern taps to minimize damage to themselves," Montero picked up, "and effectively shunt the worst of the movements to the other side of the fault—then they just sit back and watch as Westland crumbles."

Adela stared at Montero, her mouth open in shocked disbelief.

"It's worse than that, I'm afraid." Niles pivoted the small screen of the comm terminal so he could more easily read the information displayed there. "The tap stations *equalize* pressure buildups; that means additional pressure is applied to parts of the underlying structure at the same time it's being bled off others. Utilizing the control stations on the eastern edge of Arroyo in concert with Leeper, they can initialize tectonic activity as well as dampen it."

Everyone in the room sat in stunned silence; aboard *Levant,* no one spoke. Only the General seemed unsurprised by what Niles had just said.

"We'll begin severing the Leeper grouping from the control network immediately. There are . . ." Niles quickly checked the terminal, cursing softly under his breath when the figures came up on the tiny screen. "I'm afraid that when they chose Leeper, they chose well. There are forty-seven manned stations directly controlled by Leeper, but they should present little trouble. However, there are thousands of unmanned taps linked into them, and once the manned stations are taken off-line they'll have to be shut down, individually, on site."

"How dangerous will that be," Adela asked, "as far as current seismic activity is concerned? Will you be able to handle it?"

The Speaker shrugged worriedly. "We're not sure. There's no doubt that there will be an increase in minor tremors, mostly in the interior sections, but there shouldn't be any major threat. No major pressure buildups have been recorded for nearly two years, and we should be able to reroute a number of the stations to working control groupings to handle the minor ones, but . . ." He paused. "In any event, it'll take a long time to get them all." He looked up from the terminal and into the screen. "We could use help."

"You'll have it," Montero replied. "Just let me know what you need."

"Are you sure, Speaker?" The officer looked Kip Salera over with eyes that glowed with—what? The other officer seated next to him, a Major, mirrored the expression of his superior. There were others in Salera's office at the former Dominion Capitol, most of them military personnel. The only exception was Representative Blakert.

There is excitement in your face, young soldier, Salera thought, studying the man's face. *You fear the battle you know is coming, and yet you rush headlong to join it.* The man stood stiffly before his desk, his breathing fast with anticipation even though he was trying hard to keep his emotions hidden. How long had it been since he'd felt that intoxicating mix of foreboding combined with an undeniable longing that drove you on despite your best efforts at self-reason? He'd felt something similar at the final Joint Dominion, but even that could not compare with what he knew— from remembrances long past—was flowing through the man's body right now. The officer fidgeted slightly as he awaited the Speaker's reply.

"Yes, I'm certain of it, Colonel Harston. They would be stupid to attack with anything that might damage the stations themselves. If they mount an offensive at all, it will be with light weaponry. As for the starship . . ." Salera paused, gnawing momentarily on a lower lip. "I'm told that Commander Montero is sending armed personnel and equipment to help them with their efforts to take Leeper off-line, for all the good that'll do them, but the good Commander himself will take a hands-off attitude until things are settled here, one way or another."

"And after?" Blakert asked.

Salera glared once at Blakert, then regarded the Colonel, still standing before him. "You're dismissed." Harston snapped to attention, his officers following suit, and exited Salera's office immediately.

"And what about after, Speaker?"

Salera rose, crossing slowly to the large window overlooking the front of the building. Hundreds of troops were gathered on the long tree-lined parkade, awaiting their turn for the transport shuttles to take them to their assignments. As he watched, a steady stream of twenty-man shuttles landed in a cleared area on the far end of the parkade and almost immediately took off again as they filled up. "The deployment is going smoothly," he said without turning. "The shuttles are barely on the ground more than a few moments before returning to the air. They're well trained, all of them. Oh, did you know that I have a daughter in the Guard?"

Blakert went to the window and, ignoring the bustle of activity going on just a few hundred meters below them, asked again, "What about after?"

Speaker Salera didn't answer.

TWENTY-THREE

*T*he man is crazy, Adela said to herself, dragging the back of an arm across her dripping forehead. *Only a few hours past dawn, and already it's unbearable out here.* The lightweight hot-weather uniform consisting of roomy khaki shorts and matching shirt helped somewhat, but she was constantly grateful that the humidity was as low as it was. She glanced at her watch and tapped at its diminutive screen, cycling through the various functions until finding the one she wanted. *Thirty-nine degrees, and it's not even local noon yet. He really has lost it.* Louder, she called, "Hey! You're crazy, you know that?"

Woorunmarra ignored her, his attention fixed on something moving just above the horizon. The object circled back toward them and as it got nearer Woorunmarra began sprinting silently across the landscape toward it. In spite of his surprising speed, he was still several meters away when the thing hit the ground, tumbling crazily as it bounced along the surface. He scooped it up on the run, laughing giddily at the top of his lungs, and doubled back to stand before her again.

"Nah," he said, barely winded, "it feels just like home." He looked around him as if trying to decide which direction to throw the boomerang again, then added, "It's just a lot greener."

Adela followed his gaze. The surrounding countryside near station 67 was, despite the intense heat, lush with vegetation. There was a low, grassy ground cover, and clumps of large bushes were scattered everywhere. Barrel-shaped, branchless trees with leafy crowns dotted the landscape in groups of two and three, while to the west where the land became more hilly the edge of a large evergreen forest could be seen. The area around the station itself was mostly level, with only occasional hills or outcroppings interrupting the almost plainslike topography, but to the east a horizon-spanning ridge rose in the distance. A few kilometers beyond the ridge, belying the peaceful nature of the topography, lay the violent Arroyo fault.

There was a slight rise about a hundred meters on the other side of the station where a temporary shelter had been set up, housing a dozen members of the Congressional Guard that Niles had assigned to them. There were several parked vehicles— ground effect machines, or GEMs, as the soldiers referred to them—clustered nearby. Seated beneath a parasol-like canopy atop one of them, an armed soldier kept watch, glancing only occasionally in their direction. From where she stood she couldn't be sure which one of the soldiers it was, nor could she see any of the others. They were most likely beneath the protective covering of the shelter, out of the heat—just as the two of them should have been. "Let's go inside before you give yourself a stroke."

"Not yet," he replied, oblivious to the blazing sun. "I almost had it that time. A few more throws and I'll have a fair go at adjustin' to one point two *g*. Care to try?" He teasingly extended the gently curving piece of wood to her, before turning away with a laugh and whipping it into the air so fast that she barely followed the movement of his arm.

He tracked it with his eyes, his body rigid and unmoving. He wore only his khaki shorts—having dumped the rest of his uniform unceremoniously atop his discarded boots and socks—and she saw the smooth muscles rippling beneath his dark skin, glistening under a film of hard-earned perspiration.

The boomerang sailed out and slowly began angling upward, then at the very top of its flight arced gracefully to the left before beginning to circle back. As it came out of its arc, it glided downward at nearly the same angle at which it rose before leveling off for its return. "Watch now." Woorunmarra took one step to his left, studying its flight path, then another. Adela thought for a moment that the spinning blur would hit them, but at the last second Woorunmarra leaped nearly a meter off the ground and snatched it smoothly from the air. "Not bad, ay?"

Adela crossed her arms in front of her, pretending to be unimpressed. "I thought it was going to take my head off."

He grinned. "Nah. I weren't aimin' for your neck."

Adela smiled at the way his accent thickened and his speaking patterns changed whenever he was at ease and enjoying himself, as he obviously was now. In the time they'd been here at the station he seemed, almost literally, at home. "You can't really aim that thing, can you?" she asked dubiously.

"Course not." He turned again, looking away from the station. "See that tree there?" he asked, pointing at a fat-boled growth about sixty meters distant. She nodded and he handily flipped the boomerang away at a sharp angle that appeared to be taking it nowhere near the tree. It sailed out in a level arc this time, curving gently across the landscape until it impacted the tree, neatly impaling itself into the fleshy pulp of the cactus-like growth. Adela raised an eyebrow and noted that it had hit the tree at a point which, had she been standing in its place, would have been at her eye level.

"Nice." She tried to insert a tone of annoyance in her voice, but found herself smiling at him.

He laughed again and trotted off to retrieve the boomerang.

"I'm going inside," she called after him, then turned for the coolness of the station.

The pressure-tap station was well appointed and comfortable, if spartan, in its furnishings. The two-person crew had been informed by Speaker Niles himself that once the process of taking the station off-line had been completed, the station was to be used as guest quarters for the two Imperial visitors. They had cleaned the place thoroughly, even going so far as to put fresh linens in each of the small bedrooms.

Guest quarters, Adela thought sourly as she poured herself a glass of cold water. *More like a holding cell.*

She had refused to return to the ship and had attempted to convince Montero that it would be better if she and Woorunmarra were closer at hand. After all, she had reasoned, with more than a hundred *Levant* crew members helping the Westland techs in their efforts to isolate the Leeper control grouping, this whole thing just might be over before anything serious happened.

With warring factions squaring off along the length of the fault line, and with Westland troops now surrounding Leeper at a discreet distance, Montero was not nearly so optimistic. Still, with Woorunmarra echoing Adela's concern that immediate negotiations would be imperative should an agreement be reached, the Commander reluctantly agreed that the two of them should remain accessible, but safely away from any potential hostilities.

Allowing them to use one of the vacated stations had been Speaker Niles' idea. Located more than a hundred kilometers south of Leeper, they would be safe from anything occurring at the control station, and yet close enough to organize a settlement between the factions should their presence be needed on short notice. Montero had wanted to station a combat shuttle there, but Adela argued that the presence of the Imperial vehicle at an out-of-the-way spot like this was just asking for the Eastlanders to consider the station a target. The Commander had agreed with her reasoning—again, with reluctance. Besides, she argued, there were dozens of combat shuttles on standby at the Westland capital at Newcastle, and one could be sent if the Congressional Guard Captain in charge of this squad thought it necessary.

As it had turned out, the most dangerous things they'd experienced in the seven days they'd spent here so far had been boredom and the heat. And only she seemed bothered by the latter.

The centrally located control room, where Adela now stood, was dominated by a wall screen displaying a large overlay of the surface structure surrounding the station. Like the overlay they had watched in Niles' office, this one also showed the location of each station to which it was linked and extended in a four-hundred-kilometer-wide circle. The pressure tap itself was located below the station and, even though off-line from the network, she felt a humming vibration coming from below. The screen display fascinated her. While she had felt nothing since arriving on Pallatin, she knew that minor tremors occurred almost constantly on the planet, and the screen seemed to confirm that fact: Dim flashes of color appeared here and there as the automatic monitors showed even the slightest tectonic activity whenever it occurred.

The flashes came and went randomly, with no set pattern, and yet occasionally followed minor fault lines as they flickered out. The effect reminded her of the way lightning teased the distant sky on Gris whenever a thunderstorm formed. She remembered once, back home, how she and her father had sat on a hillside and watched an approaching storm sweep angrily across the de Parzon valley. The storm itself had never reached their settlement and remained in the distance, too far even to hear the thunder as the flashes played over the horizon. As a child she had always been afraid of the frequent storms on Gris, but remembered how, on that day when her father had called her up from their underground home to watch the silent lightning in the safety of his arms, she had overcome her fear.

She smiled, feeling herself becoming lost in the memory when the screen suddenly winked out, along with all lighting in the station except a dully glowing emergency lamp mounted above each doorway.

There was a low rumbling coming from outside, crossing overhead. The sound carried with it an odd presence that confused her for several long seconds until it struck her why the sound was so clear inside the station: The pressure tap beneath her feet had fallen silent. There was no reassuring vibration, no hum coming from below to indicate the station was alive at all.

Her eyes grew accustomed quickly to the dimness and she found the exit with little trouble, flinging the door wide. A wall of heat hit her in the face as she left the sheltering coolness of the station, and within seconds Adela found herself perspiring beneath the glaring sun as she sought out Woorunmarra.

He and the commanding officer had climbed atop the GEM the guardsman had used for a lookout post, and the three of them, their arms raised to shade their eyes, stared into the sky. He had put his boots back on and retrieved his shirt, tucking it into his belt. The others had come out of the shelter and were likewise trying to follow whatever it was that had attracted the lookout's attention.

"What is it?" Adela called out, trotting up to stand alongside the GEM. She leaned against the side of the machine, but pulled quickly away from the hot, sun-baked surface. "What happened?"

"Don't know," Woorunmarra replied, still gazing skyward. "An aircraft with Eastland markings circled us once at low altitude, then headed in that direction. Didn't do much, though. Captain Radaker's already called it in."

"Could it have had anything to do with the power shutdown inside the station?"

Woorunmarra and Radaker looked at each other, then scrambled down from their perch. The guardsman remained atop the GEM while Adela and the two men headed for the station.

It was still deliciously cool inside, but by the time the three of them finished an inspection of the station searching for the cause of the outage, they could tell the air was beginning to warm considerably. Unfortunately their search turned up nothing that might have been responsible for the power failure; at least, nothing that could be detected and repaired on the site. Whatever the cause of the outage, it didn't seem to be located here.

"I don't know what it is," Radaker said once they were back outside. He stared into the sky in the direction the aircraft had disappeared. "Maybe it did have something to do with it. A magnetic pulse, maybe, tuned to the frequency of the receiving dish—but there should be a buried cable backup." He cupped his hands over his mouth and called to the lookout on the GEM. "Tell Wyand to get her kit. Tell her to pick four of the others to help her do a complete check on the circuitry." A young woman, a compact electronics case tucked under her arm, and several of the others came up and, after speaking briefly to the Captain, hurried inside the station.

"Can we contact our people?" Woorunmarra sounded worried. "With the power down we can't use the station's comm terminal."

"Of course, at the shelter. The portable's voice-only, but help yourself."

"Thanks."

Radaker nodded, then followed the others inside the station.

"What's wrong?" Adela asked once they were alone. "Specifically, I mean."

"I'm not sure. Just want to call in." He picked up his step, outpacing her. Clearly, if he suspected something, he didn't want to discuss it until he'd had a chance to check it out. Adela let him go and remained outside the shelter. She wondered if she might be able to help inside the station, but decided against offering. Radaker and the others had been very friendly and courteous to both of them, but it was clear they weren't pleased with the duty they'd drawn. Best to stay out of their way, she realized.

She sat down in the shade of one of the barrel trees a few meters up the rise, her back resting against the soft, almost spongy bole. In spite of the heat, the humidity was still very low and a soft breeze made the spot quite comfortable. She leaned her head back and closed her eyes, and had been there only a few minutes when Woorunmarra came running from the shelter.

"Captain Radaker!"

He was sprinting for the station, calling out as he ran, and was about halfway to the front entrance when Adela noted a sudden sharp hissing that filled the air. She jumped to her feet, but before she could move there was a sudden *whump!* and she saw the canted roof of the station crumple as if in slow motion, followed by a brilliant flash and a shock wave that threw her backward into the tree. Dazed, she tumbled like a rag doll to the ground.

She tried to push herself up, but a dizziness and nausea swept over her and she fell forward into the grass. She tried again, successfully this time, and managed to push herself up to a sitting position. The whole scene spun around her through blurred eyes. There was a throbbing ache at the back of her head and she felt blood trickling down the back of her neck. She rubbed at it gingerly, feeling a small gash in her scalp. Her hand was covered with blood when she pulled it back, but the wound felt too small to be serious. She rose unsteadily to her feet, wiping bloody fingers on her shorts, and looked at the station. Or what was left of it.

The whole building had collapsed, the jumble of twisted plastic and metal now fully engulfed in flames. The heat was intense and pounded against her face in searing waves; she found it difficult to even look directly at it. Burning sections of the station were strewn for dozens of meters in all directions; a chunk of roofing had barely missed the shelter and hit one of the GEMs, setting it afire. Halfway between the burning vehicle and the wreckage of the station, next to a twisted support beam, Woorunmarra lay unmoving.

"Billy!" Some of the men and women at the shelter had cleared the rise and were running down to the fire, reaching the perimeter of the station just as she made it to Woorunmarra. He rose shakily to his feet, stumbling to his knees with the first step he tried to take. Adela helped him to his feet and steadied him as the first of the soldiers came to their side.

"I'm . . . I'm all right," he said, waving them away. "The station? Anybody left?"

He turned back to the flames and made a feeble move toward the wreckage before Adela stopped him. There were several people silhouetted against the fire, but it was clear that no one inside could have survived the blast itself, much less the inferno that was raging now.

The remaining soldiers came running over the crest of the rise. Adela noted they had donned battle armor and were now fully armed. The one in the lead, a woman unusually tall for a Pallatin, was shouting as she came down the slope.

"From the south! They're coming up from the south. Tell the Captain that—" She stopped cold, seeing the wreckage and realizing the seriousness of the hit they'd just taken. She came up alongside them, doing a mental nose count. "Captain Radaker? Wyand and the others?"

One of the men who had arrived at the fire first now came running back, his face red from his proximity to the inferno that just three minutes earlier had been pressure-tap station 67. "They were inside . . . *are* inside." He turned back to the flames, the others who had run down with him immediately after the blast joining them where they stood. "They . . ." He didn't have to finish.

There were eight of them now: Adela and Woorunmarra, plus the remaining six guards. The tall woman, Janners, was a Sergeant and had the highest rank among them. A look of subdued anxiety crossed her face when the realization hit that she was now in command, but she immediately sized up the situation and took charge, reluctantly and uncertainly.

"The rest of you suit up. We may have company in a few minutes. Move!" Once the others were out of earshot she turned to them, her voice apologetic. "This wasn't supposed to happen. There was no indication that—"

"Forget it." Woorunmarra rubbed at his shoulder, skinned and bleeding where he'd been thrown to the concrete apron around the station. "What information do you have?"

Adela took his arm before she could answer, forcibly leading him up the rise. "Keep talking, but let's move up to the shelter, out of the open. Sergeant, could we get a dressing for his shoulder?"

She followed, but for a moment Janners was unsure as how to respond to Adela's overt action. So much had happened in such a short time—the attack, the loss of half her squad, assuming command—that she seemed overwhelmed. Hastily catching up with the pair from behind, she caught sight of Woorunmarra's shoulder, then her gaze settled on the blood that had run down into the collar of Adela's shirt. "Come on," she barked, as if fully comprehending the situation for the first time. Her demeanor changed suddenly and she quickened her step to lead them up the rise, calling ahead of her as they approached the shelter, "I need a medical kit. Now!" She continued talking over her shoulder. "Divisional command just called, there's an enemy unit heading up from the south. They're still east of Arroyo, but command has heat-traced the missile that hit the station directly to them. It's a sure bet that the flyover computer targeted us, then relayed the information to them, and they fired while still twenty-five kilometers out."

One of the enlisted men had brought the kit at about the same time they entered the shelter and was already spraying a skin gel on Woorunmarra's shoulder and back. The wound treated, he concentrated on the gash on the back of Adela's head. The spray stung slightly for a moment, but the anesthetic worked quickly to drive away the throbbing that had been steadily increasing since she'd gotten back on her feet. She felt her scalp tighten where the injury was, indicating the skin gel was going to work closing the cut.

Woorunmarra stretched his arm and shoulder as the gel penetrated his skin, checking his range of motion. "That fits in with what I just learned from the *Levant.*" He stopped stretching suddenly and let his arm drop to his side. "I just wish I'd managed to find out a few seconds sooner."

"Don't even think about it, Billy," Adela interjected, wiping the now-dried blood from her neck with a moist pad the enlisted man had given her. "Nothing we can do about it. The question is, what happens now?"

"There's an Imperial combat shuttle on its way from the station at Taw. It's the only one close, but there are others that'll be sent as backup."

"In the meantime we get you away from the station. Listen," Janners barked at the remaining guards, "you, and you—check the GEMs; get two of them ready to move. The rest of you gather what you need." The two men, their guns clattering against their armor, ran from the shelter and Janners turned back to them. "Can either of you drive a GEM? We might need—"

Woorunmarra waved a hand to cut her off. "Nah, no good. The *Levant* scanned the unit heading our way and said they've got a fifteen-man long-range hopper. We can't outrun them in those." He hooked a thumb over his shoulder in the direction the vehicles were parked. "They're part of a larger force that's takin' out as many of the individual stations as they can. Apparently they just started movin' not much more than a half hour ago; but with several dozen of their bloody aircraft and hoppers workin' together, timin' their attacks nearly simultaneously, their hit-and-run raids managed to destroy twenty stations before anyone knew what they were up to." His eyes shifted away for a moment. "Make that twenty-one," he added soberly.

Janners considered this, then stepped across the shelter to the unit's portable comm set. A woman in armor, a Private, sat at the unit with her helmet cradled in her lap to accommodate the headset she wore. "Bring a scan up on the screen."

"It's up, but they're still too far out of range for the . . . Wait . . ." She listened in the headset for a moment, then tapped at the lower right corner of the screen with a fingertip where a pulsing blip had just appeared at the edge. "There they are, five k out and closing."

"You said hit-and-run, sir," Janners said without looking from the screen. "They're still coming."

"Yeah, looks that way."

"It's us," Adela realized aloud. "They know we're here. They monitored communications, or used satellite pictures or something."

Woorunmarra shook his head. "I don't think so." He pulled at the shirt still tucked into his belt, then slipped it on. "Sergeant, has a squad been posted at all the stations that've been shut down?"

"I don't know, but I doubt it. The individual stations are important, but they're just not that critical to the pressure-tap network." She thought a moment, then added, "There are a few stations in populated areas and they may have units assigned to them, but with so much happening to the north I don't think they'd bother with isolated locations like this one."

"There's your answer, then. They want to see what's so interestin' about this station." He buttoned his shirt, hastily tucking the tail into his shorts, and slipped the boomerang into his belt. "Sergeant, an Imperial combat shuttle's on its way, but these hoons'll be here in a matter of minutes. Could we borrow some armor?" He pointed to several pieces of battle gear near the bunks.

Janners hesitated a moment, realizing that the gear he'd indicated belonged to those who had just been killed, but nodded hurriedly and grabbed a frag vest from the nearest bunk and tossed it to him. "Put it to use, sir, ma'am. Do you need help in how to use it?"

"I'm fine," he responded, pulling the vest on and deftly snapping the catches. "How about you, Doctor?"

"Just show me what's what."

They started suiting up, with Adela needing to try a few times before finding a set of gear small enough to fit. She finally managed to find a vest that would do and Woorunmarra gave her brief directions on how the pulse rifle worked while she struggled with the vest catches. A sudden squealing from the comm set, an indication that the approaching hopper was hitting them with jamming interference, caused them to finish suiting up without further discussion.

"It's out! Gone!" The Private pulled off the headset, tossing it against the screen, and donned her helmet.

Adela finished with the frag vest and hefted the rifle, mentally going over Billy's instructions. "Where were they?"

"Two k, closing."

"Damn," Woorunmarra spat under his breath. "The shuttle won't be here soon enough if they start firin' on us. Do you have any surface-to-air weapons?"

Janners and two of the Privates immediately started to scramble for the weapons.

"No! No, wait. There's not enough time. Listen!" They stopped in their tracks. Already the unmistakable high-pitched whine of hopper thrusters could be heard from the southeast. Adela ran for the shelter door, tossing it aside like the glorified tent flap that it was and looked outside for a second, then started running out of the depression for the top of the rise leading to the station. "Come on!"

Woorunmarra, easily the fastest runner among them, was instantly trotting at her side with the rest of them directly behind. "Damn, lady," he said good-naturedly despite the seriousness of what was happening, "you even had me jumpin'. You ever think about the military as a career instead of science?"

She ignored his attempt at humor. "Billy, when they see the shelter and GEMs intact and nobody around, they're going to come in shooting from a half kilometer out. We can't fight them or even hope to hold them off till the shuttle gets here. We need *time*!"

They cleared the rise and sped down the slope to the station. It had collapsed further as the flames consumed it; the thick, black smoke from the burning plastic billowed away from the site with increased intensity as the flames began to run out of fuel to sustain them.

"Everyone! Down on the ground!" She ran as close to the radiating heat as she could and let herself fall onto the concrete apron and lay still, her gun on the ground at her side but still within reach, then unstrapped her helmet—she'd had difficulty getting it to fit properly anyway—and let it roll across the concrete. "Don't give them a reason to fire on us from the safety of distance! Make them come in close enough to see we aren't a threat that needs to be fired upon from the hopper!"

"But keep your weapon close!" Janners shouted, picking up Adela's strategy. She sprawled on the ground and, flashing a quick grin in Adela's direction, unbuckled her helmet and let it roll freely to one side.

Woorunmarra had fallen next to her. "Let's hope they circle us a few times, checkin' us out," he called out over the ascending whine of the approaching hopper. "If we can keep'm in the air for five or ten minutes until the combat shuttle gets here, she'll be sweet."

"Billy, will they be shielded?"

He smiled. "If they are, then these hoons'll be in for a big surprise when they drop out of the sky on top of them. If not, the hopper's sensors'll see it and probably turn around and get back across Arroyo as fast as they can. Either way, we just need the time."

Yes, Adela thought, *all we need is time.*

The hopper hove into view over a rise a kilometer away and skirted the flaming station in a wide circle, the whine of its jets lessening to a lower pitch as it slowed. It came to a stop and hovered at a point due west and remained motionless for several seconds. A sharp hiss split the air and one of the GEMs at the edge of the shelter jumped and spun end over end into the air as a small missile hit it. It fell heavily into the side of the shelter and fell apart, but did not explode. At the same time the hopper shifted abruptly to the side, then rapidly circled the area from the edge of a half-*k* radius and scanned the scene from a safe distance.

"A test shot," Woorunmarra said without moving. "They're buyin' it. Good job."

The hopper came in closer and settled to the ground a few hundred meters south of the burning station, kicking up a swirling cloud of dust and loose vegetation around its landing pads. Adela and the others carefully, slowly, turned heads in the direction of the hopper and watched as eight Eastland soldiers, fully decked in armor similar to their own, dropped out of the belly hatch and took positions in an advancing flank pointed toward the station. Either this hopper was not carrying a full complement of soldiers—which would seem likely if they had originally intended station 67 to be a hit-and-run mission—or there were several more still on board.

"Hello!" The shout came from somewhere in the group of advance soldiers, probably from the commanding officer. "Come forward and be recognized!"

"Everyone, stay down!" Adela admonished under her breath. Then, to the amazement of the others, she stirred fitfully, as if injured, and rose to a sitting position.

"Doctor!"

"Dammit, Billy, stay *down.* I know what I'm doing."

The advancing men fell to crouching positions as she rose.

"You! I want to see hands in the air! Now!"

She raised her hands and came up on her feet slowly, shakily, keeping up the pretense of being injured. As she stood, she made certain she'd be able to tumble sideways and grab the pulse rifle if she had to, but made a deliberate effort of giving the appearance of being unarmed and helpless. The advancing force halted well outside the apron of the station, half of them training their weapons on her, the rest—apparently on orders of their commander—aiming at the seemingly inert forms scattered on the ground around her.

"Don't shoot!" Adela pleaded. She did her best to add an edge of fear to her voice but admitted inwardly that the effort wasn't difficult. "I'm unarmed!" She ambled forward, taking each step as slowly as she thought she could get away with. She remembered something she'd seen in a video and approached with her hands clasped behind her head. She even stumbled once, purposely, dropping to her knees and milking everything she could from her "performance" as she moved toward the waiting Eastlanders.

Someone barked an order and two of the soldiers leaped from their attack positions and trotted in her direction. One of them, a woman no taller than herself, held a pulse rifle leveled at her chest as the other checked her for weapons. As they did, she heard another barked order that sent a second pair of soldiers forward to cover those lying on the ground.

Adela feined confusion as they questioned and searched her for weapons. They were rough with her and at one point during their frisking inadvertently knocked her down. Still on the ground, Adela raised herself up in time to see Billy Woorunmarra jump to his feet and pull the boomerang from his belt in one smooth motion. There was an instantaneous rattling sound as eight pulse rifles came to bear on him.

"Billy, no! I'm all right!"

He froze in place, his arm already pulled back to throw, as one of the soldiers took the boomerang away. The man handled the unfamiliar weapon gingerly, as if it might explode at any moment, and quickly gave it to one of the others of lower rank. The unlucky recipient looked no happier to be holding it than he had.

The rest of the Eastland soldiers jumped suddenly to their feet and came up to surround the two of them, half the company training their weapons on her and Billy, the rest on those lying on the apron.

With the guns holding them motionless, the commanding officer came forward. He was armored to match his company, unlike the Westland practice of distinctive armor arranged by rank. Then again, perhaps he had come into command in much the same way Sergeant Janners had, and there had not been time to receive the new gear befitting his rank. His eyes darted from her to Billy and back again, the look on his face clearly displaying his uneasiness at the presence of the two obvious off-worlders standing before him. He carried a pulse rifle identical to the others and used the barrel of the weapon to prod her as he asked, more than a hint of nervousness in his voice, "Who are you?"

"I am Dr. Adela de Montgarde, appointed representative of Javas, Emperor of the Hundred Worlds." She paused, then added slowly, deliberately, "And mother of the Crown Prince, Eric." She caught the expression of surprised shock on Woorunmarra's face out of the corner of one eye. "My companion is Lieutenant Billy Woorunmarra of the Imperial starship *Levant*. And you are . . . ?"

The young man, already stressed by at his closeness to an unexpected and unwelcome combat situation, turned ashen. The nearest of his troops likewise became increasingly ill at ease by the turn of events. What should have been a routine bombing raid seemed about to erupt into an Imperial incident.

He stared at them for what seemed several minutes before finally coming to a decision. "Corporal Tiverst," he barked at last to the man nearest him, "take three men and check the shelter."

"Sir!" The man nodded to three of the others and the group trotted over the rise, weapons at the ready. The officer said nothing, waiting until he received a shouted all-clear from the Corporal. Waving the men back down, he spoke to yet another of the soldiers, the woman who had originally come forward to cover Adela. "Take the Westies to the hopper and keep them under guard." All but two of the Eastland soldiers rounded up the remainder of Janners' unit and walked them toward the hopper, waiting where it had landed a half kilometer away.

"And you are . . . ?" Adela asked again.

He stood straighter, nodding his head at them. "I am Lieutenant Len Ellan of the Eastland Guard." He motioned to the two remaining soldiers, and they came forward, their weapons still trained steadily, if uncertainly, on them. "Doctor, Lieutenant,

I'm going to ask you to come with me, but I assure you that you will not be harmed in any way."

"Where are you taking us?" Woorunmarra asked.

"I haven't the authority to deal with you," he admitted, "so I'm taking you back to divisional headquarters."

"They won't take kindly to our being kidnapped." Adela pointed skyward, indicating the orbiting ship.

The words startled him. "You aren't being kidnapped, you're being taken as prisoners of war." He thumbed the safety on his pulse rifle as he turned away, his back already to them when the soldiers prodded her and Billy with the rifles to start moving toward the hopper.

With everything happening so quickly Adela had almost forgotten about the heat, but the full force of the sun beat down on them now as they made their way to the hopper. She stumbled once about halfway to the hopper, tripping on the exposed root of one of the barrel trees, and caused the cut on her head to start bleeding slightly again.

Woorunmarra helped her to her feet and steadied her by the arm, saying, "Doctor, are you all right?" Before she could answer, he pulled her arm forcibly to the side, making it look as though she were having trouble walking. She didn't know what he had in mind but kept her mouth shut, following his lead. They walked on, staring straight ahead. After several more meters, he squeezed her arm slightly and nodded at the hopper. The last of the prisoners had entered the craft, the soldier bringing up the rear disappearing inside afterward.

So that's what he's been waiting for, she thought, and continued walking as if it were getting increasingly difficult. After a few more steps he pulled at her arm again and both of them tumbled to the ground. Billy pushed her to the side, well clear of where he'd fallen, while at the same time rolling in the opposite direction. He twisted gracefully to a crouching position, whipping his arm back. One of the soldiers fell forward as a stone hit him directly between his eyes. Another blur of his arm and the second man went down near the first, groaning heavily and clasping both hands to his forehead.

The whole thing had taken only seconds, but it was still time enough for the Eastland Lieutenant to bring his rifle to bear on the Aborigine. Adela jumped to her feet, drawing his attention—

and the barrel of the rifle—away from Billy just long enough for him to hurl a third stone that smashed into one of the man's hands. He yelled in pain and she thought she heard the sound of the man's fingers breaking just before the gun fired, wide of her and harmlessly into the ground. She kicked the rifle, knocking it from his hands, then quickly scrambled to pick it up and covered all three of the Eastlanders—not that any of the three posed a threat at this point. The two on the ground appeared to be recovering from the surprise attack against them from the most ancient of weapons; the Eastland Lieutenant stood passively, cradling his injured hand.

Adela shot a glance at the hopper and was relieved to find no indication that they'd been seen yet, or at least that there were no soldiers coming to their commander's aid. Then again, perhaps they were aiming the hopper's guns on them . . .

A sudden, overwhelming buzz filled the air so fully that even the two men on the ground stirred and covered their ears as they gazed skyward at the four Imperial combat shuttles dropping in a diamond formation out of the sky, taking positions effectively boxing in the entire perimeter of station 67.

Several soldiers had dropped from the underside of the hopper to aid the Lieutenant, Adela saw, but now didn't know what to do—some of them dropped to the ground and attempted to cover themselves while others stared dumbly at the descending ships. Three of the shuttles formed a hovering triangle around the hopper while the fourth came to rest on the concrete apron and began a shutdown cycle as its thrusters powered down to standby.

Adela stood straighter, lowering the pulse rifle and thumbing the safety back on, and looked the commanding officer over. His eyes moved frantically from the descending array of armed shuttles to the craft on the apron, then to Adela and the others, and then back again. He was very young, she realized, like most of the soldiers she'd seen on both sides of this conflict. He nodded his head once in acceptance of his situation and turned to face the shuttle sitting on the apron and waited.

Adela couldn't be certain, because he had turned away so abruptly, but she thought she saw a look of quiet thankfulness spread over his features at being relieved of a burden he found too heavy to bear.

TWENTY-FOUR

Montero sat impassively, quiet for the first time since the briefing had begun several hours earlier. *At least he's stopped shouting,* Adela thought. *Perhaps now we can actually get something accomplished.*

Emotions finally out in the open, the meeting proceeded apace, and would end with a holoconference with both Salera and Niles. There was still much ground to cover until the two national leaders joined them, however.

The Commander was infuriated by what had happened at tap station 67, not to mention the offensive mounted by Eastland in general, although Adela suspected that it was a fury brought on by feelings of deep, intense frustration with the situation rather than a personal reaction to the blatant aggression itself.

"I can obliterate Pallatin," he was saying. "The *Levant* has planetbreakers, and I've been given full authority to use them should I deem it necessary for the successful completion of this mission." He paused again, then looked her and Woorunmarra straight in the eyes, adding as a postscript, "The last thing Commander Fain told me—with Emperor Javas' endorsement, mind you—was that Pallatin could not ultimately refuse the Hundred Worlds, that no world could leave the Empire without the Empire's approval. If Pallatin is allowed to leave, then others might follow, effectively dismantling the Empire itself. Doctor, you, of all people, should realize the effect this would have on the project to save Earth's Sun."

Adela started to protest, but he cut her off with a wave of his hand. "No. No, I understand your feelings regarding your project, and while I don't concur with the importance of it, I do agree with you and with the Emperor that a bloodless agreement from this key world would carry far more weight in swaying other members of the Hundred than would its destruction. Believe me, I don't want to do that." She stared at him wide-eyed, and he chuckled at her reaction. "Surprised?"

"Frankly, yes." Adela turned to Woorunmarra, attempting to

see if he might have known anything about the Commander's sentiments beforehand, but his normally expressive face remained impassive. "May I ask what changed your mind?"

He smiled, chuckling again under his breath. "Nothing changed my mind. Nothing at all."

She regarded him with a new respect, at the same time chiding herself inwardly not only for having prejudged him but for carrying her original impression of the man far longer than she should have. If she gained nothing else on this trip, this newfound knowledge about her character would serve her well as the project progressed. *If* it progressed, she reminded herself.

The meeting went on. Other personnel—First Officer Nelon, Weapons Master Kyovska, Imperial geologists and technicians—came and went as they were called in for their expertise, then dismissed. Many possible courses of action were suggested and discussed, and, while many had merit, none would be decided upon until after a final meeting with the two Speakers.

All other parties heard from, only Montero, Adela and Billy Woorunmarra attended that final portion of the meeting. The Speakers themselves took part from their respective capitals: Salera from the former Joint Dominion Capitol in Eastland, Niles from his own government headquarters at Newcastle. Like Salera, Niles appeared holographically, which surprised Adela somewhat. Adela remembered that his own office was not holographically equipped, and realized that he must be using another facility for this session. She wondered idly how desperate this man, who preferred simplicity in most of the things he did, must have been for a settlement of the conflict with Eastland for him to use the higher technology of holography rather than the simple flatscreen he favored in his own office.

The holoconference room aboard *Levant* was specifically designed for meetings of this type and had ceiling-mounted projectors arranged in a circular pattern rather than a holo display area located in one corner or along a single wall frame as did most of the other rooms aboard the ship. There were actual chairs here, an even dozen of them, in a semicircle on one side with an open area on the other to allow for the received projections. The room seemed half empty with only two projections on the receiving side, those of the two Speakers. The two men were projected with their chairs next to each other, although the perspective on their end was probably different. Most likely so, in fact; little chance of these two willingly sitting next to one another, even if holographically.

"We are adamant!" Salera was saying, pounding a fist on the armrest of his chair. The man had changed physically since the last time Adela had seen him weeks earlier. His face was thinner, his body gaunt, and large circles could be seen hanging opaquely beneath tired eyes. Although the Eastland Congressional Guard retained its possession of the most strategically located sites of the pressure-tap network and enjoyed virtual control of Pallatin itself, that control had not come without a price. A number of the hopper raids on the abandoned manned stations had been intercepted by Westland forces. The casualties were many, and the numbers of Eastland soldiers now being held as prisoners of war grew daily. The conflict had taken a severe emotional, and now physical, toll on the Speaker that was plain at even a casual glance. "We want neither interference from the Hundred Worlds, nor interaction. We wish simply to be left out of Imperial matters entirely. Tell me why that is so wrong!"

The question had been directed at Lieutenant Woorunmarra, but it was Niles who responded. "It is not 'wrong,' " he said levelly. Amasee Niles, like his counterpart, looked exhausted. "Eastland wishes to be an entity unto itself. That is not wrong, but it is shortsighted."

Technically, as the Imperial legal representative and negotiator, this portion of the meeting was under the direction of Woorunmarra. It was up to him to attempt to bring about a resolution to this conflict, based in Imperial law and protocol if possible. However, it was a sign of his training that he knew when not to speak as well. Recognizing that much of what he was attempting to get Salera to realize was being said now by Speaker Niles, he remained passive during their several exchanges, speaking only when necessary.

"Simply put," Niles continued, "as I've tried to convince you many times in the past: We need each other, Pallatin and the Hundred Worlds, just as our two Congresses need one another."

Salera snorted contemptuously, crossing his arms resolutely across his chest. "We don't need you anymore." He said the words slowly, almost individually, the meaning behind his words plain.

"And why is that?" Adela put in before Niles could respond. "Because you've taken over one of the most important parts of the pressure-tap network, the northern control station on the west side of Arroyo?"

"It is a matter of self-preservation!" Salera was on his feet, his face flushed. He pointed across the meeting room to a point that must have represented Niles' holographic projection from his perspective, although there was no one seated where he indicated. He looked angrily at the empty chair, adding, "I know that tremors have increased west of Arroyo. We've monitored them, but did nothing to stop them—at least as far as the effects have been felt on your side, that is. However, should you decide to join us in our opposition to the Hundred Worlds, Niles, we'll be more than happy to share the tap network."

Adela was about to counter his outburst, but the brief smile that appeared on Speaker Niles' lips stopped her before she could say anything.

"You see, Kip?" he said softly. "You need our half of the network." He paused, the smile lingering, and directed his remarks at the Eastland Speaker, although it was clear he was addressing the room at large. "You've just proven my point—we need each other. Because of the conditions here, because of the violent physical division of Arroyo, Pallatin can never truly be one world; and yet, we can never be truly separated."

Salera snorted again and retook his seat. Niles' image turned from the Speaker and, the viewing angle of his reception apparently more accurate than the other's, looked directly at Adela.

"Dr. Montgarde, several weeks ago I told you that I once felt much as my counterpart does. Do you remember asking me at the time what changed my mind?"

Adela nodded. "As I recall, you changed the subject."

He pursed his lips in an abashed half-smile and sighed. "Yes, I guess I did." He leaned forward as he spoke, resting elbows on knees. "Nearly twenty years ago—probably at about the same time you left Earth to come here—I was a junior representative to the Joint Dominion, assigned to accompany a trading delegation to Killian's World, a frontier trading world that deals in science and engineering. Specifically, I was to bring back the technology needed to develop the pressure-tap network."

"But that wasn't necessary," Woorunmarra interrupted. "You

could've obtained that technology from the Empire. You didn't need to go to another frontier world to—''

"No? It is when you'd rather conduct business outside your world, simply to avoid letting the influence of outsiders in. We . . . I was as stubborn as the rest of Pallatin in my belief that the influence of the Hundred Worlds should not be felt here, even if it meant going outside for what we needed and bringing only that one thing back. There was control that way, you see? That way there would be no danger of any outside 'contamination' from the Empire's influence.

"Killian's World is close; using one of our fastest starships, the entire trip lasted under six years. I was on my way back, less than a month out, the technology to control our world *in my hands . . .*" He thrust his hands, balled into tight fists, forcefully out in front of him. He sat like that for several moments, his fists gradually loosening as he brought the painful memory under control. "There have been many earthquakes here since Pallatin was settled centuries ago, but none as devastating in terms of loss of life as the one that occurred while I was gone.''

Speaker Salera remained quiet in his chair, and Adela noted that the anger seemed to have drained from his features as he listened to Niles. The defiance still glowed in his eyes, but behind them lay a glimmer of—what?—sorrow at Niles' story? *My God,* she suddenly realized, *there is a connection between them.* Were they related? Was there a common experience or a shared background that, despite their different philosophies, constantly tried to draw these two men together?

"We rebuilt, of course," Niles went on softly. "We always rebuilt. But the tap technology I brought back ensured that we might never need rebuild again; that we might never see the losses we saw then. Working together, controlling Arroyo from both sides of the fault tamed it, made us the masters of our world at last." He lifted his eyes, turning to face the other Speaker. "But it was something that could have been done years earlier, were it not for our foolish isolationist paranoia. Cutting ourselves off from the Hundred Worlds—and my support of the belief that it was the right thing to do—killed thousands, including members of my own family, unnecessarily. Killed them at a time when I was safe and cozy aboard a Pallatin starship.''

He hesitated, overcome with emotion, and reached outside the image for a moment. His hand returned with a glass of water, and he sipped quietly before going on. "Much time has passed since then, and in that time we in the west have gradually come to realize the folly of isolationism on a world like Pallatin." He turned again to Salera. "We can be different, we can honor different customs and ideas that are dear to us, we can live our lives as we choose. We can even disagree. But we can't continue this separation, Kip. It'll destroy us both."

The room was silent. Salera leaned back heavily in his chair, stroking at his neck and forehead with a handkerchief.

"Then join us," he replied coldly. He thumbed a control on the armrest of the chair, and his image winked out.

They spoke to Speaker Niles for several minutes longer, then he, too, signed off and the three of them considered carefully what both men had said and how it would relate to whatever actions they would ultimately have to take. The discussion that followed lasted nearly as long as the session before the holoconference.

"Like he said, they are adamant in their stance." Woorunmarra rubbed his face tiredly. "As he sees it, isolationism applies only to interaction with the Hundred Worlds; as long as both sides of Arroyo control the fault, Salera feels that they *are* united. And as long as he controls the Leeper stations, he's willin' to wait until Westland agrees with his stance."

"The man is an idiot," Adela spat. The tone in her voice took both Woorunmarra and Montero by surprise—neither had ever seen this side of her before. She became suddenly aware that they were staring at her, but didn't care. Stupidity, in whatever form she encountered it, angered her and she felt that Salera was stupidly blinding himself to the truth of everything Speaker Niles had said during the holoconference. "He feels that as long as control can be maintained on a rudimentary level, Pallatin has no need of anyone else."

"But he isn't the only one," Montero countered. Just as she had unsettled him with her angry outburst a moment ago, so, too, did he take her by surprise with the softness in his voice now. "Speaker Niles seems as adamant about what he wants as does Salera."

"But he's right!"

Montero held up both hands, palms out. "I know, I know; and

I agree with the sentiments behind his philosophy." He peered deeply into Adela's eyes. "Isn't that what this mission is all about? Holding the Empire together, just as he wants to hold his world together? But he seems, in many ways, as unwilling to bend in what he wants as Salera."

Adela was forced to admit that the Commander was correct. She glanced once at Woorunmarra, who shrugged his shoulders and nodded in agreement to make it unanimous.

Thirty-six hours later, Niles appeared in the holoconference room once more. The Westland Speaker had readily agreed, as he had in the past, to further discussion of the situation and, as he had before, came to this session full of hope. Adela felt ashamed by what they were about to tell him and, even though his image was holographic, she had difficulty looking him in the eye as he waited patiently for the proceedings to begin. Salera, on the other hand, had been nearly impossible to pin down and had made several excuses and postponements of this session. It was he, in fact, that they waited for now.

Niles sat patiently, his elbows on the armrests of his chair, hands steepled before him. Only initial pleasantries had been exchanged among them once his image had appeared in the room, but that was normal. In holoconferences planned with both Speakers, no discussion was undertaken until both were present. He seemed to sense, however, that this meeting, called at Montero's urgent request, was different and that the Imperial starship Commander had come to a decision regarding his home. He waited wordlessly, a noncommittal look cloaking his features.

There was a brief crackling in the air on the other side of the room, then a flicker of light before Salera's image took shape across from them. He, too, had a look of anxious anticipation in his eyes that he tried with little success to keep hidden. Like Niles, he did not seem surprised that Adela, Woorunmarra and Montero had been joined by First Officer Nelon and Weapons Master Kyovska. Again, a few brief pleasantries were exchanged.

"A decision has been made," Woorunmarra began without preamble, addressing the two Speakers. "It is with great regret that a satisfactory agreement could not be reached between your two Congresses, and the Empire will take no enjoyment from what it must do." The brief statement of purpose completed, he looked to Montero, turning the rest of the conference over to him.

"Thank you, Lieutenant." Montero's face was grim, and Adela noted that the man was deeply pained by what he was about to say. Far from the warmongering Imperial Commander she had first imagined him, she realized, perhaps for the first time, just how heavily this decision had weighed on him. He sat straighter in his chair and regarded Speaker Niles. "First, it has been decided that all support services, including—but not limited to—personnel, armament, transportation, medical, reconnaissance, and electronic and software services will be immediately withdrawn from Westland."

Salera allowed a smile, pleased that the decision seemed to be going in his favor. In contrast, all color drained from Niles' face. His breathing came in sharp gasps and his mouth worked futilely as he attempted to respond.

"Please remain silent," Montero said before he could utter a word. "All parties will be allowed to speak when I'm finished. The audio of anyone attempting to disrupt these proceedings will be muted." He turned then to face Salera. "Second, Pallatin is hereby notified that it will be quarantined until a resolution—peaceful or otherwise—is reached between your respective Congresses."

"Quarantine?" Salera asked, his smile fading.

"All off-planet communications will be jammed. Incoming communications, regardless their source, will be blocked. Other than orbital activity to service satellites and regular translunar traffic, all of which will be watched extremely carefully, no ships will be permitted to leave the Pallatin system. The rest of the Hundred Worlds will—"

"This is *not* acceptable!"

Montero nodded to Nelon, who touched a key on a handheld keypad. Instantly Salera—on his feet, his arms gesticulating wildly—fell silent as the audio portion of his feed was cut. Realizing he'd been muted, he sat grudgingly back down. The glow of anger on his face remained.

"Speaker Salera," Montero said calmly as if nothing had happened, "Speaker Niles, the rest of the Hundred Worlds will be informed that a state of civil war exists on Pallatin, and a general noncontact order will be issued."

Adela watched the reactions of the two men. Niles was in shock, a look of horror at what was about to happen stood immobile in his eyes. His holographic image was several meters away on the other side of the holoconference room and it was difficult to be sure, but . . . was he shaking? While Niles clearly was terrified at the prospects of what would happen, the Eastland Speaker seemed to have calmed down. Clearly he was coming to realize that the Imperial noncontact order was not all that far removed from what his goals were. Of the two, however, she wasn't sure which reaction disturbed her the most. *Are we doing the right thing here?* she wondered fearfully. *Was I right to encourage Montero to take this course of action?*

Montero leaned forward in his chair, his gaze shifting from one Speaker to the other. Again, his professional manner and the strength with which he spoke made Adela remind herself that, yes, this forceful Commander was the same man who put people to sleep at routine briefings.

"Speaker Salera," he continued, extending his hand palm-up to him, "you wish for the Empire to leave Pallatin alone, to be able to govern your own affairs without interference. I grant you that wish. The *Levant* will remain in orbit until a resolution to your conflict has been reached, at which time diplomatic negotiations will be reopened with those remaining in power. As we speak, self-contained and -powered observation stations are being established in several remote, unpopulated areas on both sides of Arroyo as well as on some of the larger islands on the far side of Pallatin. These stations will be protected by shield projectors utilizing a level of sophistication not found on Pallatin. Technology of this type is among the 'Imperial contamination' you would like to bar from your world, Speaker Salera. The stations will be untouchable. Rest assured, however, that they are being set up to monitor and enforce the quarantine only.

"Speaker Niles . . ." He turned to the other. Although Adela knew he favored the Westlander's cause, Montero's voice and manner of speaking remained the same as when he had addressed Salera. "You want only to bring the two halves of your world together, united in a common goal. I grant you your wish, as well."

A puzzled expression washed over the Westland Speaker's face. "But . . . but how?" Niles asked plaintively. Montero didn't mute him.

"Because," he replied, his voice taking on a deadly serious tone, "we feel that your forces are far superior to those of Eastland's. Officer Kyovska?"

"Sir." The Weapons Master stood, hands clasped at the small of his back, and addressed Niles. "Because of the effectiveness of their first strike against you, and because they now control a major portion of the pressure-tap network, the Eastland Guard has a tremendous advantage over your forces. However, during our brief period of cooperation, we were able to determine the full extent of your own Congressional Guard and find you to have a number of advantages. Westland's greater size and population, for example, have enabled you to draw from a greater pool of personnel for the Guard. Your industrial facilities received more severe damage during your big quake than did those of the opposition, but were rebuilt with higher technological standards than the older, existing facilities in the east. Further, your troops are greater in number and better trained than those we've monitored in the east. We've run several hundred simulations based on the statistical strength and tactics exhibited by the opposing forces, and have found that Westland will ultimately achieve victory."

"Thank you, Master Kyovska." The officer retook his seat and Montero regarded the two Speakers again. "Please understand that the loss of life in this conflict will be tremendous, far exceeding anything Pallatin has experienced as a result of all its natural disasters combined."

Salera raised a hand to speak. A nod from Montero and the muting for his transmission was canceled. "I don't accept your projections," he said, keeping his voice low and controlled. "Nor do I believe you'll merely 'wait around' in orbit until such time as we've defeated the Westland forces."

"Speaker Salera," Montero shot back, "at this point, I don't much care what you believe."

The room fell into a deep, stunned silence.

Adela felt her stomach twisting in knots. The idea of a quarantine had been hers, but Montero was eager to put it into effect as a perfect compromise to using force to bring the frontier world into line with the Empire. But the idea was hers, and the full realization at the implications, the potential destruction and loss of life, weighed heavily upon her.

"Please understand something." Adela spoke softly, but in the sudden quiet following Montero's words her voice reverberated in the room, and she felt sure of herself as she spoke to the two men. "Our project will take centuries, and will impact the lives of more people than could fill a hundred Pallatins . . ." Her eyes met Niles', and she quickly looked away. "I regret this, all of this, but we'll wait it out. I'm sorry."

Niles sat stolidly and gripped the armrests of his chair so hard that his knuckles went white. Someone appeared fuzzily at the edge of the image and he attempted to wave him away. There was an audible whispering too far out of his system's pickup range to be understood. "Not now!" he barked, then thumbed his audio off as he dealt with the interruption. He spoke for several moments, then restored his audio.

"I'm sorry, too, Doctor." He stood up wearily and regarded Montero. "I guess there isn't much more to say, then, is there?" He didn't wait for an answer. "I've just been informed that tremors have been reported near the Taw encampment. There may be injuries. Excuse me."

He reached a shaking hand to the control stud on the armrest, and his image winked out.

TWENTY-FIVE

"Can I help you with that?"

Amasee Niles had difficulty hearing the young soldier as he called from the front seat. He stopped fumbling with the restraining harness and adjusted the volume on his helmet comm, all the while trying to ignore the weight of the ungainly thing on his head.

"I'm sorry, I didn't hear you," he shouted unnecessarily into the curved mouthpiece, then returned to the tangled mess of straps crossing his chest.

The soldier from the front section, his shoulders hunched over to negotiate the restrictive cabin of the four-man supply hopper, came back to his seat. The Guard Corporal was a mere boy, surely no older than his son Clint.

"Let me help you with that, sir." The Corporal deftly pulled the harness across Niles' chest, clacking the catches and pulling the loose ends of the straps taut for him. "How's that, sir? Too tight?"

"No, it's fine. Thank you."

He smiled and climbed back into the copilot's position, and Niles heard the sound of the boy's own harness being secured.

Niles leaned back, making himself as comfortable as he could in the cramped cabin. The craft had been designed mainly for short-range transport of shipping crates and supplies for commercial purposes, and the four seats forward of the cargo compartment—two crew positions and two passenger—felt as if they'd been added as an afterthought. At least, the two passenger seats did. In truth, the original cabin had been stripped and reoutfitted with smaller accommodations to allow for additional equipment when the craft had been adapted for military use. The rear seats were redesigned as gunner's positions, but all weaponry had—on his personal order—been hastily stripped from the hopper for this trip. Niles absently fingered the mounting holes left behind when the starboard gun was unbolted from its spot below the glassless window.

Except for an occasional word or two between the pilots, the cabin was quiet; the constant vibration of the engines, on standby while they waited, was the only sound. Although the two soldiers in the pilots' positions were volunteers, they were clearly nervous about this flight, and chose not to talk. The cabin seemed empty without the usual chatter Niles had grown accustomed to when being shuttled on congressional business.

The sun was nearly overhead, and he sweltered in the confines of the tiny space. Once under way the rush of air through the cabin would cool it sufficiently, but for now the scant breeze left sweat trickling down his scalp beneath the helmet. His back, securely harnessed against the plastic of the seat, was soaked through.

"Sir?" The pilot, a young Sergeant with the name "Ponde" stenciled on his helmet, had twisted around in his seat. "The truck's here."

Niles turned in the indicated direction and saw the supply truck speeding toward them over the concrete. It slowed as it neared and looped around so it could back up to the hopper's opened and waiting cargo bay. The truck pulled to a halt a few meters from the hopper and two uniformed men jumped out of the cab. They opened the rear doors of the truck and climbed in, then directed the driver the rest of the way to the open hold. Over the soft humming of the standbys he could hear them moving about in the hold as they unloaded the truck. There wasn't much to transfer, he knew, and the hold was sealed quickly, with the truck pulling away after only a few moments.

As the truck disappeared across the concrete, Amasee said, "Anytime, Sergeant."

Sergeant Ponde gave him a thumbs-up, then nodded a silent "Good luck" to his copilot. He spoke a few words to the base controller, and they were on their way.

The hopper lifted quickly, smoothly, with the engines making little more sound than they had on standby. They flew in an exit pattern to the takeoff lane of the facility, then held position a hundred meters over the concrete, the hopper facing due east. From this height, the foothills lining Arroyo were easily visible several kilometers away, although the fault itself was still too far to be seen. Both Ponde and the copilot turned to him expectantly.

"The course is in?" Niles asked. A nod of confirmation. "All right, then. Let's go."

The engine whine climbed to a higher pitch and he felt himself being pressed back into the gunner's seat. His eyes stung, and he pulled the helmet's tinted visor down to shield his face from the wind now rushing into the cabin. With armaments stripped and minimal cargo, Niles realized, the hopper would reach top speed in only a few moments.

He reached for the small case on the seat next to him and set it on his knees, balancing it there as he flipped the latches open. He fingered the control pad of the portable comm set inside, activating the small system. "Sergeant, I'm cutting the internal two-way." The pilot nodded over his shoulder and Niles flipped a switch, cutting the static-filled signal he'd been listening to for the last half hour. Touching a few more buttons brought a quiet, breathy carrier signal into his headphones. Tied in now to the main communications station at Newcastle, he tapped in a short sequence of numbers and a voice quickly came on the line.

"We're ready, Speaker."

This is it, then, he thought, staring out the window at the landscape passing rapidly underneath. He let his eyes scan the eastern horizon, where Arroyo was just now coming into view.

"Put the call through."

"Something's happening down there," Montero said.

Adela and Woorunmarra, called to the Commander's office moments earlier, sat wordlessly and waited for him to continue.

"We've been tracking a Westland aircraft—a small shuttle or supply hopper—since it crossed Arroyo about a half hour ago. As far as we can tell, it appears to be on an approach pattern to the Joint Dominion Capitol."

"A sneak-in of some kind?" Woorunmarra asked.

"Doubtful. Anything fissionable would be scanned immediately, and it's too small to be carrying much of any other kind of threat. It could be carrying biologicals, but that's unlikely. It would be easier and more effective to launch something like that ballistically."

"How far into Eastland is it now?"

Montero glanced once at his terminal screen. "About a hundred fifty kilometers."

Woorunmarra sat straighter in his chair. "But . . . why haven't they been shot down? Are they flyin' too bloody low to be detected, or shielded somehow from ground-based monitors?"

Montero shook his head. "No. In fact, they seem to be purposely flying an easily detectable course. They're holding at a steady altitude and flying on a direct heading with no deviation at all. Whatever they're up to, they seem to *want* to be seen."

"Have you attempted to contact Speaker Niles?" Adela asked. "Or has he been in touch with you about this?"

"I've tried to reach him, but he is 'unavailable at this time.' Whatever it is he's doing, I'm not entirely sure his full staff is aware of it." Montero pivoted his chair away from the terminal, pulling at his moustache with thumb and forefinger. "We have intercepted a communication from the aircraft; it's on a coded signal, however, routed to Eastland through Newcastle."

"Coded?" Adela said, puzzled. "We should be able to break most of the military codes by now. What does linguistics make of it?"

"That's just it." Montero reached for the terminal and spun it around so the two of them could see the screen. "It's not a military code at all."

"Wait a minute . . ." Billy leaned forward, peering intently into the screen at the gibberish scrolling across its surface. He raised a questioning eyebrow and Montero nodded. The Lieutenent crossed to the desk and tapped a fingertip against the screen, causing a sequence of numbers to enlarge and redisplay themselves in a window at the bottom. "Look at the prefixes. That's a diplomatic code sequence." He stared at the screen a few moments longer, then tapped once more on the glass, freezing a second set of numbers which also reappeared in the window. He retook his seat, nodding in apparent understanding.

"I recognize those two sequences." He pointed at the terminal. "I should; I've used them enough times in setting up calls to Niles and Salera. I haven't a clue as to the rest of what's there, but this is a direct line they've set up between them. A 'hot line.' "

"My God," Adela breathed. "It's him. He's on board the craft himself."

Montero sat quietly, considering this for several moments, then swung the terminal around and jabbed at the keys, saying, "I want a class-three combat shuttle prepared immediately."

Adela glanced at Woorunmarra and, seeing that he was as stunned by what the Commander had requested as she, jumped to her feet. "But we can't," she almost pleaded. "A military strike would be a violation of our own quarantine."

The Commander stood, fastening the top button of his uniform, and crossed purposefully toward the door. It slid open at his approach. "Don't worry, Doctor," he said, turning back. "I don't intend to violate anything or anyone. We're going down as observers only, fully shielded. They possess no weaponry that can breach the shielding on a class three, at least none that can safely be used in the vicinity of the Capitol."

He exited the room, then stopped in the corridor and turned back. "Well, are you two coming or not?"

"Have us scanned again, then!" Amasee yelled into the helmet comm over the rushing wind, and stared out the window at his elbow.

They had an escort now.

Two fully armed fixed-wing aircraft had appeared from the south and now rode along at a discreet distance from the starboard side. A larger hopper, easily three times their size, shadowed them on the other. He couldn't see it, but he knew there was another craft somewhere above, and behind, them.

The two pilots watched the aircraft that boxed them in but remained calm, concentrating their efforts on flying the hopper and staying on course without alarming the escort in any way.

"I have," Salera responded finally. His voice was incongruously low and measured in his headphones; but then, he was sitting in an office or command post, and not flying squarely within the targeting sights of four armed aircraft. "But what does that tell me? You're carrying no weapons-grade fissionable material, and judging from your speed and power output you seem to be flying empty, or nearly so. Why should I trust you?"

The Westland Speaker turned at a sudden sound. Another aircraft, a fifth, passed noisily over them and took position several hundred meters in front of the hopper. Its guns, he saw, had been rotated to bear on them, and a sudden high-pitched beeping from the command console told him that yet another missile had been locked on them.

"Why shouldn't you?" was his response. "What possible threat do I pose?"

There was a long silence. "Stay on your present heading until you reach sector . . ." He paused, then, ". . . two-two-nine. Your escort will conduct you then to the military base at—"

"No! I'm landing at the facilities at the parkade!" He caught himself, forcing his emotions back down. "We have to meet at the Capitol. What I have to say is official state business and will not be conducted at an airstrip."

Salera waited a full minute before replying. "All right, then.

I've just given an order for the landing area to be cleared. Follow your escort down and land where they indicate."

"Thanks, Kip."

The other's response was immediate. "Do not deviate from the flight pattern. If so much as a stray gust of wind moves you a meter off course, you'll be incinerated before you know what happened."

Niles looked to the two pilots in front of him. He had patched the private communications channel into their comm panel when the first of the Eastland aircraft had appeared, allowing them to hear what was being said. He owed them that much. Ponde turned to him and nodded, a reassuring smile on his face.

"Do you understand, Niles?"

"Yes. I understand."

The combat shuttle *Kestrel* fell out of the sky unchallenged by Eastland forces and landed to one side of the circular parkade in front of the Capitol. Immediately upon touchdown, the shield was modified to a dome that securely covered the shuttle while it rested on the surface. Montero had informed Speaker Salera personally of his intentions to observe whatever was about to happen, and had requested a landing spot be cleared for them. Salera had balked, of course, but relented when convinced that he had little choice in the matter.

Adela and Woorunmarra rode out the landing in the Commander's post, and watched what was happening on the several viewscreens whose cameras had been trained on the parkade.

The area looked considerably different, she noticed, from when she and Billy had attended that final session of the Joint Dominion. The parkade had been a virtual garden then, but bore little resemblance now to the splendor it had once possessed. Where before stood row after row of flowering trees and rolling green lawns, a military encampment had sprung up. Temporary housing and headquarters had been placed in the area surrounding the landing field now occupying the largest part of what had once been an enormous park and gathering area centered in the roadway that circled in front of the Capitol building itself. A landing surface that extended for several hundred meters in each direction had been put down and little, if any, plant life remained.

"Here he comes."

Montero's words brought her out of her reflection and she turned to the screen he was watching. The Westland hopper was coming in, slowly and carefully, flanked on either side by East-land craft. The three ships settled on the landing surface at the same time, kicking up clouds of dust.

"I want to go outside," Adela said forcefully, prepared for an argument. The Commander surprised her, however, when he nodded and rose, leading the two of them down the shuttle corridor to the embarkation ramp located on the lower level. He selected two armed guards for each of them and gave the order for the ramp to be lowered.

The dome of the shielding was nonpermeable, allowing no breeze to penetrate it, and a wall of heat met them as they descended the ramp. She looked at the sun hanging in the late afternoon sky and was grateful they'd changed into their hot-weathers before leaving the *Levant*. She walked to the edge of the shield, accompanied by Montero and Billy, and stood quietly as the scene unfolded not far from them.

A ring of soldiers had formed around the tiny hopper, and every pulse rifle was trained on it and its occupants. The guns of the two Eastland craft that had landed with it were likewise pointed menacingly at the little craft. Other weapons, both larger and smaller than the ones that now kept the landing area in their sights, had also been brought to bear on the *Kestrel*.

Nothing moved. The occupants of the hopper made no attempt to leave the craft until a small open transport, similar in design to the GEMs Adela had seen at the tap station, entered the edge of the landing area from the direction of the Capitol, followed by several wheeled vehicles. The hopper's cabin hatch swung open when the vehicles came to a stop, and a helmeted man stepped out onto the pavement. Salera, surrounded by security, got out of the GEM and barked an order to several of the soldiers. They immediately approached the hopper.

The man was searched, a little too roughly, Adela thought. Other soldiers, their weapons leveled at the cockpit of the craft, forced the two pilots out onto the landing surface as well, their hands behind their heads. The two were taken to one side and detained, while the other man walked forward under heavy guard and stood before the Eastland Speaker. As he passed in front of them at the edge of the shield he hesitated and turned to them, lifting his helmet's tinted visor. It was Niles, as they'd suspected.

"Well, it's your move," Salera said angrily when the man stopped before him. He swept his arm to take in the whole area, adding, "We've met you as you requested. We've agreed to your conditions. We've lived up to our promises." He looked over to the shuttle, staring coldly at Adela and her companions, and bowed mockingly in their direction. "We've even been given the honor of having the high and mighty Imperial representatives attend."

"I'm glad they're here."

"Well, I'm so happy that you're pleased," he said sarcastically. He stood straighter and nodded to the soldiers at his side, who immediately brought their weapons a bit higher. "Now give me one good reason why I shouldn't take you into custody immediately and end this charade of a war."

"I'm here to end this charade, too." He pulled off the helmet and dropped it, allowing it to clatter loudly to the ground. The soldiers fidgeted, the metallic sounds of a hundred weapons being shifted simultaneously breaking through the still, hot air.

Niles came forward, his hair pasted to his scalp with sweat, and stood facing Salera. "This has gone on long enough, Kip. I've run the same simulations he has." He jerked a thumb over his shoulder at Montero. "So have you. You know you can't win. Let's stop this now before even one more dies."

Salera laughed. A soft chuckling sound at first, then he tilted his head back and roared with laughter until tears flowed from his eyes. The young soldiers at his side smiled, following his lead, but they were clearly too unnerved by this confrontation to see any humor in anything that had been said.

"That's it?" Salera demanded, wiping his eyes. "That's all this was about?" He laughed again and turned for the GEM, hopping into the open passenger seating. "I think you need to rerun your simulations. But this time, include a factor about the breakdown of the Westland Commander in Chief. I plan to." He motioned for his driver to take him back to the Capitol.

"Wait!" Several guns clattered as they were reaimed at Niles.

Salera turned in the GEM, his manner seemingly more of annoyance now than anything else. "Yes, Niles?"

The man started to speak, but stopped himself as his face changed abruptly, showing an expression of—what? Adela couldn't tell from her viewing angle just what had masked the man's features. Sorrow? Fear? Hatred?

"Open the shield," she said to the Imperial guard nearest her. The man stood dumbly, not knowing what to do, and looked to Montero for guidance. Adela followed his gaze and stared the Commander in the eyes. "Open it!"

He nodded, and the guard removed a flashlight-shaped object from his belt and pointed it at the shield in front of him, nullifying a circular area large enough for Adela to pass through. A stiff breeze, far cooler than the air inside the shield, blew refreshingly through the opening. Adela stepped through.

Woorunmarra stood by the opening. "Commander?"

"Go with her," he replied. Woorunmarra stepped through and caught up with Adela. The pair was immediately flanked by several Eastland soldiers, causing the Imperial guards nearest the opening to prepare to follow them. "No," Montero ordered, stopping the guards before they could clear the opening. "I think they'll be safer if you stay here." He nodded once to the man at his side and the opening disappeared.

Ignoring the armed soldiers covering the two of them with their weapons, Adela and the Lieutenent walked steadily to where Niles and Salera confronted each other. Niles regarded her and Woorunmarra as they approached and stood to one side, and Adela saw the look on his face for what it was: pain.

"I've brought something you need to see," he said, facing Salera again. "In the hopper." He started for the craft.

"Hold it!" Salera called at his back. He turned to several of the soldiers, ordering them to check the hopper before Niles could move any closer to the parked aircraft.

The men trotted for the craft, easily opening the hatch to the cargo hold. One handed his weapon to a companion and, covered by the others, climbed into the hold. A minute passed, then another, and he reappeared in the opening and said something to one of the others, who also climbed inside. They both reappeared a moment later and spoke animatedly to the others.

All but one of the soldiers remained at the open hold of the hopper while the first man who had inspected the craft ran back to stand panting, and fearful, before Salera.

"Well?" he demanded when the young man hesitated.

"Sir, I . . ."

"Is there a weapon? What?"

The young man stuttered, unable to speak. "There is . . . are . . . no weapons. Nothing dangerous. Sir."

Speaker Salera scrambled down out of the GEM, shoving the soldier aside as he strode toward the hopper. The men at the cargo hold moved away as he neared, futilely attempting to make themselves invisible.

Salera stood at the edge of the open hatch and stared inside, remaining there, unmoving, for several moments.

"What is it?" Adela asked of Niles. He turned to her, his eyes welling with tears, but didn't answer.

"Adela, look," Woorunmarra whispered, his hand on her shoulder, and nodded toward the hopper.

Salera had reached inside the hold, removing its contents, and was walking slowly toward them, his face a mask of consuming grief. The crowd, until just moments before abuzz with speculation and chatter, fell silent. There were gasps here and there from some of the soldiers as the Speaker walked into their field of view. He carried a uniformed woman in his embrace, her arms and legs dangling limply as he walked slowly back to the GEM.

But as he neared, Adela realized that it wasn't a woman at all. She was tiny, smaller than she was, and couldn't have been more than a teenager—eighteen, maybe nineteen years old at the most. Her blond hair hung, dirty and blood-matted, over her youthful face. The left shoulder of her uniform was blood-soaked, and her left arm swung at an odd angle as Salera stopped before them.

He tried to speak, but couldn't find the words. He gasped painfully and looked away, his eyes scanning the soldiers whose attention was now riveted on him. His lower lip quivering, he asked, simply, "What happened?" Gone was the forceful sense of command he'd displayed only moments earlier. He walked past them and sat on the fender skirt of one of the wheeled transports that had escorted the GEM, and stroked the filthy hair away from the girl's face. He looked up suddenly, his expression repeating his question.

His daughter, Adela realized. She felt tears of her own forming and turned to Billy, who put his arm around her, to comfort himself, she knew, as much as her.

Niles went to Salera, stopping just short of him, and looked down at the man as he held the broken body to his chest. "She was a member of one of the raiding parties involved in the hit-and-runs on the abandoned stations," he said softly. "Her hopper was shot down last night near station 189."

Salera knelt forward, laying the dead girl gently on the ground before him. Remaining on one knee, he rested an arm on the fender skirt and, still staring unblinkingly at her, whispered, "You've killed my daughter, bastard." He didn't rise, but looked up into Niles' face. "You've killed Lanni."

"No," Niles replied, his voice filled with pain. "She received only minor injuries in the hit; none of her crewmates were badly hurt." Niles sat on the fender and several soldiers brandished weapons, but Salera waved them off and stared again at the girl. They moved a few paces away, their weapons still held uncertainly at the ready, leaving the two Speakers, and Adela and Billy, alone.

"She and the others from her hopper were taken to a detention center at the encampment near Taw," Niles continued. "Their injuries were treated and they were being taken care of according to the Laws of War." He hesitated, his voice dropping still lower. "But this morning there was a series of tremors. The POW holding facility collapsed, as did one of our barracks. Others were severely damaged. Thirty of our people, most of them civilian support, and ten of the prisoners were killed. There was no power to the medical building, and the supplies it contained were destroyed. Medical evacuation hoppers were dispatched immediately, but eighteen more people died before they could be treated. Lanni was one of them."

Salera, his head bowed deeply, asked, "What section of the tap system runs through Taw?"

"It was controlled from Leeper grouping, on one of the sections you ordered severed two weeks ago." Niles shook his head. "There was nothing we could do to stop the tremors. I'm sorry, Kip."

Salera slid to the ground at his daughter's side and picked her up, cradling her in his arms as he rocked back and forth on his knees, causing her head to loll lifelessly from side to side. "I did it," he croaked. "I did it." His eyes closed tightly and he pulled his daughter closer, sobbing into the dead girl's neck.

A throat cleared softly at her side and Adela realized that Montero had left the combat shuttle and had come up behind them. The Commander said nothing, but stood silently with the two of them.

Niles knelt at the man's side, a hand laid softly on his shoulder. "Let her be the last to die," he said.

TWENTY-SIX

"**M**y people fought well," Amasee Niles said, looking around him at the blackened landscape. "So did Eastland's."

"It's not wrong to be proud of fighting to serve your homeland," Adela said, "even if the fight is wrong."

Niles sighed heavily, shook his head at the signs of war that had swept the area surrounding the stations at Leeper.

The ceremonies had been planned for early morning, to take advantage of the cooler temperatures. The control grouping at Leeper was the northernmost of the stations, a few kilometers farther north, in fact, than the corresponding groupings linked to it on the other side of Arroyo. The breezes that blew down from the Grande Sea, laden with the tangy smell of salt water, helped a bit, but it was already hot. The orange K-type sun that was Dannen's Star still hung low in a clear morning sky that promised an even hotter day.

The fighting at Leeper had been the first to begin and the last to stop, and had seen the greatest loss of life. It was decided to hold the ceremonies here, at the site of the worst fighting, and most of the battlefield had been left untouched. Here and there the overturned charred hulks of GEMs were scattered over the rolling hills that were more common here than at station 67. Even though the fighting had been over for months, the hulks looked as if they had only recently fallen silent. Adela supposed that the wrecks would someday be cleared, but that day would come long after the *Levant* had gone.

Someone had put white wooden markers, hundreds of them, in the ground to mark where soldiers died. In one spot a Westland hopper had crashed into a unit that must have included nearly a dozen GEMs with Eastland markings. The markers sprouted there like wildflowers, with no differentiation as to which marked Eastland soldiers and which signified the dead sons and daughters of Westland families. It was the markers, rather than the wreckage, that held Niles spellbound.

They sat in a group of seats that had been set up on the apron of the second station of the five-station grouping. The station had been the first one rebuilt, the work on the other four in the grouping still in its final stages. Where Adela sat now was a smaller section of maybe thirty portable chairs located at the front of the Westland viewing area. To her left Speaker Niles sat with his wife, Marabell. Although they sat stiffly, she held his hand as if afraid to let go; as if he might disappear and be lost from her if she did. She held a small leather case on her lap with her other hand. Carolane Pence, the representative from Leeper, along with a man she didn't know, sat next to them. There were others in the seating area—Westland government officials, several men and women in military and scientific uniforms, other guests. Montero and two officers from the *Levant* were at her right. Behind them, seated in a separate section, was the entire Westland Congress. No, not the entire Congress, Adela reminded herself. There were empty seats scattered throughout the assemblage; seats left vacant for representatives who also served in the Congressional Guard, but did not come home from Pallatin's short civil war. Behind the formal seating area stood row after row of uniformed men and women. They ringed the low area that comprised the station apron and spilled up the rise that surrounded the station like an amphitheater.

Farther down the apron was a corresponding seating area where the Eastland officials were to watch the proceedings. Like the one where she now sat, the most forward portion was set up as a VIP section where Speaker Salera and those closest to him would be watching. Woorunmarra was there, next to Salera.

The ceremonies were nearing their end. The speeches, including an address by Commander Montero, were over and a color guard made up of a mixed corps of soldiers from both sides of Pallatin was now drilling in formation for the assembled crowd. A band played; not patriotic military songs, Adela noted, but a melodic refrain that was both beautiful and haunting at the same time.

"It's lovely," Adela whispered to Niles. "What is it?"

"It's called 'Marianna Dawn.' There are lyrics, as well, that tell of a young man going off to a war that nobody wins." He listened closely a moment, determining where the band was in the song, then spoke softly in time to the music: " 'Tell me why you leave me, whene'er the hot wind blows; and I'll tell you of my love for you, to guard you when you go. But tell me you'll return to me, and tell me not to cry; and tell me we'll be one again, and I won't ask you why.' It was written not long after Pallatin was settled, by a woman who emigrated here from Hawthorne."

Adela nodded in understanding. Hawthorne was a dead world, evacuated two centuries earlier following a bloody civil war that left the planet's ecosystem unable to support human life. Survey ships had since returned there, but no attempt had ever been made to resettle it.

The song ended, the last soft notes of the horns fading away over the crowds of soldiers lining the rolling hills. As the band moved off the apron, Niles leaned over and kissed his wife, embracing her briefly before turning to Adela. "I guess this is it," he said simply. Marabell handed him the case and he walked briskly to the center of the apron, where Speaker Salera was already waiting.

Salera made some brief comments regarding the end of the hostilities and of hopes for a brighter future. He spoke optimistically about the newfound trust that had developed between the two halves of Pallatin, and of a new relationship with the Hundred Worlds. His words came naturally, as they would to a man so used to public speaking, but Adela heard the feelings behind what he was saying, and saw that he was indeed making his best effort to accept the situation.

And why not? Commander Montero had lived up to his promise to help rebuild the war-torn world. The work to restore—and improve—the pressure-tap network was nearly done. The new technology and software that had been downloaded from the *Levant* directly into the planet's data libraries would enable the

Pallatins not only to better control the violent nature of their world but to become more efficient in production at their shipyards. Further, Salera had at last seemed to accept that the Empire truly had no intention of interfering in their way of life. Genetic information, trade, technology and more would be available for Pallatins to accept—or not—as they saw fit.

When Niles' turn to address the crowd came, he echoed many of the sentiments expressed by his counterpart. While he was now realizing a goal of which he'd dreamed for more than two decades, he said nothing in his remarks that might appear to be condescending to the other Speaker.

"There is one thing more," he said as he concluded. He released a catch on the leather case and unfolded it, removing a thin rectangular slab of gleaming silvery metal that reflected the morning sunlight. "We have learned many things from those aboard the starship from Earth, but the most important things we've learned cannot be measured by technological means. The things we've learned . . . are about ourselves.

"I've also learned a great deal from the information contained in the *Levant* libraries. One thing I learned came from the writings of a man who lived on Earth many centuries ago. The people of his homeland would one day divide themselves, much as we have done, and he was destined to give up his life to reunite his people. Twenty years before his land was ripped apart, however, he wrote these lines." Niles lifted the metal plate and read the words that had been engraved onto its polished surface. " 'At what point shall we expect the approach of danger? By what means shall we fortify against it? Shall we expect some transatlantic military giant to step the ocean, and crush us at a blow? Never! All the armies of Europe, Asia and Africa combined, with all the treasure of the Earth, could not by force take a drink from the Ohio, or make a track on the Blue Ridge, in a trial of a thousand years. If destruction be our lot, we must ourselves be its author and finisher. As a nation of freemen, we must live through all time, or die by suicide.' " The crowd had fallen silent, so much so that Adela thought she heard the sound of the snaps on the leather case as he refolded it around the plate.

"The references to the nations of Earth, and to her mountains and rivers, have no correlation to our world, of course. The message *behind* the words, however, is clear; but were it not for the efforts of these people from Earth we might have destroyed ourselves before understanding that message. To them, we owe a debt of thanks."

He motioned for Adela and Montero to stand, then waved a similar invitation to Woorunmarra and the others from the starship. Some in the crowd might still have harbored a few reservations regarding those who, only a few months earlier, had been looked upon as "invaders" from the Hundred Worlds; but a resounding noise of approval arose now for the off-worlders. Even those from Eastland who had staunchly supported their secession from the Joint Dominion, Speaker Salera included, were relieved at the global tragedy that had been narrowly averted and joined in the applause.

Later, at a reception held at the Joint Dominion Capitol, Speaker Niles called Adela aside.

"I know you're leaving soon," he said over the music, "and wanted to thank you—in person, not over a holographic link."

Adela's face grew suddenly warm, and she wondered idly how long it had been since she'd last blushed. "We're all very happy that everything turned out so well. Commander Montero—"

He took her hands in his, a gentle squeeze cutting her off. "I spoke earlier to the Commander. I know that the quarantine was your idea."

A wave of cold washed over her, as if she'd just been caught in the act of committing a vicious crime. She felt a guilty lump forming in her throat and looked away to hide the tears she felt gathering in the corners of her eyes.

"I . . . I'm sorry," she began, fighting back her emotions. "I just couldn't stand to see you destroying each other; destroying all you've worked so long and hard to accomplish here. It . . . all just seemed so stupid."

"You're right, Doctor. It *was* our own stupidity we were fighting for. Dying for. As those lines from Lincoln said, we were becoming the author of our own destruction." He fished a handkerchief from the breast pocket of his formal attire, handed it to her. "Please, feel no regrets for what you did. It was your idea that terrified us enough to make us stop the killing. For that, we will be forever in your debt."

Marabell came out of the crowd, accompanied by Kip Salera and his wife. The Eastland Speaker spoke to Adela politely, introducing her to his wife, Jailene. "I thought I might find you here," Marabell said lightly once the introductions were completed. "The dinner is about to begin, whenever you two"—she indicated Niles and Salera—"are ready to join Jailene and me at the main table."

"Thanks, I'll join you in the dressing room in a few moments." Marabell smiled and turned away with the other couple. As she did, Adela noted the similarity between the two women.

"They seem very close," she said. "Have they become friends?"

Niles smiled. "They're sisters. Kip Salera is my brother-in-law."

The shimmering globe that was Pallatin began to dwindle in the display as the *Levant* picked up speed. Their mission here a success, they were leaving, heading "home" for Luna.

She would miss Billy Woorunmarra. He had stayed behind, along with several other Imperial officers, to help the Joint Dominion as they set about the task of rebuilding the Pallatin government and economy. He and the others would then become the first crew of one of the first starships to be produced in the new shipyards, and would follow *Levant* back to Sol system, arriving a few years later. His expertise at negotiations, not to mention his warmth and good humor, had made this trip bearable for her.

Alone again in her private suite, the planet glowing in the holographic display in the corner the only light in the room, she sat in silence.

The quiet was at once calming after the wearying ordeal on Pallatin, and frightening for the thoughts it now allowed to come creeping back into her consciousness after so long an absence. During the long months here she had managed, with varying degrees of success, to put Javas' message out of her mind. But now, alone, with little left to be done before returning to the tank for the long voyage home, she found the image of his message playing over and over in her mind.

"System," she said. There was an edge to her soft voice that she heard immediately. An edge that asked, what are you afraid of?

I'm afraid because I finally have to deal with this, she answered inwardly, *and I still don't know what I'm going to say to him.*

"Ma'am?" the room system responded.

"Please cancel the current display and retrieve my personal file." The image of Pallatin dissolved, leaving the room in near darkness.

"Personal files are ready for playback."

"Display personal string one-A, message one."

The corner of the room brightened, and coalesced into Javas' study at Woodsgate on Earth. Just as the first time she'd viewed this file upon waking from the long voyage from Luna, Javas sat in the leather chair, the blanket-wrapped bundle cradled gently in his strong arms.

"Adela, my love, we have a son . . ."

"Cancel playback." The image froze, and dissolved. "System."

"Ma'am?"

"Retrieve edited file of personal string one-A, message one."

"Ready."

"Playback."

Javas stood before her in the looped edit she had made of his message, smiling down at the infant in his arms. As she had before, she approached the image and looked into the eyes of her son.

He's sixteen now, she thought. *Almost a man. He'll be thirty-six by the time I return.*

She turned away from the image and went to a mirror, palming the light plate as she did. She brushed her long hair—lightened from spending so much time in the Pallatin sun—and noticed how it stood out against her darkly tanned skin. She considered changing from the hot-weather uniform she still wore, but decided against it and returned to the display area of her suite.

The edit loop was still running and she lingered a few moments in loving awe of the beautiful child in Javas' arms that was her son. Their son.

"Cancel playback and prepare to record outgoing message." Father and son disappeared and the room lights came up enough to make a clear recording.

"Ready."

Adela sat in the chair, then changed her mind and decided to stand instead as she spoke. Before starting the recording, however, she changed her mind again and went back to the chair. She remained seated for a full minute before doing anything further and breathed in deeply, then exhaled, then breathed in again, forcing herself to relax.

"Ready," the system repeated.

At the sound, she looked up into the recorder. "Record." A red light glowed above the lens.

"Hello, my love," she began.

"I'm coming home."

PART FIVE

TEST

TWENTY-SEVEN

"**C**ontinue with the tests, then," said Javas, Emperor of the Hundred Worlds. "In the meantime . . ." He turned away for a moment, as if listening to an unseen speaker. As he paused, his image on the screen stretched and distorted. His movements slowed, even froze for several seconds, before the computer reassigned the transmission matrix and brought the visual portion back up to normal speed. Unlike the recorded tachyon transmissions, which were computer-corrected before playback and could be viewed normally without undue visual or audio distortion, the realtime FTL transmissions were subject to the vagaries of the tachyons that carried the signal itself.

Even when the picture on the screen had settled into normalcy, Bomeer had to look at the image carefully to tell if the image was still frozen, or if Javas was merely holding still. *Even after more than forty years,* he reflected as he studied the Emperor's face, *you still have difficulty hiding your link to the Imperial computer net. Your father never had that problem.*

Emperor Nicholas had been adept at hiding the fact that he was consulting the Imperial computers through his integrator, often pulling pertinent information from the data banks with ease even as he spoke to someone. But not Javas. While Bomeer had seen Nicholas' son occasionally use the link unobtrusively during pauses in a conversation, he invariably stopped a conversation when something important was being relayed to him.

Bomeer tilted his head as he regarded the Emperor, then shot a glance to Supreme Commander Fain, seated at his side. The man sat quietly, patiently; he seemed to sense he was being stared at, and turned his head toward Bomeer, a faint smile crossing his lips for just the briefest of moments.

And in that moment, something became suddenly clear to the academician; something that Fain had apparently known for some time: Javas wasn't hiding the fact that he was accessing the Imperial computer through his integrator for the simple reason that he'd chosen not to.

Bomeer turned quickly away from Fain and searched his memory. He had been in attendance at hundreds, perhaps thousands, of meetings and discussions with Javas; meetings that involved dozens of attendees—and intimate chats with only the two of them present. But it occurred to him that he could recall no time during a meeting with anyone but Fain and himself when Javas had been so open with the integrator.

It's respect, he realized as he turned back to the screen to study the unmoving image of the Emperor once more. *You respect us more than I realized.* The revelation carried with it an uneasiness; although whether his sudden discomfort was caused by the fact that Javas held him in higher esteem than he'd thought, or by his own ability to recognize what now seemed abundantly obvious, Bomeer couldn't be certain. He was grateful to be spared any further introspection when Javas turned back to them.

"I've just been informed that the *Levant* is decelerating toward Sol system. Commander Montero believes he'll arrive in fewer than four months."

Fain raised an eyebrow. "They made excellent time."

Bomeer nodded in agreement. "Should we continue with the modeling, then, or wait until Dr. Montgarde arrives before we proceed to the next step? I imagine she would like to see this phase of the experimentation for herself."

Javas thought a moment; the pause punctuated by a sudden, but brief, bit of distortion in his image on the screen. "No," he went on. "Go ahead with the next phase and we'll relay your results to Dr. Montgarde on board the *Levant,* although there will still be a bit of lag time until she's in-system. I suspect she'll need a good bit of assimilation time after coming out of cryosleep anyway. A lot has happened in the last forty years, after all. No;

you're making good progress at the test site, and I don't want to slow you down any more than necessary."

"Thank you, Sire," Bomeer replied. "It is becoming increasingly difficult to hold Rice back as it is."

"Oh?"

There was an uncomfortable silence. Fain turned to face him, his characteristic raised eyebrow offering not a hint of help. Bomeer inwardly cursed himself for his loose tongue.

"Well," he offered finally, "Dr. Rice seems to have developed an . . . enthusiasm for the project that defies—"

"Academician, are you in charge of this venture or are you not?" His face impassive, the Emperor stared silently from the screen. "Perhaps you should spend more of your time on the *Kowloon,* and less on the flagship."

"What Anastasio says is true, Sire," Fain cut in, saving Bomeer further embarrassment. "Dr. Rice and the alien have become quite excited over their own progress and are quite anxious to proceed. Their enthusiasm has not been easily dissuaded."

"I see. And the attending Sarpan fleet?"

Bomeer ran a hand through his unruly hair and breathed a sigh of relief that the discussion had shifted to one of Imperial security rather than the project itself. He sat quietly in his chair and attempted to make himself as invisible as possible.

Fain straightened in his chair as he addressed the Emperor. "Actually, Sire, the close bond that has developed between Dr. Rice and the alien has worked to our advantage. While he has not been given free run of their ships, Dr. Rice has certainly been made to feel considerably more welcome than anyone in the Imperial command structure. Myself included."

Javas nodded in understanding.

"I've made no attempt to press the relationship—you know how scientists can be." Bomeer stirred in his chair at the unintended insult, but Fain either didn't notice or made no effort at this time to apologize for the slur. "Meanwhile, through careful debriefing, it allows us considerably more access to the aliens than we would otherwise enjoy."

Javas nodded again. "Very good, Commander." He turned to the academician. "In any event, please instruct Dr. Rice to proceed to the next phase of testing. Thank you both for your time."

"Sire," said both men, nodding simultaneously.

Javas' image on the screen faded immediately and was replaced with a soft blue glow. Centered in the screen was the communications code identifying the transmission number and source of the communication as having come from Luna, several light-years distant. A large Imperial crest was superimposed over the data displayed on the screen.

"I'm not adjusting to this," Bomeer offered candidly after a long silence.

"I know." The Commander of the Imperial fleet turned his chair to him, his face deadly serious. "What I don't understand is why. What is it about this"—he indicated the screen—"that bothers you so?"

Fain had never spoken this bluntly to him before. In the four decades that had passed since Javas' ascension to the Imperial throne, the two had spoken privately about their feelings to one another only on rare occasions.

Bomeer shrugged and again ran a hand absently through his thick hair. He stood and paced the room uncertainly. "I'm not sure, really. The technology. It all seems to be happening so quickly." He approached the tachyon screen, the Imperial crest and identification code from the just-concluded conference with Javas still emblazoned in the center of the blue field. "System! Screen off, standby mode." The glow disappeared instantly and Bomeer stared at the darkened plastic screen for several seconds before turning away to pace nervously again. "Maybe too quickly."

"It is happening quickly," Fain conceded, still sitting in his chair as he followed the academician's movements around the room. "But I'm not as convinced as you seem to be that it's a bad thing."

Bomeer approached another screen on the opposite wall, this one a simple viewscreen, and whispered a command that brought it to life. Against a starry backdrop, two ships glowed brightly. One of them, far enough from them that even the larger details of its construction were indiscernible, was the Sarpan vessel with the unpronounceable name. The other craft, floating only a few hundred meters off the flagship's starboard side, was one of three Imperial ships that had accompanied them to this desolate, empty point in space far removed from travel lanes. By its markings he recognized it as the science ship *Port of Kowloon,* where the testing of Dr. Montgarde's theories was being conducted. Where an *alien* was even now intimately involved in Imperial research of the highest order. Bomeer shuddered at the thought, but said nothing further.

"Progress is inevitable, my old friend." Fain swiveled around further, addressing Bomeer's back. "Do you remember when Emperor Nicholas first told us that he'd decided to back this project?" Bomeer remained silent, but the Commander was not deterred. "It was back on Corinth, nearly seventy years ago. He promised then that this project could save much more than just Earth's Sun. Had I known then how much Imperial technology would be advanced in only that time, and how close it has drawn the Hundred Worlds, I might have followed his wishes willingly from the start, instead of by his command."

Bomeer chuckled softly and turned away from the screen. "You've been seduced," he said, smiling, and came to stand behind the empty chair. "You see much of what has happened only in terms of how strong the fleet has become. This ship"—he raised an arm, sweeping it around him—"built expressly to your personal specifications." He leaned on the back of the chair, nodding at the tachyon screen. "The ability to communicate almost instantly with any ship or world that's received the technology."

"The ability to communicate with any point in the Empire," Fain countered, just a hint of ire in his voice, "is perhaps the single greatest achievement that mankind has made to date. The technology to harness tachyons for communication has spread to more than half the worlds; even now the Empire has been drawn closer together, and is all the stronger for it." He paused, checking the anger in his tone before continuing. "In a few more years, even the most remote of the Hundred Worlds will have constructed tachyon dishes. We will truly be one people then."

Bomeer raised a questioning eyebrow. "And how does one retain control of that many people, eh?"

Fain tilted his head, not quite sure of the point Bomeer was making.

"When even the closest of the worlds was many light-years distant," Bomeer went on, "it was the strength of the Emperor that drew them all together. The gift of technology from Imperial

research—not to mention the benefit of Imperial protection—
was there only for those worlds that allowed our control. But
now that instant information is becoming available to all the
members of the Hundred Worlds . . ." He straightened up,
casting a sidelong glance at the ship hanging silently in space.
When he regarded Fain once more, the Commander sat impassively, stroking his chin in thought.

Enough, Bomeer thought, *I've at least given him something to
think about.* Then, aloud: "Anyway, I think the dissemination of
technology should be handled more slowly and more carefully."

Fain turned suddenly. "The Council of Academicians has,
perhaps, been moving too slowly for too long," he snapped.

Bomeer smiled broadly, allowing that there was at least some
truth to the man's statement. "Perhaps." He turned for the
door, but when he reached it he turned back as another
thought struck him.

"You do know, Fain, why we—you and I—have been sent
here."

The Commander swiveled to face him, leaning back in the
chair and crossing his legs. "Suppose you tell me."

"We are being eased out," Bomeer replied simply. He had
expected Fain to protest, and was surprised when he remained
quiet. "You and I are part of the *old* Empire, Commander. There
may not be a role for us to play in the improved version, and
Javas knows it. Even rejuvenation has its limits. What was it you
called me earlier? 'Old friend'? That may be much more accurate
than you realize. For both of us."

Fain nodded, and it was obvious to Bomeer that nothing he
was saying had in any way come as a surprise to him. Clearly the
man must have had many of the same thoughts himself.

"Anyway," he sighed, "you may be right about we academicians being too slow. Perhaps the time has come for me to adopt
a speedier attitude toward what's left of my life."

Aboard the *Kowloon,* Dr. Templeton Rice monitored the equipment and waited patiently for Oidar to return to the open lab,
but couldn't stop the growing concern he was beginning to feel
at the length of time he'd been gone. Because they had reached
a delicate stage in the modeling, the alien had delayed going to

the fountain that had been installed for him at the far end of the room. His body moisture and temperature were maintained by his wet suit, but Oidar still needed to dampen the exposed skin of his face and neck frequently in the misty spray of the specially designed fixture. This time, however, in his excitement he had waited too long and needed to return to his quarters when he began to feel dizzy.

I hope he's okay, Rice thought. *It's as much my fault as his. I should have reminded him to go.*

The comm beeped suddenly, startling him, and he slapped the answer bar anxiously. A haziness coalesced on the small screen and Rice knew it was Oidar even before he could see his features, calling from the comfort of the Sarpan-normal conditions maintained in his room on the *Kowloon*.

"Are you all right?" he barked into the comm. A swift blur passed suddenly over the image, bringing the picture into sharper focus, and Rice realized the alien must have wiped his hand across the video pickup on his end to clear the moisture that had collected on the lens.

"I have thanks for your concern, Temple, but no worry. I am fine." His voice sounded tired. Oidar had removed his wet suit and reclined now on a small couch as he spoke. He had wrapped a brightly colored towel around his waist, but otherwise wore nothing else. "However, had I waited much longer I would have looked like—what was it you said the last time?"

Rice chuckled. "A dried prune."

"Yes. So." The alien grinned broadly and tilted his head back. Rice saw the gill slits vibrating, and a high-pitched buzzing sound came softly from the comm speaker: the Sarpan equivalent of a laugh.

The thought of comparing him to a dried fruit amused him, and Rice was relieved to see that his counterpart was feeling better, but at the same time was concerned at his coloring. Oidar was only five years old, and Rice was used to seeing his skin a bright greenish-brown color that was normal for Sarpan of breeding age. Now, however, his hue had darkened considerably to the deep gray-brown shade common to males approaching the end of their ten-year life span.

Rice had seen that coloring on only one other Sarpan—

Oidar's father, during his last months of life before his role in the experimentation was taken over by his son. "I want you back on the *Flisth* as soon as possible."

Oidar's smile faded, and he sat upright suddenly. "There is no cause to return to my ship," he said, all traces of good humor gone. The abrupt movement seemed to have caused him discomfort and he crossed his arms and grasped his sides with his hands, gently massaging the twin egg sacks located halfway down each side of his body. "I am fine."

"You are *not* fine! Look at you; you've nearly dehydrated yourself again."

Oidar's eyes widened and he tilted his head, a confused, hurt look crossing his alien features. "You are displeased," he said simply, a hint of disappointment in his voice as if he had unintentionally offended an elder.

Rice cursed himself under his breath for losing his temper—the aliens simply could not understand how humans could connect anger with concern for another's well-being. He lowered his voice, forcing a smile. "I'm sorry, Oidar," he said, and bowed his head in a Sarpan gesture of apology. "This one is not displeased. But"—he lifted his chin and looked his friend directly in the face—"I'm going to have to insist that you take better care of yourself while in the open lab. You've got to . . . I can't . . ." He had trouble expressing the worry he felt in words the alien would understand. In the screen, Oidar waited patiently for him to continue, his head tilting first one way, then the other.

Rice gave up. "Look, I can't deal with this over the comm. I'm coming up."

He punched the disconnect bar and headed for the door, unbuttoning his shirt as he walked. The open lab was generally kept several degrees above the ship's normal working temperature, to better accommodate Oidar's comfort, but he knew the alien's cabin would make the lab feel chilly. The cabin was not far, and he arrived at the door at about the same time he'd managed to slip his shirt off and sling it over his shoulder.

Oidar was expecting him and opened the door as soon as he pressed the call button, allowing Rice to enter the narrow airlock that helped maintain the room's internal environment.

The air was so hot and humid that sweat burst forth from his skin the moment the airlock door slid aside and admitted him to the room. The air was thick and dank, and had a vague swamp-like pungency to it; not unpleasant, the scent carried with it the musky odor of vegetation and mud. Other than the *Kowloon*'s captain and members of the crew who had worked with the Sarpan team to set up the cabin, Rice was one of the few people on board who had even set foot inside, much less spent any amount of time with Oidar.

The cabin consisted of a small living room—a receiving room, actually, since Oidar used it only to see infrequent guests—a galley kitchen and a bathroom. The largest of the cabin's three rooms, it was the bathroom itself that comprised the main living and sleeping area for the Sarpan. The receiving room was sparsely decorated: There were two small couches facing each other, a low round table between them. In one corner stood a tall plant with snakelike tendrils that crept up the wall, although whether it was a genuine Sarpan growth or something specially bred, Oidar had never said. A sealed lighting strip circled the room at the edge of the ceiling, and Rice noted that it had not been cleaned in some time; algae growing on the glassy surface caused it to cast a soft green glow that glistened off the moist surfaces of everything. The room was quiet, empty; the alien nowhere to be seen.

"Oidar?"

"A moment," called a voice from the galley. "Be comfortable."

Right, thought Rice, using the balled-up shirt to wipe the sweat from his face and neck. He sat on one of the couches and felt the wetness of the plastic cushion beneath him immediately soak through the seat of his pants.

Oidar appeared, and handed him a tall tumbler filled to the brim with ice cubes from the galley freezer. There was no drink in the glass, but Rice knew that none was necessary—in a few minutes, he'd have ice water.

"Thank you, friend," he said, and played the refreshingly cool glass slowly across his forehead and against his cheeks.

Oidar sat opposite him on the other couch, lacing and unlacing his fingers. There was a tiny *pop* sound as the webbing between his fingers pulled apart each time. "So?"

Rice sighed heavily. "Yes, so." A few centimeters of cold water had already formed at the bottom of the glass and he sipped before continuing. "Oidar, I must be blunt. The modeling is at a very critical stage, and we both need to be at our best if we have any chance of being successful here."

"I know that," he replied matter-of-factly.

"But beyond that, I am concerned for your health and safety." Twirling the ice cubes in the glass to make them melt a bit more quickly, he studied the alien. Was his coloring beginning to return to normal, or was the effect caused by the tinted strip light? "Why won't you return to the *Flisth* more frequently?"

Until now, Oidar had been sitting upright out of politeness to his guest, but he allowed himself to recline in a familiar slouching position Rice knew was more comfortable for him. He crossed his arms in front of him again, massaging the egg sacks. He made no attempt to avoid looking at Rice, but said nothing.

He's nervous, he thought, wiping at his neck again with the now-soaked shirt. *My God, I didn't even know they could feel that way.* He watched Oidar as he massaged his sides, then noticed something. A tiny bump appeared briefly at a spot in the left sack, smoothed out, then reappeared. Oidar massaged the spot and the bump disappeared.

"You're nearly ready to spawn, aren't you?"

Oidar stopped.

"Why didn't you say something?" Rice demanded, then quickly checked his voice to keep all traces of emotion from it. "If I'd had any idea, we—"

"A moment," Oidar replied, cutting him off. He hung his head in a shameful gesture, puzzling Rice. "I am . . . not gladly received on my home ship."

"I don't understand. You mean you're not permitted to make regular transfers over?"

"No, I am permitted. I am even welcome." He shook his head, blinked eye membranes several times. "I am not gladly received, however. I have spent much time with humans, and am"—he blinked rapidly, struggling for a word—"untrusted socially."

Rice had trouble believing what he was hearing, and sipped noisily at the melting ice while he formed a response. Was Oidar trying to say that he was being shunned? "But many of your family members are there, aren't they? Surely they don't treat you this way."

"I was spawned on the *Flisth,* yes, but none of my water group remains aboard. They have been reassigned for . . . political reasons."

"I see." Rice understood. Like Oidar, his entire water group carried much of his father's knowledge and skills, passed on genetically. The Sarpan leadership, eager to gain as much information about the humans as possible, had undoubtedly sent the others to "safe" areas within the Sarpan Realm for debriefing, far away from further human contamination. "And your spawning mate?"

"She has shown little interest in this one since I received the spawn." He sighed, the mannerism and sound remarkably human; no wonder he was considered influenced by his time with humans. "Anyway," he went on, "it has been easier for me to remain here. I will go back to the home ship when it is time to go to the water."

"And when will that be?"

He massaged at his sides again.

"Soon."

Rice lifted his glass, but noticed that the ice was gone. The water in the bottom of the glass was still cold, and he finished the last of it as the two exchanged a few last pleasantries. Finally, the room growing as uncomfortably quiet as it was hot and humid, Rice got up to leave, setting the empty glass on the table.

Once outside Oidar's cabin, he leaned heavily against the door and closed his eyes, relishing the delicious feel of the cool plastic pressing against the sweaty skin of his back.

TWENTY-EIGHT

Everything she could see, which was precious little, was a blur. As if that were not bad enough, the blur swirled around her in a sickening whirlpool.

Her mouth was dry, parched, and she coughed hoarsely. *Why am I so thirsty?* Adela wondered as she attempted to slowly climb

her way to full consciousness. She concentrated, trying to remember, and reasoned that she was still on Pallatin, sleeping
outdoors in the blistering heat.

The images were confusing, and mixed with one another as
they do during a dream. There was a bright light above her that
brought tears to her eyes, but she stared at it, blinking and
confused, until it assumed a form she was comfortable with. It
was Dannen's Star, its hot, orange light bathing her as she lay
motionless. She realized that someone stood over her, unrecog-
nizable, and her mind's eye filled in the missing details and the
faceless image became Billy, grinning from ear to ear.

"C'mon now, Doctor," her mind heard him say, "lyin' about
like that this late in the mornin', you'll wind up tucker for the
local wildlife for sure. Best to get movin'."

She tried to answer him, but her throat rasped, unable to make
any sound at all but the most feeble of croaking noises. But then
she saw that the form standing over her wasn't Billy at all; in fact,
there was no one there. She blinked, and tried to raise a hand to
rub her eyes but found that her arm still refused to work.

Cryosleep, the conscious portion of her mind told her. *I'm
waking up. Must clear my head.* She began counting silently,
trying to force herself into wakefulness. *One, two, three, four . . .*

"Adela, my love."

It was Javas, exactly as she remembered him—tall, an air of
natural command about him in his Imperial uniform. He wore
the Imperial sash, the satiny fabric complemented by his deep
blue eyes and golden hair tumbling over his collar. She felt
herself smile, causing a dry, painful cracking sensation at the
corners of her mouth, and attempted to lick her lips.

"Shhhhhh," Javas admonished when she tried to speak. He
reached out a hand, touching a fingertip lightly to her lips, then
let his fingers gently caress her cheek. "Don't talk; not now. We
have plenty of time."

"But we don't!" she heard herself plead, clenching her eyes
tightly to hold back unwanted tears. "We have almost no time at
all! Please, hold me while there's still time."

When she opened her eyes again he was gone. She managed to
turn her head and saw that she was in a room with white cabinets
running the length of the far wall. Other than the cabinets and a
low countertop beneath them, the room was empty of furnish-

ings but for two chairs and the mechanical bed in which she lay,
covered by a thin green sheet. The viewscreen on the wall nearest
her was dark and silent. Her eyes blinked up at the overhead
light, not nearly as bright now, she realized, as she'd imagined
before, but still too intense to look at directly and she turned
away. Two white-coated figures talked animatedly near the
door—one a man, the other a woman—but they spoke softly and
she couldn't make out what they were saying.

She was still aboard the *Levant*.

"Hel—hello?" Her throat ached at the effort, and she tried to
swallow.

They stopped talking immediately and turned to her, smiling.
"I'll inform the Commander," said the man, and disappeared
from the room. "Well, good morning, Dr. Montgarde," said the
other, approaching her bedside. "I'm Dr. Velice. How do you
feel?"

"Stiff. Sore. Thirsty." She managed to raise her arm, resting it
palm-out against her forehead, and experimentally stretched
anything else she could move. She shook her head to clear the
mental cobwebs that refused to release their grip. "But not neces-
sarily in that order."

One of the cabinets concealed a small refrigerator, Adela saw,
and the woman was already getting out a container of brightly
colored juice. She watched the woman, trying to decide if she
knew who she was. No, she decided; but that, in itself, was due
more to the fact that the *Levant* was a big ship, with a large crew,
and not to her post-cryosleep grogginess.

"Well, I'd say you're feeling normal, then. Would you like to
sit up?"

Adela nodded.

Dr. Velice touched a control on the headboard and the bed
smoothly came to an upright position. Adela took the offered
juice in both shaking hands, grateful that it was in a lidded
container with a straw instead of a glass, and sipped heavily of
the cool, refreshing liquid. Fruit juice. As her taste buds jarred to
life, she tried to identify the delicious mix of flavors that had been
used to disguise the electrolytes and medications designed to
both rehydrate and nourish her. The juice was, after all, her first
meal in nearly twenty years. She recognized sweet mandarin
orange. And strawberry, apple, pineapple and ginju berry.

"Are we home yet?" she asked, her throat already feeling a good deal better.

Dr. Velice was manually taking her pulse. The warm touch of her fingertips on her wrist made Adela suddenly realize she was chilly. She pulled the sheet up around her. Beneath the sheet she wore only a loose-fitting gown that was little more than a nightshirt, and long stockings.

"Almost." Velice finished her reading and entered the information into a keyed notepad. "Here, let me take that," she said, reaching for the empty juice container. "We're still eight weeks out from Luna, so you'll have a bit of time to reorient yourself before we arrive."

And I've got a lot to catch up on, she told herself. Feeling wide awake now, she swung her legs over the edge of the bed and was about to begin asking an endless stream of questions when a white-coated figure, the same man who was in the room when she first stirred, leaned through the open doorway. Thinking more clearly now than she had when she first saw him, she recognized him from earlier in the mission.

"You were right, Kinsey," he said to Dr. Velice when he saw Adela sitting up. "She is ready to hop out and get back to work. Hello, Dr. Montgarde. Good to have you back with us."

"Dr. . . ." She searched her memory, quickly finding the elusive name. "Dr. Sumatsu, hello." She smiled and, firmly grasping the edge of the bed with both hands, slid carefully to the cold floor. With no expectation of trusting her legs to hold her up, she was pleasantly surprised to see how steady she was so soon after coming out of the tank. "What was in that juice?"

"It's an improvement on what we've been using for years. We caught up with an outgoing transmission from Luna with the medical specs on the formula when we were still eleven years out. Good stuff, huh?"

Adela had to agree that it was. She tentatively let go of the bed and stretched fully, then bent over and touched her toes. The movement felt good; there was only a little stiffness left in her joints. "Listen, don't think that I'm not enjoying the plush surroundings," she said jokingly, indicating the spartan room, "but when can I get out of here?"

* * *

The recording she now watched had not been intended for her, but had been forwarded to her at Javas' request. The report had been sent to him by the science team at the test site many light-years from Earth, using the tachyon burst transmitter. She shook her head in awe at the marvelous efficiency of the device, and realized she would be able to actually be an active part of the current series of experiments from Sol system by using it. Originally she had planned to travel to the test site herself to take part, and she was grateful that many years of travel time could be avoided. More importantly, she could gain valuable lead time for the project. As it was, reports and recordings received instantly on Luna arrived on the starship as fast as conventional communications could relay them, with each batch arriving slightly sooner than the previous one due to their dwindling distance from home. The *Levant* was still two weeks out, and hence this report was slightly more than two weeks old, but Adela was ecstatic that she was able to get them this "fresh" at all.

She had hoped to get a report intended directly for her, containing specific results of some of the experiments she had designed, and had made the request in one of her first messages sent to the Moon when she awoke, but that request would only now be arriving there. Besides, she came to realize that with Bomeer directly overseeing the work on the *Kowloon,* and personally reporting all results directly to the Emperor, Dr. Rice and his alien counterpart might not even be aware that she was, even now, preparing to "join" them in a realtime sense from Luna.

"I am afraid there has been a slight setback, Sire," Bomeer was saying in the recording. The report was one-sided, merely a recitation recorded for the Emperor to review at his leisure instead of a two-way conversation and debriefing. "We've found it necessary to temporarily halt the experiment while the alien returns to the Sarpan ship to . . . spawn, apparently. We don't expect it back on board for several days." The disgust was as plain on the academician's face as it was in the way he referred to the alien scientist as "it." Bomeer's report remained impersonal and professional on the surface, she noted, but something about the way he presented it brought an amused smile to her lips. She had been immediately taken aback by his appearance when she first saw him in the recording. He had allowed his hair to gray, and she saw tiny lines at the corners of his eyes. But even though the years had managed to show in his face, it was somehow reassuring as she listened to him talk—even though much of his biased attitude was personally distressing to her—that he was the same person she remembered.

"While it is not necessary, in my opinion, that the alien even be involved with the modeling at this point," the recording went on, "Dr. Rice feels that because of the important role the Sarpan will play in the physical test phase coming up after the current series is complete, that it be there for the entire process. He's really quite adamant about it." He paused, then added, "In retrospect, I suppose the decision to wait a few days longer is for the best, as it gives me time to review the procedure with Dr. Rice with the open lab set at a temperature not resembling that found in your average oven."

The recording lasted only a few minutes longer, with the remainder of the report covering areas that, not directly related to the upcoming modeling test, held little interest to her. She paid scant attention to what he was saying as she watched the playback. *Why does he look so old?* she wondered. Bomeer *was* old, she knew, but could the time she spent traveling to Pallatin and back really account for the change she saw in his appearance?

She stopped to think of the many messages that had awaited her after coming out of the tank. As she had when arriving at Pallatin, she allowed her personal search software to select and arrange the waiting message strings in order of importance. And, as before, it was the personal message strings that she reviewed first.

Shunting the bulk of the project-related communications to the team traveling with her, she spent two full days with her personal correspondence. The messages from Javas, among the oldest waiting for her, came first in the queue and were dated from around the time of the recording containing her first look at their son. Subsequent recordings followed the first in rapid succession, allowing Adela to watch Eric's growth as he went from infant to toddler, then preschooler to adolescent. Another man appeared occasionally in some of the recordings and she learned that he was McLaren, who served as both teacher and surrogate parent. Adela realized that Master McLaren would have been present throughout much of Eric's formative years, regardless of whether she had remained behind or not, but she couldn't help feeling a loss that much of her son's upbringing had been trusted to a stranger's hands. *No,* she reminded herself. *It is not he who is the stranger. It is the mother who was never there.* As Eric got older, he appeared less frequently in Javas' communications. Javas explained in subsequent messages that he'd left the decision to contact her up to the boy, and that he wouldn't pressure him in any way. He still found time to send frequent messages of his own, however, and always went into great pride-filled detail as to their son's development. And just as she watched the changes in her son, she saw the changes in Javas, too.

She had missed the first direct message from Eric. The *Levant* had begun its journey home, and she was already in the tank when Eric sent his first recording introducing himself to the mother he had never known. "Hello, Mother," he had said in the twenty-year-old recording. "Let me tell you about myself." Adela had listened in horror as he told of the ordeal the two of them had gone through in Rihana's ill-fated attempt to place his half brother on the throne.

Finally, even as Eric's communications continued to queue up in her waiting file with increased frequency as she traveled closer to home, Javas' messages became more infrequent. She viewed them all at once over that two-day period, of course, but she noted that the dates between the Emperor's recordings grew more widely separated. At last, only a few weeks out, she viewed recordings from them both.

Eric, she had learned in recordings dating back eight years, had accepted command of a starship. His most recent recording had come, like many of those before it, from the bridge of a starship equipped with a tachyon dish and was sent first to Luna before being relayed to the *Levant.* He had grown into a fine young man, and Adela saw much of both Javas and herself in him. She was pleased to discover that his tour would return him to Sol system within a year of her arrival.

Javas' message, sent with the report she now watched, had also been upbeat. His messages had increased in number as the ship drew closer to home, and he made no attempt to hide his excitement at her coming; but behind his words in the most recent recording, appended to the beginning of Bomeer's report, lay something she could not quite identify. She could not be certain, but he seemed to fear that she would not, after all, come back; that somehow, after forty years' separation, he would not be what she had expected.

"System!" she commanded suddenly.

"Ma'am?"

"Replay current message from the beginning."

The image froze, then blanked, the corner of her cabin growing dim for several seconds before it started over. Javas reappeared in the holographic image, but before he spoke she again ordered the room system to freeze the image.

He had aged, of course, as she had expected he would, but in no way did he look . . . *old.* His hair had grayed considerably, but still reflected the golden blond she remembered. Javas' face seemed thinner, lined, but the strength she had known was still in his features. Strength radiated from him, in fact, and it was obvious he had kept himself in superb condition. Rejuvenation was no longer within his reach but, like his father before him, he took pride in himself and his appearance. Looking at him now, she allowed a feeling to surface within her that she had denied herself throughout the lengthy trip: She allowed herself to miss him. Her throat tightened and tears welled up in her eyes at how much she wanted to be with him. And as she stared silently at Javas' image in the holographic projection, it suddenly struck her what it was that had bothered her about Bomeer.

Bomeer's an old man, she realized. *He's aged, but he hasn't lived.* She had watched Javas age gracefully over forty years' worth of recordings, watched as he nurtured and taught a son whom she had also watched grow from infancy to young manhood. She should have felt older herself, realizing that the man she loved had spent a lifetime apart from her. Even knowing that she had not been there to witness Eric's development failed to make her regret the choices she'd made. For Eric, like Javas since her departure, had lived life naturally, without benefit of rejuvenation. And living life, she knew, was what was important.

Bomeer had been alive longer than them all, but it was they who had *lived.* Bomeer had merely collected years.

The stark image of the gray-headed academician flashed momentarily through her thoughts, and for the first time in her life, Adela felt pity.

TWENTY-NINE

My God, it's hot in here. How in the world does Rice stand it like this?

Bomeer frowned at Rice, seemingly cool and comfortable in his short-sleeved shirt and matching white cotton pants, and dabbed frequently at his brow as he listened to the two scientists discuss the replay of the modeling test that he was about to review. The two spoke with an excitement that eluded him, and he only half listened to what they were saying.

The playbacks of what occurred during each of the modeling experiments were among the few things Bomeer enjoyed about being stuck out here at the test site, seven light-years from Luna. Despite having to endure the environment of the open lab on each occasion, it tied him to an earlier time; a time when protocol and procedure still meant something.

The Empire of the Hundred Worlds had changed under Javas' rule, although Bomeer wasn't sure the Emperor was directly responsible for all the changes that seemed to sweep the stiff, formal behaviors away in favor of the "New Attitude" of what the Empire had become. With new discoveries had come new ideas, which, in turn, led to still more discoveries. Which, in turn . . .

He had had to be honest with himself, however, when he looked at the reasons for what had happened. Much of the changing attitude of the—what was the phrase he'd used with Fain? the "improved version" of the Empire?—had happened of their own accord as an outgrowth of a number of things: the miraculous ability to communicate instantaneously; a vastly improved understanding of medicine; a new openness among the worlds; even cooperation with the Sarpan Realm. But Bomeer had to admit that many of those things came about as a direct result of the drive and vigor possessed by the new Emperor. Javas' excitement at revitalizing a stagnant Empire was irresistible and, more importantly, infectious to all with whom he dealt, from the most powerful planetary governor to the most humble of servants on the Imperial staff.

It was in this new understanding that Bomeer felt he had no place, for it seemed that he alone was not invigorated by Javas' will. There was no question in his mind that the speed with which ↖ the Empire was changing could ultimately do it harm, but his frequent warnings fell on ears made deaf by the euphoria of the New Attitude. And so he sought refuge in those things where he still felt a certain measure of control, and he insisted in following protocol whenever possible; demanding that *B* be preceded by *A* in all cases, and that under no circumstances could *C* be even remotely considered until the lower end of the alphabet had been neatly and orderly dealt with. In this way, he still believed he had control. In this way, he could still feel important.

He wiped at his forehead again, his handkerchief nearly soaked, and promised himself that the next time he came to the open lab he would forgo at least one of the trappings of the protocol he so dearly loved: He would leave his heavy academician's tunic behind in his stateroom and come in his shirt sleeves.

Dr. Rice was describing what he was about to see and had row after columned row of figures displayed on the wall flatscreen. As he spoke, Bomeer paid little attention. He had seen these figures before, a hundred times, at least; and his mind wandered to other things.

Why doesn't it put on a damned helmet or something, he thought bitterly as his eyes strayed to the alien standing resolutely next to Rice, *so we can return this facility to human temperature?* The alien blinked eye membranes, oblivious to Bomeer's thoughts.

He leaned his head back to better wipe at his throat and felt a slight dizziness come over him. While he usually relished playing the role of overseeing the experimentation even to the point of restricting its forward motion to better suit his idea of progress, he realized that if he stayed in the open lab much longer there was a good chance of his passing out from heatstroke.

"Please, Dr. Rice," he said, holding up the hand with the handkerchief, "perhaps it would be better to see the playback and then correlate the figures with what I've seen, rather than the other way around."

The alien blinked several times in rapid succession and tilted its head inquiringly. "That is possible," it said simply, before Rice could answer.

"Thank you, Oidar." Bomeer pronounced it with three syllables, "Oh-Ih-Dar," in spite of the fact that Rice had personally attempted on several occasions—in private, of course—to help him with Sarpan names and terminology.

"Very good, then," Bomeer went on. "Perhaps the sooner we can begin, the sooner I can file my report to the Emperor."

Rice smiled politely, although Bomeer suspected he hadn't been fooled by his offer to speed up the filing of his report. The young scientist was well aware of how he felt about the environment of an Imperial facility being reset for the alien's comfort.

Rice led him to the holographic display area in the corner of the lab. There were several comfortable chairs here, and the two of them took seats facing the corner. The alien had gone to the fountain to remoisten the skin of its exposed face and neck before joining them, and Bomeer made sure to select a seat that put Rice between him and the alien. In spite of his efforts, he still felt uncomfortably close to the Sarpan, and wrinkled his nose at the scent it gave off. He wondered—again—how Rice managed to stand working in such close proximity to it.

"System, dim lights," Rice said. The lighting in the viewing area decreased by half. "Please start playback of file designated as Rice two-oh-four, version one. Normal speed."

A collection of eight red cylinders appeared in two groupings of four each. Code numbers superimposed themselves in the air above each cylinder as the groupings separated and moved to opposite sides of the projection area to form two pyramids. Once again code numbers, scrolling statistics and intensity readings appeared and changed as the playback progressed.

As the image changed, Rice gave a running commentary as to what they were watching. "This is the shielding phase of the insertion. The cylinders represent the Sarpan generators that will be used to contain the singularities before they're inserted into the star cores."

A glowing sphere, representing the contained singularities, appeared at the center of each pyramid. The one on the left was pale blue; the one on the right dark blue.

"And this shield will be enough to contain them?" Bomeer asked. "The figures bear this out?"

"Yes, sir," Rice replied. "We've been able to create microscopic singularities—both negative and positive—in the laboratory for many years. They were short-lived, of course, and served only as an aid to the study of black and white holes. It wasn't until the advanced technology of the Sarpan shielding became available to us that we even *dreamed* of being able to create anything large enough to remain stable. In any event, the Sarpan shielding should serve very well to contain the singularities until deposited in each star. The application in the next phase, the physical test, will bear this out."

Oidar leaned forward and caught Bomeer's eye. It was smiling, and even though Bomeer knew that the Sarpan tongue didn't even have a word for it, he managed to convince himself that the alien was gloating over its own importance.

When he looked back to the projection, he saw that two stars had been added to the scene. The images were not to scale for this model, and each star appeared only slightly larger than the pyramids in the projection. Again, a series of numbers and energy values scrolled in the air above them.

"All right," Rice continued. "While the scale here can't show it, the singularities are in tow to their respective stars, in preparation for insertion."

Each of the pyramids began rotating slowly, giving the appearance that they were orbiting the glowing containment in the center. The rate of spin increased, and each pyramid moved gently into the stars, taking the glowing spheres with them, until they finally disappeared inside.

Visually nothing more happened. More numbers appeared and additional statistics scrolled rapidly by, but to his eye everything seemed exactly the same.

"That's it?" Bomeer asked incredulously, certain that there must be more to the model than what he'd just seen.

The alien scientist became unexpectedly flustered with impatience and looked pleadingly at Rice. It was clear to Bomeer that his statement had upset it, but he couldn't figure out why. Rice spoke quietly to the alien, then turned back to him, the expression on his face, while completely human, reflecting the same puzzled look he'd seen in the alien's features.

"Academician, I'm not sure I follow you." Dr. Rice shook his head in frustration and glanced at the alien once more before going on. "I thought I'd made it clear a few minutes ago what we've been doing here during this stage of the modeling. Everything we've said relates to the data stick reports I've supplied to you on a regular basis. What aspect, exactly, don't you understand?"

He could not admit, of course, that he had only superficially examined the reports contained in the data sticks Rice had dutifully provided him. They had been long and tedious, rarely containing anything new regarding the original theories espoused by Adela de Montgarde, and he had only skimmed them. Worse, even though the two scientists had obviously been more excited than usual, he'd failed to give them his full attention at the beginning of their discussion here today. A wave of embarrassment washed over Bomeer at being caught, and he felt even hotter than before.

"What I review in your recorded reports and what I review personally here in the open lab are two different things," he said sternly in an attempt to cover himself. "I expect your presentations to be at least as complete as what you send me on the sticks. Is this a problem?"

A look of subdued anger flashed across Rice's face, then just as quickly disappeared. For a moment, Bomeer thought that Rice was going to call his bluff, but the scientist merely shrugged his shoulders and said, nodding in deference, "You're correct, of course, Academician. My apologies."

Oidar had said nothing through all of this, but Bomeer heard it making a faint purring sound, and knew that even though Rice had made a show of downplaying his neglect, the alien had been offended by the double dishonesty of what it had observed. Its big eyes blinked several times and its gaze shifted from him to Rice, and it was clear the alien saw little difference between the two humans right now: one overtly lying to cover an error; the other pretending not to see the lie, and in so doing, committing another untruth. The sound reminded Bomeer of a growling animal, and he made his best effort at ignoring it. "What else do you have for me?" he asked, anxious to move this meeting closer to a conclusion.

"There is another playback. System! Start playback of file Rice two-oh-four, version two, on my mark." Rice turned to face him, and when he spoke, his voice carried with it a subtle condescending tone. "The first model was based on Dr. Montgarde's original equations. As you could see from the playback, there is no visual change in either of the stars—the energy levels of the 'feeder' star into which the negative singularity, the black hole, is inserted remain constant. The same is true of the 'breeder' star. The transfer of energy through the wormhole effect is quite gradual, and serves only to replace the internal mass as it's spent, effectively increasing the life span of the breeder star. When done to Sol, it would effectively extend its life far beyond the normal range."

Bomeer nodded, and felt inside his tunic to see if he had a dry handkerchief. "And will continue to extend its life until the feeder star is depleted. This is all in her original presentation. You're telling me nothing new." He had nothing in his inside pocket and wiped again with the soaked cloth.

Rice's eyes narrowed. "Please bear with me, Academician. The model you just saw was based on the outcome of the original figures; figures based on a hypothetical field strength of the shielding she believed would be required to contain the singularities. Dr. Montgarde's figures and equations were a hundred percent accurate, but were based on a shield technology that simply did not exist at the time she did the original work. However, working closely with the shield specs provided by the Sarpan, we've been able to redo the equations based on the actual technology, as it now exists. The second computer model shows a different result." Rice paused, then pivoted in his seat. "System, begin playback."

Bomeer turned to the holo display area with renewed interest, and watched as the same scenario played itself out. The pyramids formed by the red cylinders, the glowing spheres, the two images of stars representing Sol and the unnamed feeder sun—everything looked the same. Bomeer looked closely at the figures and readings that scrolled above the images, but was unable to follow them at the speed at which the playback had been set. It wasn't until the spheres, contained in the spinning pyramids, sank into the centers of the stars that the playback differed from the one before.

Where before it appeared that little had changed, visually

speaking, it was plain to see that the two stars in this model had been affected. The one on the left side of the image, representing Sol, seemed slightly brighter than it had before the insertion, and the values of the numbers hovering above it increased. However, since Bomeer had not bothered to study Rice's reports closely enough, the values had little meaning to him. He would correct that error at his earliest opportunity. Indeed, he already was making plans to go through the two playbacks meticulously: forward, backward and at a speed slow enough that every figure, every readout, every table and chart of values could be examined one by one.

Bomeer leaned forward in his chair, resting his elbows on his knees and letting the sodden handkerchief fall forgotten to the floor, and stared at the playback image in silence for several moments, hardly able to believe what he was seeing. The sweat continued to drip down his temples as before, but as he watched the glowing stars in hypnotic fascination he no longer noticed the heat in the room.

"There is a flaw in Dr. Montgarde's theory," he said softly.

Bomeer viewed the figures again, checking and cross-checking them nervously while he waited for Javas' call.

How I have longed for this, he thought. *But now that it has finally happened, why can I not sort out my feelings about it?* Based on the results of the modeling, there was no doubt that Dr. Montgarde's equations—or at least one of them—were flawed. As presented, given the realities of the technology that had been developed and adapted to support the project, it simply would not work.

So why am I not rejoicing?

The fact of the matter was that this new development, from that moment in the open lab when he'd first viewed the model, *had* filled him with an elation the likes of which he'd not felt since Emperor Nicholas first declared his intentions to pursue the project. Perhaps now the wasteful application of Imperial funds and energies could be finally diverted from this endeavor. Perhaps now a more orderly approach to scientific study could be implemented; an approach more closely resembling the old order, and less an outgrowth of the New Attitude.

Bomeer knew better, however.

Even if the project to save Earth's Sun were abandoned today, the advances that had come from the research already done would remain. The Hundred Worlds had been reinvigorated, just as Nicholas had predicted, and it seemed to the academician that little could be done to reverse the forward trend of the New Attitude. Besides, he realized, there were few left who shared his vision of what the Empire should be. His closest ally, Plantir Wynne, his rejuvenations becoming increasingly less effective with the passage of time, had died fifteen years earlier. Many of the members of the Imperial Academy of Science, whom he'd enlisted for support at the time of Nicholas' decision to move the seat of Empire to Luna, had left the Academy. Some had been seduced by the New Attitude and had embraced the opportunity to actively delve into science once more. Others, even though they still shared Bomeer's feelings on the validity of the project, had long ago grown tired of the uselessness of continually fighting something that had proven itself beneficial to the worlds.

There were new members of the Academy, of course. But they were young and idealistic, like Rice, and put a higher value on pure research and advancement than on tradition and protocol.

So, what do I do with this information? Is it so wrong to want to learn and advance? Bomeer settled back in his chair and slapped the palm of his hand on the bar of the flatscreen reader in his lap, blanking the display, and tossed the reader absently on the desk. He leaned against the right armrest of the chair, resting his chin on his hand. Searching his memory, he tried to recall an incident that had occurred shortly after his admission to the Academy.

He had found a "shortcut" to one of the procedures he'd been assigned by a senior academician named Consol. The refinement to the research process was minor, and he had realized it, but it was an improvement and would serve to get a better understanding of the goals of the assignment at hand. He had approached Consol with a mixture of pride and foreboding when he reported his finding. Consol had laughed in his face.

"What is your hurry, Anastasio?" he had said. "Are the events of the Empire not progressing fast enough to suit you?"

Bomeer had stared dumbly at him, unable to come up with a rebuttal. "But . . . it is a more efficient way to proceed with—"

"Is there something inherently wrong with the current method of experimentation?" he had demanded.

When Bomeer had admitted that there was not, Consol had added, "What you have brought to my attention is efficiency for the sake of efficiency; tinkering for the sake of tinkering. Where is the value in that?"

The tachyon screen suddenly glowed blue, pulling him from his reverie of things past; of things that could not be changed. Of things that simply did not possibly matter now.

"Stand by for realtime transmission," the screen system advised. "Conference linkup will be completed in approximately one minute."

I have a duty, he reflected as he waited for the communication from Emperor Javas to be routed to the screen, *to be true to myself, and to what I believe. And that is* not *inconsistent with my duty to the Emperor.*

There was a diminutive beeping sound that caught his attention, and he sat straighter in his chair and faced the screen at about the same time Javas' features appeared.

"I've received your request for a realtime conference, Academician," he said, his expression serious, "and must admit that I'm somewhat concerned by the tone contained in the recording you sent. Is something wrong out there?"

Bomeer toyed with the idea of giving Javas a long-winded explanation of why he had insisted on a conference rather than merely sending a recorded report on the latest modeling, which would have been normal procedure, but decided on the more direct approach of stating the problem directly. *Look at me,* he silently mused, *after all these years I'm opting for efficiency instead of protocol.*

"We have discovered a flaw in the equations," he said without preamble.

Javas nodded. "How serious a flaw?" The Emperor, too, seemed more interested in getting to the heart of the problem than belaboring the problem itself.

"Unknown, Sire. Dr. Montgarde's theories are basically correct, but with the modeling stage now completed, we have found that the values of replenishment do not match the values that had been projected in the original equations."

They spoke for several minutes, interrupted only once by a garbled signal, as Bomeer did his best to explain what was wrong.

"The tuned pair of singularities does not behave as we expected. The wormhole is there, and the energy transfer takes place as predicted . . ."

"But?"

Bomeer hesitated, uncertain as to how to continue. "But the energy released in the breeder star is too high for the wormhole to remain stable. It works in the model, but it is difficult to say what the actual effect will be without testing it physically."

Javas nodded again. "Very well. Thank you for your candor, Academician. Dr. Montgarde will return to Luna in"—he looked to one side, checked a readout on his desk terminal—"in two weeks. Please burst me a full report on your findings so I can have them forwarded to her on the *Levant*. It'll still take a while for her to receive them, but it'll give her a bit of time to go over the results and make any necessary adjustments before she returns to oversee the next phase."

"No! Sire, I . . ." He stopped, cursing himself inwardly for responding so abruptly. But the next thing he was about to say was what he had rehearsed so carefully before sending the conference request to Javas. He also reminded himself, before continuing, that what he was about to say constituted a part of his duty; no, *was* his duty.

"Yes?" Javas asked, waiting.

"Sire, we are ready to proceed with the physical test. We had not anticipated this flaw and have already created the tuned pair for the test. As we speak they're being held in stasis by the Sarpan shielding." Again, he paused, swallowing heavily. "The modeling results tell only half the story—that a problem exists—and I'm afraid Dr. Montgarde would have no better clue as to why they are invalid than we do. May I be so bold as to suggest, Sire, that it would be more prudent to continue with the physical test? That way, Dr. Montgarde would have the full results of the flaw in the equation on her arrival."

The Emperor considered the suggestion. "You may be right," he said. "She's been out of cryosleep only a short time and probably has more to catch up on than she can handle without this added concern. You're certain that the physical test will give us more information on the problem?"

"Yes, Sire."

"All right, then," he concluded, "proceed with the next test and send me the results. Good luck."

"Thank you, Sire."

Javas' image faded immediately, and Bomeer stared at the darkened screen. He was sure that in recommending that the physical test be undertaken he was pursuing the proper course. The flaw in her equation would be dramatically revealed and, with the ability to send the results of the failed test instantly through most of the Hundred Worlds, would elicit renewed questioning into the validity of the project.

It is my duty as an academician to point out the error in this project, he reminded himself. *To do less would be to commit a lie to the Emperor, and to myself.*

He thumbed the control of the comm screen on his desk, setting it up to send a directive to Rice and Supreme Commander Fain, informing them that the next step should commence. Rice, working with Oidar, would put in place the final setup for the scientific aspects of the test. Fain, meanwhile, would coordinate with the Sarpan commander their final navigation coordinates for the event.

This is what I must do, he reflected again in an attempt to convince himself that the actions he'd taken were in the best interests of the Hundred Worlds. *To do less would be a crime against the Empire.*

He couldn't help feeling, however, as he keyed in the sequence that would send the two prepared messages, that he was acting not in the best interests of the Empire, but rather in his own best interests.

THIRTY

Rice had been aboard the *Flisth* several times since they had arrived at the test site a year earlier. Before that, in the time it had taken for the combined Imperial and Sarpan fleet to travel together from Luna, he had had ample time to get used to the ways of the aliens while dealing with Oidar's father in the earlier stages of the research. Most areas of the Sarpan ship resembled Imperial craft, and Rice supposed that there were designs inherent to space travel that were universal in nature regardless of the life-forms that rode in them. But until now, he had never seen the personal quarters of a Sarpan crew member. Oidar's cabin on the *Kowloon* had given him some insight into the aliens' way of life, and although he had never actually seen it when visiting his friend and coworker, he supposed the "bath-room" of his cabin on the *Kowloon* must have looked something like the room in which he now stood, but on a much lesser scale.

If he had not known better, if someone had carried him blind-folded and unconscious to a place like this, he would have sworn it to be impossible that he was aboard a starship. Only the entranceway where he stood held any trappings of an artificial construction.

The small pond stretched to a thick copse of trees on what he assumed would be the far side of the room. Some of the trees must be real, he reasoned, since those nearest him by the entrance to the room certainly were. But where the genuine growths ended and the holographically projected image began, he could only guess. The air was thick and heavy, and Rice touched the control plate integrated into the sleeve of his E-suit to raise his internal air-conditioning to a more comfortable level. He had a bubble helmet, as was mandatory for any Imperial personnel visiting the Sarpan ship, but once inside, away from his escort, he'd removed it and held it tucked under one arm. The cool air of the E-suit's temperature control system wafted up around the metal collar ring, offering some relief from the stifling heat of the water chamber. The room was alive with insect life, and the draft of cool air also served to deter the occasional curious flier that buzzed close to his face.

He blinked up at the ceiling, the holographically projected double star of Oidar's homeworld hazily visible through the thick curtain of air, and waited.

Oidar swam toward him, waving once as he moved just below the surface. He swam like a terrestrial frog, his hands and arms swept back against his body while strong kicks from his legs carried him forward. Rice had heard several of the *Kowloon*'s crew refer privately to the Sarpan as frogs and, while he hated the epithet, reflected that it was more uncomfortably accurate than he would have liked to admit.

"Temple!" Oidar swam into the shallows at the water's edge and sat up on the bottom of the pond. He glided his webbed hands around him as he sat, waist-deep, and the water moved around him in gentle little waves. "This one is pleased to have your visit!" He seemed genuinely happy to have Rice there, and reminded him of a small child eager to show off his room when company called.

"Hello, Oidar." Sweat had begun dripping through his hair, and Rice drew the sleeve of his free arm across his forehead. There was a low plastic bench a few meters to his left and Rice approached it, setting the helmet next to him as he sat. Oidar splashed through the shallow water to sit nearer him, and again rested on the bottom and swirled his arms to create the little waves.

Rice realized suddenly that, while Oidar was indeed stirring the water with his hands, most of the splashing around him was not of his making. Rice leaned closer, squinting in the hazy light, and saw that the alien was surrounded by several tiny fishlike animals. They swam freely over and through the alien's legs, occasionally wandering slightly away before hurriedly wriggling back to join the others. Oidar positively beamed.

"There are eleven males, Temple, that have survived. Eleven! Come see." He motioned excitedly for Rice to come into the water for a closer look, and when Rice hesitated, added, "It is all right, Temple. It is shallow and the bottom is firm." He waved his arm again.

Leaving the helmet on the bench, he waded tentatively into the murky water and was relieved to find that, although his booted feet sank several centimeters into the muddy bottom, the footing was firmer than he would have thought. He waded forward then stopped, knee-deep, in front of Oidar and looked nervously around. "Oidar, are you sure this is all right? I don't want to violate any . . ." Any what? What was he frightened of? He thought for a moment that his nervousness might be caused by the political implications of being this close to a Sarpan in his spawning area, but quickly discarded the thought. What was really bothering him, he realized, was his own discomfort at being unexpectedly thrust this far into an alien culture. He had come here, after all, only to talk to Oidar privately about the directive that Academician Bomeer had just—

"This space is mine," Oidar countered, interrupting his thoughts. He lifted his hand from the water and swept an arm around him at their surroundings. Drops of water flew from his fingertips at the motion, and the little creatures swam playfully after the tiny splashes the drops made wherever they touched the surface of the pond. "And I alone decide who visits my spawn and who does not." He tilted his head as if trying to come to a decision about something, then reached out and took Rice by the hand, pulling at the E-suit's glove. "Please to remove them, Temple?" he asked.

Rice unsealed each glove from its sleeve and pulled them off, clumsily stuffing them into one of several roomy pouches sewn into the waistband of the suit.

"Like this," Oidar said, cupping his own hands.

Rice copied his actions and held his hands out before him, watching as Oidar carefully reached into the water and scooped up one of the little swimmers. It made no effort to swim away. He extended his webbed hands and poured the water and the swimmer into Rice's.

His heart raced as he looked down at the form in his hands. Against the lighter color of his palms the swimmer was much easier to see than in the murky water where Oidar sat. The swimmer had a wide, flat tail and no rear legs yet, but otherwise was an exact duplicate of the broadly grinning Oidar himself. With water leaking through his fingers, Rice felt the slight pressure of the diminutive alien's tiny hands as it pushed itself up in his palms and regarded him carefully, tilting its little head in a mannerism he had grown used to seeing during the time he'd spent with the aliens. The little one rubbed several times against his palm, then, as the last of the water ran out of his cupped hands, wriggled back into the pond and swam to rejoin his water group. They greeted him by swimming and bumping against him and each other, friskily bumping one another and playing a game at which Rice could only guess. He felt he should say something to Oidar, but could think of nothing.

"They learn from me here," Oidar said. "You understand that." Rice nodded. "Much knowledge is passed through the blood, but much more is passed through touching. So. They learn much while I carry them, but they learn still more here." He swirled his hands through the water, brushing against them as he did. "Each new touch carries a thought, an idea."

"Thank you for sharing this with me," Rice said softly, his words almost drowned out by the buzz of a dragonfly-like insect that darted between them before disappearing in the growths to his left.

"No. It is this one who gives thanks." Oidar smiled again, his gill slits puffing out in a manner Rice had come to associate with a display of pride, and he noticed for the first time since entering the room that a single silver bob had been clipped to the skin at the edge of one of his gill slits. "You have touched one of my spawn, and have given him a bit of your knowledge, a bit of yourself. He, in turn"—he indicated the swimmers frolicking and splashing in the shallow water—"has touched the others. They all share that knowledge now and are better for it, I'm certain. Thank you, Temple."

Templeton Rice stood transfixed by the importance of what the alien had just said and forgot, for a moment, the urgent business that had drawn him to the Sarpan ship in the first place.

He is concerned for the condition of his water, and is correct to be so, Oidar reflected after Rice had left. He sat on the muddy bottom at the edge of the pond and held his free hand before him just under the water's surface, his children swimming freely through his fingers and against the skin of his hand. In his other hand he held the data stick that Rice had left with him. Oidar did not entirely comprehend the human trait "worry," and although he knew that "concern for the condition of one's water" was not quite the proper analogy, it was the closest he could come.

He had not touched Temple while he related what the human Bomeer had instructed him to do, and so had not picked up a better sense of what coursed through his friend's mind. As his visit lengthened, Rice had sat with him in the water and had, on several occasions, dipped his hands into the pond as he talked. One of his children, the one the human Temple had held previously, had been braver than the others of his group and had touched with him several times while he spoke. That one had quickly passed what he had learned to his brothers, but they kept to themselves the thoughts they shared and did not pass them to Oidar when he touched them; he could only guess what feelings they had acquired from his human friend.

As they continued swimming through his opened fingers he gently stroked at their sides, and from time to time one of them would cling to his arm or wrist and gaze upward into his eyes before jumping back into the tepid water. And as they did, he seemed to get a sense that his children shared a greater knowledge of the human feeling "worry" than did he himself.

Oidar lifted himself from the water, walking carefully through the shallows to avoid stirring up mud around the excited children swarming at his feet. They gathered at the very edge of the pond, crawling up on the stems of reeds and low grasses at the water's edge farther than he'd seen them dare before, and competed with one another for a better look at him. Their eye membranes, unaccustomed to such prolonged exposure to the air, blinked repeatedly and they made little peeping sounds that made him want to return to the water. It would not be long, he realized, before they would follow him out of the water altogether.

They stared at him, their little heads tilting first one way then the other, as if trying to tell him that they understood his feelings.

He nodded, making his decision.

So. Very well, Temple. I will send the message for you.

He checked the room controls, hidden in a clump of leafy fronds growing to one side of the entranceway, and satisfied himself that the children would be all right while he was gone. Then, taking a last look at the tiny faces at the edge of the pond, he quietly slipped out of the room and headed for the communications center of the *Flisth*.

* * *

They were nearing Luna rapidly, but it had still taken nearly a week for the transmission to reach them.

The message from Dr. Templeton Rice, Chief Researcher at the test site, had been sent instantaneously in a recorded tachyon burst to a Sarpan ship in Earth orbit, then relayed by normal communications to the *Levant*. There was a great deal at the beginning of the transmission that Adela did not comprehend, but Montero assured her that it was normal protocol intended mostly for his benefit.

"Dr. Montgarde," the recording began once the aliens' introductory material had concluded, "I have circumvented Imperial directives to see to it that the information contained in this communication reaches you. I considered going around Academician Bomeer, the director here at the test site where your theories are being put to practical demonstration, and filing this with the Emperor's staff directly; but I had no assurances that it wouldn't be intercepted by the academician. He is a man of extraordinary scientific genius, but he is also cunning in a way that would be difficult for me to describe at this time."

Adela smiled. Rice had no way of knowing it, of course, but she knew only too well how formidable an opponent Bomeer could be.

"For that matter," Rice's transmission went on, "I have no guarantee that this will reach you at all, but I felt it imperative to make the attempt." He paused and seemed unsure as to how to continue, then took a deep breath and said, almost apologetically, "We have found an error in your calculations. Because of our findings, my colleague and I recommended that the physical test be delayed until your return, so that you can join us via the tachyon link to discuss the figures and adjust the testing accordingly before proceeding further. However, the academician wishes to proceed with the physical test based on your original equations, stating that it would be better for you to have complete results to review upon your return. Personally I get the feeling that he wishes for the test to fail, although I admit that I can't explain my suspicions."

Rice turned in the screen and tapped out a command on the control pad set into the desktop in front of him, then slipped a data stick into the keypad input port.

"In any case, the test is scheduled to proceed," he went on, his eyes downcast. "The test will fail. We'll have an extensive recording of the entire experiment, beginning to end, for review waiting for you when you arrive. Perhaps the academician is right, and the full results will serve you better; I can't say. But I'm appending to this file the full report of the modeling tests to date"—he indicated the data stick—"to give you an idea of what you might expect on your return. Have a safe conclusion to your journey. Thank you."

His image faded out and was replaced by a notification indicating that several data files followed the verbal communication.

"That's it," Montero said. "System. Screen off." The screen obediently darkened. "I've taken the liberty of routing this recording, as well as the associated files, directly to your ID node in the computer, Doctor. You'll find them waiting for your personal attention whenever you want them."

"Thank you, Commander," she replied, her voice subdued. "And thanks for bringing this to my attention so quickly."

Montero sat, quietly pulling at one of the tips of his moustache. "This is highly irregular, you know." He nodded at the darkened screen. "A communication from an Imperial researcher who, purposely sidestepping his superiors, sent it through the facilities of the Sarpan without the knowledge or permission of those closest to the project . . ." He let his voice trail off when he noticed she wasn't listening.

"Doctor?"

She hadn't heard him, and concentrated instead on the feeling of sudden fear spreading uncontrollably through her.

An error, he'd said. *An error. An error. An error.*

It was there.

Adela ran the figures that accompanied the modeling, and it was there. Plain as the sun in the sky.

As Dr. Rice and the alien Oidar had noted in the results of both of the models, her original figures had been correct, but only so far as it theoretically applied to a technology that had yet to be developed. There had been blanks in the equation for which there were no currently available figures to plug in. Her theories took into account that shield technology would have to be developed to put her ideas to practical use, and much of the generations-long research had taken this into account. But there had been no way to project—at the time—how the application of the nonexistent technology itself would affect the results.

Adela had needed to make several educated guesses as to how the necessary shield technology, required to make the theory work successfully, would behave. She had guessed incorrectly.

"It is the character of the shield generating process itself," she recited into the recording lens, "that accounts for the difference in energy levels between the two stars. I had assumed that the shielding used to keep the singularities stable would be nonintrusive, and that the energy transfer would occur at a ratio of one to one.

"However, I was only half right. The shielding containing the negative singularity introduced into the feeder star is impassive, in that the energy needed from the star is drained off in a one-way manner in the expected amounts without being affected by the shield itself. What I could not anticipate, not having a working shield concept at the time, was that the emitted energy of the shield generating process is also drawn into the singularity, resulting in more energy being sent through the wormhole to the breeder star. This extra energy in the breeder star, however, is not only released by the positive singularity, but is further amplified by the reflective nature of the shielding there.

"The net result is that the amount of energy released in Sol, the breeder star, is far greater than anticipated. The total effective release is a factor of . . ." She paused and glanced at the readout displayed in the handheld in her lap, compared it to the figures floating in the air above the frozen image of the second model Rice had sent her, still displayed in the holo viewing area in the corner of her stateroom. "A factor of approximately one point nine one."

Adela paused to check her notes, confirming that she had covered all the points she wanted to make in her report. Satisfied that she had included all the pertinent information, she said, "The complete figures and energy projections are included in the data file attached to this recording." She snapped the cover closed on the handheld. "System, please end current recording and send it immediately to Dr. Rice at the test site." She hesitated, a knowing smile gracing her lips. "Encode it for personal delivery to Dr. Rice's ID *only.* " She had no reason to suspect that Bomeer would intercept communications intended for other members of the research team without their knowledge, but she felt better at having added the encoding.

According to Rice's clandestine communication, the physical test was to take place in a few days, and even though she was now less than a week away from Luna—where her report could be sent immediately to Rice using the tachyon link—the file she'd just encoded wouldn't reach him in time to be of any benefit to him for the test itself. However, her findings would arrive shortly after the testing was concluded and might help him to sort out the results of the failed test; and, no less importantly, verify the new figures.

She felt much better now than she had when Montero had given her the recording the previous day. As it turned out, the unavoidable flaw in her original equations would work to their advantage: The small-scale physical test that Rice was about to conduct, while minuscule in scope compared with the reality of what would be done to the Sun itself, was still the largest implementation of the Sarpan shielding that had yet been attempted. The "real thing" would require far more immense shield generating facilities to contain singularities of the size that would be required for success. But her new figures—which would be borne out by the test, even when it failed—indicated that a smaller set of tuned singularities, and therefore lesser shielding, would yield the same amount of energy needed to save Earth's Sun.

In fact, now that she thought about it, she wondered just how much more economical the process could be, based on the new figures. After all, if much of what she hoped to do could be done on a smaller scale, it could quite possibly be done years sooner. And since there was no way of knowing exactly how much time Sol had left, every year sooner they could move up the process would greatly increase the window of safety they had.

Adela regarded the image still displayed in the corner and took a light pen from the breast pocket of her uniform.

"System."

"Ma'am?"

"Replay current file and activate cursor, please."

"Ready, ma'am."

The model began again, the red cylinders forming the perfect pyramids she'd already viewed nearly a hundred times in the last twenty-four hours. She allowed the playback to continue, pointing the pen to the set of figures over the leftmost pyramid, the one at the representation of Sol, at three points—when they first arranged themselves in the geometric figure, when the shielded singularity first appeared inside it, and just before the singularity was inserted inside the star.

"Stop playback and give me a full readout of the requested statistics. Direct the feed to my handheld." She snapped the cover open once more and studied the figures as they scrolled by: mass of containment, energy of singularity contained, length of time to arrange and insert, required distance and power of shield generators and a hundred other relevant aspects of what was happening during the model.

Once the download was complete, she requested that a new model be created, under a different file name, using the same values as the one from which she'd just extracted the key information she needed to change the model to conform with the new energy equations. *Let's see,* she mused as her fingers flew over the keypad, substituting a new figure here, a different value there. The new figures were sent to the model and each change slightly altered the image, followed by a new set of readouts floating near the changed items.

Hours passed, but Adela was so excited and involved in what she was doing that she barely noticed.

"Run the model, please," she said once satisfied with the changes she'd entered. The image played out and a feeling of elation swept over her as the results matched the first model: There was no apparent change in the image representing Sol; the energy output reading remained as constant and steady as it had before. Only the rapidly scrolling statistics below the projection gave any indication that the star had just been given the boost of a secondary power source, a helping hand designed to keep the star healthy and stable for eons to come.

Grinning now, she ran the model once more to verify her findings, and nearly danced giddily across the room when assured that the new numbers were valid.

She would send the redesigned model to Rice, of course, so he could set up another physical test utilizing the new figures, but there was no hurry. Rice and Oidar, not to mention Bomeer himself, would be actively involved in the final setup for the test at this very moment.

There was an angry rumble in her stomach and Adela glanced at her wrist, surprised at how late it had become. All right, then, she decided; she'd head to the mess for something to eat and put together another recording containing the new model and all the figures she'd substituted when she got back. She hadn't realized it, but she was nearly as exhausted as she was hungry. Adela stretched aching joints held much too long in a sitting position hunched over the handheld. The next time, she promised herself as she left the cabin and headed for the mess, she'd walk around the room with the handheld to avoid the cramped feeling she now felt in her back and shoulders.

Adela rubbed at her neck and wished, not for the first time since the *Levant* had left for Pallatin, she was back in Javas' chamber. The untimely murder of Emperor Nicholas and the importance of the upcoming trip had weighed heavily on her before she'd left, and he had rubbed her neck and shoulders then, his strong but gentle touch bringing life into weary muscles. She felt herself smiling at the memory and stopped to lean against the wall of the deserted corridor. Still smiling, she closed her eyes and tried to imagine the touch of his fingertips, the scent of him and the soft caress of his breath against her neck as he whispered into her ear . . .

"Doctor? Are you all right?"

She snapped her eyes open, startled, and stared with embarrassment into the face of a young Ensign she did not recognize. She had grown accustomed, since coming out of the tank, to how empty the ship had seemed. Many of the nonessential members of the crew would not be awakened until they were actually in orbit around the Moon, which, combined with the fact that a large number of the ship's complement had remained behind on Pallatin, almost made the *Levant* feel like a ghost ship. Other than Montero and the bridge crew, some of her personal team and the medical staff—all of whom were already "up"—she had seen few people aboard the big ship and had simply not expected anyone in the corridor at this late hour.

"Oh. I . . . I'm fine." The young man, his face pale and

anemic-looking from cryosleep, reached a hand to steady her. "I was dizzy for a moment, that's all. Hungry, I guess."

The Ensign smiled in understanding. "I know what you mean, ma'am," he replied brightly. "I haven't been able to stay away from the mess since I got out of the tank myself. You sure you'll be okay?"

"Really, I'll be fine." She gave him a reassuring smile and thanked him for his concern, then watched as he headed in the opposite direction.

It was probably just as well that he brought me back to reality, she told herself. The Javas who awaited her would not be the same man who lived in the memory of a night she'd left more than forty years earlier. But it wasn't fair; from her perspective, taking cryosleep and the near-relativistic speeds the *Levant* traveled into account, it seemed as if only two years had elapsed. And yet, she knew better. For him, four full decades had passed.

Four decades.

She put the thought out of her mind, reminding herself that even now the Emperor would be so intimately involved in the final setup for the physical test of her theories that he couldn't spend idle time wondering about her even if he wanted to.

The test, while simple in nature, involved many critical aspects other than the application of her equations. There was the tuned pair of singularities, for example. Rice's files had indicated that they had already been prepared and were being held in stasis, and that would occupy many of both the Imperial and Sarpan scientists.

There was also the coordination of the ships. It was critical that each be in place at precisely the correct distance, at the exact moment required, when the singularities were inserted into the artificial stars created for the test. Adela had no doubts, however, about Fain's abilities in that regard. From the reports that awaited her when she woke up, she'd learned that Fain had become one of her project's staunchest supporters, and had taken it upon himself to learn a great deal of the scientific principles involved in the effort.

And then there were the two artificial stars themselves. The test was being undertaken on a scale that would make the parts involved seem almost microscopic compared to a real sun. It was not normally possible to create a G-2 star of the size needed for the test, and keep it funtioning at the reduced size for very long, of course: The stable, sustained reaction needed to simulate a star would quickly dissipate in space. Utilizing the marvelous shield technology of the Sarpan, however, a star could be created and contained—a "bottled beam" was what some of the younger researchers had jokingly dubbed it—for the amount of time required for the test. Once the test was concluded, the test site would be evacuated and quarantined and the two mini-stars and the tiny singularities they contained would be allowed to dissipate once the timed shield generators expired.

But for now, the formation and containment of the two test stars was critical, and Javas would be in constant realtime link with Bomeer and Fain to ensure that everything was going properly—

Adela stopped dead in the corridor.

The shield containments for the mini-stars were powerful; they needed to be to contain the fury of the constant fusion reactions occurring within them. But the test that was about to take place was based on her old equations, and the singularities being used, as she'd just recalculated back in her cabin, were too big. Had the increased energy levels that would be released by the breeder star during this test been taken into consideration?

She spun about and started jogging back toward her stateroom, her mind racing. *I've got to look at the values for the shielding for the mini-stars,* she thought desperately. She overtook the ensign she'd chatted with moments earlier, and he started to say something to her, but she quickly left him puzzled as she rounded the corner and increased her pace to a full run. *One point nine one . . . almost double the amount of energy they're expecting. Surely they've recalibrated the shielding.* But then—if they hadn't set up a new model—reconfigured with the new values, as she had done—they might not even be aware of how much greater the release would be.

"System!" she shouted the moment she burst into her cabin. She had already pulled the handheld from its belt pouch and had flipped the cover open. "Redisplay most recently viewed file! Cursor on and feed the statistics to my handheld." She had changed the values for almost everything in the new model to achieve an energy transfer ratio of one to one. The one thing she hadn't needed to alter was the value of the shielding containing the two mini-stars; they were the same as the values intended for the test that would begin soon.

The playback started immediately, and she stabbed the light pen at the image the moment the two stars and their associated readouts were added to the display, the numbers she highlighted going directly to the unit in her hand. She turned away from the image and tapped frantically at the keypad, ignoring the playback as it continued unheeded behind her.

In her haste, she hit several wrong keys, causing the handheld to beep angrily at her. Adela closed her eyes tightly and forced herself to breathe more slowly. She swallowed drily and entered the required commands again, more carefully this time. It took a few seconds to get it right, and then another moment for the value she was looking for to appear in the unit's tiny readout. She gazed at it for only a split second, then, muttering fearfully under her breath, cleared the machine and ran the same commands over the figures again, being extremely careful to hit just the right keys. Again, the same value as before appeared in the readout.

"Dear God," she whispered, feeling her throat tighten. She sank back against the arm of the chair, letting the handheld fall clattering, forgotten, to the floor.

THIRTY-ONE

J avas, Emperor of the Hundred Worlds, sat in the holograph viewing chamber that was the very heart of his personal quarters on Luna. His father had enjoyed a similar chamber on Corinth and had often programmed it to display a peaceful Earth forest, spending many long hours there strolling through the projected greenery. Javas had never realized it while his father was alive—he had, he admitted regretfully, never even been interested in how his father had lived during those earlier years—but recognized now that the forest being displayed was the backwoods that surrounded Woodsgate. The file for the display was in the Imperial computer, and Javas had literally stumbled upon it years after Emperor Nicholas' death.

The sounds of birds and the creaking of the tall trees in the wind above his head filled the chamber and he looked up, squinting when the branches parted enough to allow a shaft of holographic sunshine to pour through the leaves. There was a soft thump to his left that caught his attention and he turned in time to see an acorn roll beneath a pile of leaves. He looked up for the source of the acorn and met the eyes of the gray squirrel that had let it slip from its paws.

The file had been enhanced, he noticed: There were trees and wildflowers here that had never seen a misty Kentucky morning, but it was all so very real. The sound of the boughs rustling overhead, the scent of dry leaves beneath his feet, everything. For some reason, Javas felt very close to his father right now; closer than he'd felt in years.

I wish you were here today, Father, he reflected. *A major part of your dream will come true today.*

Emperor Nicholas had been right all along. In the many years that had passed since his father had sent him to Luna, officially putting the project in motion, so much of what he'd predicted had come to pass. Technology had been reborn. The worlds had drawn closer together in pursuit of this joint goal than they had been in centuries. The Empire's strength had grown, and that strength was respected by the Sarpan, ushering in a new era of peace and cooperation with the aliens.

Even the test that was about to take place was a sign of their progress. Although flawed, it illustrated better than anything else the advancements they had made, and the results would point out the exact areas that needed to be reworked. And he was certain that Adela would have no trouble, once she was home and in realtime contact with the test site, reconfiguring the equations to their best advantage.

Adela . . .

There was a beeping, more felt through the integrator than heard, that told him the tachyon link had been established with the wide-scan array set up for viewing the test.

Javas took one last look around him at the forest, inhaled one last time of the cool fragrant air, then silently ordered the holographic file canceled and stored. The empty chamber appeared in its place—stark, barren, metallic—and he walked to the single plush chair that had been placed here for this event. The forest scent still lingered, but the recirculating fans were already venting the pleasant aroma out of the chamber.

He received notification that the link was ready and reclined in the chair as another silent command through the integrator plunged the chamber into sudden darkness.

The room had transformed into deep space itself. Nearly in front of him the artificial mini-star that would represent Sol in the test glowed fiercely. Above and to his right, and graphically farther away than its counterpart, another yellow star shone brightly. The intense light of the two miniature suns washed out nearly everything else in the image, and the sheer brilliance was almost too much for him; he was forced to shield his eyes with a raised arm until he could issue a command for the projection to be dimmed.

The level of brightness dropped immediately to a more comfortable setting, and allowed him to see everything with a much greater degree of detail, with a unique perspective of the test site not seen in nature. The view had been "constructed" by taking tachyon signals from two different vantage points and computer-blending them into a single vista, overlaying the images to give a picture that, while not to exact scale as far as the distances between the two stars were concerned, nevertheless allowed him to take in everything at once.

Javas was also aware, now that he could view the image without squinting, that there was much more to be seen. He could not quite tell on the farther star, but on the nearer of the pair he could see the Sarpan shielding itself, arranged around the miniature thousand-kilometer-wide sun like concentric soap bubbles nestled one inside the other. It was the inner layers of shielding, he realized from the scientific briefings, that kept the reactions contained at the right levels to simulate Earth's G-2 star.

The shield generator ships were visible, already arranged in the distinctive pyramid shape, and were in the process of emplacing the positive singularity in the right orbit for insertion. The singularity itself was much too small to be seen, but the pale blue sphere of its shield indicated its location in the exact center of the pyramid. As the pyramid swept across the face of the Sol mini-star, the Sarpan ships were silhouetted against the bright, roiling surface.

He knew that Adela would view the playback of the event in this very room when she returned in a few days, and the grandeur of what he observed now would be in no way diminished by the fact that it would be a recording. But he couldn't help wishing that she were beside him now, watching this with him.

"All goes well," Oidar told his sons.

The holographic image of the Sarpan pond had been partially removed, although the projected trees mingling with the real plants lining the water's edge still gave the impression more of a natural body of water than an artificial construct. Above them, where the projection of the twin suns had been, an image was forming that gave them an outside view of what was taking place ten thousand kilometers from the *Flisth*.

Oidar did not know that the projection was not as sophisticated as the one the Emperor enjoyed, nor would he have cared if he'd known. It consisted only of the single image of the ministar representing the humans' home Sun. The other artificial sun, placed for the test at a distance of 900,000 kilometers from this one, was but a bright dot that mingled with the many true stars that swept across the "sky." As the projection became more defined, the little swimmers gathered around Oidar and held onto him, growing still and silent as they watched wide-eyed and open-mouthed at the magnificent spectacle above them. The image now completed, it looked to them like a new night sky, with a strange bright star where their suns had been.

The insects in the water chamber seemed puzzled by what was happening and buzzed frantically at the unnatural light.

"All goes well," he said again, even though they would not fully understand speech for many months.

"And look there. Do you not see the generator ships?" He pointed to the pyramid formed around a pale blue sphere orbiting the glowing orb. "One day, when it comes time, the humans will build much greater generators and learn to pilot them from a distance. But for now, it is we who steer them." Oidar looked down at his children, stroking each of them tenderly with his hands.

"This is called cooperation," he whispered. "Remember it, for it will be your legacy."

The holograph frame located at the front of the *Port of Kow-loon*'s small lecture room projected two separate images, displayed side by side. One showed the mini-star representing Sol, the other presented the hypothetical G-2 feeder star.

"They're ready to insert the singularities, Academician," Rice said. He turned away momentarily and spoke softly into the headset he wore, then returned his attention to the images. "I've instructed them to begin with the negative singularity."

"Why?" Bomeer asked, then added quickly, "Forgive me, I don't mean to sound critical. I'm merely curious as to why the feeder star was chosen first."

Rice shrugged. "The shielding for the feeder is the more critical of the two, as far as permeability is concerned. If scanning shows a problem with the shielding once the negative singularity has been inserted, we'll stop everything then, before attempting anything with the breeder."

Bomeer nodded, and regarded the projections.

The two men watched the image on the right as the pyramid made a gentle spiral around the star, each pass taking it through the outer layers of the shielding and bringing it closer to the surface. Just when it seemed, from the aspect of the holograph, that it would touch the star itself, the pyramid began to expand and flatten into a pattern closer to that of a square with the blue sphere still held equidistant from the four individual generators. The square continued its expansion until the dimensions were greater than the star, all the while still orbiting the glowing orb as a huge flat sheet might circle it.

As the orbit of the generators altered, the sphere brushed the star at about the same time the four generator ships completed the adjustment to their course that took them in a full orbit around the star. Then, like a hoop being drawn over a floating ball, the ring of generator ships drew the sphere at its center into the star, slowly, slowly, until it finally disappeared into the interior. The ships increased speed, widening their orbit considerably around the star.

"I'm curious," Bomeer inquired. "How far away can the generator ships get and still maintain their hold on the singularity?"

"At this scale, with generators rated only for this experiment, they can go about four thousand kilometers out and still maintain the integrity of their lock on the sphere. They'll need to go much farther out when we do this with Sol, of course, and we'll need to increase the size of the generator ships, but that's still very far away. These ships will hold the pattern at a distance of three thousand kilometers."

As he said this, the four Sarpan generator ships reached their apogee and revolved smoothly around the star, waiting for the next step to begin.

Supreme Commander Fain was pleased, as he watched the insertion at the feeder star, with how smoothly the operation was going. He was no less gratified at the way the combined efforts of science and military meshed, not to mention the careful cooperation of the crews of the five-man generator ships—or, more accurately, crews consisting of one man and four Sarpan pilots. As much in favor as he was of this joint effort, and as much assimilation time his handpicked officers had experienced, he still could not help the nagging feeling of trepidation going through him now.

They know their jobs, he admitted inwardly. *I could not have chosen better people.* Likewise, Fain had been satisfied with the crewmates that the Sarpan captain had selected. The two of them had worked carefully with their respective crews and had every right to be proud of them.

Visible in the viewscreen less than a thousand meters to starboard was the Sarpan flagship. This was the closest the two ships had come to one another during this mission. For reasons of protocol or practicality, the two had been widely separated; but now they floated together—along with the science ship *Port of Kowloon*—to view the physical test that would signify the end of this mission.

As he watched the insertion phase beginning at the Sol star, he realized that there were really two tests going on here. One was the research necessary for the success of the project, of course; but the other test was perhaps even more important. The joint mission was a test unto itself, and would prove that the two races could indeed work together.

Fain's attention remained on the viewscreen, but he couldn't help wondering if the Sarpan captain could feel pride.

It's nearly over.

Academician Bomeer stared at the twin displays, and saw that the insertion of the singularity into the Sol star had gone as smoothly as it had on the feeder. He turned to Rice, heard the scientist speaking rapidly into his headset and knew that final readings were being taken of the shields containing the singularities. Once completed, the generator ships would move into final position in preparation for allowing the shields to go permeable and start the wormhole effect that would link the two mini-stars.

The test would fail. Rice already knew it. Emperor Javas, Fain and all the scientists at the test site—both human and alien— knew it would fail. And, according to the surreptitiously gained information he'd received from a source close to Rice, even Dr. Montgarde would know by now that this test was destined to be unsuccessful.

He had no way of knowing what Dr. Montgarde's reaction was when she had received the illegal communication his source told him had been routed through the aliens. But if the mood of those now observing the test—from those around him here at the site, to Emperor Javas back on Luna—was any indication, the effect was not what he had anticipated.

Bomeer had hoped to bring about a questioning of their goals, a review of the project itself and the value it would serve compared with the obvious choice of merely evacuating Earth as he and Fain had originally proposed on Corinth a century ago. What he found instead was an attitude that what was about to happen was not a failed experiment, but rather a data-gathering endeavor that would better hone the experimentation process for research and development yet to come.

How could I have been so wrong? he asked himself. *There was a time when a failure like this would have stopped all forward motion; the Council of Academicians would have demanded that more study be done, that nothing further be attempted until a full reevaluation of the stated goals was presented, reviewed, dissected and then reassembled for still further study.*

But things were different now. There was the New Attitude,

after all, now being openly embraced by the member planets of the Hundred Worlds.

Fain and Javas are right. And before them, Emperor Nicholas. Bomeer nodded slowly in the darkened room, admitting for the first time that it was he and the last holdouts among the academicians who were out of step with the Empire, and not the other way around. *We were blind to it all— No,* he silently confessed, *we blinded ourselves.*

"Academician?"

He felt a hand on the sleeve of his tunic and turned to see Rice staring at him.

"Academician?" he asked again, his hand covering the microphone of his headset. "Did you hear me, sir?"

Bomeer smiled softly in resignation. "I'm sorry, Doctor, my mind was elsewhere. You were saying?"

"Everything is in place. We're ready to allow the shields to permeate and begin the test. As the ranking member of the science team, the order is yours to give, Academician."

The irony of the situation struck him that it would be he who gave the order for the test. A test that everyone involved in the research—indeed, everyone now watching in realtime through the tachyon link—already knew would be a failure. He felt suddenly old and wondered how he would be remembered for his actions this day.

"Begin," he said simply.

Rice spoke into the headset, his eyes not leaving the twin projections before them.

Nothing happened visually. They continued watching, and Rice received reports over the headset almost as rapidly as the figures scrolled through the air around the various parts of the display. The readings were changing, much as they had in the second model, but still no visual changes occurred.

Ten minutes passed. Then fifteen, twenty, twenty-five. Nearly thirty minutes had gone by before Bomeer noticed that the glow of the Sol star had increased slightly.

The radiance grew steadily, becoming almost too bright to watch before the computer-controlled projection dimmed the image on the left. The brightness still increased, the familiar yellow glow lightening to a whiter shade as the energy heightened.

"Academician . . ." Rice started to say, then hesitated and cupped his hand over the headset's earpiece. He stood suddenly and stared, not at the Sol star where most of the effects were being manifested, but at the feeder star.

Bomeer followed his gaze, puzzled by the expression visible in the glow cast from the bright objects. The feeder star was visibly unaffected, the energy drain having the effect of speeding up its aging process. There should not be a noticeable change in a feeder star until much later during its lifetime; certainly, since this mini-star would be dissipated at the conclusion of the test, nothing would be seen here. But still Rice stood riveted, his mouth open.

What is he—? Bomeer stopped himself when he saw what had captured Rice's attention. Where was the fourth generator ship?

"System! Increase right side image!"

"What magnification would you—"

"Double it!" Bomeer demanded, cutting off the system's query. The image enlarged immediately and the remaining three ships were easily visible. All were clearly in trouble.

One was breaking up in space, the wet Sarpan atmosphere puffing out in a frozen crystalline cloud for a brief second before dissipating. The craft crumpled, as if being squeezed by a giant invisible hand, its size shrinking as it formed a tight ball of debris before he lost sight of it. The other two ships managed, through either their pilots' skill or good fortune, to get farther away and, although they suffered nothing like the damage that had just occurred to the other ship, they now appeared to be dead in space.

The two men stood transfixed at the sight, unable to speak until a warning claxon jarred both of them.

"System!" Bomeer yelled. "What's happening?"

There was a brief pause as the room system analyzed his voice patterns, determining if he had clearance for the requested information. "Commander Fain has ordered the *Port of Kowloon* to begin an immediate pullback." It offered nothing further and Bomeer knew that asking for additional information would be fruitless.

"Academician!" Rice had grabbed him by the shoulder and was pointing to the image of the Sol star. Bomeer turned, incredulous at what he saw.

The mini-star glowed nearly white-hot, and had expanded to the limit of the innermost of the concentrically arrayed holding shields. The generator ships were moving away, but as the energy level increased, the inner shield disintegrated before his eyes, the star "jumping" in size to fill the space to the next shield. With more room inside the shields, the glow softened slightly and the brightness lowered, but immediately began to build again.

The energy released by the ruptured inner shield traveled out from the mini-star in an invisible wave, catching the nearest of the fleeing generator ships in its grasp. The ship flared instantly, incinerated. There was a second flare on the opposite side, then a third and fourth as the energy wave caught up with them.

The next shield burst, like the thin bubble it was, much the same as the first had minutes earlier. Two more flares followed and, although he hadn't seen them in the projection because the system had steadily dimmed the projection in response to the intensified brightness, Bomeer knew that the two Imperial support ships had just been destroyed.

The two projections had begun shrinking in size, and Bomeer reasoned that the *Kowloon* was accelerating fast enough now that the distance between them and the test site had been widened significantly. He hadn't realized that he'd risen to his feet, and he fell wearily back into his chair as he regarded the receding stars. He didn't bother to order the system to compensate the projection for the distance.

There were no more flares as he watched the image fall away.

Commander Fain's holographic image at the front of the viewing chamber remained so still that for a moment Rice wondered if the system had malfunctioned. He stood—had remained standing, in fact, since the conference started—lost deep in thought as they awaited the next report from the shuttle now surveying the test site.

In contrast, Academician Bomeer, seated next to him, refused to sit still and fidgeted constantly. The man was severely distraught by what had happened and became increasingly so as the reports of additional fatalities came in. There were dark circles under his red eyes and his academician's garb was untidy for the first time in memory. Rice knew Bomeer had gotten no more sleep in the last day than he had. The academician ran his hand for the hundredth time through his disheveled hair, the sudden motion catching Fain's attention.

There was no one else in the room, and although only the three of them were involved in this conference, Rice knew that everything they discussed would be relayed to the Emperor's top scientific aides on Luna. Emperor Javas himself had not been available for this conference. Rice had no way of verifying it, but he suspected that the Emperor was at this moment occupied in intense discussions with the Sarpan.

"Commander?" The sudden disembodied voice of the reconnaissance shuttle pilot filled the chamber.

Fain raised his head. "Yes, Captain?"

"Sir, the craft the Sarpan sent out is between us and the two generator ships that tried to get away from the feeder star. They've got them in a gravity harness and refuse to allow us to get any closer. We've done a complete scan, though, and as far as we can tell there's no life on either of them."

Fain nodded to himself, then, "No sign of the other two generator ships?"

"No, sir; nothing appears on our scans and the gravity field here is too distorted for us to safely go any closer to the feeder to mount an effective search. We're having a hard time maintaining this position as it is."

"Very well, Captain. Return to the ship." Fain, still on his feet, turned to face them. "I think we can assume that there were no survivors inside a radius of four thousand kilometers at either star," he said bluntly. "All the Sarpan on the eight generator ships, thirty-two of them in all, were killed; along with the eight human crew members assigned to accompany them."

Bomeer shifted again uneasily as Fain listed the casualties.

"The Imperial support ships *Dendam* and *Powell* were incinerated in the flare, with the loss of all hands—more than three hundred."

He hesitated and, although there was no outward change in his features, it seemed to Rice that Fain was pausing in a moment of reverence and respect for those killed in the accident—human and alien alike.

Fain's mouth tightened into a straight line for several seconds, then, "I'm ordering that preparations for the return trip to Luna be finalized immediately, Dr. Rice. We should be ready to leave in under two weeks. Is there anything else your analysis requires here at the test site before we depart?"

"What more analysis could you possibly want?" Bomeer demanded angrily before Rice could respond. He was on his feet and gestured at Fain in frustration. "The mistake we have made here should *never* be repeated! We should be the master of technology, but in our attempt to move technology too quickly into the future, we allowed technology to become master over us."

Fain shook his head at the academician's outburst, but said nothing.

"I've been warning of a failure like this since the beginning of the project."

"May I remind you, Academician," Rice countered, "that it was you who rushed this experiment to its completion?"

Commander Fain arched an eyebrow. "Is this true?"

Bomeer stood speechless. He tried several times to refute what had been said, but gave up before turning back to his seat and falling heavily into it. "Yes," he said finally, his voice shaking.

"Then you've not only interpreted the data incorrectly," Fain said, staring down at them, "but you are also a fool with blood on his hands." The Commander said nothing more for several moments, then silently broke the connection.

Rice stood, inhaling deeply and rubbing at his sore eyes, and regarded the academician. He sat slumped in his seat, his shoulders drooping, and stared at the darkened display area. Everything that Rice had come to associate with him—the arrogance, the self-assured air, the importance of his position—seemed to drain from him as he watched. The man was a mere shadow of the figure he had been when they left Luna.

"You think this was a failure?" Rice asked in a tone of voice he would never previously have dared use with the academician.

Bomeer didn't turn, and continued staring wordlessly at the empty area in front of him.

"A tragedy, yes," Rice went on, "a senseless act of stupidity that could have been avoided if you had put our goals ahead of your own. But this was no failure. We have the proof that Dr. Montgarde's theories are valid, and we have the figures we need to restructure the equations to allow for the characteristics of the shielding. Far from bringing this project to an end, or even slowing it down, the test shows us that what we've done here is only a beginning."

Rice walked to the exit of the viewing chamber. "What we've accomplished here was worthwhile, and your efforts to stall us can't change that." He thumbed the control to open the door, then turned back to Bomeer one last time as the door slid aside. "You've only succeeded in changing its cost."

Rice turned away and, although not bothering to close the door as he strode away, didn't see Bomeer bury his face in his hands.

"Temple? Do I disturb you?"

Rice sat upright at his desk in the open lab, blinking rapidly at the light, and looked at Oidar standing before him in a Sarpan E-suit. The last two weeks had been busy ones. He had been going over some last-minute details before the *Port of Kowloon* prepared to return to Luna and had fallen asleep over his hand-held. The alien stood motionless, his arms gently cradling a bulge in the front of the suit, and waited for him to come fully awake.

"Oh . . . Oidar. No, no; I'm fine." He hadn't been expecting a visit from the alien and as he became more awake he suddenly remembered that the temperature settings in the open lab would be uncomfortable for Oidar once he'd removed his suit. "System! Increase lab temperature and humidity to—"

"System! Cancel!" Oidar said, cutting him off. The room system beeped once as it reset itself to accept the alien scientist's voice pattern. "I am sorry, Temple, but I cannot stay." His voice was tinny as it came from the suit's small speaker, but Rice could easily tell that he was uneasy.

"Oidar, what's wrong?"

He took off the E-suit's bubble helmet and set it on the corner of the desk. Water dripped from the helmet's collar ring and ran in a thin trickle over the edge. Rice ignored it.

"There is something here for you to see." Oidar pulled a data stick from a sleeve pocket and handed it to him, then again caressed the suit bulge. "It is a recording of the accident at the breeder star. I am sure you have such recordings, but our scans"—he paused briefly, a hint of apology in his tone—"are better at penetrating our own shielding than yours. It is not visible, but please to note if something strange appears in the readout."

Rice took the stick and inserted it into his handheld. "What should I be looking for?" Oidar shook his head, and Rice understood that the alien didn't want to influence him. Perhaps Oidar wasn't sure what it was either.

He started the playback and the figures ran through in the same sequence and values as on the Imperial recordings of what had happened. "I'm not sure I understand what it is you want me to—" There was a sudden anomaly in the readouts that stood out sharply from the familiar sequence. "What was that?" Oidar smiled and nodded. Rice reversed the playback a few increments and started it again. Again, the anomaly appeared. Rice removed the stick and replaced it with another, then watched as it played back and compared the two. When it finished, he set the handheld back on the desk.

"What did you see?" Oidar tilted his head curiously.

"I'm not sure," Rice replied. "Everything matches the figures we got. The energy levels in your recording, made at the time the shielding ruptured, are the same as ours. The energy released by the destroyed ships shows up at the same intensity as in ours. But where our recording showed six explosions—the four generator ships and the two Imperial craft—this one shows a seventh."

"So."

"Yeah, 'so' is right." Rice leaned against the desk and crossed his arms as he considered what he'd just seen. "Can I assume your scans of the feeder star are as good as this one, and that you've detected no trace of the generator ship that disappeared there?"

Oidar nodded.

"Could it be the missing ship?" Rice asked, more to himself than to Oidar. He looked up, then, "Do your people think it could somehow have been drawn through the wormhole when the energy balance went critical, only to be incinerated with the other ships at the breeder star a few seconds later?"

"They do, Temple. But—" He hesitated, his voice again taking on the apologetic tone. "But they do not wish to share this information with you at this time."

Rice understood. The feeder star had been separated from the breeder by a distance of 900,000 kilometers. If the anomaly on the data stick proved to be the missing ship . . .

"Temple?"

Rice looked up and saw that Oidar was shaking. The air in the open lab was dry, and his skin no longer glistened as it had when he'd first removed his helmet.

"My God," Rice said, grabbing the helmet, "you'll hurt yourself. Put this on. Now." He snatched the helmet from the desk and tried to slip it over his friend's head, but was stopped by Oidar's arm firmly grasping his shoulder.

"A moment more, then I promise to put it on." Rice stopped, but continued to hold the helmet. Oidar's hands moved to the bulge in the E-suit, and he rubbed at it in a circular motion. Rice noticed that the bulge moved slightly at his touch.

"They move now without benefit of tails," Oidar said, and Rice knew that meant they were walking on newly developed legs. There was both pride and sadness in Oidar's voice. "They will be mature soon and will choose their way. I am hoping they will all choose science and will investigate what we have found here. When you are again back at Luna I will be gone, but they will work at your side as I have done. As did my father before me."

"And they will be . . ." Rice groped for the phrase he'd once heard Oidar use. "They will be gladly received."

There was an awkward silence that seemed to last forever before Oidar reached for the helmet and lowered it over his head. The helmet sealed at the collar ring, he inhaled deeply for several seconds, then held out his hand, palm forward. Rice placed his own palm flat against the other's in a Sarpan gesture of final touching. Their hands parted, and Rice grasped the alien's hand in a firm handshake. Oidar said nothing when he released his grip and walked for the door. Rice remained standing at the desk.

When he reached the door, Oidar stopped and turned back. "Temple," he began tentatively, his voice again thin and tinny in the suit speaker. "I have studied your medical records most thoroughly . . ."

"Yes?" Rice crossed the lab and stood facing his friend. "And—?"

"Your rejuvenation methods. They would not be as effective on this one as on your species, but they would work, no?"

Rice exhaled heavily, his cheeks puffing out, and shrugged uncertainly. "I . . . I'm not sure. It's never been tried, but I don't see why it couldn't be adapted for Sarpan chemistry."

"And cryosleep could be used to make the rejuvenation more effective, no?"

Rice nodded nervously. What Oidar was suggesting represented a level of interspecies cooperation that was unprecedented.

Oidar twisted off the helmet and held it under one arm as he stroked the front of his suit with the other. He lifted his chin in a way that suggested both pride and courage and said, "Temple, this one wishes to work with his children, and to remain a part of the project until its conclusion."

PART SIX

HOMECOMING

THIRTY-TWO

"**T**his is wrong," Adela said as the small transport shuttle was brought in a mere sixty meters away from where they now stood. She turned to go but was stopped by Javas' firm but gentle hand on her arm. "Please! Let me go; I shouldn't be surprising him like this. It's not right."

Javas smiled at her in that way he had that said he understood what she was feeling, but at the same time told her that he felt she was overreacting to a given situation. He said nothing. He didn't need to.

She stopped and looked up into his face, then turned her eyes back to the ship being pulled into the receiving tube of the auxiliary landing bay. The other shuttles, those with the support personnel and crew of lower rank, had landed and departed hours ago. This transport, the last to come down from the starship now in a parking orbit above them, would be carrying the officers and bridge crew. The landing procedure was being handled remotely from the main bay, and except for a few technicians and support personnel, the bay was deserted.

"I'm being silly, aren't I?" The ship's thrusters were still in shutdown cycle and her voice was almost lost in the receiving bay.

"No. You're not being silly." Javas stood behind her and put his hands on her tiny shoulders, turning her around to face him. "I understand how scared you are right now, but you needn't be afraid of taking him by surprise." Javas smiled, and the tiny

wrinkles at the corners of his eyes seemed to make them sparkle.
"I probably shouldn't tell you this," he confessed, nodding at the
shuttle, "but he was hoping you'd be here to greet him."

Adela hugged Javas, partly for the warmth and moral support
she needed right now, partly in gratitude for his admission that
he'd anticipated her concern and had spoken to Eric before the
transport shuttle left the starship. Was there nothing about her
that he did not know, could not anticipate?

"My entire life has been one of waiting," she said at last. "But
this last year . . ." She let her voice trail off without finishing the
thought.

He said nothing in reply, but she knew that he understood.

Adela had spoken to Eric frequently since her return a year
earlier and the two of them had grown close, or as close as a
separation of millions of kilometers would allow. The tachyon
dish aboard his starship had made their communications instantaneous, and the transmitted images were frequently crystalline
in their clarity, but they were a poor substitute for the warmth of
his touch, the feel of his fingertips, the scent of his hair.

Javas held her, silent and unmoving. After forty years' separation from her with only recorded holographic messages and images to give them some small semblance of closeness, he
understood only too well the emotions going through her right
now. She tightened her embrace, thankful for his insight, and
closed her eyes as she thought, *But this is even more difficult, my
love, than you can know. The two of us have shared each other in
so many ways . . . but I have not shared even a day of my life with
my son. And it frightens me.*

There was a sudden loud hissing as the holding tanks on the
shuttle were purged. The two of them turned in time to see the
noxious gasses, contained in an air shield, form a hazy sphere
around the shuttle's nose before being swirled away into the
bay's recycling system. It was the last technical function that
needed to be performed before the air shield was lowered and the
passengers disembarked.

"Are you sure you wouldn't like me to stay?" Javas asked,
taking one of her hands in his. "Just until you've had a chance
to greet him?"

"No." She shook her head firmly, a determined smile coming

to her lips. "I'll be fine. I've been looking forward to this for a long time."

"Until dinner, then." He kissed her softly, and with a quick squeeze of her hand turned to go.

The two Imperial escorts that had been standing unobtrusively behind them now snapped smartly to attention, and one of them formally fell into step at the Emperor's side as he headed toward the guarded corridor that would take him back to the Imperial section. The other man remained at attention behind her, but discreetly made a show of observing the activity of the bay technicians.

She heard the sound of laughter ring out over the constant background noise of the bay and returned her attention to the shuttle. A group of nine, in obvious good spirits to be back home, trundled down a narrow ramp that had appeared just behind the nose of the craft. Eric was in the center of the group, his uniform jacket slung casually over one shoulder. Most of the others still had their jackets on, and even from this distance Adela could see the colors of rank on their collars. The fact that the group was of mixed rank pleased her, as Eric seemed to show as much friendship and respect for the lowest ranking members of his bridge crew as he did for his closest officers. She could tell, in the way they shared a sense of comradeship with one another, that the respect and admiration were mutual. They gathered in a tight knot at the end of the ramp as he bid them farewell one at a time, shaking the hand of each in turn.

Adela caught the eye of one of the crew, a young woman whose collar indicated that she was First Officer. The woman whispered something into Eric's ear, and he turned quickly in her direction, easily picking Adela out in the nearly empty bay. He stood straighter then and slipped on his jacket, hastily fastening the gold buttons.

Eric smiled at her and raised his hand in an eager wave, then politely excused himself from the group. The others seemed to sense the importance of this meeting and quietly dispersed, heading for the crew exit hallways on the opposite side of the bay.

Adela felt her heart pounding in her chest as Eric approached, and clasped her hands in front of her to hide their shaking. She prayed that he wouldn't notice how nervous she was.

It's just not the same, she reflected as he neared. After a full year of realtime communications with him, in holographic settings that gave the superficial appearance of someone being in the same room, she came to realize everything they had said to each other had been a poor preparation for this moment.

"Hello, Mother," he said in the powerful tenor she had come to know so well these last months. He took both of her hands in his and kissed her on the cheek, and as he pulled back and looked into her face, it suddenly struck her that he was as anxious about this meeting as she was.

"Eric."

She studied his face, and saw herself in his features as surely as if she'd peered into a mirror: the dark hair and deep brown eyes; the wide mouth which, like her mother's, was quick to turn up into a smile; the fair complexion that ran in her family. But it was also as if a part of Javas was standing before her as well. Eric had grown tall, and while he did not reach his father's height he had Javas' strength in his broad shoulders. The structure of his face, the high cheekbones, the waviness of his thick hair as it touched the collar of his gray-blue commander's jacket, all spoke of the Emperor. But above all else, behind his eyes lay the same fire she knew to be in Javas' eyes.

Adela opened her mouth to speak, but was cut off by a loud, steady whine from the shuttle receiving tube as the lifters engaged to rotate the craft for later departure.

Eric nodded sharply to the escort, dismissing him. "Walk with me, somewhere quieter," he said over the noise, indicating the guarded hallway that Javas had taken a few minutes earlier. He released her hands, then fidgeted for a moment as if he didn't know what to do with his own, and finally clasped them behind his back as they walked toward the exit.

Neither spoke as they walked across the noisy bay. The guards snapped to attention when they passed, then resumed their position once the soundproof doors closed behind them. In silence at last, Adela wondered if her son could hear her heart as easily as she could.

"You look well . . ." "I'm glad that you . . ." they said at the same time, then stopped and faced each other in the corridor. Both of them burst into laughter, the spontaneous pleasure of the sound reverberating in the corridor relieving the tension she felt. There was another set of double doors several dozen meters down the hallway, with another set of armed guards stationed on the other side, but here they were alone, mother and son.

For the first time.

"I'm sorry," he said, still chuckling nervously. "You first."

"Eric, I . . ." Adela began. Even though she had rehearsed this meeting a hundred times in her imagination, she still wasn't sure where to begin.

He seemed to sense what she was trying to say, and again took both of her hands in his. "There's no sense in trying to rush things," he said, smiling.

As he spoke, Adela heard both the strength and tenderness to which she had grown accustomed in Javas' voice. He was so much like his father.

"You want to say so many things. You want to put so many years into so short a time." He chuckled again, then smiled in admission. "Believe me, Mother; I'm fighting the urge to do exactly the same thing." He paused, lowering his gaze to the floor. "I have so much to tell you about my life and my goals, my dreams. And I want to hear everything about yours. I want you to tell me of Pallatin—not what I've already read in the reports and data files, but what it was like and what you felt and what you thought when you were there. I want to hear of Gris and my family. And I want you to tell me of your project and of what my role will be someday. We have so much to say to each other—"

Adela touched a finger to his lips to silence him, and said, "And so much to *be* to one another."

They embraced, and as they did Adela tried to push away the thought that she never had the opportunity to hold him as an infant, to hug him as a child. But with the regret she felt for the years and experiences missed, she also felt comfort in the knowledge of what a fine son Javas had raised, and what an excellent Emperor he would one day make.

Above all else, Eric was right: There really was no need to try to force a lifetime's memories into this brief moment. There was a lot of work to do before Rice and the scientific team returned from the test site, bringing this phase of the project to a close. It would be several years before she had to go into cryosleep.

And for once, perhaps for the first time in her life, she knew that there really was time to get to know someone.

EPILOGUE

LUNA

Adela's office was almost bare.

Most of the furniture, the pictures and decorations she'd personally selected, all of the little touches she'd added to reflect her own tastes and make the working environment as pleasant as possible were gone now, stored away. The terminal was silent, its screen dark. The desk had been cleared and its drawers emptied, their few remaining contents filling the small box at her feet, and she sat in a room as devoid of emotion and personality as a vacant apartment.

She held a small figurine, hand-carved from Grisian rockwood, and fidgeted with it as she waited for the academician to arrive. Having already made all of her good-byes to friends and staff, the meeting with Bomeer would mark the end of her stay on Luna. As she turned the object over in her hands it tapped occasionally against the surface of the bare desktop, the sound echoing hollowly in the room.

There was another sound, this one unfamiliar and intrusive, and it took a moment for Adela to realize that someone was knocking at the office door.

"Coming," she said, even as she rose from the desk and approached the door. She thumbed the control in the door's frame and it slid open, revealing her secretary and Academician Bomeer standing outside in the reception area. Her terminal now disconnected and silent on her desk, it was her secretary who had knocked. "Thank you, Stase. Academician, please come in."

"Thank you, Doctor," he said politely, and entered, allowing her to conduct him to one of the room's remaining chairs. He waited until she seated herself behind the desk before sitting. "And thank you for agreeing to see me."

Adela nodded, studying the academician, fairly shocked at his appearance. Adela had consulted with him at length in realtime links immediately following the test, but during the lengthy voyage back to Luna he had spent the trip in virtual seclusion. He had been back on Luna for six months, but she had not met with him personally during the entire time since his return, confining whatever discussions they had had to recorded messages and electronic communications.

He had aged more than she might have expected, and she guessed that he was years past due for a rejuvenation. This was not the same Bomeer she had met on Corinth nearly a century earlier. His hair, always an unruly mop, was longer, grayer now and combed straight back over his head. He wore the trademark academician's tunic, as he always had, but the outfit seemed less fastidiously tailored, more comfortable. And he seemed to smile more easily as he spoke than she remembered, or maybe it was the slight wrinkles at the corners of his eyes and mouth that made it seem so.

"I see that you've just about closed up shop," he said with the air of a man at peace with himself. "May I ask when you'll be going into cryosleep?"

"You're right," she replied, returning his smile. "I am just about finished here. My appointment with you is my last bit of official business before I go down to Earth."

"You'll be staying at Woodsgate?"

"Yes. It'll be the closest thing I've had to a vacation since . . ." She stopped, suddenly realizing that she hadn't had anything even approximating a vacation in recent memory.

Bomeer chuckled softly. "I think I understand the feeling."

"Anyway, to answer your question, I'll be going into the tank in about a month."

"I see." He seemed to hesitate, unsure of himself for the first time since he'd entered. There were several data sticks in the breast pocket of his tunic; two had brightly colored rings near the pocket clips and he pulled them out. "Please accept these as a token of my esteem."

She took them, noting the color coding.

"The red one is a full accounting of everything that occurred at the test site," he said. "I have checked all the figures and have compared the results with your own findings to verify your original equations. Further, I have extrapolated the necessary projections as to the proper course of the project—I realize that most of this will duplicate what you've done in the years since the test, but this is meant to confirm your theories. I've included with it my personal endorsement, and recommendations for the Imperial Council of Academicians."

Adela was almost speechless. "Thank you, Academician," was the best she could manage.

"The other, coded blue, contains our full investigation into the anomaly of the seventh flare on the scan recording provided by the Sarpan scientist working with Dr. Rice."

"Oh?" Adela had reviewed some of the earlier findings sent to her by Rice while the *Port of Kowloon* was still in transit. While her work setting up the next phase of the project had occupied most of her time since she'd returned from Pallatin, the possibilities surrounding the mystery of the seventh flare had intrigued her and she wished there had been more time to look into it. "Have any conclusions been reached?"

Again, Bomeer smiled. Not the arrogant, I'm-better-than-you smile she had frequently associated with him, but something pleasant, genuine.

"It is the missing Sarpan generator ship. I've personally examined Rice's work and have confirmed his findings. There is no doubt that the ship was drawn through the wormhole, instantly crossing a distance of nearly a million kilometers, before it was destroyed along with the other ships in the flare-up."

"That's . . . incredible."

"Discovery leads to discovery," Bomeer said. "The theories that have proven to be valid for the project—*your* theories, Doctor—are directly responsible for yet another development, one of immense importance to the Hundred Worlds."

Adela felt her excitement blossom, then just as quickly tempered her feelings of elation. "But the cost! More than three hundred died to learn this—"

"Their deaths were not your fault. You will be remembered as the person who made one of the greatest contributions to science;

I will be remembered for the tragedy that resulted. This is a fact that will be with me for the remainder of my life."

Bomeer was silent for several moments, and seemed to wrestle with his guilty burden before he was able to continue.

"However," he went on, "we've only proven that wormhole travel occurred. It will be years before we can analyze the mechanics of how it works, even longer before we can put what we've learned to practical use. If ever." He paused, then looked deep into her face. "I have made my official recommendation to the Academy that the investigation of this phenomenon be made their top priority. I wanted you to know this before you went into cryosleep."

"I appreciate that, Academician . . ." Adela started to say, but was cut off when Bomeer held up his hand.

"Please, let me finish," he said softly under his breath, the sound reminding her more of a weary sigh. "I have fought the natural scientific growth of the Empire for so long that I can remember little else. But I fought the wrong battle. In attempting to keep the Empire from moving too quickly, to keep scientific development on what I thought was a safe and steady course, I succeeded only in battling myself." He looked at her once more, relief in his eyes at having unloaded this personal burden. The smile returned to his lips as he added, "I am very tired, and I am through fighting."

"Fighting against one's self is the most wearying fight of all."

"Besides"—Bomeer looked at her, a twinkle of excitement in his eyes—"I've seen the changes that instantaneous tachyon communications have brought to the Empire, and I must admit that the changes have been good ones. But imagine: to travel from one point in the Empire to another in the blink of an eye! I am forced to confess that the siren song of faster-than-light travel has captured me. Research. Discovery. The acquisition of knowledge. These are the things that first attracted me to science, and these are the things that will guide the Empire in the centuries to come as the wormhole is studied. Somewhere along the way I lost those things, but I have them back now—thanks to you—and I want to be a part of it all again. To contribute to the future, instead of merely maintaining the present."

Again, Adela had trouble finding the right words to fit this surprising situation. She was about to simply thank him again, but was stopped by another series of insistent raps on the office door. She smiled politely at Bomeer in way of apology and turned almost automatically to the darkened terminal before remembering that it was useless.

"Excuse me a moment." The door slid aside before she reached it and Stase immediately stepped inside, obviously agitated. There was someone standing behind him, but from her viewing angle she couldn't make out who it was.

"Dr. Montgarde, I—"

"That won't be necessary," barked the man as he pushed Stase authoritatively aside. "I will speak with Dr. Montgarde directly." Her secretary looked about ready to grab him and toss him forcibly out of the office, but Adela shook her head, dismissing him. Once Stase stood back from the doorway the uninvited guest allowed a broad, insincere smile to spread across his features, and his demeanor changed instantly as he dipped his head to her in just the slightest suggestion of a bow. She had seen him before, years earlier, and recognized his plastic smile almost immediately.

Oh, not now. I don't need this now. "Poser, isn't it?" Adela demanded angrily as she strode the rest of the way to the door.

He bowed slightly. "Dr. Montgarde, you honor me and my House by remembering—"

"Shut up." She started past Poser for the reception area, but stopped when the man, utterly nonplused by Adela's rebuke, entered her office and approached Bomeer.

"Good day, Academician." Again, a short formal bow. "My Mistress will speak to the Doctor alone."

Bomeer had barely begun to rise from his chair when Adela grabbed Poser's arm with a grip that surprised even her and spun him around. "I'll decide who stays and who doesn't." She flung his arm aside and enjoyed the sight of what was probably the first genuine expression of emotion the man's face had revealed in years: stunned shock. "Now, if your Mistress wishes to speak to me, then she had better be quick about it. I plan to leave this office in five minutes."

He made a feeble attempt to recover his composure as he almost scurried from the room into the reception area. Bomeer remained standing, but had difficulty hiding his amusement.

Poser returned almost immediately, his all-purpose smile conspicuously absent. If his Mistress had been upset by the information that she wouldn't be speaking to Adela alone, he gave no indication of it. "Mistress Rihana Valtane," he said simply, then quickly stood aside for her to enter.

The former Princess had changed little, it seemed, since the last time they had spoken more than four decades earlier. Her glowing copper hair, her poise and grandeur, the way she carried herself with absolute authority and, above all, her youthful beauty were all exactly as Adela had remembered them. Her outfit gave the appearance of being spun from molten gemstones, and was tailored in such a manner as to seem alive when she moved, if not an actual living part of her. The ensemble was completed with her signature sapphire earrings and necklace, the precious metal of their settings matching the bracelets on each of her wrists.

Adela said nothing, but led the woman into the room as Poser exited and closed the door behind him.

Bomeer approached a few steps and stood straighter when she neared, bowing deeply. "Mistress Valtane," he said respectfully, "it is good to see you once again."

Rihana walked past him as though he wasn't there, and Adela understood now why she'd raised no objection to Bomeer's staying in the room when she called: The woman had absolutely no intention of acknowledging the academician's presence. She instead went directly to one of the two remaining chairs before the desk and sat, waiting for Adela to take her own seat behind the desk. Bomeer remained on his feet about halfway to the door.

Adela nodded her head curtly in a motion that was not quite a show of respect before taking her own chair. "It's been a long time, *Mistress,* but not long enough." She made sure her voice carried with it as much scorn and sarcasm as she could summon up, then added bluntly, "What do you want?"

"I want nothing but to give you a parting message. Something to think about while you sleep."

"And what would that be?"

The former Princess smiled and shrugged nonchalantly, settling back into the chair. "I wanted to remind you of the cost of your dream. I know how long you plan to remain in cryosleep.

There will be little left of what you remember when you wake up.
Javas will be long dead, as will most of your friends and associates."

"You've told me this before. I've not forgotten."

"I'm glad to see that you have a good memory, but you are not
the only one. I have a good memory, too." Rihana crossed her
long legs and smoothed the fabric of her gown. When she spoke
again her smile had vanished. "I understand that you have became very close to your Eric. Well, remember this while you
sleep, Adela: He murdered my son. *I* do not plan to forget."

Adela felt a chill sweep over her at the thought of Rihana
hurting Eric. She rose shakily, and found it necessary to lean on
the desk for support. "You'll do nothing to hurt my son," she
said forcefully, her words feeling like jagged ice in her throat.
"I'll see to it myself."

Adela had expected Rihana to threaten the power of House
Valtane against her, but when the woman gazed up at her over
the bare desktop she did the one thing Adela never expected. She
laughed. Adela shook her head in disgust at whatever it was in
her words that had so amused Rihana.

"I swear it, *Mistress,*" she spat, her sudden fear replaced now
with unbridled anger. "If I have to forgo cryosleep entirely,
you'll not get close to my son!"

Rihana's laughter faded, and she made a pretense of wiping
tears from the corners of her eyes. "Come now, Doctor; do you
really think that I would have any interest in your precious
offspring? Eric was but the tool that took my son's life, a weapon
wielded by someone else who owes me a debt. Besides," she
shrugged, and again smoothed a fold in her gown, "I am not so
foolish as to have frozen but a single fertilized ovum. My only
mistake was in my timing; I'll do better next time."

"Not with my family, you won't." Adela was appalled at
Rihana's complete lack of emotion regarding Reid's death, and
at how the woman apparently thought of him only as a means to
an end.

"Really, you value yourself and your young Prince much too
highly. No, it is Javas and what he's stolen from me that I want."
Rihana stood, her bracelets jingling musically at the movement.
And as she continued, Adela became aware that anger made
itself plain in her voice only when she spoke of Javas. "He has

taken from me that which is rightfully mine—my position in the Empire, guaranteed me by my birthright. I mean to have it back!"

Rihana stood ramrod straight and smiled again, as if the anger and emotion she'd displayed only moments before were but parts of an elaborate act. When she spoke again, her composure had returned. "In any event, Doctor, feel free to sleep; preserve yourself for your project to save the world. But understand that I mean to have what is mine, and that I'll permit nothing to stand between me and that goal. Not Javas. Not your project. Nothing. And understand something else . . ." She stopped, her icy blue eyes piercing Adela's soul. "Once I regain what has been taken from me, you may not recognize the world into which you'll awake. I'll see to it."

"Will you?" Bomeer, until now remaining quietly in the background, came forward. "And you think that those loyal to Javas and to the Hundred Worlds will merely stand aside while you attempt to regain this—what did you call it?—birthright?" He stood resolutely only a meter from her, his chin lifted and his hands clasped behind him defiantly.

She was taller than he, taller than many men, and she looked down on him in more ways than one. Her eyes narrowed disapprovingly and she said, her words dripping with sarcasm, "Do I know you?" Without waiting for an answer she turned for the door. Poser snapped nervously to attention and fumbled with the door controls until finally getting it open and jumping out of Rihana's way just in time for her to clear the door frame, then followed her out like an obedient dog.

Again, Bomeer and Adela were alone in the barren office, surrounded by an uncomfortable silence that seemed to last for several minutes. "I've not looked forward to going into cryosleep this time," she admitted at last. "I've always known that saying good-bye to everything close to me would be hard." Adela came around the desk, leaned heavily against the front of it as she faced the academician. "But I've never been *afraid* to go into the tank. Until now."

"Don't be," Bomeer replied. He held out his hand, escorting her to the door. "A little while ago I said I was tired of fighting, and I meant it. But the more I consider what I have just seen and heard, the more I realize that there is still a fight to be joined.

Somehow, I have a feeling that fighting for a worthy cause for a change will not be nearly so wearying." At the door, he stopped and faced her, taking both her hands in his. His hands were warm, not the cold unfeeling hands she had always imagined of the academician.

"Don't worry for Javas," he said firmly. "He is much stronger than she believes, and he has more support on his side than Rihana can ever imagine."

"And now he has you on his side," Adela added.

Bomeer smiled. "Yes, I suppose he does at that." He thumbed the door open, then, "Sleep well, Doctor."

The academician turned abruptly and disappeared down the corridor, leaving Adela alone in the quiet, empty office.

EARTH

Adela sat on a limestone outcropping on the grounds of Woodsgate and watched the receding thunderheads of storm clouds as they drifted away to the southeast. It was raining heavily beneath the black sky to the southeast, and occasional lightning punctuated by softly rolling thunder several seconds later told her how far away the storm was. The clouds had threatened when they'd passed overhead an hour earlier, but no thunderstorm had come. Now, as the sky above her cleared, the sunshine beamed down once more.

She wore Earth clothing of soft denim jeans and a white linen blouse, with a leather vest and riding boots. She inhaled deeply of the clean afternoon air. The weather front associated with the passing thunderstorms had brought with it cooler, less humid air, and she reveled in what had turned out to be a perfect early summer day.

She had visited the family estate several times during the eight years following the test, and each visit here made her long to return. Adela had always realized the planet's importance and had studied its people and geography for years, but it wasn't until she had completed her work, until she had *lived* for more than a month on Earth, that she found that she had come to love it as intimately as she did her own Gris.

The eight years had been wonderful. Every moment she wasn't

involved in overseeing the project team and analyzing the test data she had spent with Javas; and with Eric upon his return. But this part of the project was over, and Javas had implemented security measures to ensure that Eric would be protected. She was further comforted by the fact that Eric had selected Billy Woorunmarra as his First Officer. Whether the choice had been Eric's idea—the two had become fast friends shortly after Billy returned from Pallatin—or had been Javas' doing, she had no way of knowing. But now that Eric had returned safely to his ship . . .

There was a scrabbling noise farther down the outcropping, the heavy sound of boots on rock, and she turned to see Javas approaching. He, too, was casually attired in Earth garb and looked more like a plantation owner than the most powerful man in the Empire. Adela smiled as he walked the length of the outcropping. He was older, but he was so vibrant and alive that their age difference mattered little to either of them. Javas reached her at last and sat at her side on the bare rock, swinging his long legs over the edge of the outcropping.

"It's turned into a beautiful day," he said, taking her tiny hand in his. He squeezed her hand gently, three times, in a gesture that said a silent "I love you."

Adela gazed up into the sky. "I want it to be a day like this when I wake up."

Javas didn't reply, but she knew that whatever request she made on this, their last day together, would not be refused. Her theories had been validated—at a terrible cost—and all that remained now was to select the feeder star from a long list of candidates and to construct the actual hardware for the full-scale version of what was needed to save the Sun. It would take nearly two centuries to complete the task, two centuries of routine work that did not require her presence, but she knew that on the day she awoke from cryosleep, the Sun would be shining just as it was now.

She sighed and slid from the outcropping to stand before him, then encircled him with her arms and hugged him tightly. It was time, past time; the medical attendant had been waiting in the special room set up for her in the House. Adela had needed some last moments of solitude and Javas had given her those moments, and more, before coming to find her.

"I don't want to leave you again," she said, still lost in his strong embrace.

"I know; and I don't want to lose you." He slid from the outcropping and took both her hands in his. "Say the word and I'll arrange for someone else to take your place: Dr. Rice or any one of your team you feel is competent. Just ask it."

Adela shook her head. They both knew better.

They walked silently, hand in hand, back to the House, passing through deserted halls and empty rooms on their way to the new cryosleep chamber. The entire staff had been dismissed. Other than the guardsmen still at their posts, only Master McLaren remained in the House. He had met them at the door and now escorted them personally to the chamber, saying nothing. He smiled once, weakly, when they'd reached the massive oak doors masking the chamber and took position outside once the doors had closed.

She had expected the stark white walls common to cryosleep chambers, but her heart flew when she entered. Javas had ordered that the holographic display of a forest be implemented in the room, giving it a sense of quiet serenity.

"My father often found peace here," Javas said, and Adela knew that he was speaking of the forest scene and not the House itself. "And I've been here a great deal myself in recent years. I've had the display edited." He looked around him and, with a sweep of his arm, indicated the clearing that allowed the sunlight to come streaming down from above. There were enormous white clouds floating above their heads, and the Sun would occasionally go behind one before reappearing brightly a few seconds later. "I thought you might like it."

She looked around her. The medical attendant stood dutifully to one side, waiting to prepare her for her long sleep. She knew there should be a lot of equipment here: monitoring devices, room systems, additional furniture . . . and the coffin-like cryosleep tank itself. But the only unnatural object in the idyllic surroundings was a low bed, its Earth-made flannel sheets drawn back for her. The other trappings of the chamber were surely here, but were—for now—being masked out of sight by the hologram.

Javas followed her to the bed, and she fell into his embrace one last time before sitting. She nodded once at the attendant.

"It's time," she whispered.

He brought her a glass, and Adela quickly downed the fruit-flavored drink. Aided by the juice she would fall asleep naturally. Once asleep, she knew, the holograph would be switched off. Her clothing would be removed, replaced with the cryosleep gown and stockings, and she would be put into the tank.

And Javas would leave and return to the day-to-day business of running the Empire of the Hundred Worlds, preparing everything that would greet her on her awakening two centuries from now. He would not be there when she awoke, she knew; would not witness the project brought to a successful conclusion. But he would be remembered, as she had told him that night on Corinth, as the man responsible for saving the Sun. It seemed so long ago, that dinner, and she tried to recall when it had taken place but her mind was becoming fuzzy.

She yawned sleepily, then stifled a giggle as Javas sat on the edge of the bed. She was lying on the bed now, she realized, but didn't remember having done it. "I'm sorry," she said, "I didn't mean to—"

"Shhhhhh." He touched her lips lightly with his fingertip, just as he had in a dream nearly a decade earlier. "It doesn't matter." She closed her eyes and tried to remember the dream she'd had when coming out of cryosleep on the *Levant* at the conclusion of her trip home from Pallatin, and seemed to recall that she'd been upset in it, but remembered nothing more.

She opened her eyes, blinking sleepily, and realized that they were alone now; the attendant had apparently left the room.

"I do love you," Javas whispered, and kissed her softly. He had never said the words aloud before, and as Adela looked up into his face she saw that his eyes glistened. Behind him, a cloud passed lazily in front of the Sun and she felt a smile come to her lips.

The cloud moved away and Adela closed her eyes tightly at the sudden brightness. She felt light, disconnected, as if floating free of the bed.

With the image of the Sun still in her mind, Javas' face silhouetted against its brilliance, she let go finally, allowing the deep peace of cryosleep to fall gently over her.

TETON COUNTY LIBRARY

JACKSON, WYOMING